NEVADA!

The eighth thrilling novel in the WAGONS WEST series—heroic sagas about the brave men and women who risked their lives in their search for freedom and justice on the new American frontier.

★ ★ ★ ★ ★ ★ ★ ★ ★ ★ ★ ★ ★ ★ ★ ★ ★ ★ ★

WAGONS WEST
NEVADA!

BOLD MEN AND WOMEN SHARING A GLITTERING DREAM... AND ANSWERING THE CALL OF THEIR COUNTRY

GENERAL LELAND BLAKE
—A wagon train of silver must cross the war-torn West to New York. The future of the Union Armies rests on the success of his near-impossible mission.

WHIP HOLT
—The wagon master risks his life on a blazing trail of greed, deception, and death.

SUSANNA FULTON
—A violet-eyed newspaper editor who is torn between devotion to duty and her love of two worthy men.

LADY ALISON WHITE
—The young, lovely English widow who, against her better judgment, is forced to perform an act of espionage.

BERNHARD von HUMMEL
—A dashing Prussian businessman, whose fondness for Susanna creates jealousy and a bitter dispute that upsets his true mission.

★ ★ ★ ★ ★ ★ ★ ★ ★ ★ ★ ★ ★ ★ ★ ★ ★ ★ ★

ANDREW BRENTWOOD
—A bold young soldier whose love for an impetuous woman spirals his life toward violence.

SCOTT FOSTER
—Publisher of the Virginia City *Journal*, endlessly passionate, hopelessly romantic, he epitomizes the grand spirit of the American West.

DOUGLAS de FOREST
—A man of violence, a man no one seems to know, whose treacherous plan for the valuable wagon train turns to blood.

TOBY HOLT
—Whip's quick–tempered son, whose battle with Andrew over a woman threatens to smash everything—his life, his career.

BETH BLAKE
—Leland Blake's high-spirited daughter. She erupts in bitter disputes with temperamental Toby Holt—the one man everyone hopes she will someday marry.

EZEKIEL
—A former slave who, with his wife, Patricia, suffers inhuman abuse before he rises to challenge the worst of men at a time of crisis.

CAROLINE BRANDON
—Fabulously beautiful, undeniably seductive, the highest paid courtesan in Nevada, she pays an expensive price to save the gallant wagon train from certain doom.

★ ★ ★ ★ ★ ★ ★ ★ ★ ★ ★ ★ ★ ★ ★ ★ ★ ★

Bantam Books by Dana Fuller Ross
Ask your bookseller for the books you have missed

WAGONS WEST

★

VOLUME 8

NEVADA!

DANA FULLER ROSS

Created by the producers of
White Indian, Children of the Lion,
Saga of the Southwest, and
The Kent Family Chronicles Series.
Executive Producer: Lyle Kenyon Engel

BANTAM BOOKS
TORONTO • NEW YORK • LONDON • SYDNEY • AUCKLAND

NEVADA!

*A Bantam Book/published by arrangement with
Book Creations, Inc.*

Bantam edition/January 1982

2nd printing ... January 1982	4th printing . September 1982
3rd printing .... March 1982	5th printing ...... July 1983
	6th printing ... January 1985

*Produced by Book Creations, Inc.
Chairman of the Board: Lyle Kenyon Engel*

ISBN 0-553-25089-2

Published simultaneously in the United States and Canada

Bantam Books are published by Bantam Books, Inc. Its trademark, consisting of the words "Bantam Books" and the por-
trayal of a rooster, is Registered in U.S. Patent and Trademark
Office and in other countries. Marca Registrada. Bantam
Books, Inc., 666 Fifth Avenue, New York, New York 10103.

PRINTED IN THE UNITED STATES OF AMERICA

H   15 14 13 12 11 10 9 8

NEVADA!

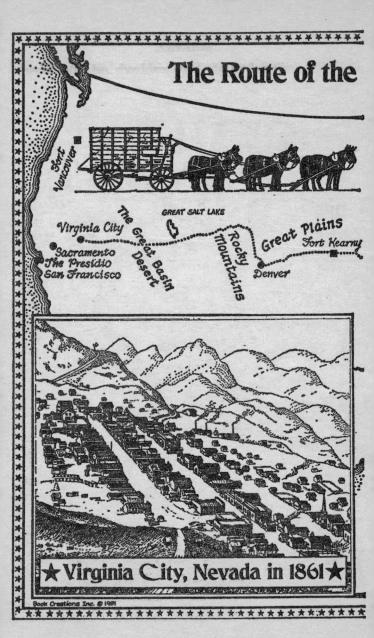

The Route of the

Fort Vancouver

GREAT SALT LAKE

Virginia City

The Great Basin Desert

Rocky Mountains

Great Plains

Fort Kearny

Sacramento
The Presidio
San Francisco

Denver

★ Virginia City, Nevada in 1861 ★

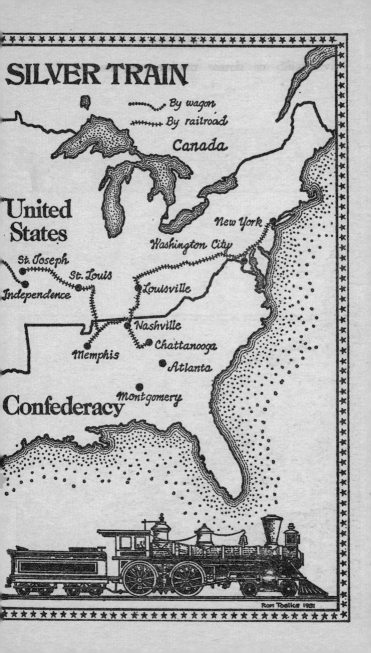

I

"Eustace," the old miner said as he looked up and down the length of the crude saloon and sipped his beer, "I swear I never seen nothin' like it!"

His companion, a chubby gray burro, placidly drank his own beer from the soup plate that his master had provided for him.

"First off," said the old miner, whose name was Bingham, "war is comin', sure as hellfire is on the way for sinners, and it's goin' ta tear this country ta shreds. Folks knew that's what'd happen when they elected Abraham Lincoln president, an' you know blamed well that state after state is leavin' the Union an' formin' a new, separate country." Gloomily he signaled to the bartender for two more beers, then carefully poured one into the soup dish for Eustace.

Drinking in silence, the miner rubbed the stubble of beard on his face and surveyed the crowded bar. "You'd think that with Armageddon threatenin', folks would be a mite careful and would mind their manners," he declared. "But you look around this here town an' you'd never guess that a war was comin'. Drink up, Eustace! The world is so crazy we're better off drunk than sober."

There was a kernel of truth in the remarks of the old man, who was a veteran of the gold rushes of both California and Colorado. Virginia City, the wildest, most active town in Nevada, which had just become a federal territory in March of 1861, was unique. It was a boom town, no question of that, due to the gold and silver—

particularly silver—that had been found in such quantities there. But what made Virginia City even more extraordinary was that it sat, literally, on its own fortune. The town was built on the side of a mountain, and that mountain was the site of the fabulous Comstock Lode, the richest find of silver ever discovered by prospectors.

The first prospectors to arrive had not been looking for silver. These men had been gold seekers, who were sorely disappointed as they washed their sieves and noticed a heavy black mud that made it nearly impossible to separate the gold from the rest of the earth. These men left the area disgusted and forlorn, never learning that the heavy black mud was rich in silver.

There were two miners, however, who were not discouraged so easily. James Finney, nicknamed "Old Virginny," and Henry "Old Pancake" Comstock discovered that the mountainside mine they had dug was rich in silver, and that was the beginning of the fabulous Comstock Lode. Learning the news, Old Virginny fainted to the ground, breaking his bottle of whiskey in the process. When he came to, he used his remaining liquor to christen the spot Virginia City.

So one of the great towns of the West was born, and it grew by leaps and bounds. By 1861 a semblance of order had been created out of the usual mining town chaos of shanties and tents, and Virginia City boasted over one hundred shops and stores, saloons, restaurants, boarding-houses, and offices, all built on the side of a mountain. The community lived and ate, made love, and fought aboveground, and under the surface of the earth, huge tunnels were constructed by the men who worked for a score or more companies that had bought the rights to explore and develop the lode.

The miners, as Bingham was the first to recognize, were a somewhat different breed from the individual prospectors who had come to California and to Colorado in the hopes of striking it rich. Here they split their proceeds fifty-fifty with the proprietors of the mining companies, which meant that they earned far more for their physical labor than they could earn for comparable work anywhere else on earth. Consequently, Virginia City was crowded; newcomers continued to arrive daily, and huts were erected hastily to house them under conditions that were far from satisfactory. But no one cared. The get-rich-quick fever covered a multitude of sins.

Of the thousands of men who came to the Comstock Lode in the early 1860s, many were businessmen, gamblers, and speculators. Gentlemen in starched collars, stovepipe hats, and somber suits of wool stood shoulder to shoulder in the saloon with roughly clad miners, and they all stared at the rather heavily made-up young women who drifted into the bar. The establishment hired no hostesses, but a discreetly placed sign in the window proclaiming "Ladies Welcome" was a signal understood by everyone that women would be present to offer their services. There were a few decent, honorable, and law-abiding women in Virginia City, but they had a difficult time and rarely ventured out without an escort. There were so many brothels in town that no one could keep track of the number, and no one tried. The prostitutes—like everyone else—lived off the earnings of those who took the rich silver ore from the earth and refined it. Virginia City was a miners' paradise, and nothing was allowed to interfere either with the removal of silver from the earth or with the pleasures obtained by the men who worked so hard to remove it.

The old miner drained his mug. "I reckon me an' Eustace will each have one more for the road," he told the bartender, who silently handed him two more containers of beer.

In the more sophisticated cities of the United States—in New York, Chicago, or San Francisco, for example—the sight of a burro drinking beer would have created a sensation, but Virginia City's motto was Live and Let Live, and the residents behaved accordingly. A few people stared at the burro and shook their heads in wonder, but by and large the patrons of the bar minded their own business. Few of them noticed the old miner as he staggered out into the street, followed by Eustace, who wove amiably from side to side.

As Bingham and Eustace left the saloon and stumbled down the main street of Virginia City, the townspeople stared at them, and a young boy pranced down the street behind the duo, laughing and pointing. A dog trotted alongside, barking at the inebriated, wobbling burro.

They soon left the town and went the short distance to the site Bingham had claimed halfway up the mountainside. To date the old miner had found very little silver—just enough to purchase food and equipment and to stand Eustace and himself to a few drinks at the saloon every now and then—but his philosophy had always been "Ya git what ya git," and he never complained about his lot.

The old miner stretched and yawned. "I think it's time ta take me a little siesta," he said to Eustace, and wrapping himself in his blankets, which had been piled next to a burnt-out campfire, he lay on the ground and fell fast asleep. Eustace, meanwhile, stood nearby, eyes squeezed shut, tail flicking at the flies. Neither of them heard or saw the two masked men as they approached, then concealed themselves behind a large boulder.

"That there is the ugliest-looking man and beast I ever did see," one of the bandits said.

"Tain't likely there'd be anything more than a pint of liquor and some chewin' tobaccy in that burro's saddlebag," his partner responded.

"Maybe, maybe not. You never know with these old coots. I say we go and investigate. We got nothin' to lose, and iffin we only find a bottle, I ain't had a drink all day."

The two men approached stealthily, though they could have cursed and shouted for all Bingham would have heard. But Eustace had become suddenly alert, his ears pricking up at the sound of footsteps behind him.

Just as the two masked men came up to the burro and snatched the saddlebags, Eustace went into action. He brayed loudly, managing to waken the old miner, and

4

kicked his hind legs into the air, knocking one of the bandits off his feet and causing the other man to run. Meanwhile, Bingham had sprung into action. Grabbing his beat-up rifle, he aimed it at the two startled men.

"Now you jest drop that there saddlebag," he said to the bandit who had attempted to flee. "Otherwise, I'll put some metal in ya, and I don't mean silver."

The masked man quickly complied as his partner scrambled to his feet.

"Ya wouldn't a found much in them there bags anyway," Bingham said, holding the rifle tightly with both hands, his eyes squinting down the gunsight. "There's only a pint o' whiskey, but it belongs ta Eustace an' me, an' we don't take kindly ta people stealin' our liquor, do we, Eustace?"

The burro brayed.

"Now if ya don't want Eustace here ta do any more kickin', I'd advise ya both ta clear out and stay out."

With this, Eustace once again launched his hind legs into the air, baring his teeth and braying angrily. The two desperadoes had seen all they needed, and they quickly turned and fled, a shot from Bingham's rifle following just above their heads.

"That's jest ta warn ya," Bingham shouted after them. Then he turned to Eustace, who had stopped kicking and braying, and said, "Mighty good work, Eustace. Them two won't bother us anymore, that's for damn certain." With that, he returned to his blankets and soon was fast asleep, while the burro stood nearby, grazing on some blades of grass, fighting hard to keep his eyes open.

By rights, Leland Blake should have been a happy, contented man. As he made his way down the corridors of the War Department headquarters in Washington City, he wore two stars on each shoulder, just awarded to him in a ceremony by the Chief of Staff. Lee Blake was a professional soldier who had spent his entire adult life in the United States Army; being promoted to major general was the culmination of a lifetime of hard work and devotion.

A friend and colleague in the War Department summed up Lee Blake's appearance completely when he said, "You know, Lee is the only major general in the army who looks like a major general. Most of the officers of two-star rank bear a strong resemblance to hunters or trappers or leathery old master sergeants, but Lee has just the right amount of gray at his temples and sprinkled through the rest of his hair, he carries himself as though he were still a cadet at West Point, and he has a real knack for wearing his uniforms with distinction."

Far more than his appearance, however, was responsible for the respect that Lee Blake was given by colleagues and subordinates at the War Department. His record was brilliant, and he had achieved a measure of renown far greater than that of most generals. He had made a major contribution to the security of the first wagon train that had crossed the continent to Oregon, he had fought with distinction under General Zachary Taylor in the Mexican War, and he had commanded the Presidio in San Francisco during the difficult days of the California gold rush. He was, as everyone associated with him knew, reliable in all things at all times and an officer to be reckoned with.

But Lee felt no sense of accomplishment. On the contrary, he could not rid himself of a cold, hard feeling in the pit of his stomach. He knew all too well that ordinarily he would have had to wait many more years before being eligible for a promotion from brigadier general to major general. The imminence of a terrible civil war was resulting in promotions for many senior officers, and he knew that the prospect of war was responsible for his own rise. Sober and unsmiling, he entered his own suite and started into his office.

The officer who sat in the adjoining room glanced up, saw the new stars on Lee's shoulders, and hastily joined him. Colonel Henry Hayward was Lee Blake's deputy, and his pleasure at the promotion of his superior was genuine. "Congratulations, sir," he said. "You've made it at last."

Lee nodded and shook his hand firmly. "I must admit, Henry, I'd be far more pleased if you and I were going to continue working together."

A cloud passed over Colonel Hayward's face. "As it happens, Lee, I've tendered my resignation to the general staff today. Effective immediately. I'm leaving at once for Richmond, Virginia."

Lee stiffened as he nodded. Richmond had just become the capital city of the Confederacy.

"I've been informed on excellent authority," Colonel Hayward said carefully, "that I shall be offered the star of a brigadier general in the Confederate Army."

Lee sighed. "For whatever it's worth to you," he said, "you deserve a promotion, but I'd rather you received it from the U.S. Army."

There was an awkward silence. "I would to God," Colonel Hayward said, "that this terrible schism weren't happening, but we seem powerless. The South Carolinians swore they'd secede if Lincoln was elected, and now they've done it. They've been followed by other states, and I've got to be loyal to my native Georgia."

Lee stared at him and spoke somberly. "Be sure you give my very best regards to Mary," he said. "And tell her I regret dreadfully that the atmosphere makes it impossible for us to get together for a farewell celebration, as we would have done in normal times."

Colonel Hayward said, "I know you'll give my love to Cathy and to your daughter. God only knows when we shall meet again, but tell Cathy please to rest assured that I shall think of her often."

"I'll tell her," Lee replied huskily, scarcely able to believe that he was bidding farewell to a brother officer he had known well since they had both been cadets at the military academy at West Point.

Now they were on the verge of becoming sworn enemies, each under oath to thwart the efforts of the other and, if necessary, to kill him. The nightmare was just beginning, and Lee had a feeling that it would grow much worse. Hayward straightened, brought his right hand to his forehead in a crisp salute, and then extended it.

Lee saluted smartly in return and then grasped his deputy's hand. There was no need for words; in fact, neither was able to speak in this moment of farewell. When they next encountered each other, they would be foes.

Lee turned aside brusquely and decided to call it a day; he was too upset to do any more work. As he made his way out of the War Department headquarters and mounted his horse for the ride to the military compound where he and his family were supplied a house by the government, the stars on his shoulders felt very heavy indeed.

The many political foes of Lord Palmerston, prime minister of Great Britain and leader of the Whig party, claimed that he was so wily he confided in no one. They did not underestimate his cleverness, but their assertion was not true. He was inclined to speak freely to one man, William Gladstone, a former Conservative now a Whig, who held the number two post in the Cabinet, that of chancellor of the exchequer. Gladstone was much younger than Lord Palmerston, but he was endowed with as quick a mind, and he was so ambitious that Palmerston already knew Gladstone would succeed him.

The prime minister drummed lightly on his leather-top desk and spoke softly. "I'm afraid," he said, "that the Americans are creating a mess from which we cannot totally escape. There is no way that we can fail to become involved in their coming war."

"Our embassy in Washington confirms the articles we read in the press," Gladstone said. "There appears to be no question that the entire South is intending to secede from the Union to join the new Confederate nation."

Lord Palmerston nodded. "We shall be required to walk on very thin eggshells," he said. "Ostensibly we shall be obliged to remain on good terms with the Union, but in actuality we'll be offering our full support to the Confederacy."

This was news to Gladstone. "We have enjoyed amicable relations with the United States for some time," he said. "If we should incur the displeasure of Washington, Canada certainly is vulnerable. Although President Lincoln is an unknown entity at this point, I wouldn't blame him in the least if he sent troops to occupy Canada if we step out of line."

Palmerston's smile was tight. "That, my dear Gladstone," he said, "is a risk we'll be obliged to take."

The chancellor of the exchequer fingered a gold watch fob hanging from his waistcoat pocket and made no reply. He wanted to hear the prime minister's full reasoning before he expressed himself.

"Britain," Palmerston said, "has made remarkable strides during the Industrial Revolution. I'll grant you that the munitions industry has grown rapidly in the American North, but even America cannot hold a candle to us. We've become the foremost industrial power on earth, and I need hardly tell you that our wealth is based on our manufacture of cloth. We make virtually all the cloth worn by Europe and by Asia."

Gladstone thought he was being patronized and became somewhat annoyed. "With all due respect, sir," he said, "I can do without a lesson in basic economics."

Palmerston accepted the rebuke without a murmur, which was unlike him. "I've gone to great pains to explain our basic situation in order to stress to you, my dear Gladstone, the importance of the South in supplying us with the raw materials we need for our continued economic health and well-being." The prime minister lowered his voice and spoke very softly. "The future of Great Britain depends on cotton," he said. "The primary source of cotton is the Confederacy. Without this raw material our factories will close, and we shall go into a decline that will make us a second-rate nation. Consequently, we are firmly tied to this new American nation. Regardless of any other consideration, we must support the Confederate States of America!"

Gladstone frowned. "The move won't be popular, you know," he said. "People here sympathize with the Union because they loathe the institution of slavery as much as do the people of the North."

"That can't be helped," Lord Palmerston said. "We've got to do what's necessary. Our munitions factories will be obliged to turn out guns, ammunition, and powder for the Confederate armies, and our shipyards will be required to build warships for the Confederate Navy. Our banks will be obliged to lend large sums to the Confederacy and to make credit easily available to her. In other words, we must do everything in our power to help her, short of going to war on her behalf ourselves."

Gladstone was relieved. "You agree with me, then, that it would be dangerous for us to arouse the ire of the United States?"

"Very dangerous," Palmerston said. "But the danger is one that we'll be required to face to one degree or another, because I'm willing to go still farther than I already outlined to you on behalf of the Confederate cause. I don't mind if Britain engages in espionage on her behalf, and I'd be inclined to be blind to any acts of sabotage that our subjects might commit for the Confederate cause."

Gladstone whistled softly under his breath. The prime minister was playing a risk-laden game indeed.

"Thank you, my dear Gladstone," Lord Palmerston said brightly, "for not delivering me a lecture on the morality of the position I've taken. Just as the Americans are in a fight for survival, so are we. Our need for Confederate cotton is of paramount consideration and must come ahead of everything else!"

The inauguration of Abraham Lincoln on March 4, 1861, had been a gloomy affair. The President's inaugural address, delivered in a downpour of rain, had been cautiously worded in order to prevent the defection of the four remaining Southern states that had not yet declared their plans to secede, but his efforts were in vain, and now it was obvious that these states would join the rest of the South in establishing the Confederacy. There was no longer any question about it—America was going to be trapped into fighting a vicious and bloody civil war.

The President conferred at length with his secretaries of war and the navy. Then, disregarding the lateness of the hour, he summoned William H. Seward, secretary of state, and Salmon P. Chase, secretary of the treasury, to the executive mansion.

Seward and Chase were startled to find President Lincoln in his carpet slippers. He offered them mugs of hot chocolate, which they gratefully accepted, and then he immediately got down to the urgent business at hand. "Well, gentlemen," he said in his flat, nasal accent, "the fat is in the fire for sure. I am afraid there is no way we can avoid a war with the Confederacy—unless we admit the unthinkable and grant the Southern states the right to secede at will."

Seward shook his head. "That's impossible, of course," he declared flatly. "We've taken the position that the Union is indissoluble, and we must hold to that position at all costs."

Chase nodded. "It won't be easy; in fact, it will be damned expensive, but I'm afraid Mr. Seward is right. This is the greatest crisis the United States has ever faced."

President Lincoln scratched his cheek. "What concerns me at this point is whether we'll be able to afford the luxury of waging an expensive war. I've read your report," he added to Seward, "to the effect that the British are going to give quiet support to the Confederacy."

"I've confirmed that unfortunate fact from several impeccable sources, Mr. President," Secretary Seward replied, "and I'm afraid it is so. The British will keep their aid as quiet as possible, but I think you can depend on it that they're planning to support the Confederacy to the hilt."

Lincoln nodded, and there was a faint trace of a smile on his lips as he said, "Can't say as I blame them. If I were the prime minister, I might be tempted to support them, too. However, I daresay we'll fool a great many people before this war ends. What concerns me is the financing. I shudder to think of what it's going to cost us to pay for all the uniforms, rifles, cannon, and munitions that we require."

Secretary Chase nodded somberly. "I've spent a great deal of time adding up columns of figures, Mr. President," he said, "and the totals I've reached are astronomical."

"Do we have the money we need?" Lincoln demanded.

Chase shook his head. "Not in cash in hand," he replied, "but it's there, and it belongs to us."

Lincoln looked at him quizzically.

"It's in the best of all possible places, Mr. President," Secretary Chase said. "It's in the ground, in mines owned by the United States government. There's gold still to be found in California. There's plenty of gold in Colorado, and now we have the silver in the Comstock Lode in Nevada. One way and another, the fortune adds up to millions of dollars, and I assure you, sir, it's ample to pay for uniforms, food, weapons, and munitions for a vast army and navy."

Lincoln stared up at the ceiling of his office. "It relieves me to hear it, Mr. Chase," he said, "because we're going to need every last penny that we can accumulate before we win this war. I guess the Almighty is watching over us."

Chase was a devout man, and he well understood what the President meant. "I don't doubt it, sir," he said. "The Lord will provide."

"Just think of the fix we'd be in," President Lincoln continued, "if gold had not been found in Colorado and silver had not been discovered in the Nevada Territory. Both lands are safely in the Union camp, and the precious metal is our lifeblood. Without it the Union well could lose this war. With it I don't see how we can fail to achieve our ultimate victory, no matter how difficult the task may be for us!"

C Street, the principal public thoroughfare of Virginia City, was located partway up the side of the mountain on which the town was built. It was quiet at noon, the occupants of most offices having gone to eat their midday dinner, but at the offices of the Virginia City *Journal*, there was a flurry of activity. The editor-in-chief and part owner, Susanna Fulton, daughter of the principal proprietor, Wade Fulton, a successful Denver publisher, was busy in her office, scribbling a story for the following morning's edition. Although clad in an open-throated man's shirt and trousers and boots, Susanna's figure was obvious, and her short, tousled auburn hair and enormous violet eyes caused any man seeing her for the first time to stare hard at her.

Susanna was already something of a legend in Virginia City, where people found it hard to reconcile her beauty with her profession. She had no idea of the whispers that she created, however, and certainly would have shrugged them off had she known. She was totally committed to the newspaper that she had started with Scott Foster, a colleague who had accompanied her to Nevada from Denver a few months earlier, and she placed that commitment above everything else.

She was not impervious to the attentions of men, however, and Scott was still her persistent suitor, as was Andy Brentwood, the nephew of General and Mrs. Lee Blake, who had just been promoted to the rank of captain in the United States Army. But Susanna, as always, devoted herself to her work with such intensity that she continued to give romance a second place in her life. She knew she was fortunate to have two such eligible suitors rather than one, but so far, at least, she was interested primarily in her career and was not ready to settle down and raise a family.

In fact, she was now so preoccupied with her article that she paid scant attention when the door to her inner sanctum opened. Scott Foster, a tall, husky young man, formerly a California rancher before he had gone to work for the Fultons in Denver, entered and lowered himself into a chair opposite her desk. She continued to write, and Scott deliberately hoisted his feet onto a corner of the desk, only inches from the paper on which she was preparing her article.

The success of the *Journal* was important to Scott Foster, also, but it was mixed in his mind with his deep feelings for Susanna Fulton. He had known when they had worked together in Denver that he was in love with her, and his feelings had become even deeper since they had come to Virginia City.

He knew Susanna was not yet ready to settle down, and he forced himself to exercise patience, a quality that did not come easily to him. He knew better than to push too hard or try too much to influence her. It was enough, Scott constantly reminded himself, that they were friends and worked together in perfect harmony.

Susanna's sigh was exaggerated, and she raised her head. "All right, Scott," she said, "I can take a hint. You want to talk."

He grinned at her, and she couldn't help returning the smile. There were many people in Virginia City who thought Scott and Susanna were a perfect match, and Scott's sister, Sarah Rose Atkins, confided to her husband, Isaiah, that she expected the couple soon would be marrying and that the Atkinses would be losing Susanna as a boarder. What they failed to take into account, however, was the determination of both Susanna and Scott to make the *Journal* as successful as its Denver predecessor. They had both agreed to take on the challenge of establishing a newspaper in the Nevada Territory, and that meant romance would have to wait.

"Do I gather you're writing a big story?" Scott asked.

Her reddish-brown hair danced as she shook her head. "No, I'm preparing an editorial actually," she said. "Another of those senseless arguments broke out between miners who support the Union and those who support the Confederacy. A really vicious quarrel was developing when I went by the entrance of the F Street mine. I'm moved to preach that the business of Virginia City is mining and that the quarrels of the Union and Confederacy have no place here."

"Well," Scott replied judiciously, "that could be ar-

14

gued in a number of ways. I happen to agree with you, but I'm sure there are a great many people in town who wouldn't."

"They're entitled to their opinions," Susanna snapped, and there was a note of finality in her tone.

Scott knew better than to argue the point with her. She knew her own mind and could not be swayed, so he changed the subject. "Isaiah and I have just had a very interesting lunch with that young Prussian nobleman," he said.

Susanna studied him with interest. "You mean Bernhard von Hummel, the representative of the Prussian munitions industry?"

"The very same," Scott replied.

Susanna leaned forward in her chair, tapping her pencil on the edge of her desk. "I'm dying of curiosity," she said. "What on earth is an official of the munitions makers of Prussia doing here in Virginia City? This must be the far ends of the earth for him."

"I guess it is," Scott replied, "but his business here is not for publication. He told us in confidence that he's making a study of the silver mines."

"Whatever for?"

"He's seeking to assure himself and his employers that the Union will be able to pay for the large orders for cannon that are beginning to be placed in Berlin," Scott said. "The Northern factories are working overtime, but there's such a great demand for arms that the War Department has placed some millions of dollars' worth of orders for the latest Prussian cannon—which comes under the heading of a military secret, so you can't publish it. I gather von Hummel's directors wanted to make certain that the U.S. government could pay for what it's ordering."

"I should hope so," Susanna sniffed.

Scott shook his head gently and ran his fingers through his wavy, dark brown hair. "As Americans we anticipate the Union will live up to its debts," he said. "But the orders for the foreign munitions are so huge that naturally the Prussians don't want to become in-

15

volved until they're quite positive that the Union is able to stand behind its orders. Anyway, Bernhard was asking Isaiah and me for information, and we were happy to oblige him. I told him if there's anything else that he'd like to know, to feel free to drop in here for a chat with you."

"Why me?" Susanna asked in surprise.

"You're too modest," Scott told her, laughing. "You're the best informed person in the whole Nevada Territory, and you know better than anyone else what's going on."

She could not deny the statement and shrugged. "It's my job to be well informed," she said.

As Scott was about to reply, he happened to glance out the plate-glass window, and he chuckled in surprise. "Well," he said, "von Hummel is losing no time showing up here, I must say."

Susanna also caught a glance of the Prussian through the window and tried to smooth her ruffled hair with one hand, as her fingers crept to her shirt front to make certain that it was discreetly buttoned. It was small wonder that Bernhard von Hummel created such an instant effect, but it was obvious that Susanna reacted to him as did virtually every other young woman who saw him. He was tall and slender, with a wiry, athletic build. He looked very distinguished, with pale blond hair, electric blue eyes, and a mysterious scar on his left cheek that in no way diminished his dashing good looks. He entered the building and smiled when Scott beckoned to him, crossing to the editor's office with quick, firm steps.

"I hope I do not intrude," he said, speaking with a faint but distinct trace of a crisp German accent. "Scott assured me I would be welcome here."

"You're indeed welcome, Mr. von Hummel," Susanna assured him, "and as we have several hours until the deadline for tomorrow's paper, this is as good a time as any for interruptions."

He bowed to her, removed his fawn-colored gloves of thin leather, and placed them carelessly but elegantly in his well-fitting jacket breast pocket. "I have long sought the opportunity of a chat with you, Miss Fulton," he said.

Scott was surprised by his warmth and was equally disconcerted by Susanna's obvious interest in him. The young publisher felt thoroughly ill at ease. He already had enough competition for Susanna's hand from Captain Andrew Brentwood, and he didn't need another rival in the Prussian. However, knowing there was nothing he could do about it, he shrugged, then rose to his feet and excused himself, going off to his own office at the opposite end of the *Journal* building.

"Scott tells me that you're interested in the solvency of the federal government and of its participation in the profits of the Virginia City mines," Susanna said. "What can I tell you that Scott and Isaiah haven't already described to you?"

Von Hummel smiled at her and spoke without apology. "You might say that my inquiries are a trifle more personal. I have been fascinated by the fact that this newspaper has an exceptionally attractive young lady as its editor, and I wondered how you happened to hold such a post. It is a very unusual position for a woman."

"I've been a newspaperwoman all my life," Susanna told him. "I worked with my father in Sacramento, and then I helped him found his new paper in Denver, so you might say I'm an old hand."

Bernhard was impressed. "You do not find the rugged frontier quality of Virginia City a handicap, then?"

She shook her head. "I've survived two gold rushes," Susanna replied, "one in California and one in Colorado. So I'm quite able to manage in a town like Virginia City."

"Incredible," Bernhard muttered, shaking his head.

Susanna concealed her annoyance. Scott had learned, as had Andy Brentwood, that she was well able to look after herself under almost any conditions, but von Hummel's reaction was that of the typical protective male, who assumed that just because she was a woman she was helpless. She saw no point in making her view known, however, so she let the matter slide.

The front door of the *Journal* office burst open, and a young man hurried in breathlessly and raced into Susanna's office. "Miss Fulton," he declared, "I don't know how you do it, but you sure do have a nose for a breaking story. You were so right when you told me to go to the entrance of the F Street mine. The argument between the Union men and the Confederates there has really erupted into a first-class fight."

Susanna brightened. "Is it a riot, or isn't it that well developed?"

"It'll be a sure enough riot before they're through," her informant declared emphatically. "They're heaving paving blocks at each other now, and they'll be using firearms pretty soon, sure as hell."

Susanna was on her feet instantly, reaching for her broad-brimmed hat, which she fastened with a leather strap under her chin. "I guess I'd better see for myself," she said. "This will not only lend greater authority to my editorial, but it may turn into a whale of a story itself."

Bernhard von Hummel moved to the door with her. "Have I your permission to accompany you?" he asked. "It seems to me that a riot is no place for a young lady."

"By all means, come along," Susanna told him. There was nothing like giving him a practical lesson in her ability to look after herself, she thought. She dashed into Scott's office, and as she emerged again, Bernhard was astonished to see her strapping on a Colt six-shooter. He had never before seen a woman handle firearms and was too astonished to comment.

His horse was tied to a hitching post in front of the *Journal* building, and as Bernhard mounted, Susanna dashed to the rear for her own mare. She emerged onto the street, already riding at a rapid clip, and Bernhard had to hurry in order to keep pace with her. She negotiated the narrow streets of Virginia City with aplomb, and when she began to climb to the next higher level, she handled herself and her mount like an expert.

As they drew nearer to the F Street entrance to the mines, the loud, ugly sounds of a major fight greeted them. Men were shouting and cursing, their voices raised in anger, and occasionally their exchange of insults was accompanied by a pistol shot.

Von Hummel instinctively drew his mount closer to Susanna in an effort to shield her. It was obvious that they were heading into real trouble. The beautiful young woman was undaunted, however. She did not slow her pace and seemed intent on going as far forward as she could into the milling crowd of angry miners.

Susanna's arrival on the scene created an immediate diversion, and the miners surrounded her.

Bernhard von Hummel was an expert rider, but before he quite realized what was happening, a half-dozen men created a wedge that separated him from Susanna. Then one of the miners snatched the reins from the young woman's hands and in a loud voice crudely invited her to dismount.

Susanna was equal to the occasion. Continuing to sit her mount, she surveyed the men milling around her horse calmly. "I'm here to get a story for the *Journal*," she said. "I have no intention of becoming involved in your quarrels or of contributing to your day's entertainment." She addressed the miner who had taken her reins and was still holding them tightly. "If I were you," she said, "I'd release the reins at once."

The man laughed coarsely. "Now, now, girlie," he said, "you and me is gonna get real friendly."

Susanna's expression did not change as she drew the Colt six-shooter from its holster. "I don't intend to warn you again," she declared, and put a bullet through the crown of the man's hat at short range.

He was astonished, as were his comrades, and they fell back several paces, giving her more room.

"That was just a warning," Susanna said amiably. "Next time I'll shoot to kill, and there isn't a jury in the whole of the Nevada Territory that will condemn me for protecting myself and my honor."

Realizing he had misjudged the young woman, the miner hurled the reins at her, then hastily withdrew. His comrades followed his example, and there was a long, shocked silence, with the two opposing groups forgetting for the moment to exchange insults.

All at once the members of the opposing factions became aware of each other's presence again. Paving stones flew, and loud curses filled the air. The Confederate adherents formed a wedge and tried to clear a path for themselves through the lines of their foes, but scores of miners hurried to the defense of the Union. Fists swung, and miners began to use crowbars and clubs.

The fight developed so swiftly that Susanna was almost caught in the midst of the fray. Bernhard had the good sense, however, to snatch her reins and to lead her mount a short distance away from the swirling, ugly mob.

Susanna was forced to admit that the Prussian's help had been timely and useful, and she had the grace to thank him. Then, before he could reply, she turned her full attention to the struggling mass of men. One of them fell, another staggered and went down, and it appeared that soon the riot would become sufficiently serious to cause casualties.

Bernhard could think only that this was the last place on earth where a young lady should be, and he wondered how he could persuade Susanna to withdraw. Surely the risks she was taking were too great for the news story she would obtain for the *Journal*.

All at once they heard the clatter of horses' hooves, which became louder and louder, and a full troop of United States Cavalry appeared, riding in formation with the tall, thin Captain Andrew Brentwood in the lead. It seemed that Andy was accustomed to such disturbances. He shouted an order, and his troop, responding as one man, drew their sabers.

Bernhard von Hummel, long accustomed to the maneuvers of cavalry in his native Prussia, admired the precision and skill of the cavalry troop. The riders advanced very slowly now and, using only the flats of their sabers, forced the mob to back off. The soldiers did not hesitate when they reached the entrance to the mine just beyond the corner, and before any of the men in the crowd quite knew what was happening, the mob was successfully dispersed. The troop then returned their sabers to their scabbards and spread out over the immediate area to make certain that a crowd did not reconvene.

Andy had been quick to note the presence of Susanna Fulton at the scene; he raised his hand to his broadbrimmed cavalry hat in salute as he approached her. "I might have known you'd be here right in the middle of the furor," he said. "I swear, Sue, you have a genius for going where there's danger."

Fortunately for Andrew Jackson Brentwood, he had inherited some of the best qualities of both his parents. He was cool and poised and always kept his head in emergencies, as did his father, Sam Brentwood, a former mountain man who had guided the first wagon train to Oregon as far as Missouri, then had given the post to his close friend, Whip Holt. His wife, Claudia, the older sister of Cathy Blake, was a wise woman who rarely gave in to impetuosity and who believed in the motto of looking long and hard before she leaped.

Certainly these qualities had stood Captain Brentwood in good stead in his military career, and they were more helpful than he knew in his relations with Susanna Fulton. He had fallen in love with her and had waited for more than a year for her to make up her mind. He was content to wait even longer—as long as was necessary. She was the right woman for him, he had decided, and nothing would ever change his opinion, unless of course she decided to marry Scott Foster—or even someone else.

Andy now turned to the dashing young Prussian sitting his mount next to Susanna's. "Good afternoon, Baron von Hummel. If I may, let me give you a quick word of advice. If you want to stay healthy, avoid Miss Fulton as you would the bubonic plague. She has an instinct for going into nasty situations."

Bernhard, who was already acquainted with the young cavalry officer, grinned and nodded. "Thank you for the advice, Captain," he said, "but I am afraid you have given it a little too late to do me any good today. I thought for sure that we were going to have to shoot our way into the clear."

Andy cocked his head to one side and peered at Susanna. "No doubt," he said, "you were merely obtaining a story for the *Journal*."

"Of course!" she replied hotly.

Andy sighed. "Sorry to spoil your pleasure, as well as your news story," he said, "but I'm glad that I got here in time to avert serious problems." He called an order to his men, who formed a column three deep and started back in the direction of their barracks.

"I suppose," Andy said, "it's useless to offer you an escort back to the *Journal* office."

Bernhard von Hummel intervened. "I shall be delighted to escort Miss Fulton," he said.

"Thank you," Susanna said sweetly, "even though I don't really need an escort." She included Andy in her smile and then started back in the direction of C Street.

As Andy Brentwood rejoined his troop, he frowned. He was long accustomed to the rivalry of Scott Foster for Susanna's hand, but now he had another, even more serious, rival. How could a captain of cavalry, who relied on his army salary, hope to compete with a Prussian nobleman who represented the munitions makers of his country? Andy clamped his jaw and told himself it was his own fault for having developed an interest in a woman as provocative and attractive as Susanna.

That same evening Bernhard von Hummel took advantage of an invitation from Isaiah Atkins and his wife, Sarah Rose, and accompanied them to the theater. The young lawyer had come to the Nevada Territory with the other members of the wagon train party from Denver. He had already established a thriving practice here, working also on behalf of the firm of Chet Harris and Wong Ke, who had bought a number of mining properties in Virginia City before returning to California. Sarah Rose, Scott Foster's very pretty younger sister, had been happy to accompany her enterprising young husband to Virginia City. Before marrying Isaiah, she and Scott had originally journeyed to Colorado from California in order to locate their outlaw brother, but after Tracy Foster's capture and execution, Denver had become haunted for the young woman, and she was only too glad to leave Colorado behind her.

Bernhard von Hummel met Isaiah and Sarah Rose outside the entrance to Virginia City's large, open-air theater, where entertainment-hungry residents flocked to see the performers who toured the rapidly growing towns and cities of the American West. The Prussian was curious about all phases of life in Virginia City, and Isaiah had told him that if he attended the concert that evening, he would have an experience he would not forget. So he purchased a ticket and accompanied Isaiah and Sarah Rose to a seat only a half dozen rows from a large, bare stage.

The theater itself was extraordinary because the seats, which were arranged in a large semicircle, consisted of plain wooden benches. Along the sides of the stage were the "boxes," where more comfortable chairs were set up for the patrons willing to pay a higher admission price. There was no roof on the auditorium, which was surrounded only by a high wall to prevent people from watching performances free of charge. In an orchestra pit were several fiddle players, and the Prussian also caught sight of a spinet and two harpsichords. The concert, he was told by Sarah Rose, was the social event of the month.

The lady who was singing, Sarah Rose continued, was a well-known theatrical celebrity, who had performed often in London and in New York. She was currently on tour in the United States, and naturally she included Virginia City.

Bernhard raised an eyebrow. "Naturally?" he demanded. "I would have thought a community as barbaric as this would have been the last to hold a successful theatrical performance."

Both Sarah Rose and Isaiah laughed. "You'll see what we mean," Isaiah promised.

The concert was a startling revelation. The singer was

a rather good-looking, buxom lady in her late thirties, who was endowed with a large, clear voice, and she gave the audience of enthusiastic miners their moneys' worth, eliciting loud cheers after every number. At the intermission Bernhard was astonished to see the miners hurling heavy objects at the performer. "Are they trying to kill her?" he asked in alarm.

Sarah Rose shook her head. "Not at all," she explained. "They're actually rewarding the lady."

Bernhard glanced again at the stage, then looked to Sarah Rose for an explanation.

"They're throwing raw silver to her," she said, smiling as she saw the reaction of the startled European nobleman.

Bernhard looked again at the stage. The miners received part of their pay in unrefined silver ore, and they were bestowing it now on the performer as a sign that they enjoyed her performance. An assistant appeared on stage with a large basket, and when the shower ended, he quickly scooped up the raw silver.

"This is astonishing," Bernhard muttered.

Isaiah agreed. "Just about everything in Virginia City is astonishing," he declared. "I imagine the singer will earn as much from these freely given gifts of the miners as she will make from the fee that she is being paid."

"Now," Sarah Rose said, laughing, "perhaps you understand why entertainers are so eager to play in Virginia City. If they win the favor of the audiences, they can earn as much in a single night here as they can make in several weeks in San Francisco or in Chicago."

"And if they do not please the Virginia City audiences, what then?" Bernhard asked.

Isaiah shrugged and looked grave. "In that case, they're advised to leave town without delay," he said. "It can be dangerous for them when an audience turns into an unpleasant mob."

Bernhard von Hummel shook his head, convinced that the atmosphere of a frontier mining town in America was unlike that of any community he had ever known. He was about to comment to that effect when an extraordinary woman caught his eye. He gaped quite openly.

Sarah Rose saw the direction of his gaze and smiled a trifle sadly. "I might have known," she said. "I've never yet seen a man who fails to be fascinated by Caroline."

Bernhard's throat was unaccountably dry. "Caroline?" he asked hoarsely.

Sarah Rose nodded. "Her name is Caroline Brandon," she said.

"She's a widow," Isaiah added. "Her late husband was killed in Denver, and we learned on very good authority that she was employed there by a sporting house, where she enjoyed great popularity."

"She was a member of the wagon̄ train that brought us to Virginia City," Sarah Rose said, picking up the recital. "She made a great point of saying that she had reformed and intended to lead a new life for herself when she arrived here, but it's very obvious that she has done no such thing."

Bernhard nodded but continued to stare at Caroline Brandon. She had long, flaxen-blond hair and luminous green eyes, and she wore a velvet gown of deep green that was so tight that her figure left virtually nothing to the imagination. She was seated in one of the boxes at the side of the stage and appeared to be its only occupant. Now, as she rose to her feet, the astonished Bernhard saw that she carried a short, ugly whip in one hand and that she appeared to be prepared to use it. As she left the box, apparently intending to stroll through the audience during intermission, a phalanx of three burly men formed a wedge in front of her. These hirelings were strong and well armed, and their attitude indicated that they had no intention whatever of permitting any miner to molest the woman.

Caroline strolled slowly up the aisle, looking from side to side, her walk provocative. Her smile was radiant as she spotted Sarah Rose and Isaiah from a short distance and waved at them. She peered at Bernhard at length with considerable, obvious interest.

Bernhard felt as though he had been struck by a bolt

of lightning. The impact of Caroline Barndon was enormous, unlike anything he had ever experienced.

Her step slowed, and her eyes lingered on Bernhard, but ultimately she moved on and disappeared in the crowd. "Naturally," Isaiah Atkins said in a low voice, "you find her fascinating. You'd be less than human if you didn't. I'll just give you a word of warning: everyone here in Virginia City knows, that she's a prostitute, and the talk about her is not kind."

Bernhard thanked him and tried hard to concentrate on the stage as the candles that were used in the footlights of the theater dimmed and the performance resumed.

The second act proved to be much like the first, and the audience applauded the singer rapturously. Again chunks of metal were thrown at her. Had one of them struck her, she would have been injured, but she chose to take the risk. As she made repeated curtain calls, the amused Bernhard realized that she had earned herself a small fortune. He admired her courage, if not her wisdom.

Isaiah had to make an early appearance in court the following morning, so he and Sarah Rose said good night and went on their way.

Bernhard lingered behind awhile, continuing to observe the crowds of people as they made their way out of the theater and onto the dusty Virginia City streets. This frontier-town auditorium was a far cry from the elegant, ornate theaters in Berlin, and Bernhard was relieved that he had no need to draw his sword cane from his innocent-looking walking stick. Miners made up the bulk of the audience, and Bernhard had already seen how rowdy these men could become, but tonight they had enjoyed themselves thoroughly and, consequently, were on their good behavior.

Bernhard was about to head for the exit gates when someone approached him from another direction, and he paused instinctively to stand aside for Caroline Brandon, who was preceded by her three husky bodyguards.

As Caroline came face to face with the young Prussian

nobleman, she slowed her pace, and her full, pouting lips parted in a smile. She eyed him again, taking everything in, and then she said demurely, "Good evening."

Bernhard removed his stovepipe hat and clicked his heels as he bowed.

His gesture obviously pleased Caroline, who continued to walk past him without missing a step, and she indicated with a backward glance and smile that she would not object if he cared to accompany her. He promptly fell in beside her. "You are new to Virginia City?" she asked.

He nodded. "I have only recently arrived here. I am Baron Bernhard von Hummel."

Caroline was quick to note his title and to observe that his clothes were very expensive. "I am Mrs. Brandon," she said. Managing to look appropriately abject, she added ruefully, "I am a widow."

He nodded. "So I was told by Mr. and Mrs. Atkins, who I gather came to Virginia City with you."

"Yes, they are dear people," Caroline said, then sighed. "Life isn't all that easy for a woman on her own."

He was vastly amused by her remark. It was obvious by the way she dressed that she did not find widowhood a hardship and had no trouble meeting her financial obligations. As he would learn, she was one of the primary attractions of Virginia City.

"You don't live in America, I take it?" Caroline asked, companionably taking Bernhard's arm.

"My home is in Berlin," he said. "In this country I know only New York and Chicago, and only very slightly. I have come directly to Virginia City from the ship that transported me across the Atlantic."

"How fascinating," Caroline murmured. She was not putting on an act. Not only was this titled foreigner handsome, but he was unlike any man she had ever met, so he was of great interest to her. There was no need for her to feign absorption in him.

Bernhard von Hummel's pulse beat more rapidly. He was well aware of the fact that the woman on his arm was a prostitute, available to any man who could pay her price, but by recognizing only that aspect of her, he was doing her an injustice. She was by all odds the most luscious, enticing woman he had ever encountered; her appeal was overwhelming and irresistible. In addition, she spoke like a lady, and her manners appeared to be those of a lady, although her clothes were far from lady-like, to say the least. Bernhard hadn't spent any time with a woman since he had left Berlin, and he knew that he needed one. He felt no shame at being seen in the company of this fascinating creature, and he made that fact apparent in his attitude. In fact, he seemed to be proud to be walking with her.

Caroline's instinct told her all this about him, and more. She knew that he would be an experienced lover and that she would enjoy herself thoroughly with him, so her grasp tightened almost imperceptibly on his arm, and she said, hesitating prettily, "I don't wish to intrude on your plans, Baron, but if you are not otherwise engaged for the rest of the evening, I would like nothing better than to entertain you at supper."

Bernhard gallantly rose to the occasion. "I must insist," he said, "on entertaining you as my guest."

Caroline knew she had hooked him and was able to relax. "You're very kind, sir," she said, "but obviously you don't know Virginia City. There is no place in this town where a lady and a gentleman can go to dine in peace. The only eating places open at this hour are frequented by miners who will soon be drinking themselves into an intoxicated state and will be creating trouble. Therefore, I must insist that we go together to my house, where we'll not only be assured of a decent meal but also of privacy."

The relationship was developing more rapidly than Bernhard had dared to hope, and he smiled broadly. "Very well," he said. "You are most gracious, and I would be a boor if I did not accept."

She called out an order to her bodyguards, then devoted her complete attention to the man beside her as the trio skillfully led them down the street.

Bernhard was surprised by Caroline's house. Her home, which was unlike any other in Virginia City, was a small, well-built mansion complete with a brick wall surrounding a large garden illuminated by Chinese lanterns. Two more guards were on duty at the entrance, and she led the way through several tastefully furnished rooms to the garden, where she waved her guest to a seat on a large white divan. Then she clapped her hands together, and almost instantly a maid in uniform appeared, bringing them a pitcher of a drink that turned out to be a mixture of brandywine, whiskey, and various fruit juices. It was a potent combination, but Bernhard had no problem handling liquor. He noted that Caroline drank quickly and showed no ill effects.

They discussed the evening's concert at length, and the young nobleman found that his hostess was exceptionally well informed on the theater and the arts. She was an easy, amusing conversationalist, and she certainly knew how to put a male guest completely at ease. He began to realize that she was endowed with an exceptional art: she might be a prostitute. but she was able to handle herself and could converse brilliantly.

The maid served the meal, and enjoying himself thoroughly, Bernhard ate heartily. He found that the sauce on the meat accompanying the omelet was a match for any that he had ever tasted in Berlin, Paris, or London. His inquiry elicited the information that Caroline had imported a chef at considerable expense from New York. Clearly her establishment was anything but cheap to operate, and he imagined that her fee was exorbitant. He wondered how to discuss her fee with delicacy, and gradually he led the conversation toward the subject.

Caroline realized precisely what he was doing and permitted herself to be guided accordingly. She had already decided on a fee in her mind and was prepared to cite figures to him at the appropriate moment. She was in no rush. Her experience told her that the longer she waited to tantalize this potential customer, the more eager he would be to bed her. She refilled their glasses with the potent punch, and leaning back on the divan beside him, her shoulders bare, she smiled steadily, allowing her guest to take in all her abundant charms.

Suddenly they were interrupted by the sentry who was stationed at the front door. "Excuse me, Miss Caroline, ma'am," he blurted, "but we got plenty of trouble!"

Caroline frowned at the interruption, which had come at a most inopportune moment. "I'm sure the problem, whatever it is, can wait, Robert," she said severely.

The man shook his head. "I tried to stop him, ma'am, but it was like trying to call a halt to a bull buffalo that's gone loco, I swear it."

Caroline couldn't conceal her annoyance. "Whatever on earth are you talking about, Robert?"

The sentry waved an arm wildly. "It's that no-good fellow from Mississippi who hangs around here," he said. "That Douglas de Forest. He insisted on seeing you right off, and he wouldn't take no for an answer, even though I told him you were busy. So he's going through the house right now, room to room, and he'll be out here any second."

"Oh, dear," Caroline murmured, looking distressed.

"Me and Eddie could slug him real good, ma'am, and knock him out, but you gave us orders we're never to rough up the customers, and so we kind of hesitated, you might say, and we couldn't stop him. The only way you can halt that one is to knock him unconscious."

Before Caroline could reply, footsteps sounded loudly, and Douglas de Forest burst into the garden.

He was good-looking, with thick, wavy hair and flamboyant attire. His gestures and words were theatrical, and his smile, which revealed a mouthful of bright, white teeth, was obviously exaggerated. He claimed to be the son and heir of a prominent Mississippi plantation owner, and occasionally acquaintances wondered why he was in Virginia City, since he had no interest whatsoever in silver. "At last," he said loudly, "I found you."

Caroline faced him sternly. She rose to her feet and looked him up and down, her green eyes suddenly glacial. "There was no need to search so diligently, Douglas," she said. "I'm entertaining a guest here, and as I believe you've been told, I've given strict orders that I'm not to be disturbed. Needless to say, you are disturbing me."

De Forest refused to be cowed by the severity of her tone and her lack of hospitality. "I've been waiting all evening to see you," he declared. "I even followed you to the concert and then lost sight of you in the crowd afterward."

"You know I'm not beholden to you in any way," Caroline told him, "and I find your attentions quite embarrassing." She turned to her Prussian guest and gave him an apologetic smile. "I'm so sorry, Bernhard," she said. "There's really no need for you to be subjected to this boor or his outlandish conduct."

Bernhard thought that he should at least offer to rid her of the unwanted company of Douglas de Forest. The man obviously was incensed, and perhaps he was intoxicated; it was difficult to tell for certain. "If you wish," he said, "I will put him out."

"Will you, now!" de Forest said loudly.

Caroline was so grateful to Bernhard that she ignored the danger signs. "You're very kind and considerate, sir," she said, "but my own security guards can well protect me. I see no need for you to become involved." She turned back to her unwelcome guest. "I bid you good night, Douglas," she said flatly.

De Forest responded by planting his feet far apart and defiantly folding his arms across his chest. "You're not getting rid of me all that easily," he said. "I have rights, and you know it."

Caroline's temper flared. "You have rights, sir?" she asked icily. "What rights do you have? I am beholden to you? No! I am beholden to no man. I call my soul my own, and I entertain those whom it pleases me to have here as my guests. It does not please me to have you here, and I bid you good night at once, sir."

De Forest continued to stand unmoving.

"If need be," Caroline said, "I'll have my guards put

you out. I hate to create a scene, but you're forcing my hand. Now, sir, either you go peacefully, quietly, and quickly, or you will force me to act accordingly."

Douglas de Forest responded by laughing loudly. Then suddenly he stared at Bernhard, who had risen and taken his place beside the young woman. Taking his gloves from his pocket, de Forest flicked them deftly as he struck the Prussian across the face. "I brook no rivals for Caroline Brandon's affections," he shouted. "I challenge you to a duel, sir, to be fought at once, this very night! And I assure you it will be a duel to the death."

Bernhard could scarcely believe he was involved in such a bizarre incident. He found it difficult to comprehend that this apparent madman, who was claiming Caroline Brandon as his own, did not realize that she was available to the highest bidder. Bernhard was embarrassed by the prospect of a duel over such a woman, no matter how attractive she might be. He knew the furor that would be created at the court in Berlin and in the circles of munitions makers there if it became known that he had fought a battle for the favors of a courtesan. He had no choice, however, because of Douglas de Forest's insistence that the issue be settled by force of arms. As far as Bernhard was concerned, there was no issue, but that apparently was beside the point. What was more, his honor was at stake.

The one aspect that did not bother Bernhard in the least was the possibility that he might be wounded or otherwise incapacitated. He felt certain of his ability to take care of himself, regardless of what weapon was used in the duel.

He looked helplessly at Caroline, silently appealing to her to call off the hot-tempered young Southerner. Her slight shrug, however, spoke volumes. There was nothing she could do to curb de Forest's temper. That meant, like it or not, a duel would have to be fought here, on the courtesan's property, and now, in the small hours of the morning.

"As the challenged party," Bernhard said, "I believe I

have the choice of weapons." His matter-of-fact calm had an immediate effect on Douglas de Forest.

"To be sure," he said. "I assumed, naturally, that we would fight with pistols."

Bernhard's smile was icy. "I have no objection to pistols," he said, "but in this instance I would insist on using my own, and I'm afraid that I would be required to return to my lodgings for them. I don't ordinarily make it a habit of traveling about with a pair of dueling pistols in hand." He smiled broadly.

The sober-faced Caroline appeared stricken, however, and did not share his sense of humor.

"I believe," Bernhard said, still speaking crisply but quietly, "that circumstances will make it necessary for us to use swords. I have my blade, which is serviceable enough, and I see that you carry a sword of about the same length. I'm willing to accept these weapons and deal accordingly."

The arrangements were absurd according to any code of dueling, but that did not matter. There were no legal seconds; no qualified physician was in attendance; and no attempt was being made to reconcile the differences between the principals. In fact, the whole incident, Bernhard thought, was as wild and as unreasonable as everything else in Virginia City.

Not waiting for further discussion, de Forest stalked off to the far side of the garden, where he drew his sword and waited impatiently, tapping a foot on the gravel path. Bernhard had no choice but to follow him, and Caroline reluctantly trailed after the pair. She dreaded the bloodshed, but she knew of no way to quiet Douglas de Forest.

Bernhard halted a sensible distance from his foe and inquired politely, "I assume you abide by the customary rules of swordplay?"

"Naturally," de Forest snapped. "Shall we begin?"

"Not so fast," the baron cautioned. "He who first draws blood, regardless of whether the wound he inflicts is major or minor, will be regarded as the winner of the duel. That must be understood and mutually agreed upon before we cross swords."

The Mississippian found it impossible to curb his temper. "You insist, sir, upon reciting the obvious. I've already informed you that I abide by the customary rules of swordplay. Now, sir, you will either fight me at once, or I shall brand you publicly as a coward!"

Bernhard's patience was exhausted, and he was growing weary of the other man's ranting. However, there was no escape for him, and so he decided to do his best.

That best, as Douglas de Forest discovered almost immediately, was formidable. The young baron had been trained in a hard school and had gained great expertise as a swordsman. He easily deflected his opponent's fierce opening lunge. His wrist moved no more than a slight fraction of an inch, and de Forest's blade slid up the length of his own, virtually immobilized.

For some time Bernhard was content to remain on the defensive. His foe was none too accomplished a swordsman, but he made up in zest what he lacked in subtlety. He telegraphed every move in advance, which made it a simple matter for the Prussian to protect himself and remain unscathed.

Caroline stood near the garden wall, one hand at her throat, her lips parted, her breathing heavy. She was badly frightened and was expecting the worst.

Bernhard wanted to reassure her but did not want to risk taking his gaze from his foe. "You may relax my dear," he called. "I assure you that all will be well and that you will have no problems with which to contend."

Caroline knew he was trying to soothe her but refused to be consoled. De Forest, however, considered the observation deliberately demeaning and redoubled his efforts.

Bernhard continued to parry methodically, and his enemy's blade did not touch him. Suddenly, however, he grew tired of the sport. He could continue to play this same senseless game for hours, but he saw nothing to be gained by it. The hour was late, and it was time to end the farce. So he called softly, "En garde, sir!" Then he shifted from the defense to attack, and feinting cleverly, he drew his blade down the cheek of his opponent. He inflicted a scratch about a half inch in length, and it began to bleed. "I have fulfilled the requirements of the duel," Bernhard announced and, stepping backward, disengaged.

Douglas de Forest was so furious, however, that he rushed forward and lunged at his foe. The astonished Bernhard barely managed to raise his sword in time to deflect the blow that otherwise would have killed him. He, too, lost his temper now, and his sword flailing, he swiftly disarmed the young Mississippian, sending his sword flying through the air and leaving him helpless.

De Forest struck a theatrical pose. "I am defenseless now, sir, so you may kill me at your leisure."

Bernhard wanted no more of his false heroics. "You will leave at once, sir," he declared, "or I shall be obliged to tan your backside with the flat of this blade." He advanced toward de Forest as if to make good his mortifying threat.

De Forest, robbed of his dignity, bowed coldly to Caroline. Paying no further heed to the Prussian, he marched off.

It was very quiet now in the garden. Then Caroline Brandon's peal of laughter sounded loud and clear, and both she and the baron relaxed.

Bernhard was relieved that the incident had ended and that no complications had developed. The hour was late, he had a busy day awaiting him again in the morning, and the time had come for him to withdraw to his own quarters.

Caroline, however, had other ideas. Bernhard had emerged the victor and according to her criteria, he deserved the spoils. She went to him slowly, deliberately slid her arms around his neck, pressing close to him, and rewarded him with a lingering kiss on the mouth.

Startled by her initiative and aroused by her blatant sexuality, Bernhard responded in kind to her gesture.

"You will spend the night with me?" Caroline murmured.

Only a boor would have refused, and Bernhard von Hummel prided himself on being a gentleman.

"We'll settle mutually on a fee that's agreeable to both of us," the young woman murmured carelessly.

Bernhard realized that she had injected the statement into the conversation in anything but a careless mood, but he was in no position to object. Obviously her fee was her primary objective, and at no time did she forget it.

She smiled at him warmly and then led him into the house. He followed her to a huge chamber on the second floor, dominated by a mammoth four-poster bed. Thoughts of sleep left his mind.

Caroline quickly rearranged the lighting, and soon the room was bathed in soft candlelight. With marvelous dexterity she changed into a clinging, ruffled silk negligee, and when she slowly approached the seated, staring man, her lips parted in invitation.

Bernhard knew that he was being rewarded for winning the duel, and he accepted his victory graciously as he rose and folded the luscious creature in his arms.

II

Canadians regarded the town of Victoria as unique. Located in the Royal Crown colony of Vancouver, part of British Columbia, the town combined the dignity of the Old World, which was reflected in its formal flower gardens and neat rows of houses, with the raucous brashness of the New World. Certainly Victoria was a boom town by any standards, for it was the takeoff point for gold seekers in the Canadian Northwest. Consequently, it was filled with miners and with men of every age and every vocation, all of them planning to make their way to the profitable gold fields that lay to the north. The town fathers struggled hard to maintain the civilized ways of the Old World and frowned on brothels, saloons, and gambling houses that characterized such communities as Virginia City in the Nevada Territory of the United States. The town fathers, however, fought a losing battle; human nature was too strong for them, and the greed of the gold seekers was all-consuming.

The dark-haired, black-eyed Lady Alison White, whose fair complexion identified her instantly as English, stood at the windows in the parlor of the white clapboard house and looked pensively beyond the rose gardens to the street beyond. She felt, with good cause, that she was a prisoner in Victoria and that she was suffering from a nightmare that would never end.

She had come to the New World with high hopes, accompanying her husband, Sir Charles White, who had been selected as managing director of a supposedly prosperous gold mine in the rugged Northwest Territory. The couple had paused in Victoria for the winter, intending to go on again when the weather became warmer in the spring. Then Charles, who had never known a day of illness in his life, suddenly dropped dead of a heart attack.

Alison had borne the tragedy well, thanks in part to the loyal support of Sid and Martha Sewell, investors in the mine, who had promptly opened their home to her. By now, thanks to the continuing kindness of the older couple, she had overcome the shock over the loss of her husband. But there was no telling how much longer she would be required to linger in Victoria. She had received a letter to the effect that the directors of Charles's company would be sending her a return ticket for London and funds for the long journey. Until that money arrived, however, she was obliged to remain in Victoria, for she had no funds of her own.

"Thank God for you and Sid!" she said as Martha Sewell came into the parlor.

Martha knew that her lovely young guest had been brooding again, and she spoke with forced cheerfulness. "We've done nothing that others would not do," she said. "Now, do stop dwelling on it."

Alison shook her head. "I'm not thinking about Charles, and I'm not allowing myself to become depressed. Honestly. All that I'm thinking is that I wonder how much longer I'll be obliged to stare out at this same view."

"Sid feels, and I agree with him," Martha said patiently, "that you're too young and too pretty to be left to wander freely through Victoria. These days the town is crammed with men who are undesirables, and you know that you'll just create complications for yourself if you go off traipsing through the streets."

"I take your word for it, Martha," Alison said, sighing. "I'm not the most patient of women, and it certainly isn't easy for me to stay cooped up here. The weather has become nice, and ships have been calling here for weeks now. I just can't understand why I haven't heard any more from the directors of Charles's company. So many weeks have passed since they wrote to tell me that they were sending me funds for my return to England."

Martha Sewell had expressed the same wonder to her husband in private, but she assumed a confident air for Alison's sake. "They'll get to it soon enough. So in the meantime, you might as well enjoy yourself as best you can."

Alison knew she was right and tried to force herself to relax, but it was difficult. She was young, alive, and alert, and she had her whole life ahead of her. She supposed that if she had really been in love with Charles, she might feel differently about her situation, but he had been many years her elder, and she had married him at the insistence of her parents. Thus, when he died she felt a sense of freedom as well as loss.

Well, she was stuck in Victoria, so she sighed and said, "If you pass any magazine vendors today or tomorrow when you go into town, Martha, I would be grateful if you would see if they've received the latest installment of Mr. Dickens's *Great Expectations*. It's my favorite of his books so far, and reading it does so help to pass the time."

A maid brought in a pot of steaming tea, and as Martha observed the ritual of pouring, the two women, by mutual, unspoken consent, changed the subject. They discussed the latest fashions from London and Paris, although they were far behind the times. They mentioned the civil war in America, but both admittedly knew very little about affairs in the United States. Their talk necessarily was confined mainly to the prospects of finding gold in the Northwest.

While they chatted, a man paused near the gate, then entered and slowly walked up past banks of roses on both sides of the front door. A short, lean, dark man, he was impeccably dressed. At first glance, at least, he did not appear to be English. He rang the doorbell, then the maid went to answer it. A moment later she returned.

"A Mr. Poole is here to see Lady White," she announced.

Alison and Martha exchanged glances, and the former shrugged. "I'm not acquainted with the gentleman," Alison said. "In fact, I don't recall ever hearing his name before. Did he state his business?"

The maid shook her head. "No, ma'am."

Martha took charge. "Be good enough to show him in," she directed, rising to her feet.

The man followed the maid into the room. He was carrying his hat and his gloves in one hand. At least, Alison decided, he had manners.

"Lady White?" he asked, looking at Martha.

"I am Mrs. Sewell," she said. "This is Lady White."

Alison inclined her head. The man reached into an inner breast pocket and removed a sheet of parchment, which he unfolded and handed to her. It was an exceptional, impressive document. It bore the official seal of the British prime minister at the top. The message contained was succinct and to the point: *Mr. Poole is my representative. Please deal with him accordingly. Palmerston.*

"Well," Alison said, "your credentials are certainly impressive." Her heart was beating fast as she thought that this at last might be the man who was bringing her the funds to return home.

Poole inclined his head slightly but did not smile. "Perhaps," he said, "you'd care to accompany me on a stroll, milady? I'm obliged to converse with you in private."

Martha Sewell promptly took charge. "Her Ladyship will not leave this house with you, Mr. Poole," she said. "With all due respect, in spite of your credentials, we don't know you, do we?"

He nodded slowly, grudging admiration in his eyes.

"I shall be pleased," Martha continued, "to leave you here privately in this room with Her Ladyship, where you may discuss what you will in the full knowledge that no one is overhearing you and that what you have to say may be treated in confidence. But that's the extent of what I'm prepared to do for you. Her Ladyship's protection is my responsibility, and I do not intend to treat it lightly."

The stranger's solemn mood changed abruptly. "Good for you, ma'am," he declared, grinning broadly. "I accept, by all means."

Martha insisted on pouring him a cup of tea and then withdrew from the parlor. The man sat opposite Alison and regarded her steadily. "I have come a long distance specifically to see you, milady. In brief, I've come all the way from London."

Alison made no attempt to hide her growing excitement.

"I trust you understand that everything I say to you is in complete confidence. I must stress to you that none of what I say to you is to be repeated."

Now she was mystified. This did not sound like the kind of talk that had anything to do with providing her the means to go home. She folded her hands in her lap and waited for him to continue.

"I regret to inform you," Poole said solemnly, "that contrary to a popular belief, the late Sir Charles White left no estate of consequence. He allegedly was a man of considerable wealth, but that wealth was strictly a myth."

"I see," Alison said. She was neither surprised nor disappointed in this news. She had suspected for a long time that Charles was not endowed with the funds that had made her parents believe he was such a fine catch. But that still did not explain why this man had come all the way from London to see her.

Although no one was within earshot, Poole lowered his voice as he continued. "I don't know how familiar you may be with your late husband's business affairs," he began.

Alison cut him short. "We were married only a short time before Sir Charles's unfortunate death," she said, "and during that time we had little reason to discuss business. He wasn't the type to bring his office affairs home with him."

Poole nodded somberly. "You knew him, then, as the managing director of a large gold mine in the Northwest?"

"Yes, of course," she replied, somewhat irritated by his manner and impatient for him to explain the nature of his visit.

"The position of mine director was a front, a pose, Lady White," he said. "Sir Charles was actually in the employ of Lord Palmerston and was one of the prime minister's most efficient and effective intelligence agents."

Alison had no reason to doubt the stranger's wild statement, but she was completely stunned by it. "I—I had no idea," she murmured.

"Lord Palmerston regrets the delay of your departure from Victoria, but he has been searching everywhere—in vain—for a suitable replacement for Sir Charles. Frankly, he can find no one."

"Oh, dear." The remark was inane, Alison knew, but she didn't know what else to say.

"I am requested by Lord Palmerston," Poole said, a note of urgency creeping into his voice, "to ask you to act as your late husband's replacement."

The idea was absurd, and she laughed aloud, shaking her head. "I'm afraid I know nothing whatever about being an intelligence agent for a government," she said. "I've had no training for such work, and I'm in total ignorance of what is required."

Poole sipped his tea appreciatively. "I'm aware of your handicaps, Lady White, and I assure you that the prime minister is even more conscious of them. Believe me, he would not ask you to do anything beyond your capabilities. As I understand your background, you enjoyed a rather successful career as a singer prior to your marriage."

"Yes, I did," she replied modestly, "If you can call eleven weeks at Covent Garden a sign of success. I daresay I would have moved several notches higher in my profession, but I gave up my work when I was married.

I had been intending to resume it when I returned to London."

"Perhaps you will have an opportunity," Poole said mysteriously, "to resume your career long before you go back to London."

"I'm afraid I don't understand," she said.

"Ah, you will, Lady White," he assured her. "Your work will not be arduous, and the government will pay you well for it. Furthermore, you'll have a chance to earn double fees because you'll be paid as a singer, as well."

The offer sounded almost too good to be true. Perhaps she would have a chance, after all, to acquire the money for her passage to England.

"Have you heard of a town in the western part of the United States called Virginia City?" he asked. "It's located in what is known as the Nevada Territory."

Alison nodded. "I've read an occasional article about it in the *Victoria Press*," she said. "It's a silver mining town, I believe."

"Your belief is correct," Poole said briskly. "Arrangements will be made for you to go there. You will be engaged as a singer at one of the popular theaters. All that you earn will be yours, and let me assure you that the miners there have a custom of rewarding singers whose work they like."

"I look forward to an early resumption of my singing career," she said, "but you haven't told me the nature of my work for the prime minister."

"That should be very simple," Poole told her. "Lord Palmerston is very eager to have you find out precisely how much of the newly mined silver is being acquired by the United States government. As we understand it, some mines are owned by the government, and the Treasury takes all of the silver that is mined from the ground and smelted. We understand, also, that the government buys other quantities of silver from private owners for a special price."

"How do I go about learning these facts?" Alison asked.

"In any manner that you see fit, Lady White," he said. "The information that the prime minister seeks is vital to the policy-making procedure of Great Britain, but it is not particularly secret in any sense of the word. I should think that the information is available to anyone who seeks it, although I doubt very much that the figures are automatically made public."

"Well," the young Englishwoman said dubiously, "it sounds simple and aboveboard. I'm not certain that I'm capable of obtaining the data that Lord Palmerston wants, but I have no objection to trying to gather it for him."

"Splendid," Poole said. "Be good enough to remember that the future of Great Britain depends—far more than you could believe possible—on the acquisition by the prime minister of the simple facts that I have outlined for you."

By no stretch of the imagination was Alison happy to have been thrust into the role of an espionage agent, but she had to count her blessings. At least she was going to be resuming her career as a singer and would be active far sooner than she had anticipated. Even more important, she would be leaving the stifling atmosphere of Victoria, and then after she carried out her assignment, she would finally be able to go home.

Poole rose briskly to his feet. "Stay here for the present," he told her, "and say nothing to anyone about our meeting. You will receive a letter before long, inviting you to sing in Virginia City, and you will of course accept the engagement. I'm sure that you will find that the fee offered to you will be generous and satisfactory."

"Where do I make my report to the prime minister?" she demanded.

"I shall contact you," Poole replied, "and then you will tell me what you have learned."

The Civil War had begun, and Washington City, the capital of the Union, was bustling. At the executive mansion, Abraham Lincoln had announced his intention of keeping his doors open to all who wanted to see him, but Major General George B. McClellan and the General Staff had ruled otherwise. Confederate agents were everywhere, and the President of the United States was a prime target for assassination. Lincoln was careless of his safety, but the army was not, and troops surrounded the White House twenty-four hours a day. Major General Lee Blake became aware of the security precautions when he rode his horse up to the main gate of the White House and was politely asked by a stern-faced young captain to show his credentials. Only when he had satisfied the young officer was Lee Blake allowed to proceed, and he noted that there were other troops stationed at strategic intervals inside the building as well.

At last he was admitted to the President's inner office, and he saluted smartly. Lincoln peered at him owlishly, his spectacles sliding down his nose, and he removed the glasses and waved an arm. "Sit down, General," he said. "You will find that the brown chair is comfortable. The official furniture in this place left a great deal to be desired, you know. I can't understand how my predecessors ever got along with it. That brown chair comes from my own law office in Springfield, and it's as comfortable as any you'll find."

"Thanks, Mr. President," Lee said as he sat.

The President shoved aside a mound of papers and grinned at him. "I suppose you're curious as to why I sent for you?"

"Well, sir," Lee replied, "I know I'm due for a transfer to a new command, and I assumed that you wanted to discuss it with me yourself rather than letting it come to me from the regular War Department channels."

Lincoln chuckled. "That's my excuse," he said. "If you want the truth of the situation, I've heard only good things about you, and I'm discovering that's very unusual when an officer reaches your rank, Blake. So I was curious to see you myself."

Lee smiled and then reflected that the stories he had heard about the new President undoubtedly were true. Lincoln liked to play the role of the small-town lawyer, but he was an exceptionally shrewd man.

The President picked up a single sheet of paper. "Let me stress to you the command you're being given is relatively temporary," he said. "Ultimately I'll need you for a combat command, so you can expect a transfer at an appropriate time, when the need becomes great."

"I see, sir."

"For the present, a new command has been created for you. We're calling it the Pacific Command. It comprises territory with which you're thoroughly familiar—the states of California and Oregon, the Washington Territory that lies north of Oregon, and the Nevada Territory, as well. It covers a pretty big area because the whole of the Idaho country is also included in the Washington Territory."

Lee was pleased because he was being returned to the part of the land that he knew and loved.

"I'm giving you a choice," Lincoln said. "You can either make your headquarters at the Presidio in San Francisco or farther to the north at Fort Vancouver, Washington, opposite Portland on the Columbia River."

"If it's all the same to you, Mr. President, I prefer to make my headquarters at Fort Vancouver."

Lincoln was surprised. "I'd have thought the lure of San Francisco would be irresistible."

"If I am to be responsible for the safety of the very large western territories, I prefer that my headquarters be more strategically located for military purposes, sir," Lee said.

Lincoln looked at him and obviously respected his judgment. "That makes a great deal of sense," he said. "You'll glean specifics from the records at the War Department. All that I can tell you is that we're expecting the Rebels to be kicking up a fuss just about everywhere, and that means there are certain to be sabotage attempts in your territory, from time to time. You'll handle them as you see fit."

"Thank you, sir," he said.

"One of your most important jobs," the President said, "will be to organize a special wagon train that will travel east to the railroads and then will proceed by rail."

The procedure seemed unusual, and Lee's curiosity was piqued. "What cargo will this wagon train carry, Mr. President?" he wanted to know.

"Silver bullion," Lincoln replied succinctly. "A vast quantity of silver bullion. You will need to have special freight wagons built to carry the silver, and you'll have to arrange with the railroads to have special cars constructed for you. Silver is a very heavy metal, and there's one whale of a lot of it that's going to be transported. Needless to say, you'll take the greatest security precautions possible to protect the bullion, which is going to be vital for the Union's prosecution of the war."

"Yes, sir."

"You'll work out the details strictly as you see fit. I'll provide you with a confidential directive giving you the order, and from there you'll be on your own. Needless to say, I'm sure you realize that the country depends on you, General, and that you're going to have a delicate and difficult mission."

"I won't let you or the country down, Mr. President," Lee replied as he rose to his feet, saluted, and left the office of the overworked Abraham Lincoln.

That evening at dinner, Lee repeated to his wife and daughter the news that they would be traveling to the West. Cathy Blake listened in silence. Still attractive, with blond hair and blue eyes, she had gained only a few pounds since the days, long ago, when she had driven the lead wagon on the first train to cross the United States to Oregon. She was delighted at the news.

"How wonderful," she exclaimed. "Going to Fort Vancouver, so close to where we once lived in Oregon, is a dream come true. It really is. How in the world did you ever wangle the assignment, Lee?"

"I didn't." He grinned. "As I understand it from the personnel people at the War Department, the President selected me for the post from the available candidates."

Beth Blake, who had just completed her third year at college, was an exceptionally handsome young woman who greatly resembled her mother. She grinned insolently at her father and asked, "Why do you suppose President Lincoln wanted you in particular, Daddy?"

Her mother frowned and would have reprimanded her but knew it was no use: in her father's eyes Beth could do no wrong.

Lee grinned at her. "I'd answer your very fresh question, young lady, if I could, but there are matters of national security at stake that are none of your business. So let's just say that the President figured that I'd fit the bill."

"It's not fair to claim national security," Beth protested. "But there isn't much that I can do to stop you, is there?"

Her father laughed and then turned back to his wife. "We're being sent by warship as far as Panama," he said. "We and the members of my staff whom I elect to take with us. The government is providing us with a special train to carry us across Panama, and another warship will pick us up on the Pacific side and will carry us straight to Fort Vancouver."

"How lovely!" Cathy exclaimed.

Beth helped herself to vegetables and shook her head. "It's pretty wonderful the way the government lays out a red carpet for an officer of your rank, Daddy," she said. "You really do get the best of everything, don't you?"

Her father chuckled and shook his head.

Cathy replied quickly. "There were a great many years after your father and I were first married when we didn't have warships and special trains assigned to us, believe me," she said. "As for Fort Vancouver, that was a British fort when we lived in Oregon and built the first buildings there ourselves. They were little more than log cabins."

"That's true, Beth," Lee added, reminiscing. "You were just a little tyke when we left there. You wouldn't remember it as it was then."

The young woman smiled. "I remember the times we went back to visit. There was that nasty little boy, Toby Holt, who constantly teased me and pulled my hair. He threatened to throw me into the Columbia River when I insisted on accompanying him whenever he went fishing."

Lee roared with laughter. "I knew nothing about all that," he said. "Good for Toby."

"I thought at the time that Toby was rather brutal," Cathy observed. "I'd have spoken to his parents, but Eulalia and Whip were such good and special friends that I didn't want anything to come between us and disturb our relationship."

Beth remained indignant. "What's so funny, Daddy?" she demanded.

"If you must know," Lee said, "you really could be a terrible little nuisance when you chose to be. I don't blame Toby Holt in the least for threatening you when you tried to pester him when he was going fishing. By the way, did he ever succeed in throwing you into the Columbia?"

Beth sniffed and looked stern. "He wouldn't have dared," she said. "Granted that he was a boy, so he was bigger and stronger than I was, but I was always a far better swimmer, and I told him that if he tried to throw me in, I'd drag him into the water with me, and what's more, I'd hold him under it until he drowned."

Lee chuckled again, and Cathy forced a pained smile.

"I'd have done it, believe me," Beth said earnestly. "If anybody had tried to throw me into the river, I'd have forced him to pay for it—the hardest of hard ways!"

Eulalia Holt sat in the kitchen of her Oregon ranch house and shook her head in silent wonder as she watched her husband and son eat. She had prepared a large pot roast for supper—at least it had been large by a normal family's standards—and it was disappearing quickly, even with one person less at the table. Her daughter, Cindy, was not at home, as she was spending the summer with a girlfriend whose family had moved to Olympia in the nearby Washington Territory. That left Eulalia with her two men: Whip, her husband, and Toby, her son, who was home for vacation from the University of Michigan.

For a long time, Eulalia had thought that Whip's large appetite was due, at least in part, to the years he had spent as a hunter, trapper, and guide in the mountains of the West. He had eaten enormous quantities of food then, and there had been no diminution of his appetite since he had arrived in Oregon as the guide of the first wagon train and had settled down with Eulalia to raise horses on their ranch.

What galled her was that he gained hardly an ounce, no matter how much he ate. Even in recent years, when his arthritis had slowed his physical activity, he had continued to eat heartily. Eulalia privately envied him. She herself looked far from middle-aged: her figure was still svelte, her dark hair was still thick and shining, and her blue eyes were as bright as they had ever been, but she only had to look at food, and she gained weight.

Toby, their son, who was tall and husky and as athletic as his father had been in his prime, had an appetite that matched his father's. He, too, never gained an ounce, but she knew that that was normal for someone of his age. She watched the pot roast disappear, and with it the two men consumed huge baked potatoes and a large platter of corn. She had completed her own meal and, in contented silence, watched them eating.

Whip saw the humor in her eyes, but long experience with her had taught him to ask her no questions. Instead he concentrated on his meal.

Toby stared out at the familiar view to the east through the kitchen windows. He could see snow-covered Mount Hood plainly and thought how he had taken the view for granted when he had been younger. Now, having been away from home attending college for more than three years, he appreciated the beauty of the Oregon wilderness, loving it as much as his parents did.

Eulalia spoke suddenly, breaking the silence. "We'll miss you when you go back to school, Toby," she said. "I know we ought to be accustomed to your coming and going by now, after all these years, but it's always the same."

Toby looked at his mother, glanced at his father, and

then drew in a sharp breath. "I've been putting off telling both of you something for the past few weeks," he said, "but I can't delay any longer."

Eulalia braced herself for the worst. Her husband, however, followed his lifelong principle of refusing to worry until he had good cause for his concern. He grinned at his son in order to encourage him and waited tranquilly.

"I'm scheduled to receive my Bachelor of Science degree in another few months," Toby said, "and that would win me a job with any railroad in the United States, particularly the companies I'm interested in—the new roads that are coming to the West. But what I'm doing can't be helped: I'm not finishing school."

His mother had been prepared for this announcement, since Toby had already discussed the possibility of his leaving school in the event war broke out, but Eulalia still let out a sigh when she heard the news. The expression on Whip's leathery face remained unchanged, he continued to gaze serenely at his son, and the only indication that he gave of being perturbed was to run a hand through his silver-colored hair.

"As you know, it's the war," Toby explained. "The President hasn't yet called up the reserve militia of the individual states, but it's obviously just a matter of time now until he does so. The way I hear it, the Oregon militia is undoubtedly going to be called to duty within a month. Certainly they'll be called before I could win a degree."

Whip nodded. "That's true," he said, explaining for his wife's benefit. "I still have some connections with the militia, even though I've been retired as its colonel, and I believe Toby's information is correct. The regiment and the supplemental battalions will be subject to active, full-time military duty within the next four to five weeks."

Their display of calm encouraged Toby. "That's about the size of it," he said. "As I once explained to you, I feel that my duty to my country must take precedence over any duty that I owe to myself. I know you've both

51

been anxious to see me win my degree, but that will have to wait. I still hold a commission as a first lieutenant in the state militia, and that must come first."

As much as Eulalia hated to see her son go off to war, she knew he was right. "Of course," she said, as though she had suffered no doubts regarding his plans.

"Toby," Whip said with hearty heaviness, "I envy you, boy. If my damned hip didn't cripple me so badly, I'd insist on going off to war with you, with or without a commission."

Eulalia kept her counsel but privately was vastly relieved that Whip's ailment had forced him to retire as commander of the Oregon militia. He had spent enough years fighting, and he deserved his rest now. He wouldn't agree with such sentiments, naturally, so she knew better than to express her thoughts aloud.

"So I'll be staying home until I'm called," Toby said. "I'll make myself useful around the ranch, naturally, until I leave."

His mother smiled at him. "You always do," she said.

He nodded and then twisted in his seat slightly to face his father. "Pa," he said, "tell me truthfully—what do you think the chances are that the Oregon militia will see any real action in the war?"

Whip stared out at the view with unseeing eyes as he sorted his thoughts. "That all depends," he said. "All I know about the military situation is what I read in the papers, but I would doubt if any troops from the West—including ours and the units from California—will be sent to the eastern theater of war. A new commander is due to take charge of the Pacific district in the immediate future, and I would think he would hold all of his troops for possible action here. California presents a tempting target to the Confederacy, and Oregon is a rich prize, too. For that matter, so is the Nevada Territory. All that silver they found at Virginia City—a whole mountain of it—makes it a very tempting prize, too."

Toby looked disappointed. His father grinned at him. "I know just how you feel, boy," he said. "You're itching to be in the thick of the action. When I was your age, I felt just exactly the way you feel now."

Eulalia laughed aloud. "Age is totally irrelevant. If you had your way, you'd go marching into battle for the Union this very day, and you know it."

Whip smiled at her sheepishly.

"I know you, Michael Holt," she said. "I know your bloodthirsty ways."

Whip turned to his son. "Your mother," he said, "is a splendid woman. She's more intelligent than most ladies, and she sure as shooting is better looking. In addition to that, she's a fine wife and mother, but she has no understanding whatsoever of what makes a man tick. She can't grasp that it isn't bloodthirstiness that motivates me in wanting to do what I can for the Union. It's a sense of obligation to a country that has been very good to me and to mine."

"Indeed it has, and I'd like to remind you that you've been very good to the United States," Eulalia replied firmly.

Toby intervened diplomatically. "I wonder if either of you has seen tonight's Portland newspaper," he said. "There's an article in it speculating on who the commander of the Pacific district is going to be, and whoever wrote the piece suggested what a welcome move it would be if President Lincoln decided to give the appointment to General Blake."

Whip smiled broadly and leaned back in his chair.

"Lee and Cathy were among the original settlers here, you know, and there's nobody in the army more deserving of the command than Lee Blake, I can tell you that much," Eulalia said flatly.

A mischievous expression appeared in her husband's eyes. "Lee is such an old and good friend," he said, "that I reckon I could persuade him to grant me a special mission, arthritis or no arthritis."

Eulalia smiled a trifle primly and shook her head. "I'm sorry, my dear Michael," she said. "I don't care how good a friend he is. Cathy is an even better friend of yours, as well as of mine, and you can be sure that she wouldn't permit her husband to do any such thing. Much as I hate to say it, you're going to have to act your age and sit out this war."

Again Toby felt compelled to intervene. "The only thing I object to in the Blakes is their daughter," he said. "Beth is just about the most spoiled, opinionated brat I've ever encountered in all my life."

His mother sighed. "I think she's a charming girl, and so does your father," she replied severely. "Unfortunately you and Beth have never hit it off."

"You know why, don't you?" Whip inquired, speaking mildly.

"I haven't the vaguest idea," she replied.

"Because you and Cathy decided when Toby and Beth were small that you wanted to see them get married someday. Every time the Blakes visited us here, you threw Toby and Beth at each other, and I can't say as I blame either of them for rebelling."

Although Eulalia looked hurt, she confined her reaction to a loud sniff and a shake of her head.

Toby decided it was the better part of wisdom to keep his views to himself, so he helped himself to one more slice of pot roast and concentrated his full attention on his meal.

The man who called himself Poole not only kept his word but worked efficiently and with great speed. Within a remarkably short time after his visit to Victoria, Alison received a contract from the open-air theater in Virginia City, Nevada, offering her ten concerts and paying her the very liberal sum of five hundred dollars per concert. She signed the document, sent it on its way, and was further elated when Poole sent her funds that would see her from Victoria to Virginia City and would pay her expenses until such time as she began to earn a salary.

She bade a warm farewell to the Sewells, promising to write to them when she was able. She had told them as little as possible about the purpose of Poole's visit, saying only that the Englishman had indeed provided her with the funds to return home.

Alison sailed from Vancouver Island to San Francisco on one of the regularly scheduled steamships that traveled along the Pacific Coast. Then, instead of boarding a ship that would take her to England, as she had told the Sewells, she went on to Virginia City in a convoy of wagons that included a dozen trappers who were familiar with the mountains and deserts. Fortunately the party included an itinerant minister and his wife, and they acted as chaperons and protectors of Alison, seeing her to Virginia City without incident.

There, calling herself Alison White rather than Lady White, Alison took a small suite of rooms in the Virginia City Hotel.

Alison was struck immediately by the primitive, violent nature of life in Virginia City, and it amused her to remember how protective Sid and Martha Sewell had been about her welfare in Victoria. She knew that now she no longer could hide behind the respectable, sheltering façade of widowhood, and she forced herself to accept Virginia City for what it was.

She was aided in achieving this attitude by her sense of excitement over the resumption of her career. When she had married, she had assumed that her career had come to an end, and she had stifled her deep, lingering regrets at giving up something that she wanted so desperately and for which she had struggled so long. Now she was being given a new opportunity to make her girlhood dreams come true, and she was determined to succeed, even in Virginia City. As a matter of fact, she knew that if she could attract and hold an audience here, she would be able to do so almost anywhere.

As she began to rehearse for her opening concert, Alison found she was rusty, since she hadn't used her voice for so long, and she was glad that she had ample time for practice. In fact, she became so absorbed in her work and her new life here that she very nearly forgot all about the information Poole wanted her to obtain.

On the third day of her Virginia City stay, Alison received a visitor who introduced herself as Susanna Fulton, the editor of the *Journal*. She asked permission to write an article on the Englishwoman, and Alison graciously allowed herself to be interviewed as they sat together in the noisy hotel dining room, where they both ordered tea. She answered Susanna's questions with such forthright bluntness that the two young women, who were about the same age, soon struck a close rapport. Before long they were chatting about subjects other than the interview.

"Perhaps you'll be good enough to tell me something, since I've answered all of your questions," Alison said. "Don't you loathe Virginia City?"

Susanna was amused by the directness and lack of tact of the question and laughed. "I've known worse places," she said. "I don't find the town particularly objectionable. May I ask what it is that you don't like?"

Alison waved a hand disdainfully. "The men here drive one mad. Men, men, men! When I walk to the theater, I'm accosted on the street. When I eat a meal, regardless of whether I dine in a restaurant or eat right here in the hotel, men seem to pop out of the woodwork and annoy me. I've never known such brazen, forward, insistent men in all my life."

Susanna nodded sympathetically. "I know what you mean," she said.

Alison stared at her. "You're very attractive," she said. "Surely you get your share of attention—and more."

"I'm afraid I do," Susanna said, "but I'm inured to their advances. I lived in Sacramento during the California gold rush, and then my father and I moved to Denver in time for the inundation by gold seekers there, so I've come to regard the persistent attentions of males as a part of life that's normal and that I must tolerate."

"I'm afraid I shall never become accustomed to it," Alison replied. "There's been a certain amount of attention that one creates automatically when one appears at Covent Garden, or elsewhere in the theater in London, but it's nothing like the furor that the mere presence of a young woman creates here. I've never encountered anything like it."

Susanna was sympathetic. "I'm afraid it doesn't help much that you are living in the Virginia City Hotel," she said. "You're more or less in the very heart of things, and there's no escape for you."

"Do you mean to say that you've found a place to reside where you're safe from all this pestering?" Alison asked.

"As a matter of fact, I have," Susanna replied. "I live in a house with Isaiah and Sarah Rose Atkins, newly-weds who are quite good friends of mine, and so I do manage to get away from all the fuss and bother."

"You're very fortunate," Alison said enviously.

A sudden thought struck Susanna. "The house is quite large," she said. "Large enough for at least one more person. We have a bedchamber there that isn't being used, and I'm sure that Sarah Rose and Isaiah would be delighted—as I certainly would—to rent it to you, if you're interested."

For a moment Alison looked as though she would burst into tears. "Interested?" she demanded. "My dear, I accept your offer at once without even seeing the quarters. That's how anxious I am to leave the hotel."

"Wait here," Susanna said, rising. "I'll just go tell Sarah Rose and Isaiah, and I'll meet you back at the hotel in half an hour." Susanna dashed out of the dining room and rode her horse at a gallop to the spacious house on B Street. Residents of Virginia City had become accustomed to seeing the pretty, petite woman in male attire always going somewhere in a hurry, so they paid her little heed as she raced through the streets.

As she had suspected, Sarah Rose and Isaiah proved amenable to the arrangement, and Susanna returned to the hotel as quickly as she had left. She told Alison that everything was settled, and the two women went at once to Alison's room and packed her belongings.

Then, using a cart that belonged to the *Journal* and asking one of the printers for assistance, Susanna helped the young English widow move to the Atkins residence.

Alison was introduced to Isaiah and Sarah Rose, who were about to leave for a social engagement, and then she went up to her new room and unpacked her belongings. She completed the task in a short time and then went downstairs in search of her benefactress.

Seeing Susanna sitting in the parlor, Alison called out to her, "Ah, there you are. I've been looking for you. The peace and quiet here are absolutely wonderful. You can't imagine how much better I feel." She entered the room and stopped short when she saw two strange young men staring at her with obvious interest.

The expression in Scott Foster's eyes made it plain that he thought Alison White was an exceptionally attractive young woman. He jumped to his feet as Susanna introduced them, and he was annoyed with himself because he actually stammered when he addressed her.

Captain Andy Brentwood made his own interest in the woman equally plain. A slow, lazy smile lit his face, his eyes glowed, and when he clicked his heels as he bowed, his spurs jangled musically.

There was no doubt in Alison's mind that she had made two quick, legitimate conquests. Both of these young men stood head and shoulders above the miners who had made her life so miserable at the Virginia City Hotel, and she was secretly pleased that she had created such a definite stir. It had been a long time since any gentleman had looked at her twice, and it was comforting to know that she was still attractive.

She answered Scott's and Andy's questions demurely, and slowly her conversation with them became more animated. She was beginning to enjoy herself in the company of these two bright and good-looking young men.

Susanna Fulton sat in something of a daze. The last thing on earth she had expected was that either of her devoted beaux would respond so strongly to Alison. She realized that she was spoiled, of course, that she had come to take Scott's and Andy's devotion for granted. Unfortunately she had regarded them as "her" young men, and she had to admit now in all fairness that she had no claim to either of them.

Perhaps she would have been less quick in offering the hospitality of the Atkins home to the pretty English singer had she realized that her suitors would respond with such obvious enthusiasm to Alison's presence. Well, what had been done could not be undone, and she had to make the best of the situation. It felt strange, however, after having Scott Foster and Andrew Brentwood to herself for so long to have to deal with a potential rival.

And Susanna was forced to admit to herself that Alison White was a formidable rival indeed. She was pretty, talented, unaffectedly charming, and very feminine. The combination was a hard one to beat.

Old-timers—those who had spent more than two decades in Oregon—rejoiced when the official announcement was made in Washington that Major General Lee Blake had been given the Pacific Command and intended to make his headquarters at Fort Vancouver. The general and his family arrived by United States warship from Panama, and as the vessel made its way up the broad mouth of the Columbia to Fort Vancouver, a large crowd gathered to meet the Blakes.

Lee and Cathy were greeted with loud, prolonged cheers when they appeared on deck, and old friends and acquaintances swarmed around them when they came ashore. They were inundated with invitations to come to dinner or to see friends' new babies, and Lee was hard put to attend to his official duties and to begin organizing his new command. But there was no question as to which invitation the Blakes would accept first. That night, Lee and Cathy, accompanied by Beth, crossed the Columbia by ferry and were driven in the general's official carriage to the Holt ranch, where Whip, Eulalia, and Toby were on hand to greet them.

The years fell away as the four old friends lifted glasses of sack and toasted each other in the parlor before supper. They had endured so much together on the long trek across the face of America from the Eastern Seaboard to the promised land of Oregon that Cathy felt closer to Eulalia than she did to her own sister, Claudia Brentwood. Several years had passed since the Blakes had last visited the ranch, but the passage of time meant nothing to people who were so attuned to each other's thoughts and desires. They had faced so many dangers together on the wagon train that they were bound by unbreakable bonds.

Only Toby and Beth, to their mothers' private consternation, failed to enjoy and appreciate the reunion to the fullest. The young couple were too well bred to be rude to each other, but they were reserved and stiff with each other, both of them unyielding in their attitudes.

"I had no idea that you were in this part of the world," Beth said, struggling to be civil.

Toby was aware of her complete lack of interest in him, and he certainly returned her feeling. There was no girl who interested him less. "Oh, yes," he said stifling a yawn, "I've been home from Michigan for some time."

"Too bad that we don't keep in touch," Beth said, forcing a smile, "I'm not too far from you in Ohio, and we might visit each other from time to time."

"That would be nice," he said vaguely.

They continued to be polite to each other on the surface. During dinner, Toby inquired about Beth's life at Antioch College, and she replied equally politely. By the same token, she pretended to be interested in his university, and she feigned an interest in his coming career as a railroad man. Only when he revealed that he was dropping out of the university to go on active duty with the Oregon militia did Beth come to life and display genuine sympathy for him.

Eulalia and Cathy exchanged an occasional pained glance, but there was no need for either to comment on what was all too obvious to them. They realized that they had only themselves to blame for the attitude that Toby and Beth were displaying. Toby and Beth's antipathy toward each other, which appeared to be deep-grained, was a natural result of the pushing of mothers who fondly hoped their children would grow up to marry each other.

As Lee remarked after dinner, when Toby politely took Beth off to the stables to see some of the Holt horses, the irony of the situation was that the young couple were well suited for each other, and they might have shown some interest in each other if their relationship had been allowed to develop naturally.

The four older people maintained a steady conversation all through the leisurely evening in the Holt dining room. The Blakes had to catch up on the news of so many of their old friends and acquaintances in Oregon, and the Holts were equally eager to bring them up to date. As they strolled toward the parlor of the ranch house for an after-dinner drink, Lee remarked casually, "I wonder if I could have a word in private with you, Whip?"

Instantly aware of the underlying significance of Lee's tone, Whip immediately nodded. "Come to think of it, Lee," he said, "I've got some special whiskey in my study that I've been saving for years. I reckon this is a sufficiently auspicious occasion to open the bottle. Come along." They disappeared in the direction of the study, leaving Cathy and Eulalia to go to the parlor without them.

The two men took their time and observed all of the amenities. Whip opened the bottle of whiskey, removing with a sharp knife the wax that sealed it, and poured small quantities of the amber fluid into two glasses. Then he offered his humidor to his guest. Lee selected a cigar, and after Whip had also chosen his, they lighted their cigars, sipped their whiskey, and at last were ready to talk.

"I've been given an unusual command," Lee said, speaking almost casually. "I'm free to organize it as I see fit."

Whip nodded. "That'll be an interesting challenge."

"Very," Lee said. "I also have a specific assignment that's an even bigger challenge. It goes almost without saying that what I am going to tell you is in the strictest confidence. It concerns a secret matter that is vital to the Union."

Whip nodded. "I reckon you know I can keep my mouth shut."

Lee grinned at him. "If I weren't roughly familiar with that fact, I wouldn't be saying a word to you now, believe me. Are you familiar with the situation in Virginia City, down in the Nevada Territory?"

"I reckon I know what most people know, that there's a whole mountain of silver there that's worth more millions of dollars than anyone has been able to count, and that several companies are busy excavating as fast as they can. There are a number of smelters in the town, too, so the silver, as I understand it, is refined before it ever leaves Virginia City."

"That's correct," Lee said, instinctively lowering his voice. "What isn't generally known is that the federal government desperately needs that silver. The government is the proprietor of several of the mines, and every ounce of silver produced is needed by the Treasury Department to pay for arms and munitions. The bill for our munitions needs is astronomical. The only way we can afford to fight the Confederacy is by paying for rifles, cannon, ammunition, and gunpowder with silver."

"I see," Whip said.

"The administration," Lee continued, "is planning to refine and move a great many millions of dollars' worth of silver from Virginia City to the bank vaults in New York. In other words, they're going to have it transported right across the continent."

Whip was impressed. "That's going to be one hell of a job," he said.

"Indeed it is," Lee replied. "Even under the best of circumstances, moving metal that weighs a great many tons is no mean task. Naturally, the Treasury and War Departments want the transfer to be kept as quiet as possible because it offers a perfect target for Confederate sabotage."

Whip nodded, his face grim. "I'll say it does," he said. "A small number of heavily armed men could create real havoc, and of course the temptation is always there, too, for the Confederates to want to steal the silver for their own purposes. How they'd go about doing that, I don't know, but these days I reckon we can expect just about anything."

"Exactly," Lee replied, then paused. "The command of the wagon train that will carry the silver is an enormous responsibility. President Lincoln has made me ultimately responsible for moving the silver and has given me a free hand to deal with the problem as I please. I've already sent out orders to have special freight wagons and special railroad cars made."

Whip shook his head. "I don't envy you," he said. "You have a rough job ahead."

Lee smiled wryly. "The potential headaches that present themselves are enormous."

"That's true," Whip replied, "but the challenge is what counts most."

"You think so?" Lee spoke lightly—too lightly. "How would you like to take personal charge of that silver train?"

Whip cocked his head to one side and laughed aloud. "I must say it would be a bit like old times, wouldn't it?"

"I'm serious," Lee Blake assured him. "I'm offering you the command of the silver train and with it the responsibility for moving the metal from Virginia City in the Nevada Territory all the way to New York."

The humor faded slowly from Whip Holt's face, and his eyes took on a steely look that anyone who had traveled with him in the wagon train he had led across the continent would have recognized instantly. "Well, now," was all he managed to say.

Lee carefully studied his boots and said nothing, giving his old friend as much time as he needed to reach a decision.

"If it's feasible," Whip said slowly, "I'll accept, of course. I've never yet turned down a request from my government, and I don't aim to start now."

"As I see it," Lee said, "it's very feasible. You were retired as a full colonel in the Oregon militia, and I can simply reactivate your commission. It'll be up to you to decide how many officers and men you'll want to make the trip with you, whether you'll want separate arrangements for the wagon train and railroad segments of your journey, and so on. I have total faith in your competence to deal with this matter—over and beyond my belief in the competence of anyone else, obviously—so I'll leave all details to you. I'll simply assure you that you'll have my complete backing and support in whatever you decide. I can't stress strongly enough the importance of the silver train to the Union's war effort."

Whip seemed lost in thought. "It's like a dream come true," he said softly. "I've been longing for a chance to activate my commission and do something useful for my country when she's at war, and here you're offering me this opportunity. I'm flattered by your confidence, Lee."

Lee smiled and shook his head. "Don't be," he said. "I've given the matter a great deal of thought, and I assure you that you stand head and shoulders above anyone else I could possibly select for this key job."

Whip hooked his thumbs into his belt in a characteristic gesture. "I'll do my darnedest," he said.

"I know you will," Lee told him. "That's one of the reasons I selected you." He hesitated and then asked, "How is all this going to sit with Eulalia?"

Whip frowned. "She'll tear the roof right off this ranch house," he declared. "But I reckon I can handle her. Offhand, I don't know how, but we've been married long enough that I guess I'll have to rely on my instincts and hope for the best."

"I won't intervene unless you give me the word, then. Just remember that I'm available for any help that you might want in the domestic quarter."

Whip grinned and sounded far more confident than he felt. "It'll work out all right," he declared. "After all, my wife is a sensible woman, and after she gets through blowing off steam, she'll listen to reason."

He had good cause to remember his words after the guests departed and he and Eulalia retired to their bedchamber. He was silent, lost in thought, as he tried to determine the best way to present the issue to her.

Eulalia sat at her dressing table, removing her makeup. "You're very quiet tonight," she observed, glancing at him in her dressing table mirror.

Whip nodded but made no reply.

She tried again. "You and Lee Blake spent quite a bit of time in your study," she said. "Were you talking about anything special?"

She was giving him his chance, and he seized it. "As it happens, we had a very special talk," he said. "Lee was telling me about his new command and some of his responsibilities. He was particularly concerned about the charge that President Lincoln has given him, a job that isn't going to be easy to perform." He paused, swallowed hard, and went on. "As a matter of fact, he did me the honor of asking me for my help. He'll see to it that my old commission is reactivated."

Sheer astonishment registered on Eulalia's face, and Whip hastily averted his eyes from the mirror.

She twisted on her stool in order to face him. "Be more specific, if you please, dear," she said. "Just what are you driving at?"

"I'll be commissioned as a colonel in the Union Army," Whip said, his tone unconsciously defensive. "I'll have a specific job to perform that'll take me a number of months to do. I'm not prepared right now to say exactly how long it'll keep me busy, and when I'm finished I suppose I'll revert to a civilian status again. The reason I'll be commissioned is because I'll have a number of officers and enlisted men under my command, and it's easier to establish discipline if I'm commissioned."

Eulalia stood slowly, removed her dress, and slipped into her dressing gown, which she tied with great deliberation around her waist. "I won't hear of it," she said flatly. "Apparently Lee Blake isn't concerned about your arthritis."

"My arthritis be damned," Whip said. "I can do this job just fine, regardless of the arthritis."

"You've already served your country long and honorably," Eulalia declared, her mouth set in a straight line. "You can't tell me that of all the millions of men available in the Union, only you are capable of doing this mysterious whatever-it-is for the government."

"I suppose there are others who could do the job," Whip conceded, "but Lee Blake doesn't know them. He knows me. He's done me the honor of asking me to accept a responsibility in a secret and hazardous undertaking, and I'd be shirking my duty to my country and to myself if I refused to accept it. I'm not getting any uniform for the duration of the war. I've already told you that. This is a matter of my attending to this one responsibility, which will take some months—I don't know exactly how long—and then I'll come back here to the ranch. I've already accepted Lee's offer, and I've given him my hand on it."

Eulalia knew she was fighting a losing battle, but she persisted valiantly. "Then you'll just have to disappoint him," she said.

He shook his head, and his voice was unyielding. "You know me better than that," he said. "I've never gone back on my word in more than a half-century, and I don't aim to start now." He paused and looked at her, uncertain whether she intended to burst into tears or to unleash her temper at him. Either prospect was unnerving, and he tried to avoid any further unpleasantness. "I'll tell you what I'm willing to do," he said placatingly. "I'm free to select my own subordinates for this assignment, and Lee told me I could have anybody in the whole army that I want, so I'll ask for Toby as an aide. How does that suit you?"

Eulalia well knew that he was offering her a sop in order to calm her, but she had to admit that his offer made sense. She would be able to speak privately with Toby, who could look after his father, keeping an eye on him and making certain that he did nothing to aggravate his arthritic condition. "Your offer," she conceded, "is better than nothing. Will the assignment be suitable for Toby?"

Whip took care not to reveal that he was pleased he had won the argument. "It's right up Toby's alley," he said. "The job is made for him, just as it's made for me. I tell you, I haven't been this happy in years."

Loving him, Eulalia couldn't help thinking that he was like a small boy who had been offered a great reward. Michael Holt, she knew, was a member of a very special breed. He was a man who required excitement and adventure in order to be truly content. He had to pit himself against forces that were strong almost beyond measure, forces that would cow a lesser man.

The following day Whip, anxious to begin his new duties as soon as possible, announced at breakfast that he was going to pay an official visit on General Blake at Fort Vancouver.

Eulalia's frown was partially eased when he glanced down the table and said to his son, "If you have nothing better to do, why don't you come with me?"

Toby had outlined a number of chores for himself on the ranch for that morning and started to explain to his father that he was too busy to accompany him.

Whip silenced him with a wave. "I'll expect you to have your horse saddled and to be ready to leave in about ten minutes," he said. His wife's smile was his reward.

Father and son rode to the near bank of the Columbia River, and they were carried across to the army post by a commercial ferry. Whip well remembered when Fort Vancouver belonged to the Hudson's Bay Company and served as a barracks for the small British garrison stationed in the area. Now, however, the post had expanded and grown so much that it was hard to recognize it as the same place. There were quarters for infantrymen, artillerymen, sappers, and cavalrymen, and the barracks were full now with the volunteer and militia troops that manned the post. The headquarters building bustled with activity, and a respectful young aide-de-camp informed the visitors that General Blake would be with them shortly.

"I'll find myself something to do so you can talk privately with General Blake," Toby said.

Whip shook his head. "I think not," was his only response.

He became somewhat more articulate, however, when they were seated in Lee's private office. "I managed to quiet my wife," he said, smiling, "by promising her I'd take Toby with me."

Lee's nod was enthusiastic. "Come to think of it, that's a first-rate idea," he said. "He'll be a useful addition to your company."

Toby looked bewildered.

"I'll swear both of you into federal service together," Lee said. "Please stand and raise your right hands."

Whip was pleased, proud he and his son were being sworn in together. Toby, however, became even more confused. He had expected to enter federal service with the Oregon regiment, but for some reason he did not understand, he was being sworn in as a first lieutenant and being called to active duty now, a month earlier than he had anticipated.

When the ceremony was completed, Lee told him to sit, then carefully explained the nature of the mission.

Toby whistled under his breath. "This is great," he said. "I'm grateful to you, Pa, and I'm grateful to you, General, for giving me a chance to participate in a mission of this importance."

"Never fear, you'll earn your keep," Whip told him, then turned back to Lee. "How soon do you want me to begin?"

"At once," Lee answered crisply. "There are four special freight wagons, each of them drawn by twenty mules, that have been built in Portland and have been delivered to this post. I suggest that you and I go to Virginia City ourselves and inaugurate this enterprise."

Whip could scarcely control his eagerness. "There's no time like the present," he said.

III

The Confederacy was only partly organized but was already functioning, and until new buildings could be constructed in Richmond, the larger private homes of the Virginia city were being used as offices by the military, the Treasury, and the other branches of the new government.

The military intelligence section of the Confederate Army headquarters occupied the third floor of a former mansion. It was so crowded that as many as eight officers shared a single room. Only one office was private, and that was the sanctum of Brigadier General Henry Hayward, who had last seen service as Lee Blake's deputy in the Union. He sat now behind a closed door with two subordinates to whom he listened with great care.

"We have it on impeccable authority, General," the young major declared, "and we have no reason to doubt the authenticity of the story."

"What is the source?" General Hayward demanded.

The lieutenant colonel who sat opposite him looked embarrassed. "I know how you feel, sir, about data that we acquire from officers who haven't yet given up their commissions in the Union Army, but they're valuable—extremely valuable—and we have every reason to believe that the information they have given us is authentic."

"I don't for a minute doubt its authenticity," General Hayward declared quietly. "I simply regret the lack of ethics involved, but I'm afraid this is a war in which ethical standards will play a very small part. Go ahead with your information."

The major, his eyes gleaming and his voice trembling with excitement, outlined the Union plan to transfer a huge sum of money in silver bullion from Virginia City to New York City. "The plans are being completed right now," he said, "under the direction of General Blake."

Hayward shook his head ruefully. "It would be Blake," he murmured, "but those are the fortunes of war. What specific information do you have on the operation?"

The lieutenant colonel looked apologetic. "Our information ends with what we gleaned from the War Department, sir. The specific plans are being made in the western theater of operations, and they're known only to a very few trusted officers in Virginia City."

General Hayward shook off his lethargy. "Then it behooves us," he said, "to get our own operatives busy and to find out exactly what the enemy plans are. Do we have anyone stationed in Virginia City?"

The lieutenant colonel consulted a sheet of paper that he was carrying. "We have no active espionage agents in the Nevada Territory at present, sir," he said. "However, there is one competent officer of the reserves who happens to be living in Virginia City and who has not been recalled to the Confederacy for active duty."

Henry Hayward brightened. "That sounds promising," he said.

"The officer is a Captain Douglas de Forest, General," the lieutenant colonel declared. "He's had considerable experience in intelligence, and he's under orders to stay in Virginia City until he receives a specific military assignment."

The general nodded vigorously. "Good," he said. "I'll write to him at once and tell him to find out all he can about the moving of the silver bullion. I'll make some funds available to him, and in order to make certain that he receives the orders quickly, I'll send my communication to him by special messenger!"

* * *

Alison White's first concert gave every promise of being successful. It did not matter that she was unknown. The miners of Virginia City were so starved for entertainment that virtually every seat in the open-air auditorium was sold well in advance of the occasion. Alison had worked hard in preparation for her performance, and she was outwardly calm.

Susanna Fulton, who had come to know and understand her fairly well, suspected that she was apprehensive, but at the same time the young newspaperwoman had no doubts that her friend would do her best. On the evening of the performance, a box had been reserved by Alison for her friends, and Scott Foster and Captain Andrew Brentwood escorted Susanna to the theater.

Scott and Andy seemed to have quickly forgotten their initial attraction to the charming, dark-haired Englishwoman, since Alison had to spend many hours at the theater for rehearsal. Susanna supposed she was glad she no longer had competition, but sometimes the rivalry between Scott and Andy for Susanna's attentions created rather ludicrous situations.

Tonight was no exception. When they had made certain that Susanna was comfortably ensconced in her seat, both young men excused themselves. They encountered each other suddenly and unexpectedly moments later at the bar, where both had gone for the purpose of purchasing a drink for Susanna. They vied for the attention of the bartender, with Scott slapping a coin onto the bar while Andy waved a paper dollar bill. The bartender, adept at avoiding trouble, poured them identical cups of claret at the same time.

They took the drinks back to their seats, and then simultaneously, like two characters in a comedy, they presented the cups to Susanna.

Not daring to laugh, she thanked them gracefully, and not wanting to show favorites, she reached for the two glasses at the same time. Aware that they were continuing to watch her, she set the cups on the ground beside her, deliberately confusing the issue so that neither of her suitors knew which cup was which when she picked one of them up and took a token sip.

All three were disconcerted when, a few minutes prior to the beginning of the performance, the occupant of the adjoining box appeared and created an immediate sensation in the theater. Caroline Brandon was wearing a skintight cloth-of-silver gown, and every man in the audience was dazzled. Aware of the stir she was creating, she pretended to be oblivious to it, and she nodded to her former companions on the wagon train that had brought them to Virginia City from Denver. They returned her greeting, but none of them engaged in conversation with her.

Caroline was aware that they did not approve of her and her occupation, but she didn't care. She was earning vast sums of money, and that was what mattered.

The footlights were dimmed, the candles in the spotlights were lit, and the performance began. Alison's first songs were simple and quiet, but she struck a plaintive note that gripped her audience, and the miners did her the courtesy of listening intently.

Susanna was greatly relieved. She hadn't told Alison that when a performer failed to please an audience of miners, they were known to react violently and that some artists had been chased from the stage and forbidden to return.

Gradually Alison became livelier and more forthright. Her voice grew stronger, she became far more self-confident, and when she actually began to enjoy herself, the miners roared their approval.

As she hurriedly left the stage at intermission, the storm of sustained applause that sounded throughout the auditorium told Alison that she had indeed achieved a signal success. Indeed, had she not been so eager to exit from the stage and retreat to her dressing room—needing to regain her equilibrium after all the opening-night excitement—the miners would have thrown her chunks of silver. As it was, they would wait for their chance to reward her at the end of the performance, when she took her bows.

No sooner were the lights along the walls of the auditorium lit than a visitor appeared at the entrance to the box occupied by Susanna and her escorts. Bernhard von Hummel had noticed the trio from his seat in the auditorium and had come to pay his respects to the young newspaperwoman.

The Prussian nobleman obviously was pleased to see Susanna again, and his interest in her predictably caused both Scott and Andy to bristle. They were united, at least temporarily, by their intense dislike of a possible third rival for her hand. But Susanna seemed impervious to any tensions and was her usual, unaffected self. As she exchanged cordial greetings with Bernhard, they were interrupted by a voice from the adjoining box.

"Bernhard, darling! How nice to see you!" Caroline Brandon's smile was ravishing.

The young baron flushed until his face was crimson. He managed to click his heels and bow to Caroline, but he did not address her or approach her box. He felt certain that the greeting she had given him let Susanna Fulton know that he had been intimate with Caroline, and he cursed the bad luck that had placed these two adjacent to each other.

Scott Foster and Andy Brentwood recognized the cause of Bernhard's embarrassment. Caroline Brandon had a habit of causing complications for gentlemen, and Susanna's suitors were secretly amused to see the normally self-assured Bernhard completely flustered.

If Caroline was aware that she had been snubbed by her recent customer, she gave no sign of it and left her seat to wander as far as the bar, escorted by her bodyguards. She soon returned, however, and looked somewhat perturbed. "I'm afraid there's going to be trouble tonight," she said to those in the adjoining box.

"What kind of trouble?" Scott demanded.

"There are Union sympathizers and Confederates in the audience, and they're making it plain that they dislike each other thoroughly," she replied. "They'd reached the name-calling stage by the time I got to the bar, and things were getting so unpleasant that I hurried back here instead of ordering my customary lemonade."

She had never had a lemonade in her life, Susanna thought, but that was irrelevant. Caroline had provided some interesting information, At least, in the event that trouble developed, they could see everything that happened from their box. She examined the audience critically, her newswoman's instincts taking over.

Alison was unaware of any growing problem as she began the second half of her concert, but not even the most experienced of veteran theatrical stars could have held the attention of that audience on that particular occasion.

Hostilities between Union and Confederate sympathizers continued to smolder, and names were called softly from one side of the auditorium to the other. As luck would have it, Susanna realized, the miners loyal to the Union appeared to be sitting in a block on the right-hand side of the auditorium, while the Confederate adherents were on the left.

The sentiments of men from every segment of society in both North and South were involved, and events quickly proved that no matter what an individual's background, he could not remain neutral. As the crude, untutored miners began to hurl epithets at each other, men who should have known better soon became involved. Supposedly distinguished mine owners found themselves taking sides, as did land speculators and businessmen who ordinarily went to great lengths to maintain dignified façades.

Neither then nor later did anyone know for certain exactly what sparked the riot. Susanna, whose attention was distracted from Alison's performance, knew only that both the Confederates and the Union sympathizers seemed to erupt at the same instant. As she said in her *Journal* article, it was a case of spontaneous combustion.

All at once men were on their feet, shouting curses and threats at each other. Others tried to silence them, and some miners, in an attempt to reward Alison for her efforts, began to throw chunks of raw silver onto the stage.

Susanna had warned Alison of this phenomenon, so the young Englishwoman wasn't too surprised, but the heavy pieces of metal flying through the air were so dangerous that they sent her toward the back of the stage.

The musicians accompanying her sensed that a full-scale riot was developing, and they hastily took themselves elsewhere. Alison was alone.

In a calm, courageous display of good sense, she advanced to the footlights and repeatedly requested the audience to resume their seats. But the shouts of the angry men drowned the sound of her voice, and the chunks of silver landing around her drove her toward the rear of the stage again. The management of the theater realized that the problem was getting out of hand, and the lights were lit. The opposing factions met in the center aisle and clashed, their fists flying. Benches were overturned as men stumbled and fell. The rioters surged toward the stage.

Captain Andy Brentwood was the first to realize that Alison was in danger. Leaping from the box onto the stage, he drew his sword and took a protective stance in front of the singer.

Suddenly the fighting broke out everywhere. Several Union and Confederate partisans began exchanging blows in the rear of the boxes. Scott had the good sense to realize that the boxes were too exposed for the good of their occupants. He shouted for Susanna to follow him and, taking her arm, dragged her onto the stage.

Caroline Brandon, in the meantime, was becoming panicky and didn't know how to react. Bernhard von Hummel's deepest instincts were those of a gentleman. He leaped into Caroline's box, brandishing his sword in order to clear a path for himself, then thrust Caroline after Susanna onto the stage. Soon the singer, the courtesan, and the young editor were huddled together while Andy, Scott, and the baron formed a phalanx in front of them. Andy and Bernhard kept the rioters at a distance with their swords, and Scott, who normally carried a pistol, wielded his weapon in one hand and gripped Andy's service six-shooter in the other.

The rioters were not so bereft of reason that they lost their common sense, however. They hurled epithets with hatred and vigor at their fellow miners as they fought with their fists, but they avoided the determined trio onstage, who would apparently kill in order to protect the young women who were huddled there.

There appeared to be nothing to do except to let the riot run its course. There was no real constabulary in Virginia City to restore order, and as the theater was private property, the army could not intervene. A few sensible men joined the determined group onstage, and somehow all of the rioters, including Union adherents as well as Confederates, were prevented from stepping onto the apron.

Fortunately neither side resorted to the use of firearms, or men on both sides would have been killed. But even under the circumstances, the results were grisly as the miners lashed out with their fists.

Gradually the fighters seemed to be losing their passion for the riot, and the men on the stage relaxed their guard and began to step forward. Then all at once the fighting erupted again with even greater force, and a score of miners landed on the stage.

A slender, dark figure wielding a saber hurled himself at the rioters on the stage with such determined frenzy that they retreated. He then went up to the huddled group of men and women and bowed, and Bernhard instantly recognized his dueling foe, Douglas de Forest. Caroline quickly introduced him to the others, and Andy Brentwood expressed his gratitude. "You intervened right smartly," he said. "That was good thinking."

De Forest accepted the praise of the Union officer and nodded his head stiffly.

Then, as suddenly as it had begun, the riot ended. A dozen men had received bashed heads, and one or two had been knocked unconscious.

Even the aplomb of Susanna Fulton was shaken. "I've

seen a great many riots," she said, "but that one was a little too close for comfort. Thank you, gentlemen."

Caroline nodded and spoke in a voice that shook. "I must admit that I was badly frightened," she said. "I don't know what I would have done if it hadn't been for all of you. I shall certainly remember your gallantry."

Alison White remained numb and silent, and Scott was the first to realize what must be going through her mind. "The riot was in no way a reflection on you or your performance," he said. "That's just Virginia City in these trying times."

Alison nodded. "I've endured occasional catcalls on the London stage," she said quietly. "Everyone in the theater has, but this was a new experience for me, and I must admit, I didn't care for it in the least."

As stagehands emerged to clean up the theater and to collect the silver for Alison, the young men conferred hastily and privately. They decided to escort all of the women home. First they took Caroline to her house, where de Forest remained with her, and then they went on with Alison and Susanna. When they reached the house, they found a short, dark-haired man awaiting them in the parlor, and the surprised Alison was forced to present Poole to her companions.

Alison had been so preoccupied the last few weeks that she had given very little thought to Poole or to her espionage assignment. But now she realized the man could not be avoided any longer, and after explaining to the others that Poole was her theatrical agent, she led him into one of the reception rooms, where they could talk in private.

"I made it my business to be in Virginia City in order to attend your performance," he said, "and when the unfortunate disruption occurred, I had occasion to speak with the proprietor of the theater. You'll be relieved to hear that he attaches no blame of any kind to you for what happened this evening."

"That's good," Alison murmured.

"On the contrary," he said, "I was assured that you created an exceptionably favorable impression and would have been richly rewarded at the end of the performance, instead of receiving merely a few pieces of silver. You can be sure that the audience will remember that you were cheated out of the full portion of your silver, and they will reward you the next time you give a show."

"I don't believe there will be a next time," Alison said. "I'm really not accustomed to such hooliganism."

"I certainly don't blame you for feeling as you do," Poole said. "I sympathize with your feelings as an artist. Let me remind you, however, that you have another and even more important profession at stake. I was afraid you'd feel as you do, and that is why I have come here to see you. You must stay on here and live up to your contractual agreements. The prime minister," he added, lowering his voice, "is anxiously awaiting your initial report."

Alison didn't have the heart to tell him that she hadn't even begun to come up with an "initial report," that privately she had been hoping the British request for information about the silver would be forgotten and that she'd just be left alone to continue her singing career and eventually to return home to England. But now things were becoming hopelessly complicated.

For one thing, there was the riot tonight, which might have cost her her life. By being assigned to do espionage work in Virginia City, she had clearly been thrust into a role that might cause her untold dangers.

Then there was her friendship with Susanna, and her growing respect for Americans like Andy and Scott, who believed in the preservation of the Union, not in the establishment of the Confederacy.

So Alison felt trapped. She had promised Poole that she would acquire the information he requested, and she had accepted the money he had given her. She was a British subject, and even though she had been recruited into the espionage service against her will and even though she had been in danger during the riot, she realized she had to carry out what she had promised to do for her country.

She was, after all, Lady White. It was true she had been married to the late Sir Charles for only a short time, but she still bore his name and had certain obligations to fulfill.

Most Nevada residents were loyal to the Union, and there was a movement afoot in Congress to make Nevada a state, with Carson City as its capital. With statehood imminent, the number of federal troops stationed in the area would be doubled, and justices of the circuit court would begin to visit the territory regularly. The status of Nevada having been clearly determined, most of the Confederate sympathizers decided to take themselves elsewhere. The military was promptly reorganized, and Captain Brentwood received a promotion to the rank of major. At the same time that he received General Blake's order, he was also the recipient of a private communication from his aunt, Cathy Blake, extending her warm congratulations to him.

Scott Foster had been pondering the future for some time, and his own Union loyalties impelled him to take action. He kept his views to himself for a time, and finally he told Susanna Fulton that he wanted to confer with her privately. She came into his office, and he closed the door.

Scott was afraid of the way Susanna might react when she learned that he was abandoning their precious newspaper in order to enter the army. Perhaps he was hurting his chances with her, but that couldn't be helped. A major principle was at stake, and he had to hold to it firmly, regardless of whether it destroyed his personal happiness or not.

"I've decided," he said, "to apply to the Union Army for a commission. I've discussed the matter with Andy, and he tells me that he can grant me a captaincy right off."

Susanna was stunned. "I have my hands full as it is, editing the *Journal*," she said. "I don't have the time to publish the newspaper as well."

"I realize that," Scott replied. "I also realize that it's been a struggle to obtain a foothold here."

"Much as it was in Denver," she said.

He nodded. "But as both you and I know, the Virginia City situation is quite different from what we found in Denver. Here, almost the entire population is male. In Denver whole families have settled, and that's created a far more stable influence."

Susanna was silent for a moment, then said sadly, "I've hated to admit it to myself, but when the mines are exhausted, and they're certain to be after a few years, Virginia City will atrophy, and so will Carson City. Once the miners leave, there won't be much of anything left—including opportunities for the *Journal*. I've seen the handwriting on the wall for some time. We're breaking even right now, of course, but that's a temporary situation. I've written to my father that my days are numbered here."

"As I once mentioned, I've also written to your father," Scott said. "He's been kind enough to keep the door open to me in Denver anytime I want it. But I've already notified him that I feel my place is in the army right now."

"What did you have in mind for me?" Susanna made an effort to speak lightly and humorously.

"I'm afraid that when I'm called to duty," Scott said, "we'll have to close the doors of the *Journal*, and you'll be obliged to go back to Denver. I'm sorry. I hate to sound like a quitter, but the situation here is far, far different from what we faced in Denver, and we'd be foolish if we didn't recognize it and act accordingly."

Susanna stared out the window. Her first reaction was one of bewilderment and loss. The idea of closing the *Journal* was a major blow to her pride and her professionalism. She also realized that Scott might be sent on a military assignment far from her, and she knew that she would miss him more than she wanted to admit. "I'd be extremely selfish," she finally said, "if I failed to do my duty appropriately. You'll be doing yours by going into the army, so I guess the least I can do is to call it quits at the *Journal* and go back to Denver. I ought to be glad that I have a good job waiting for me there."

"The worst of it," Scott said solemnly, "is that we'll miss the fun of trying to create the *Journal* together. At least I'll miss it."

Susanna smiled painfully as she struggled to her feet. "I know what you mean," she murmured. "I'll miss it, too." She turned away, opened the door, and fled to her own office.

Scott was distressed. The last thing on earth that he wanted was for Susanna to be hurt in any way. But he also couldn't help feeling encouraged by her reaction. Perhaps he was gaining ground on Andy Brentwood after all. But that question probably wouldn't be settled for a long time. Andy would have less time to spend with Susanna now that he'd been made a brevet—or temporary—major, and Scott had no idea where he himself would be stationed.

He tried to put such personal considerations out of his mind as he picked up his hat, strapped on his pistol, and went out to unhitch his horse for the ride to the small headquarters of the military garrison.

When he arrived, Andy was busy fixing his new insignia to his shoulder boards. "I seem to have come here at an opportune time," Scott said.

"It's better than most," Andy admitted. "The one good thing about a war is that academy graduates are promoted several times faster than they are during peacetime."

Scott took a deep breath. "I've come here, Andy, following our conversation of the other day. I definitely want a commission in the Union Army."

Andy stared at him intently. "You realize you'll be making a great many sacrifices. Your career will be in abeyance, and you'll be earning a great deal less money." He paused, hesitating for a long moment, and then he added, "And you'll have fewer opportunities to pursue your romantic interests."

Scott smiled wryly. Clearly their rivalry for Susanna would be in no way diminished by the new turn of events. "I'm well aware of all the handicaps," he said. "But I thank you for reminding me of them. I have an old-fashioned patriotism, I guess. When my country is in trouble, I can't stand aside and let others do my fighting for me."

Andy sighed and then grinned at him. "I've got to admit I'm glad you feel that way," he said. He rummaged in his desk, found a blank form, and handed it to the young publisher. "Fill this out, if you will, and then return it to me, and I'll swear you in."

Scott was surprised. "That's all there is to it?"

"Well, yes and no," Andy Brentwood said. "I have no idea when you'll be called to active duty or where you'll be stationed, but after you've been in the army about six months, you might ask me that question again. You might find that the army is more difficult and more complicated than you think."

Scott secretly agreed with him and began filling out the long, detailed War Department form. When he completed it, he went in search of Andy and found him in the outer office. Never one to stand on ceremony, Andy Brentwood requested him to raise his right hand and swore him in then and there.

"You are now a captain in the army reserve," he said, when the brief, informal ceremony came to an end. "I advise you to go to the supply master and get yourself a couple of uniforms and be prepared for a call to duty. I don't pretend to know when or where you'll be summoned, but I know the need for competent manpower is pressing these days, and I can't see General Blake letting you sit idly on the sidelines."

IV

The arrival of the special wagons, each of them pulled by a team of twenty mules, created something of a stir in Virginia City, especially as the wagons were accompanied by a military escort that contained two very high-ranking officers. Major General Lee Blake, commander of the Pacific District, had arrived in the silver capital, and with him was Colonel Michael "Whip" Holt.

Whip Holt and Lee Blake reacted almost identically to the chaos and lack of discipline they found in Virginia City. Both were reminded of the more unsavory elements of the gold rush in California. Whip vividly recalled the lack of law and order in Sacramento, where miners were inclined to run riot after spending weeks in the gold fields. Lee remembered the trying conditions in San Francisco and his need to call out his troops from the Presidio regularly in order to hold disorders to a minimum.

First Lieutenant Toby Holt, who had accompanied the older men, had never seen anything quite like the Virginia City scene, and he was stunned by it. Never had he encountered such drunkenness, such open licentiousness, such a lack of standards. Although far better educated than his father, he was still Whip Holt's son, his jaw set in firm lines as he looked with quiet contempt at the scene around him.

Susanna Fulton, undaunted by her recent conversation with Scott about the *Journal*'s future, immediately sought an interview with both General Blake and the

83

renowned mountain man. It was Toby Holt's unpleasant duty to inform her that no interviews were being granted under any circumstances, and Susanna was disappointed.

Immediately after the wagons were made secure, Lee took possession of a large unoccupied office in the little Virginia City headquarters and called in his wife's nephew. Andy Brentwood had been waiting for his summons and was surprised when he saw that Colonel Holt was present, too. Whip Holt, who succeeded somehow in making even his trim blue and gold full colonel's uniform look shaggy, rose to his feet and grinned broadly. "Major," he said, "you have no idea how good I feel just seeing you. Your father is about the best friend I've ever had in my life. I can thank him for everything good that's happened to me because he was responsible for getting me the job of guiding the first wagon train to Oregon."

"I know, sir," Andy replied. "I've heard about your exploits ever since I was old enough to understand that two and two make four. My father has a special regard for you, too."

They beamed at each other. Lee Blake hated to break the spell, but urgent business was waiting. "Sit down, Andy," he said, "and listen carefully. What I have to tell you is strictly confidential." He proceeded to outline the mission he had been given by President Lincoln, that of delivering a large amount of silver bullion to the banks in New York.

Andy Brentwood listened carefully and nodded. "That's a tall order, sir," he said. "No two ways about it."

"I've called Colonel Holt to active duty," Lee said, "because he's the only man I know who will deliver the silver precisely on time and without fuss. We're handpicking a staff for him, and of course we agreed to choose you."

Andy was pleased, but his military training had been so intense that he did and said nothing to interrupt.

"We're going to provide Colonel Holt with a full battalion of troops," Lee said. "They'll protect the caravan on the trail. The number of troops will be reduced somewhat, of course, when the switch is made in Missouri from wagon train to railroad." Lee paused a moment, then continued. "We want to give you the command of that battalion, but you'll have to volunteer for the job. What do you say?"

Andy grinned broadly. "I volunteer, sir!" he said heartily. "Do I ever!"

Whip chuckled and impetuously reached out to shake his hand. Lee watched as Andy Brentwood grasped the old mountain man's hand, and he felt confident about the success of the expedition. He knew of no two men whom he trusted more completely than he did this pair.

"Colonel Holt had an idea that we'd like to try out on you, while we're about it," Lee said.

Whip leaned back in his chair. "I needn't tell you that the Confederates would give their eyeteeth and a whale of a lot more if they knew about the silver train," he said. "So it struck me, for the sake of protective coloring, as you might call it, that we should form a legitimate, civilian wagon train. It will accompany the expedition as far as Missouri, where we'll switch to the railroads. Needless to say, none of the civilians who will be taking part will be told anything about the presence in the train of a fortune in refined silver. Of course, there are bound to be questions about the contents of the special wagons, just as there will be comments about the presence of the military, but we'll have to maintain strict confidentiality."

"I see," Andy said.

Lee stared hard at his wife's nephew. "Well," he demanded, "what's your reaction?"

"I have two reactions," Andy said. "From a military intelligence point of view, a civilian wagon train is sound and should add to the deception we're trying to create. On the other hand, the civilians may cause more damned trouble than they're worth."

To his surprise, both of the others started to laugh.

"Lee and I both felt that way many times," Whip said, chuckling, "on the trek across the continent to Oregon, but in retrospect those civilians were well worth the problems they caused. I'm willing to cope with them, and I reckon I can handle them"—Whip smiled wryly, and Lee winked at Andy—"so there'll be no need for you to deal with them any more than you want to. We've weighed all the pros and cons, and we think the advantages far outweigh the disadvantages, so we'll give the story to the local newspaper, and we'll ask for volunteers. I imagine that quite a few people will find the prospect attractive because the military escort will be strong enough to prevent attacks by either Indians or Confederates."

"How soon will we leave, sir?" Andy asked.

"As fast as we can get organized," Whip told him. "From now on, every day counts!"

The three men shook hands, but now as Andy left the major general's office, he braced himself for an ordeal that he dreaded. He had to tell Susanna Fulton that he had received orders and soon would be leaving Virginia City. He had no idea how she would react, but he was afraid that she would shrug away his departure, and that would mean the end of an already fragile romance.

At Andy Brentwood's suggestion, Whip Holt interviewed Scott Foster without telling the younger man what he had in mind. He was impressed by the forthright, direct young reserve officer and finally admitted the purpose behind the discussion. "I hear that you're eager to be called to active duty," he said.

Scott nodded. "I guess I am, Colonel," he replied. "With the war becoming more involved every day, I'm anxious to do my part."

"Maybe I can accommodate you," Whip said. "There are some Nevada troops being added to the protective units assigned to my wagon train, and I'd be happy to give you command of the company, if that suits you."

"Yes, sir!" Scott beamed. "That would suit me just fine."

Whip extended his hand. "Consider it done," he said, "We'll start processing your orders immediately."

NEVADA!

Scott went directly to the *Journal* office and related his news to Susanna Fulton. She was silent for a moment and shook her head slowly. "Well, I guess this is it," she said. "The end of the *Journal*. I've been bracing myself for this day, but now that it's here it's still something of a shock. However, I'll get over it."

"Does this also mean an end to any possibility of our getting together?" Scott asked clumsily.

Susanna looked down at her desk. Andy had also just told her of his imminent leave-taking, and now with the *Journal* closing down and the two young men in her life going off into active service, she felt quite forsaken and bereft. "They say that absence makes the heart grow fonder," was all she could manage, determined not to break into tears.

"Well, I sure can't be any fonder of you than I already am, Sue," Scott said, taking a step forward. He wanted to take her in his arms and ask her to marry him once and for all, but he felt that would be taking advantage of the situation. He assumed Susanna would be returning to Denver to work with her father on the *Tribune*. He had no idea when he would see her again, but he realized he would just have to bide his time. At least there was consolation in knowing that Andy Brentwood would also be accompanying the wagon train and would have no chance to further his suit, either.

Suddenly Susanna looked up from her desk as she was struck by an entirely different prospect. "Where are you going with this wagon train?" she asked, all her former vivacity returning.

"I didn't inquire," Scott said.

"And why are so many troops being assigned to protect it? I find that highly unusual."

He shrugged. "Colonel Holt didn't tell me, and I didn't ask him. When you're a reserve captain, you don't pester your commanding officer with questions."

"I think," Susanna said thoughtfully, "that the time has come for me to request another interview from Whip Holt. I've been curious ever since I learned that he had come to Virginia City, and my curiosity is

87

greater now. I can't for the life of me understand why a mountain man with his national reputation should be assigned by the army to command this wagon train."

Scott grinned at her. "You'll have to ask him, not me."

"That," Susanna replied emphatically, "is precisely what I shall do."

The following day, somewhat to Susanna's surprise, Whip Holt readily granted her time for an interview and was the soul of amiability.

"Ask anything you like," he invited. "We're hoping that when you write your piece in the *Journal*, it will inspire a number of civilians to join the wagon train."

"What's your destination, Colonel?" Susanna asked without preamble.

"Missouri," Whip replied promptly.

"I'm curious by profession," Susanna said. "It's instinctive in my kind of work. You're known all over the country as a hunter, trapper, and guide. How does it happen that the army selected you to command this particular train, Colonel?"

Whip grinned guilelessly. "You'll have to ask my superiors for the answer to that one, ma'am. All I can tell you is that I was called to active duty, and here I am."

Susanna tried another tack. "On my way here to see you," she said, "I happened to notice some perfectly enormous freight wagons, and a lieutenant—I believe he was your son—told me that each of them will be pulled by a team of twenty mules. May I ask the nature of the cargo that you're carrying to Missouri? I think the *Journal* readers would be very interested to find out."

Whip hesitated, then faced the issue squarely. "Miss Fulton," he said, "you're a good newspaperwoman—too good, if you ask me. I wish that you hadn't made that inquiry about the heavy freight wagons, and I'll be obliged to you if you'll just forget the question. I'd prefer not to lie, and I'd rather that you didn't force me into an embarrassing situation. Let's just say that with the Union at war, there are certain matters that are confidential—that it's better not to publicize."

"I didn't know," Susanna assured him hastily, "and under the circustances, naturally, I'll refrain from asking anything."

"Thanks very much," Whip said, smiling slightly.

Susanna's mind raced. There could be only one reason for the army troops and the heavy freight wagons to be in Virginia City, Nevada, and that reason was silver—silver to help finance the Union war effort. Clearly, Susanna was sitting on the lid of a story, which, when it could be published, would be major news. Inasmuch as the calling of Scott Foster to active duty meant that the *Journal* would close its doors, she would be leaving Virginia City in any event and would be heading back to Denver. So, on sudden impulse, she said, "If it's all the same to you, Colonel Holt, I'd like to join that wagon train myself. At least for a part of your journey, if you'll have me."

Whip grinned. "There's nothing I'd like more," he replied gallantly. "You'll be a very welcome addition, Miss Fulton."

As she thanked him, the thought occurred to Susanna that she would be in constant touch with her source of news and that this big story wouldn't escape from her. The fact that she would also remain in close touch with Andy and Scott struck her forcibly, as well.

Whip was delighted when he saw the article that Susanna prepared for the *Journal*. She described the coming journey in glowing terms and emphasized that here was an opportunity not to be missed by any family intending to move to the eastern part of the United States.

Lee Blake was both amused and impressed. "You sure did a fine selling job on the young lady from the *Journal*," he said. "We couldn't have written a more favorable piece ourselves."

"We did even better than that," Whip told him, grinning. "Miss Fulton has decided to join the wagon train caravan herself."

Lee's smile faded. "Be careful of her," he said. "I don't doubt her patriotism, not for a minute, but she is first,

89

last, and always a newspaperwoman. I knew her from Denver, and I suspect she is joining us on the march because she either knows or suspects something about the wagon train's real mission."

Whip was instantly alert. "You really think so?"

"I know so," Lee warned him. "Watch your step."

"Thanks, I will," Whip said and nodded somberly.

"While we're about it," Lee declared, "I wonder if I could ask a favor of you?"

"Hellfire," Whip said, "you know you don't even have to ask."

"The time is approaching for my daughter, Beth, to go back to school for her last year of college. So I thought I could accomplish two things at the same time. If she joins the wagon train to Missouri and then takes the railroad with you as far as Ohio, you'll not only pick up another civilian, but it will be a great convenience for Cathy and me. I don't like Beth to travel unescorted, and it really isn't convenient for Cathy to take her all that distance when we're just getting organized at Fort Vancouver."

"By all means, send her with me," Whip assured him. "She'll be no bother, and the idea makes a great deal of sense."

"You're certain you don't mind?" Lee asked.

"Dead positive," Whip assured him flatly, and that was that.

In the meantime, other less orthodox plans were being made to join the wagon train. Douglas de Forest was looking in the mirror, waxing his mustache and combing his hair with a straight part down the middle, when his butler announced someone was waiting to see him, a man who was dressed as a civilian but who had official papers from the Confederate government in Alabama. De Forest ran the comb one more time through his hair, then went to see the man, who he guessed was a messenger from his superior officers. Clearly an assignment had been found for him, and as he went down the staircase to the front hall of his house, de Forest grumbled to himself, thinking that his days of leisure were over.

But as it turned out, the assignment that the Confederate messenger brought to him did not pose that much of a hardship, and de Forest was able to find out all he needed to know, without having to take too much time off from purchasing new clothes or flirting with every pretty woman he encountered.

Realizing that barber shops were always great sources of information, de Forest went to his barber for his regular haircut and mustache trim. With only a little digging, and a bribe of a twenty-dollar gold piece, he ascertained the basic facts about the wagon train that was being assembled in Virginia City's little army garrison. His barber told him that one of his customers, a harness maker, had learned that the wagons were specially constructed to carry very heavy loads, and a miner who had hit pay dirt and was treating himself to a haircut and shave revealed that huge quantities of silver were being smelted and that a number of army personnel were visiting the mines and the refineries.

Douglas de Forest realized that the army had specific plans for the silver, and he quickly was able to surmise that it was being brought by wagon to the Union Treasury in the East.

Sooner or later, of course, at an appropriate time and place, he would have to commit an act of sabotage that would halt the train and would deprive the Union of the silver bullion it so desperately needed. However, he needed to be informed of the train's whereabouts at any given time, especially after it left the Nevada Territory, where it could follow any one of many different routes to the East, and that meant that he would be required to find some subordinate who would be willing to make the journey. Thus, he resorted to a scheme that, in the long run, would serve his purposes well.

Calling on Caroline Brandon, he complimented her on her beauty and told her how he had missed her since their last meeting. Then, sitting on a divan in the private living room, de Forest reached up casually, caught hold of Caroline's wrist, and drew her down beside him. Still behaving with apparent spontaneity, he slid an arm around her shoulders. "I've been quite worried about you lately," he said.

"You have?" she asked, her eyes widening as she responded to the pressure of his hand on her shoulder and leaned against him.

"Yes," he said, stroking her arm. "It's been obvious that you haven't been any too happy in Virginia City."

That wasn't quite true, as Caroline well knew. She had earned enormous amounts of money from miners who had made financial killings here, so she had achieved a measure of financial independence that she had never before known. However, it appeared to her that the Southerner had something in mind, and she was curious, so she agreed with him.

"How clever of you to know the way I feel," she murmured, and made no objection when his hand closed over a breast.

"You know," he said, "the time for you to leave the Nevada Territory has come. You have a perfect opportunity to go east with the wagon train going to Missouri, and I suggest you avail yourself of the chance."

His suggestion dropped on surprisingly fertile ground. The truth of the matter was that Caroline was very tired of the violence and crude behavior that were a part of day-to-day life in Virginia City. She had longed for the dignity of cities in the East, where she would be able to ply her questionable trade subtly and would be able to live in quiet comfort and dignity. So she was delighted at the idea.

Caroline stared at him wide-eyed, with feigned surprise. "You must be a mind reader!"

De Forest smiled. "Not at all," he said. "A lady of your refinement would find Nevada living to be obnoxious."

"To be honest with you," Caroline said, "I look forward to resettling in the East."

"I have an even better idea," Douglas replied. "Marry me, and I'll take you to my family's plantation in Mississippi. You'll live there in comfort for the rest of your days."

"Why, Douglas!" she cried prettily. "I do declare, this is a very unexpected proposal!" Caroline's mind worked rapidly. Certainly she was no more in love with Douglas de Forest than she was with any man, but she had known for some time that he enjoyed independent means, and the prospect of becoming mistress of a very large plantation was rather exciting. She promptly placed both hands on the velvet lapels of his jacket, and her green eyes were wide and innocent as she murmured softly, "I'm very touched by your concern for me."

He knew his scheme was working perfectly and was quietly elated. Sliding both hands around her waist, he returned her gaze. "You can't imagine," he said, "how anxious I've been to get you out of the business that you're engaged in. I realize that you were trapped into it, that you had no choice, but enough is enough. The time has come for you to put it behind you and settle down into domesticity for the rest of your days."

"I wouldn't even consider a domestic existence with any man except you," Caroline lied.

"Then it's all settled. I will provide you with a wagon and horses so that you can accompany the wagon train to Missouri, and I will follow shortly after, as—ah—I have some business matters I must first settle. We'll take the railroad to Mississippi, and the plantation will be getting the mistress it deserves." Under no circumstances did he intend to take her to Mississippi or to introduce her to his family and friends as the mistress of his ancestral plantation.

The bargain was better than any that Caroline had anticipated. Not only would she be leaving Nevada, which she urgently desired, in a wagon that would cost her nothing, but in time she would be marrying this wealthy young suitor and, in effect, would become an heiress. She raised her face for Douglas's kiss. As he embraced and kissed her, sealing their bargain, he told himself he was very fortunate. He had found the perfect person to travel without suspicion on the wagon train. It would be easy enough to contact Caroline on the road after the wagon train set out, for there was only one route they could follow through eastern Nevada. Then he would get her to use her wiles to learn the train's itinerary as it continued eastward. She need never know the actual contents of the oversized freight wagons, and as for her ultimate disposition, he refused to worry. Once she parted company with the silver being carried in the wagons, she would be of no further use to him, and he would abandon her without troubling his conscience. He had erred for the last time when his jealousy had gotten the better of him and he'd made a fool of himself in a duel with the Prussian baron. He had sworn then that he was not going to behave this way over Caroline again, and he fully intended to keep his pledge to himself.

The discussion that Whip Holt held with Major Andrew Brentwood was brief. "Andy," he said, "I know it's customary to give an officer the privilege of selecting his own deputy, but this is no ordinary mission. I wonder if you would mind if I assign you someone."

Under the circumstances there was little that Andy could do to object. Certainly he had no reason to mistrust the judgment of the mountain man of whom his father thought so highly, and he responded quickly, "I'll leave it strictly up to you, Colonel."

"Good," Whip smiled. "In that case, I'll assign you First Lieutenant Toby Holt."

They went their separate ways shortly thereafter, and Andy seethed inwardly. There was no way that he could object to the assignment without creating difficulties for himself. After all, Toby Holt was Whip's son. On the other hand, as Andy well knew, Toby held his basic commission in the reserves militia in the state of Oregon, and Andy had the traditional regular army officer's contempt for militiamen. What rankled even more was the fact that here was a young man—a mere novice—who apparently had to do nothing to acquire an estimable place in the United States Army. In Andy's book a man proved himself by what he did, not whom he knew, and as far as he was concerned, Toby would have to do something extraordinary in order to earn the respect of his superior officer.

Well, he was stuck now, and there was nothing he could do about it. He supposed he could use influence himself and complain to his uncle, but Lee Blake was an officer of the old school and would frown on any attempt to use his influence for private purposes. Andy had to resign himself to his fate.

Besides, Andy had matters far more important to him than Lieutenant Toby Holt on his mind. He had just learned of Susanna Fulton's intention to join the wagon train as a civilian. The prospect of having Susanna nearby during the journey was almost too good to be true and filled him with fresh hope.

Perhaps on the trail he would have opportunities to pursue his courtship, opportunities that were lacking in Virginia City, just as they had been lacking previously in Denver. What those conditions were, exactly, he wasn't sure, but he was determined that this time he would not miss his chance.

The bar at the entranceway to the open-air theater was crowded, as usual, at Alison White's next-to-last concert. Miners slapped down silver coins for beer, while businessmen ordered whiskey and the mine owners, together with a handful of miners who had suddenly struck it rich, confined their drinking to imported champagne.

It was difficult, if not impossible, for any newcomer to get near the bar, where men stood four and five deep awaiting their turns. But all at once the crowd parted to allow a strange-looking pair to approach.

In the lead was an elderly man whose hair and beard had recently been subjected to a much-needed trimming. He was clad in a tailcoat of expensive black worsted, with which he wore a white shirt with a stiff collar and a flowing, black silk cravat. His waistcoat was of silk, and hanging from one pocket was a fob of gold, a sure sign that he had made his fortune with a lucky strike in the mines. His trousers fit him to perfection, and his feet were shod in expensive boots of English manufacture that only the well-to-do could afford.

The old miner named Bingham had finally come into his own.

So had his constant companion. Eustace, the burro, who happily followed him, also advertised their new prosperity by proudly wearing a collar of thick leather studded with nuggets of alternating gold and silver. The collar clearly was worth a small fortune.

Man and burro reached the bar together, and Bingham moved to a place that several miners made for him. "We'll have the usual," he announced, and dropped a bill of large denomination on the bar.

The bartender nodded and hastened to do his bidding. First he opened a new bottle of chilled champagne, which he placed, together with a glass, near the old miner's elbow. Then he carefully filled a large glass bowl with more champagne, which fizzled and bubbled as it rose to the surface.

The old man took the bowl and placed it on the ground carefully, making certain that he spilled no champagne. Then taking his own drink, he exclaimed, "Here's mud in your eye, Eustace!" He raised his glass and drained its contents.

Eustace wasted no time, either, and in the silence, the lapping sound of the burro's tongue could be heard plainly all over the bar.

The patrons who regularly frequented the theater bar paid no attention to the couple, but those who were here for the first time gaped at Eustace and his master. Bingham and the burro were oblivious to the strangers, however, and when they finished their champagne, they turned away with one accord.

Both the man and his pet maintained their great dignity, as great now that they were flush as it had been through the long, lean years of adversity. They made their way into the theater itself, walking down the outside aisle, and entered their private box. Bingham sat on one of the velvet-cushioned chairs, and Eustace seated himself on his haunches, his ears pricking up as the house lights were extinguished and the performance began.

The audience cheered loudly when Alison White came on stage, attired in a long satin gown and white gloves. There was no question that she had overcome the nervousness she had suffered during her first concert. She had become more and more popular, and now, with only one concert remaining in the series, she was well established as a favorite artist of the miners.

They showered her with raw silver at the end of her performance, as they did each night. Alison was able to sell the silver for an appreciable sum to the mine owners, and to her pleased surprise she found that she had accumulated a nest egg of considerable size.

After her last interview with Poole, she had made a few halfhearted attempts to learn what she could about the silver being taken by the United States government. She had attempted to speak to both Andy and Scott, hoping she might be able to take advantage of the interest they had shown in her, but their military activities totally preoccupied them, and she was unable to get either man alone for any length of time. And when she spoke to Susanna about the silver, the newspaperwoman admitted to total ignorance about what was going on.

She realized that the money she had accumulated from her concerts might very well offer her freedom from the espionage work she was being asked to perform for Great Britain, and once again she began hoping that she might be able to get off scot-free. Her hopes were dashed, however, when, during her curtain calls, she caught a glimpse of Poole sitting in the audience. A feeling of dread mounted inside her. She tried not to display her feelings when, after the performance, Poole knocked at the door of her dressing room, then opened it, stuck his head inside, and said in his most saccharine voice, "May I come in?"

Wearing an old robe, Alison sat in front of her dressing table mirror, removing her heavy stage makeup, and she did not pause in her task as the spymaster came in without waiting for an invitation.

Poole stood, hooked his thumbs in his waistcoat pocket, and beamed at her. "You were quite good," he announced, "First rate, in fact. I'm delighted that I set up this whole arrangement for you. You've been worth every penny that the theater has paid you."

Alison inclined her head in silent acknowledgment.

"As a matter of fact," he continued, "everyone has benefited from the arrangement." He paused momentarily. "Everyone, that is, except the parties most directly concerned, the people in London whom I have the honor to represent."

He stood directly over her, breathing down her neck, and Alison retreated behind a screen while she shed her robe and donned street clothes.

Poole continued to direct his forceful remarks to her. "Fortunately, however, you're going to have an opportunity to repay your benefactors at last." He paused, and when she made no reply, he inquired quizzically, "Aren't you pleased that you're going to have a chance to repay your debt?"

"I'm overwhelmed," she said.

He chose to ignore her sarcasm. "I daresay that you are familiar with the fact that a wagon train of considerable consequence is going to be departing soon from this town for the eastern section of the United States."

"Yes, I know about it," Alison replied.

Poole smiled and nodded. "You're going to have the rare opportunity to see a side of American living that is offered to very few foreigners," he said. "You're going to be a member of the wagon train, and I've already purchased a handsome wagon, travel essentials, and a team of spirited, matched horses for your use."

The woman finished dressing and came out from behind the screen. "May I ask why I am being given this—rare opportunity, as you call it."

Poole preferred not to explain that he had managed to learn about the silver being carried on the wagon train; it was his belief that his agents worked best if they remained uninformed about the specifics of an assignment. "Let it suffice," he said, "that you will be informing us of

98

the train's movements by sending us letters via one of the overland postal services. You can mail the letters whenever the train makes a stop at an army post or a city, and you will remain with your party, if possible, after it reaches Missouri."

"I don't think that will be possible," Alison declared. "As I understand it, the civilians are being granted the right to accompany the train only as far as Missouri. I'm not sure what is happening to the basic train then, but I've heard rumors that they may switch to the rails."

The spymaster smiled. "You are a young woman of considerable charm and very considerable beauty," he said. "I should think you'd be able to persuade the officers in charge of the train to allow you to continue to accompany them."

She was shocked, and it was apparent to her that her real work for the British Crown was to begin now in earnest. "I can make no promises regarding the attitude that American military officers will take."

"Indeed, and all I ask is that you try. I think that the results will please you. You'll be asked to mail the cards you send to an address in Chicago, and if, as I assume, you travel east of Chicago, you will send them to New York. It will be quite simple, really."

"I think I have the right to know what this is all about," she said, a challenge in her voice.

Poole thought quickly and decided to accommodate her, up to a point. She was sufficiently intelligent that she would work better and more willingly if she understood something of what was at stake. "Obviously," he said, "the contents of the very large wagons are of great interest to the Union government. It is our understanding that they are providing three hundred well-armed soldiers to guard the contents of those wagons. Let us just say that they're also of interest to my employers, who want to keep themselves informed as to the precise whereabouts of those wagons from one day to the next."

"I see." Alison saw far more than she was willing to reveal. What bothered her most was her deepening friendship with Susanna Fulton, as well as with Isaiah and Sarah Rose Atkins. She was fond, too, of Scott Foster, and she had developed great admiration for Andy Brentwood. All of these people, without exception, were strong Union supporters. She had known nothing about the sectional disputes in the United States prior to coming to Virginia City, but since she had been here, she had learned a great deal about the issues that had split the United States asunder.

Her sympathies were with the Union, heart and soul—presumably, she guessed, because of her friendship with so many Northern adherents. Fair enough.

Now however, her services would be used to keep Lord Palmerston's government in London notified of the movement of the wagon train. No matter what the large freight wagons contained—and their contents did not matter to her—she felt that she was being disloyal to people who had taken her in and offered her unstinting friendship. She felt very uncomfortable, and a streak of rebellion came to life within her. "I'm being asked," she said, "to do something terribly sneaky."

Poole was surprised by her reaction but was able to deal with it. "Not at all," he replied. "You're being a patriot. More of a patriot than you've been so far, I might add. To date, you've either been unable or unwilling to provide us with any information about the silver."

Alison, however, had made up her mind. She had had enough of this smarmy and insistent man, and she decided she would do no undercover work for Great Britain, even if she was Lady White. So she shook her head and said flatly, "I prefer not to comply with your request, Mr. Poole."

His eyes smoldered, and his lips parted slightly in an ugly snarl. "I regret to say that your desires, or lack of them, are irrelevant, my dear Lady White," he declared. "My employers have kept their end of the bargain, and your career has not only been launched again, but you have been well paid for your efforts. Now you shall keep your end of the bargain."

"What if I refuse?" she demanded defiantly.

"I assure you, Lady White, that you will not refuse,"

he said, a strident note creeping into his voice. "You would offer me no choice but to see to it that you are banned for life from returning to London—in fact, you will be prohibited from setting foot anywhere in the British Isles."

The reprisal that he suggested was so severe that she could only gape at him. "Surely you don't mean that, sir?"

"Indeed I do mean it, and quite literally," he told her. "I regret the need to threaten you, and I certainly dislike becoming unpleasant, but I simply inform you flatly that my employers regard it as urgent that you accompany this wagon train. Look at it another way, if you will. Had Sir Charles been alive, he would have been ordered to accompany the train, and he would have done so. Therefore, you would have made the overland journey across the United States by wagon train in any event, so I urge you to be gracious and accept the small task that you have been given. You're not being requested to dishonor yourself in any way or to break any laws. So, be glad and do what you're told to do."

Alison knew she was trapped. She wished, however, that she could rid herself of the feeling of guilt that threatened to overwhelm her.

About that time, Beth Blake arrived in Virginia City, her presence there making it certain that at least four young women would be in the civilian wagon train party. Word had spread regarding the train's intentions, and somewhat to the pleased surprise of Lee Blake and Whip Holt, more than twenty families were on hand, all of them planning to head east and start their lives again. Like almost everyone else who had come to Nevada, these people had hoped to make their fortunes in the mines, the difference being that the men had brought their families with them. But like so many others, these men had been unsuccessful, just as they had also been unsuccessful in their attempts to earn a living for their wives and children on the bleak, unproductive soil of Nevada. These ninety persons, along with the four young women going for special reasons, provided a nucleus.

Whip conferred on the guard arrangements with Andy Brentwood and Toby Holt.

"Our chief concern at all times is going to be the four freight wagons," the train commander said. "The silver they'll be carrying is worth millions, and its safety is of prime importance to the Union."

Andy nodded. "I'm well aware of that, sir, but I think that the three hundred men we have on hand will be adequate to protect the wagons. All except seventy-five of them are regulars, and those seventy-five are Nevada volunteers. I don't have much use for militia, but the Nevada lads are different. Most of them have spent time in the mountains, and they're tough."

Toby resented his superior's attitude toward militia but kept his thoughts to himself.

"First off," Whip said, "there's the question of who will drive the silver wagons. What do you suggest, Major—do we hire civilians, or do we use soldiers?"

"Soldiers by all means, sir," Andy replied firmly. "We have much greater control over them, and we won't run into all of the troubles that civilians can cause."

Whip grinned and nodded. "That's fine," he said. "Matter of fact, that's already what General Blake and I had decided, but I was curious to see your reaction. Since we have four individual companies of soldiers—with approximately seventy-five men in each company—I suggest we assign each one of them to guard a specific wagon, and just to keep the men alert, we'll shift the units from one wagon to another from time to time."

"That makes a great deal of sense to me, sir," Andy replied.

"Do I take it," Whip inquired, "that you knew Captain Foster in Colorado before you headed out this way to Nevada?"

Andy nodded. "Yes, sir."

"You think he's competent to command a company charged with the responsibility that our units will have?"

"He may be a reserve officer, Colonel Holt," Andy

said, "and ordinarily I'd regard that as a strike against him, but in this instance, no. Scott Foster is a thorough, competent man, and I'm sure he leaves nothing to be desired as a company commander."

Whip had no idea how much the admission cost the younger man. Knowing nothing of the rivalry between Andy and Scott for Susanna Fulton's hand, he didn't know that Andy Brentwood was going far out of his way in order to be fair.

Toby had been listening to the conversation in silence, as befitted his junior position, but he couldn't help interrupting now. "Excuse me, gentlemen," he said. "According to our latest figures, we've got about ninety-five civilians making this trip in individual covered wagons. Do I understand correctly that we're making no effort to provide them with guards on the road?"

Andy looked slightly scornful but made no reply.

Whip chuckled. "I reckon that by now," he said, "hundreds of thousands of people have come West on the wagon trails. So many wagons have crossed the country that they've made permanent roads where there were no roads. So it strikes me that the civilians will make out just fine without specific guards assigned to them. The army troops will be nearby, guarding the freight wagons, and in case of need they can provide cover for the civilians. And, of course, we'll provide monitors to look after the civilian wagons. I reckon that will suffice."

Andy nodded vigorously, and Toby was very much surprised by the casual attitude that both his father and Major Brentwood displayed toward the people who were, after all, being encouraged to accompany the wagon train. However, he had to admit that his father's expertise in such matters was second to none, and he would not question his father's judgment.

A short time later the meeting ended. Andy, accompanied by Toby, left Whip's temporary office, and the two young men made their way across the busy military compound. The entire battalion was encamped now, the eighty mules being used to drag the silver wagons were being exercised regularly, and the civilians were already setting up their own camp prior to the train's departure.

As the two officers rode across the bare field, they slowed their mounts to a walk when someone hailed them. Andy saw a young man in his late twenties whose hands and face were tanned from long exposure to the sun. The man was riding rapidly toward them. "Do you happen to know who he is?" Andy muttered.

"Yes, sir," Toby answered. "His name is Ted Eannes. He's one of the newcomers to the wagon train, the only single man in the group of civilians. Like everyone, he came out here looking for silver and, failing at that, bought a farm. Had a ranch about one hundred and fifty miles northeast of here and nearly starved to death. He's a bachelor with no family, and he's traveling alone." There, he thought, was a report complete enough to satisfy even an officer who held his commission in the regular army.

"What can I do for you, Mr. Eannes?" Andy called. The former rancher looked pleased that he had been recognized and greeted by name.

"I was wondering, Major, how soon we're going to take off with this here wagon train?"

Andy could hardly explain to him that they were waiting now for the silver that was being smelted to be transferred to the freight wagons, a task that, necessarily, would be performed at night.

"We're rounding into shape nicely," he declared. "I'd say we're going to take off in the next couple of days at the most, but don't you worry, Mr. Eannes. I give you my word you won't be left behind." To Toby's surprise the rancher joined Andy in a hearty laugh. Toby saw nothing funny in the remark.

The two riders turned away, intending to resume their interrupted ride to their destination, but they paused when they saw someone else approaching them: a young woman riding a mare sidesaddle, her appearance so striking that both officers gaped at her. Caroline Brandon wore a bright pink band that held her flaxen hair in place and was attired in a gown of matching pink linen with a low neckline and full skirt, and a pair of matching high-heeled pumps. Her outfit was exceptionally attractive and enhanced her prettiness, even though it was completely inappropriate for someone riding a horse.

Andy Brentwood regarded her sourly and, barely civil to her, raised his hand briefly to the brim of his hat in salute. Toby, however, immediately removed his broad-brimmed uniform hat, bowed to the young woman, and grinned broadly. Caroline rewarded him with one of the dazzling smiles that she reserved for her favorites.

Had Toby been alone, he would have lingered for a conversation with Caroline, but he had to observe the amenities with his superior officer, and because Andy did not pause, he, too, had to continue on his way. Toby looked back again over his shoulder at the young woman, noting that she was slowing to a halt near Ted Eannes, and he waved again. Caroline lifted a hand, and her handkerchief caught the breeze as she returned Toby's greeting.

They rode on in silence for several minutes, and Andy finally said, "I see you've become acquainted with Caroline Brandon."

"Yes, sir," Toby replied. "I've been making it my business to know everybody who's going to be making this journey with us. I speak with all of them as they enter camp in their wagons."

Andy chose his words carefully. "You're doing the right thing, Lieutenant Holt, but be careful."

Toby was surprised. "Careful, sir?"

"I knew Caroline back in Denver, when her late husband was still alive, and I've been acquainted with her through all the fuss, fume, and furor that resulted when he was found murdered."

Toby bridled. "Surely you're not accusing her—"

"Of course not," Andy said hastily. "All I'm trying to get across to you is that the lady developed a rather unsavory reputation in Denver, which she deserved." He hesitated for a moment, still choosing his words with care. "She happened to join our party coming to Virginia

City from Denver, and I've seen her here from time to time as well. Her reputation in Nevada isn't the very best, either."

Toby shrugged. He looked amazingly like his father. "I never give a hang what people say about anybody," he said.

"Well," Andy replied, "in this case you might say where there's smoke, there sure is a fire, too. You know, no doubt, that Caroline is a trollop."

Toby thought his language was unnecessarily harsh. "I sure got the idea that she's worldly, all right," he declared. "You can tell that from her makeup and the way she dresses, but you've got to admit, Major, that she sure is pretty!"

Andy shrugged. "Her beauty—or lack of it—is entirely a matter of personal taste, I suppose," he said.

Toby marveled that such an officer should be the son of his father's closest associate and friend, and the nephew, even by marriage, of General Blake, whom he admired. Major Brentwood, in his opinion, was an opinionated prig, whose tastes left a great deal to be desired.

Meanwhile, Caroline Brandon continued to sit her mount quietly, making no move. She deliberately kept her horse still because she wanted to be in the same place when Lieutenant Holt glanced around at her again and yet again. She continued to strike a pose, and each time he gazed at her, she smiled at him in return. Someone on horseback came up beside her, but she didn't respond to Ted Eannes until he said, "Afternoon, Miz Brandon."

He was a man, so she smiled at him, too. He was neither wealthy nor influential, and as nearly as she could judge from her one previous talk with him, he was nobody of any consequence, but she nevertheless wasn't in the least rude to him. That went against her basic principles, which impelled her to treat all men with great consideration at all times.

Eannes was shy and struggled for something to say. "I just can't get over it," he said. "You being on this here wagon train."

Caroline was intrigued. "Why should my presence be so surprising?" she demanded.

He floundered as he sought an explanation. "Well," he said, "most of the folks who are going to be traveling East came West to make their fortunes and obviously failed. Take me for instance. I've been out here now for nine years. I've worked harder and for longer hours in these nine years than I ever worked in all the rest of my life put together. But what have I got to show for it? I ain't got a blame thing to show for it." He paused and moistened his dry lips. "So when I heard tell that this wagon train was going East and when I knew we'd be safe from Indians and bandits and Rebels, I sold my land claim for next to nothing, and I came here to join."

His story was ordinary, but Caroline treated it as something special and pretended to listen intently, her green eyes fixed on his.

Her steady gaze made Eannes even more uncomfortable. "It's like I say," he stammered. "Here's a great lady like you, you got all the money and fine clothes and jewels that a body could ask for, it's plain to see. But you're putting yourself a distance from Nevada, too."

The young woman smiled and said, "Fine clothes and jewels don't mean much, you know, especially when they're inherited, so to speak." He looked at her blankly. "I'm a widow," Caroline continued, and she spoke the truth, although she couldn't help adding, "All my finery was bought for me by my late husband." That was, of course, untrue, but the unsuccessful rancher had no way of finding out the truth.

Ted Eannes was deeply impressed. "I'm right sorry, Miz Brandon," he said. "I sure didn't aim to upset you none."

"You haven't upset me in the least," Caroline assured him. "You're very sympathetic and very sensitive, but please, I beg you, no more of this Mrs. Brandon talk. My name is Caroline, and I hope you'll remember it."

He swallowed hard and didn't know quite what to say. Caroline leaned slightly toward him so that he could catch a whiff of her expensive scent. She smiled at him warmly, put her hand on his arm for a fleeting instant, and then turned quickly, riding off in the direction of her new wagon without a backward glance. Ted Eannes sat unmoving, his mount rooted to the spot as he stared after her in open-mouthed wonder. He had known few women during his long, grueling sojourn in Nevada, and the few for whose favors he had paid small sums bore scant resemblance to the lovely, impeccably attired Caroline Brandon. He would have been astonished had he known that she was a courtesan and that in the upper-class circles she had acquired a notorious reputation as the heartbreaker of many men. All he did know, and it was quite good enough for him, was that she was the loveliest creature that he had ever seen, and he was smitten with her—so smitten that he would do her bidding in all things without hesitation.

On the second evening of Beth Blake's stay in Virginia City, her father thoughtfully invited her cousin, Major Andy Brentwood, and Whip's son, Toby, to dine with her at his temporary quarters. Whip was present, too, and the atmosphere, thanks to Beth's presence, was festive.

"I couldn't believe it, Daddy, when you wrote me suggesting that I join the wagon train," Beth said, beaming with excitement. "I would have sworn that you'd have a hundred objections to my traveling on a train."

Lee chuckled, aware that as so often happened, children had preconceived notions of their parents. "I discussed the idea with your mother before we left Fort Vancouver," he said. "She approved, and when Colonel Holt proved willing to have you with him, there were no barriers in the way."

Beth turned to Whip and said sincerely, "I'm very grateful to you, too, Colonel Holt. I grew up on stories of the first wagon train to Oregon, and it's almost too good to be true that I'm going to be traveling with you on a wagon train now."

Andy Brentwood peered at her over the rim of his glass of dry sack and said quietly, "If I had known that you were going to be cluttering up the train, I'd have requested a transfer, preferably to another theater of operations, but by the time that you showed up here and confirmed my worst fears, I had already accepted my new assignment, and I was stuck."

Beth, long accustomed to such raillery from her cousin, instantly responded in kind. "The one bad feature of making this trip is that you're going to be on it, Andy," she replied. "But I'm hoping that I'll be lucky and won't have to have too much to do with you."

Toby Holt looked first at his superior officer, then at Beth. Their conversation confused him and not until he heard them carrying on at some length did it finally dawn on him that they were teasing each other. Then he became annoyed for having taken their jibes seriously.

It was odd, he thought, but Andy and Beth were very much alike. Both had high opinions of themselves, but there was scant foundation for their self-regard. They were both opinionated and—well, he supposed he could go on criticizing them for some time, but he knew only that he disliked both of them intensely.

Certainly Andy's warnings about Caroline Brandon had been rough and unnecessary. He was a grown man and needed no advice from anyone on how to deal with any woman.

Toby was beginning to think that this journey wouldn't be nearly as pleasant as it had promised to be. He couldn't believe his good fortune to be serving in the military under his father's command, for this had been a lifelong dream of his. But now that this dream had come true, the pleasures were being spoiled by Andy and Beth. Not that they were deliberately causing him trouble; on the contrary, both seemed so superior to him that they were scarcely aware of his existence. That, perhaps, was the root of the trouble.

Well, he couldn't allow his attitudes to interfere. After the silver bullion was safely delivered to New York, his father would return to Oregon and would be demobilized; undoubtedly he wouldn't serve again for the duration of the war, so this assignment was precious, and Toby realized that he would be wise to savor every moment of it.

Susanna Fulton was delighted to learn that Alison White would be traveling on the wagon train, ostensibly to see some of the United States before leaving the country to return to England. The two women helped each other prepare their personal belongings for the journey, packing dresses and other items of apparel into boxes that could be fitted into a covered wagon. While they were engaged in these endeavors, Alison asked suddenly, "What living arrangements are you making for yourself on the wagon train?"

Susanna grinned. "I have a beat-up old wagon that I used when I came to Nevada from Denver," she said, "and Scott has promised to check it over for me. If he thinks it'll last for one more trip, I'll use it. Otherwise, I suppose I'll buy a new wagon."

Alison beamed at her. "I have a lovely, brand-new wagon," she said, "and it has two beds in it. I know a little something about horses, and there are two first-rate packhorses to pull it, so I'd be delighted to share it with you."

"That's very sweet of you," Susanna said, "but I wouldn't want to impose on you."

"Impose?" Alison raised an eyebrow. "You took me in here when I was desperate for a place to live, and you scarcely even knew me at the time. I think the least I could do is to return the favor and show my gratitude to you."

Susanna saw that she was sincere in making the offer. "I just don't want to be in the way," Susanna murmured.

"Fiddlesticks!" Alison declared heartily. "I'll enjoy your company, and there will be someone to spell me in driving the team of horses. Not only that, but you know the United States, so you'll be able to tell me all about the territories we're passing through."

Susanna laughed. "You give me more credit than I

deserve," she said. "I know the territory between here and Denver, it's true, but I was very young when my father and I went out to California, and I remember virtually nothing about the territories that lie east of Denver. It will be as new an experience to me as it will for you."

"Well," Alison said, "I'm hoping it will be fun—something for me to remember." She had made up her mind that since there was no way she could avoid making the overland journey by wagon train, she might as well make the best of the situation and enjoy herself to the fullest extent possible. "Anyway," she added forcibly, "the issue is settled. You and I will be traveling together."

"Thank you," Susanna replied. She was silent as she packed sweaters and scarves into a box. Then she asked, "May I confide in you?"

"Of course," Alison said quickly.

"Some women," Susanna said, her voice becoming confidential, "enjoy the excitement and fuss of being courted by several suitors at the same time. I've never been that way myself. I've always preferred to deal with one man at a time because I feel as if I can evaluate him more fairly that way, if you see what I mean."

Alison smiled and nodded. "I know the feeling you describe," she replied. "But frankly I'm afraid that my ego is flattered when I'm the center of attention from more than one male. That may be wicked of me, but I confess—between us—that I like it."

"Most women do," Susanna replied. "I've become accustomed to it, you might say, because I've had two such persistent suitors for a very long time. Scott Foster makes no bones of his feelings toward me, and Andy Brentwood, although he is somewhat more reserved, is also very clear."

"You're fortunate," Alison replied. "They're both exceptionally attractive men." She refrained from adding that she herself was drawn to both of them and had a hunch that either would be a suitable husband.

"I'll let you in on a secret," Susanna said. "I'm delighted that both of them are going to be accompanying the wagon train. I'll have ample opportunity to see both of them and to make up my mind—once and for all—which of them I prefer. I don't think it's right to keep both of them dangling on a string, and I'm going to be very firm with myself. Before my wagon train journey comes to an end, I intend to make a final choice between them."

Alison thought her attitude was commendable but naive, so she worded her reply carefully. "More power to you if you can meet that self-imposed deadline. I'm not so sure I could do it."

Susanna looked very serious. "I will, because I must," she said firmly. "I've encouraged both Scott and Andy long enough, and it simply isn't right. I know it makes me sound like a spoiled brat," Susanna confessed, "to be flaunting two suitors, and I hope you don't think that I'm bragging."

"Hardly," Alison told her. "But you're far luckier than you know. You have a free choice and can marry the man you truly love." Somewhat to her surprise, she found herself telling the story of her marriage to Sir Charles White, which had been foisted on her by her family and which she had accepted in obedience to their will.

"I had no idea that you'd been married," Susanna said.

"Well," Alison replied slowly, "I haven't been publicizing the fact, especially as my husband died unexpectedly and tragically in Victoria, up in British Columbia, some months ago."

Susanna looked stricken. "How dreadful."

Alison was unwilling to confess that she had never loved Charles and that, therefore, his loss had been far less shattering than it otherwise would have been. She smiled vaguely. "One learns to do what one must in the world," she said, managing to sound very matter-of-fact.

She had a resilience, a hard core that Susanna envied. "I wish I could be more like you," she confessed. "I've acquired a surface toughness in the newspaper business, but I'm afraid that, underneath, I'm still too soft for my own good."

"Well," Alison said, "for whatever my advice is worth to you, be very certain of where you stand, of what you want before you make up your mind. Once you decide between Andy and Scott, there will be no turning back for you."

"I'm well aware of it," Susanna confessed, "and the knowledge makes me more than a little bit panicky. What can I do to overcome the feeling?"

Alison considered the question at length before she replied. "I'm no expert on love and romance," she said. "Once a woman has been married and widowed, she's supposed to be knowledgeable about these matters, but that simply isn't the case. All I can tell you is what I believe myself, and that is when you fall in love with a man—genuinely in love, without reservation—you'll know it. You won't need to be told or guided or advised. That's why I've said to you to let your decision grow gradually. Don't force it. When you've chosen the right man, you'll know it, and a team of wild horses pulling in the opposite direction couldn't force you to change your mind."

Major General Lee Blake planned to leave for Fort Vancouver before the wagon train was scheduled to depart. He held a long, final conference with Whip Holt and then dined in private with his daughter, whom he subsequently consigned to Whip's care. His aide was busy packing his belongings, and Lee was attending to some last-minute chores in his temporary office when the battalion sergeant major interrupted him.

"General," he said, "there's a Baron Bernhard von Hummel who's here to see you. He apologizes for coming without an appointment."

Lee was well aware of Bernhard's value to the Union cause. The Prussian arms manufacturers whom he represented had received requests for large quantities of vitally needed field artillery guns, and the orders had

113

not yet been filled. It was Lee's understanding that Bernhard's approval would be necessary before the guns would start to be sent across the Atlantic for the use of the Northern Army.

He received the young Prussian without delay and shook hands with him warmly.

"I apologize for calling on you so abruptly, General," Bernhard said, "but I just learned that you are not accompanying the wagon train and instead are going back to Fort Vancouver. The misunderstanding is my own fault; I have no idea why I thought that you were going to go with the wagon train."

Lee assured him that the interruption was in no way disconcerting.

Bernhard braced himself, then spoke succinctly. "General," he said, "I shall not mince words. You and I both know that your War Department has placed some very large orders with my employers for cannon. The orders are so large, in fact, that I was sent to America for one purpose—to make certain that the Union Government can afford to pay for what it has ordered. You will forgive me, but your President and treasury secretary are new, and we know nothing about them. We must be very certain that we will be paid."

Lee faced a dilemma. The best way to convince the young Prussian nobleman that the government of the United States was indeed able to pay its bills was by telling him the secret of the silver hoard that was being entrusted to Whip Holt's care for the journey to New York. He decided that his superiors in the War Department would want him to speak candidly and to reveal the complete truth to von Hummel.

Rising from his desk, he walked to the window, gestured for the baron to join him, and pointed at the mammoth freight wagon that was very much in evidence on the grounds. It was several times larger than the conventional covered wagon. Also, it had a permanent, hard roof of wood rather than a roof of canvas stretched on supple poles. It was an impressive-looking vehicle.

"I will tell you what very few people know," Lee said. "That wagon and three others like it will be filled with silver bullion. The real purpose of this wagon train is to transport the silver—which is government owned—to the Treasury Department's vaults in New York City."

Bernhard was awed. "Four wagons of that size filled with silver bullion," he said, "will be a vast fortune—it is bound to be worth many millions of dollars."

Lee nodded but made no comment.

Bernhard was silent for what seemed like a long time. "General," he said at last, "I appreciate your confidence, and I assure you that I shall not destroy it."

"Thank you," Lee said. "I knew of no better way to assure you that the United States will be able to pay for the field artillery pieces ordered from your Prussian munitions plants."

Bernhard grinned. "I feel a trifle foolish now for having even raised the subject. Of course," he continued thoughtfully, "much could happen in the Nevada wilderness before the arrival of the bullion in New York."

"Indeed," Lee replied. "That's why Colonel Holt has taken command of the train, and that's why he will have a full battalion of experienced troops at his disposal. We intend to make very certain that nothing happens to the silver en route to its destination."

"Do you suppose it would be possible," Bernhard asked thoughtfully, "for me to accompany the wagon train? I assure you that I would be no bother, but it would give me an opportunity to do my duty as my employers conceive it."

Lee was willing, and he felt certain that Whip Holt would feel as he did. "By all means, join the train," he said, "but I don't know that there's going to be enough time for you to obtain a covered wagon for yourself. The caravan is scheduled to leave Virginia City early tomorrow morning."

Bernhard shook his head and smiled. "I will require no wagon and no assistance. Thank you all the same, General. I have my own horse—a very reliable animal—

and I carry my own equipment, including a blanket and cooking utensils. I shall be self-sufficient on the road."

Lee admired his thoroughness. "Then you'll be more than welcome," he said. "I'll notify Colonel Holt that you'll be accompanying him."

V

The raw, untamed beauty of the Nevada wilderness was never more evident than at dawn. As the sky brightened in the east over the endless rock formations and deserts of the huge territory, eventually casting light on the towering snow-covered peaks that lay to the west, the man-made structures of Virginia City seemed flimsy and temporary.

The settlers who were returning to the East could look at the view that unfolded for them without regrets: they had never been able to appreciate the beauty of the Nevada wilderness, finding it instead a bleak, desolate place where they had been unsuccessful at making a living. There were others who loved Nevada and were determined to live nowhere else; they, of course were the settlers who were staying in the territory and were establishing deep roots.

Now, at dawn, the sharp, crisp sound of a bugle floated across the compound, and within moments the military camp was astir. The bugle call awakened the few civilians who were not already up and dressed for the beginning of their journey. A military cooking detail built up the fire that had been deliberately allowed to die down after the previous evening's meal had been cooked, and the civilians were apportioned chores. Children emerged from their wagons and gathered silently around the adults as the entire camp sprang to life. The mules had already been fed and watered and were harnessed to the huge freight wagons. The example set

117

by the soldiers impelled civilians, also, to hitch up their teams to their covered wagons.

Susanna Fulton and Alison White emerged from the wagon they shared, the former wearing pants, as always, and the latter dressed for the road in a sturdy gown of plain wool. Beth Blake, her blue eyes shining with excitement, her lifelong dream about to come true, burst from her own wagon wearing a boy's shirt, trousers, boots, and a hat. She had a spare horse in addition to the team that would pull her wagon, and in her eagerness she saddled it now. Susanna and Alison, noting her excitement, half expected her to vault into the saddle prematurely.

Caroline Brandon created a sensation when she emerged from her wagon. Her makeup had been impeccably applied, her hair had been carefully brushed, and her gown of pale green silk was as startling as it was inappropriate for the beginning of a journey across the Nevada wilderness. But Caroline, as usual, cared nothing about the proprieties. She had managed to attract the attention of virtually the entire company, and that was good enough for her.

Soon breakfast was ready, and the cooks served bacon and biscuits, as well as the more customary military fare of hot oatmeal. The civilians stood in line and patiently received their rations and then spread out to eat. The soldiers were served quickly and efficiently, and then the battalion adjutant suddenly called them to attention.

Whip Holt, clad in faded buckskins, worn boots, and a broad-brimmed hat that had seen better days, rode up to the fires. Those who were unacquainted with him were impressed by the sight of the long rawhide whip hanging from the side of his saddle. Those who knew him realized that he could wield it so expertly that it became an extension of his arm.

He halted his stallion, then ordered the troops to stand at ease.

"Today," he said in a loud, clear voice, "we're starting a journey—an adventure—together. I'm not one for making speeches, so I'll be brief. The officers and men of the

118

battalion know what's expected of them and will do their duty accordingly. Any man who wants to see me for any reason will apply through appropriate channels, and I'll be glad to talk with those who have Major Brentwood's approval." He transferred his gaze to the civilians. "You folks aren't in military service, but you're going to be subjected to some pretty hard and fast disciplines, too. When you're told to do something, please do it immediately, without discussion and without argument. If you encounter problems of any kind with the battalion, don't come to me. Go at once to Major Brentwood, the battalion commander, and complain to him." He paused, then scanned the ranks of the civilians slowly. "Monitors will guide you in starting and stopping for rests and in halting at the end of each day. Just remember this—everyone carries his own weight in any wagon train that I command. Every man has responsibilities. Every woman has her jobs. Even the children have tasks to perform that aren't beyond their abilities. You're expected to carry your weight at all times. I will not hesitate to expel from the wagon train anyone who creates disturbances or who causes troubles either for himself or for others. Anyone who is forced to leave our company will have to go it alone. If you think I'm harsh, I'm sorry, but we're going to be crossing some rugged terrain, and our safety depends on the obedience and cooperation of all." He settled his hat firmly on his head and turned away. His speech was the first and last that he would deliver on the entire wagon train journey.

Now Toby rode up and quickly revealed to Whip and Andy Brentwood the assignments he had made, placing two men on each of the freight wagons as drivers and giving five others the positions of monitors, those who would ride up and down the line of wagons, patrolling their sectors to make sure that the wagons stayed the proper distance apart, that they halted and started on schedule, and that nothing untoward was happening to any of them. Whip nodded in satisfaction; Toby had done his job well.

Toby was still speaking, concluding his report, when

Beth Blake rode into their midst and interrupted him in mid-sentence. "Colonel Holt," she said breathlessly, her eyes shining brightly, "I looked for you last night, but I couldn't find you anywhere." Toby frowned at the interruption.

Whip remained tranquil. "I was having a last chat with your father, I reckon," he said mildly.

"Just in case you're looking for another monitor," Beth said, "I want to volunteer my services. I've arranged for someone else to drive my wagon, so I'm free to serve as a monitor."

Her eagerness was so obvious that Whip couldn't help grinning. He could understand how Beth felt. She had grown up listening to countless stories told by her parents of the many adventures experienced on the original wagon train to Oregon, and now she had a chance to share those experiences herself.

Toby made no effort to conceal his irritation, and Andy Brentwood frowned at his young cousin and shook his head in mock despair. He was secretly pleased, however, that she had volunteered her services, but he had no intention of letting her know it.

"It'll be fine with me if you want to serve as a monitor, Beth," Whip said, chuckling, "but the decision isn't up to me. The battalion is determining those things, and Lieutenant Holt here is in charge."

Beth's face fell as Toby regarded her stonily. She glanced inadvertently at her cousin, silently appealing to him, but Andy Brentwood was not one to overrule a subordinate, and his shrug spoke louder than words.

"I guess I'm willing to try you out, Beth," Toby said at last. "The reason I hesitate is because all of our other monitors are soldiers and you'll be the only civilian in the company. If you can follow orders and not create a ruckus, however, the job is yours."

The young woman bridled, and she gave a toss of her long blond hair. "What makes you think that I'm going to create a ruckus?" she demanded.

Toby shrugged. "I'm not saying you are, and I'm not saying you aren't. I'm just telling you my conditions for taking you on as a monitor and keeping you working." She had an infinite ability to annoy him, he thought, and he wondered why she was always so willing to quarrel.

A nod of Beth's head told him that she accepted his conditions, but her indignant sniff indicated her real opinion. Toby saw no need to burden his father and Andy with the details of what was required of a monitor. "Come along," he said, "and I'll get you started right now." As he rode off with her, he patiently explained her duties.

Watching the young couple as they rode off, Whip shook his head. "You know," he said, "it wasn't so long ago that my wife and your aunt had a big romance planned for those two. I think it still bothers both of them that Toby and Beth can't stand the sight of each other."

"They're a little immature, if you don't mind my saying so, sir," Andy replied. "I think they've got some growing up to do."

"I know," Whip replied, chuckling. "Just so you're prepared for some fireworks between here and the East Coast. I expect one or the other of them is going to explode someday, and I hope for the sake of the whole company's peace that they don't let loose at the same time."

The line of wagon trains was a familiar scene. It had been repeated countless times over the decades. There was one difference, however, between this wagon train and the others: while immigrants by the thousands had made their way to Oregon and California, Colorado and Nevada, this wagon train was moving in the opposite direction; it was traveling from west to east.

Ahead of the column, sometimes well out of sight of the caravan itself, were the scouts. In this instance they were professionals who knew their business thoroughly. All were noncommissioned officers of the battalion, and all were experts at reading various signs on the trail. At the head of the line itself, Whip Holt rode easily, his pale eyes constantly alert as he scanned the horizon, searching for trouble. His rifle was looped under his arm, his buckskins made him appear inconspicuous, and only those who knew him realized that here was one of the legendary heroes of the West. Behind him on his left and right, respectively, rode his son, Toby, and Major Andy Brentwood, both in uniform. The monitors reported to Toby in an unending stream, keeping him busy, while the major concentrated on searching for signs of potential trouble. The fortune that was being carried on the train was so enormous that he had to be braced for any eventuality.

The large teams of mules, twenty to a wagon, hauled the heavy freight at a surprisingly lively clip, and the mules were so accustomed to trail travel themselves that they required very little goading or urging from the drivers who sat on the boxes of the four wagons. The soldiers, approximately seventy-five men assigned to each wagon, tended their business and maintained military silence in the ranks. They were certainly aware of the cargo they were carrying, some of the soldiers having helped load the wagons in Virginia City, but that was not what was important. Major Brentwood had impressed them with the fact that they were engaged in a service that was vital to the future of the United States and could mean ultimate victory or defeat in a war with the Confederates. That was all they needed to be told in order for them to keep close watch over the wagons.

Their officers also maintained a vigil, each in his own way. A tense knot had formed in the pit of Scott Foster's stomach at the beginning of the journey, and it refused to dissipate now. He, like Andy Brentwood, anticipated serious trouble sooner or later. In fact, he was quite willing to wager that the Confederates would launch a concerted attack on the wagon train before it reached its final destination. It was too much to hope that the contents of the wagons had been kept a secret from Confederate intelligence agents, and the bullion was so important that the Rebels undoubtedly would make every effort to take it and apply it to the Confederate cause.

Scott was conscious of Susanna Fulton's proximity, and he was aware, too, of the presence of the alluring and pleasant Alison White, but he did not allow himself the luxury of spending more than a few token moments at a time with the young ladies. He took his responsibilities as a company commander seriously.

Susanna Fulton, sitting on the open box of her covered wagon, the reins in her hand, had no question in her mind about the contents of the heavy freight wagons. She noted how the troops surrounded each of the four wagons at all times and kept them under surveillance, and she observed that at stops—even the pause known as "nooning," when the caravan halted for rest and light refreshments—the soldiers did not relax their vigil but continued to guard the contents of the wagons, rifles ready for immediate use. She was eager to begin writing her big story about the silver train, but she knew that until she had authorization to do so, her hands were tied. She was much too loyal to her country to do anything that might jeopardize the mission. In the meantime, she would have to content herself with making observations and jotting down notes.

Alison White, sitting on the box beside her, was far more relaxed, at least on the surface. She was awed by the vastness of America. She had known that the United States was a huge country, but crossing it by wagon train was an experience that she would never forget. The train covered twenty to twenty-five miles per day, but it seemed to rumble endlessly across the wastelands of Nevada, on which the sun invariably shone out of a cloudless blue sky.

Alison was ever conscious of the presence of Scott and Andy on the wagon train. It amused her to see how frequently Captain Foster and Major Brentwood found a seemingly valid excuse to visit Susanna, and no sooner did one appear than the other showed up on his heels. Alison couldn't help envying Susanna, who had two such devoted swains.

Even more, Alison envied her friend the peace of mind she could enjoy because her conscience was clear.

When the wagon train arrived at the first post office station, Alison would be required to mail a letter to an apparently innocuous address in Chicago, and she dreaded performing that act because when she did she would be acting as a spy against the best interests of the United States, a country she was beginning to like and admire.

One person who seemed totally unaffected by the rigors of wagon train travel was Caroline Brandon. She was never seen by anyone except when wearing full makeup, and as the other women in the train told each other, she was "dressed to kill" at all times. The wagons bounced and swayed over the rough terrain, and water had to be conserved in the Nevada desert, but Caroline seemed untouched by the hardships that affected everyone else. She continued to look as she had when preening in her box at the theater in Virginia City.

Some of the women concluded that Caroline had set her cap for Lieutenant Toby Holt. Certainly she came to life instantly in his presence, chatting animatedly and flirting with him openly. But what her critics failed to realize was that Caroline was not smitten, nor was she determined to make a conquest of Toby. The facts were simple: of all those who were drawn to her, he was by far the most attractive, so she preferred his company, and she exerted herself more in his presence than she did with any of the other men.

"We'll travel at about half our usual pace this afternoon," Whip announced to Andy and Toby one day as they resumed their journey after the nooning rest. "You'll note the ground seems level enough, but it's rough. There are rocks and ruts that can throw wheels out of alignment and can break axles, so we'll anticipate trouble by going at a crawl. Lieutenant Holt, make sure your monitors keep a sharp watch on every wagon and that no one drives faster than he should. Any animal that breaks a leg on this terrain will just plain have to be shot."

"Yes, sir," Toby replied, then hastily fell back to the head of the line to communicate the orders to his line monitors. He spent about an hour with them, moving incessantly up and down the length of the column. He resumed his place at Andy's side, behind Whip, only when he had satisfied himself that the train commander's orders were being obeyed.

The procedure to be followed was simple enough: the individual wagon drivers were required to adjust their own speed and to travel at the pace that Whip set. But after a time it became apparent that the half-dozen lead wagons containing civilians were traveling far more rapidly than Whip had decreed, which forced Toby to slow them down and adjust their pace accordingly. His irritation with them grew, and finally, half turning in his saddle, he beckoned to the monitor for the sector.

Beth Blake cantered to the head of the line, smiling happily.

Toby addressed her more harshly than he realized. "If you would pay a little attention to Colonel Holt's speed," he said, "you wouldn't be having these problems with the folks in your sector. Please follow orders!"

Beth became annoyed, and her temper flared. "I can't crawl at a snail's pace, and neither can those wagons!" she exclaimed.

It was obvious that she was being deliberately disobedient, and Toby became stern. "Beth," he said, "you're kicking up a fuss, and you're going to cause trouble. I didn't ask you to set your own speed; in fact, I made it quite clear to you that you were to adjust your pace to Colonel Holt's. You've been given a direct order, and you're expected to carry it out."

Whip, overhearing the conversation, silently applauded his son, who was, in his opinion, handling the situation admirably.

Beth did not think so, however, and began to sputter. "It's very difficult to drag at a funeral pace across this desert," she declared.

"Frankly," Toby told her flatly, "I really don't care what pace you find convenient for yourself or for the wagons under your jurisdiction. God Almighty, girl, you come from a military family, so you sure as shooting ought to know by now how to obey a direct order."

Beth became nasty. "Perhaps," she said, "I'm accustomed to taking orders from generals, not from lieutenants."

Andy Brentwood had remained silent through the exchange, but suddenly he could stay quiet no longer. "Beth," he said, exploding in anger, "you're just about the most spoiled brat I've ever seen in my life. I'd urge Toby to whale you proper if I thought it would teach you manners, and I don't mind telling you I'd be tempted to take a hickory stick to your bottom myself. There were good and valid reasons why you were told to hold your wagons to a certain pace. There was no need to explain to you why Colonel Holt wanted that pace kept, and I see no reason to go into it all with you now. Let it suffice that you were given an order, and you sure as hell weren't expected to go out of your way to disobey it."

Beth stared in astonishment at her stern-faced cousin. She had known Andy only as a jovial, extremely pleasant young man, and she was seeing a side of his nature with which she was thoroughly unfamiliar. He pushed his broad-brimmed campaign hat back on his head and eyed her stonily. "We're not going to waste time with a girl," he announced. "All we need is one accident to one wagon under your control, and the whole train will suffer. Lieutenant Holt!"

"Sir?" Toby inquired.

"I'll leave the decision regarding the future employment of Beth Blake strictly in your hands," Andy said. "If you want to give her another chance and think she's capable of behaving herself, then you're free to keep her on as a monitor. If you're as disgusted as I am and want to get rid of her, however, don't keep her on the job for either my sake or her father's. She obviously doesn't know the meaning of the word discipline."

His rebuke was so severe that the color flamed in Beth's cheeks.

Toby couldn't help feeling sorry for her. He knew that she had gone too far, not realizing the seriousness of her offense, and he knew how she was reacting to her cousin's withering scorn. "I reckon just about everybody has to learn sooner or later," he declared, "and I hope that Beth has truly learned a lesson from this experience. I have no intention of discharging her as a monitor now."

The embarrassed, mortified Beth was less grateful to him than she should have been, and she curtly nodded her thanks to him. Her gratitude, however, was the last thing that Toby wanted or expected. A principle was at stake, and as he had learned from his parents, principles were all-important.

"I'm giving you another chance, Beth," he said. "Slow down your wagons now and see to it that they stay slowed." Rather than prolong the difficult conversation, he turned away from her abruptly and devoted himself to studying the terrain directly ahead.

For a long moment, Beth rode in rigid silence. Then ignoring Andy and hoping in vain that Whip Holt—the close, lifelong friend of her parents—had not heard too much, she turned suddenly and spurred back to the column.

Out of the corner of his eye, Toby saw her pausing and speaking earnestly to each of the wagon drivers for whose safety she was responsible. He knew that she was cautioning them to adjust their pace to Whip's.

Whip appeared unconcerned by the interlude, and Andy grinned quietly to himself, occasionally shaking his head, but he made no comment.

Toby himself was in no way surprised at Beth's behavior. As far as he was concerned, she was indeed a spoiled brat, and he supposed that he had been foolish not to discharge her immediately. He hoped that he wouldn't regret his leniency, but he had handled the incident as he had believed right, and that was all that mattered.

In the days when Whip Holt had led the first wagon train to Oregon, he had grown accustomed to mounting his stallion after a hasty breakfast and not leaping to the ground again until the end of the day's journey.

Now, however, he could no longer do that. In the almost inaccessible mountain heights, as well as in the broad valleys below, the sun beat down mercilessly on the dry land. The terrain itself was so rough that the horses had to watch their steps in order to avoid stumbling and breaking a leg. Whip discovered, soon after the wagon train left Virginia City, that he lacked the stamina and resilience that he had taken for granted for so many years. Now, the jolting gait of his stallion caused his arthritic hip to throb, and he had to control a strong desire to squirm in pain. At noon when he called a halt, he was relieved that he could dismount and stretch out on the ground, and often he found that he had to exercise great willpower to set the train in motion again. He hated to admit the truth but the facts were plain—all too plain: Eulalia had been right, and he had been wrong; he had become too old and was not in good enough physical condition any longer to lead a wagon train. He was capable of leading a company against a vastly superior force of Indian warriors; he could find his way through a wilderness morass where others rapidly became lost; but he could not overcome the reality that his body could no longer function as it once had.

But the United States of America was depending on him to lead the wagon train with its silver from Nevada to Missouri, then to travel by train to New York. He had no choice; he had accepted the assignment from General Lee Blake, and the responsibility was his, regardless of his physical condition. Therefore, he was obliged to continue the journey, no matter how much he suffered. Eulalia could say "I told you so" all she pleased when he returned to the ranch in Oregon. Between now and that time, he still had a job to do for his country, and he intended to do it.

Concealing his discomfort, hiding his acute pain, he carried on and continued to lead the wagon train. Others in the company did not suspect that he was in torment. Andy Brentwood, who spent virtually every waking moment in his company, knew only that Whip was a silent man. Andy found nothing unusual in this because his father, Sam Brentwood, was of the same breed as Whip and often—especially when traveling—remained silent for long hours on end. Toby Holt should have known that his father was suffering, or at least he might have guessed, but Toby had only the external signs to go by. He had promised his mother that he would keep a sharp watch on his father, but he lacked Eulalia's instincts. He saw his father eating and sleeping, he observed him as he kept the entire wagon train company under the rule of his benevolent tyranny, and he appeared to be very much at peace with himself.

So even Toby did not realize or suspect the torment that Whip suffered. His father's hip throbbed intolerably; the pain eased somewhat only in the small hours of the morning after he had rested, rolled in his blanket; and the torture began anew the moment that the ride was resumed.

Whip was relieved beyond measure that he had succeeded in fooling his son and Andy. That meant no one would interfere with him or try to persuade him to cancel his journey. Under no circumstances was he willing to turn over command of the train to someone else. The responsibility for the bullion was his, and he would discharge it without flinching, as he had discharged his duty so often in the past.

Whip Holt knew he had no real alternative. He had always done his duty, regardless of what happened to him personally.

As the Civil War increased in intensity and the fighting on both sides became more furious, the feelings of people about the conflict grew at a rapid rate. Almost no one in the Union was neutral anymore, and even in towns and cities remote from the great population centers of the East, the war's partisans became increasingly vehement.

This was true of Denver, a wild frontier community tasting respectability and responsibility for the first time. A portion of the city had been settled initially by Southerners, but their day had long passed, and by mid-1861

Denver was firmly and without qualification in the Union camp.

Of all the partisans in favor of the North, there was no one whose loyalty surpassed that of the young black giant known only as Ezekiel. A former slave who had run away from his Southern master and had been befriended by Miss Prudence Adams, the New England proprietress of Denver's first general store, Ezekiel had grown with the town. After working for Miss Prudence as a handyman, he had gradually risen to the position of chief clerk, at which time he had married an exceptionally bright and attractive woman, Patricia, who had worked as a lady's maid for Cathy Blake.

Now, suddenly, life was changed overnight for Ezekiel and Patricia. Miss Adams had died and had named them as her sole heirs. So they found themselves the owners of the largest and most prosperous general store in all of Colorado. Ezekiel said nothing about his good fortune until several days after Prudence Adams's funeral. He seemed to withdraw into himself and was lost in deep thought for hours at a time.

Patricia, who knew him well, was seeing a side of him that she had never before encountered, but she generally bided her time and hired a couple to help out in the store. One night as they sat in their private quarters behind the store eating their supper, Ezekiel suddenly began to unburden himself. "The way I see it," he said, "we're kind of rich. I imagine if we put this place up for sale, we'd get one whale of a lot of money for it."

Patricia was astonished. "Why on earth would we want to sell?" she demanded. "Miss Prudence, God bless her, has given us financial security for the rest of our lives. We'll be able to earn a good living from this place for years and years to come."

Ezekiel was silent and pushed food around on his plate with his knife and fork. Ordinarily he had a voracious appetite, but this evening he seemed to have no interest whatsoever in food. "Hear me out, Patty," he said. "I got some thoughts that are eating holes in me."

His wife nodded sympathetically and leaned back in her chair, prepared to listen.

"The way I see it," he said, "the Union Army needs men and needs them bad. So I've got me a mind to enlist."

Patricia was shocked. "Don't do anything hasty, Ezekiel," she replied. "We have security now for the first time in our lives. With all the millions of men who are living in the Union, surely the army will be able to meet its quotas."

"You don't understand," he said, shaking his head slowly. "Miz Pru, she didn't understand it, either. Both of you came from New England. There are no slaves in Massachusetts, and there haven't been any there since the United States was founded, so you can't imagine what slavery is like."

Patricia's smile was taut. "Let's say I have a rather vivid imagination," she said. "I think I can picture it."

He shook his head stubbornly. "Unless you live through it you just plain don't know, and me, I've lived a bellyful of slavery. I know it for the vicious, rotten, no-good, foul, contaminating—"

"Please, Ezekiel," Patricia interrupted. "Don't get excited."

Ezekiel took a series of deep breaths, then said, "I'm sorry, honey, but I feel strong about it, and feeling the way I do, I've got to act. I'm a big man, and I'm about as strong as they come. I have me an idea that the army will be glad to find a place for me. There aren't many black men who can read and write, you know, and I owe that to you, for teaching me after we were married. So the army's sure to have a real use for me."

Patricia understood the way he felt and couldn't help agreeing with him, at least to an extent, even though his enlistment in the army would interfere with their future.

"The way I see it," Ezekiel said, "we sell the store and get as much as we can for it. Then I go into the army, and you go home to your family in New England."

"That doesn't make too much sense," Patricia protested. "I can understand your desire to enter the army, but why don't we keep the store, and I'll operate it while you're in service?"

"No, ma'am!" Ezekiel was emphatic.

"Why in the world not?" she demanded.

"You can answer that question yourself by taking a good, long look at yourself in the mirror, lady. You're attractive. You're as pretty as they come. In fact, there're few women anywhere as pretty as you. Denver is still a wild frontier town in many ways, and you just plain couldn't protect yourself if you stayed on here without me."

"Oh," she murmured.

"The way I see it," Ezekiel continued forcefully, "is for us to handle all this by selling the store, which will give us enough money to keep you in comfort for the rest of your days. You'll be safe with your family in New England, and you'll have everything that you'll need while I'm at war."

"I hate the thought of giving up this store," she said.

"So do I," he told her, "but it can't be helped. Let's just say that that's one of the wartime sacrifices that we've got to make."

She sighed deeply but made no comment.

"I've given the whole problem a lot of thought, and I can't come to any other conclusion than the one that I've reached. I'm sorry. I know that I'm asking a lot of you, but I don't know any other way to do it. I wouldn't rest easy if I thought you weren't safe when I go off to war."

"Where do you plan to enlist?" Patricia asked.

"Well, now," he replied. "I guess I'll just take me down to the local garrison and get myself sworn in and maybe even get me assigned to active duty."

"That soon?" Patricia was surprised.

"The sooner the better," he said emphatically. "This is one war that the U.S.A. has got to win, and I want to do my part!"

Chancellor of the Exchequer William Gladstone was said to be imperturbable, but he confounded his immediate subordinates by his reactions to a meeting he held with an unnamed representative of his ministry. There were many such semianonymous men who had curious, blank faces, who dressed nondescriptly, and who came and went in mysterious ways. No member of the regular staff quite knew the functions that these persons performed, but everyone was wise enough to ask no questions and to make no inquiries.

Gladstone was closeted with one such man for the better part of an hour, and when he was alone again, he immediately rang for his assistant. Awaiting him impatiently, he sat drumming on his desk of polished mahogany. As usual the desk was bare, in keeping with his principle of staying ahead of his current work load at all times.

His subordinate hurried into his office, and to his surprise, William Gladstone was red-faced.

"Be good enough," he rasped, "to find out how soon it will be convenient for the prime minister to see me." The assistant knew from his tone that something very much out of the ordinary had happened. He asked no questions, however, and promptly clapped his high-crown beaver hat on his head and hurried to the prime minister's office, which was located in another building behind the Whitehall government complex.

While he waited, Gladstone, contrary to his custom, read no reports and conducted no interviews with anyone. Instead, he impatiently paced the length of his office, his hands clasped behind his back. He halted, scowling, when his breathless assistant appeared.

"The prime minister is scheduled to make an appearance in the House of Lords in the next half-hour," he said, "but his office assures me that he can see you now, Your Excellency, if you have an urgent matter you wish to discuss with him."

Gladstone wasted no words. He snatched his stovepipe hat and lightweight cloak from the wall peg on which they were hanging, took his walking stick from the umbrella holder just inside the door, and hurried out into the street. He was so distraught that he failed to mention to his private secretary how long he intended to absent himself from his office. This was extraordinary, in no way typical of his usual conduct. He hurried the two blocks down Pall Mall, the broad thoroughfare on which the huge stone buildings that housed the government of the British Empire were located. Several officials whom he passed en route to his destination were delighted to see him and would have taken advantage of the chance meeting to press business of their own, but Gladstone gave them no opportunity.

Lord Palmerston was signing a stack of documents when the chancellor appeared, and he looked up calmly. "I gather," he said mildly, "that an emergency of sorts has arisen."

"I sincerely hope it has not, sir," Gladstone replied. "I have just received a detailed report from my man in North America. He has learned from our senior agent, Poole, that a wagon train laden with huge quantities of silver bullion is currently traveling from the silver mining country of Nevada and is being transferred all the way to New York."

Palmerston smiled faintly and nodded. "Quite so," he said. "I received a similar report and intended to pass the word along to you at our regular meeting tomorrow."

Gladstone's impatient gesture indicated that he was not concerned by the prime minister's failure to notify him of the development immediately. "I have also learned—to my great surprise, sir—that Poole has assigned a young female British agent to accompany the wagon train. Poole has instructed the agent to travel all the way to New York with the silver, if that is possible."

Lord Palmerston leaned back in his chair and fingered the heavy gold watch fob that dangled from his waistcoat pocket. "That is also my understanding," he said.

"The presence of a British espionage agent on that wagon train," Gladstone said with deliberate emphasis, "places the entire situation in a new and menacing light."

He was so definite, so somber that the prime minister was surprised. "How so?" he demanded.

134

"The primary function of an agent—whether male or female—is to commit acts of sabotage. In this case I assume it would be performed for the purpose of interrupting the wagon train journey and somehow interfering with the delivery of the silver bullion to the U.S. Treasury vaults in New York."

Lord Palmerston shook his head. "I've given Poole no orders to that effect," he said. "It would suit our purposes, obviously, if the silver failed to reach its destination. I have little doubt that the Americans are intending to use that bullion to pay for some of the extensive munitions they're ordering from plants in Prussia, but I have deliberately refrained from giving Poole specific orders for the simple reason that I now think it's best that we not become too deeply involved in American affairs."

This was a reversal from the prime minister's earlier intentions to go to great lengths to assist the Confederacy, but Gladstone was still far from satisfied. "We must assume, must we not, that our agent Poole is endowed with slightly better than ordinary intelligence. Consequently, he knows that Her Majesty's government—Lord Palmerston and William Gladstone in particular—would not be displeased if the delivery of the bullion were delayed or interrupted."

Lord Palmerston failed to understand what he was driving at, but he nodded. "I suppose you're right," he said. "Most agents would draw rather obvious conclusions, and I don't think there can be much question about that."

"Let's make another assumption," Gladstone said, becoming even more perturbed. "We know that Poole is a man of some ambition. He hopes to further his career, win promotions, obtain better assignments, and receive higher pay for his activities."

The prime minister nodded.

"Therefore," the chancellor said grimly, "it's virtually inevitable that he will instruct the young female agent to commit some act of sabotage against the wagon train." Gladstone tried to control himself but could not. He began to pace up and down the edge of the rich Oriental rug on the floor of his superior's office. "I know nothing about the particulars of this wagon train," he said, "but it stands to reason that the American government isn't leaving it unguarded. The War and Treasury Departments undoubtedly are taking special precautions to see that the bullion is safe and that it will be delivered intact to New York."

The prime minister still couldn't see what the chancellor was trying to tell him and became somewhat testy. "I'm due on the floor of the Lords, where I'm scheduled to make a policy address, so please be brief, if you will."

Gladstone spoke with great emphasis. "An act of sabotage conducted against this particular wagon train is sure to be noted by the American authorities, who will act accordingly. I see virtually no chance that any agent in our employ would be so deft and clever that he or she could perform such an act and escape without detection."

Comprehension began to dawn in Lord Palmerston's eyes.

"We well may face the wrath of the Union government," Gladstone said. "The Americans have their backs against the wall now, and they're certain to lash out furiously at anyone who interferes with the attainment of their goal. So an act of sabotage—that is almost preordained to fail—may involve Great Britain in a new war with the United States. Our people are totally unprepared to fight such a war, and in fact it well could cause the downfall of this government."

"There's little doubt," Palmerston replied, "that the sentiments of the British public on the slavery question make the cause of the North highly popular here."

"I'm very glad that you are aware of the facts of the matter, sir," Gladstone said severely. "The agent traveling with that wagon train, whoever she may be, must be instructed by Poole to commit no act of sabotage and to do nothing that will impede the transfer of the silver bullion to its destination. I regard that as imperative."

Lord Palmerston rose slowly to his feet. "I think I can assure you that our agent traveling on that train is completely harmless. You see, what I know that you do not is that Poole has given the assignment to Sir Charles White's inexperienced widow, Lady Alison White."

Gladstone shook his head. "There is no such person as a harmless agent," he declared. "To call any secret agent harmless is a contradiction in terms. Our entire foreign policy will be in a shambles if the agent, acting out of misguided motives or instructions, does anything to interfere with the delivery of the silver. The Americans will be wild if they find out what we're about."

"I can only repeat that I've been informed on the best possible authority that the agent Poole is working with is harmless," Lord Palmerston said.

Gladstone glared at him. "I urge you, sir, to take no unnecessary risks. If you please, send specific instructions to Poole at once and make it very clear that there is to be no sabotage, no interference of any kind with the bullion."

The prime minister was tired of the subject and had what he regarded as far more pressing problems of state on his mind. "Very well, William," he said soothingly. "I shall take your advice, and I'll send instructions accordingly, immediately."

A look of vast relief crossed Gladstone's face. "You won't regret this, sir," he declared. "This is one instance where an ounce of prevention is worth many pounds of cure." Satisfied at last, he withdrew and returned to his own office.

As soon as he departed, the prime minister's private secretary bustled into the room. "Excuse me, milord," he said, "but you're due to speak in the House of Lords in less than five minutes, and you'll have to hurry to reach the Houses of Parliament on time."

"So I shall," Palmerston said. "Now where the deuce are the confounded notes that I made?"

The underling handed him a file folder, and the prime minister snatched it eagerly, accepted his hat and cloak, and rushed out of his office with all of the dignity that he could muster. His mind was already fully occupied with the policy address that both the Whig and Conservative parties had been awaiting, and the espionage agent who was attached to the American wagon train faded rapidly from his mind. He did not think in terms of the agent again and completely forgot his promise to Gladstone that he would issue instructions to Poole to curb any possible act of sabotage against the silver bullion.

VI

Although temperatures soared by day beneath a scorching sun in the Nevada desert, the nights were invariably chilly, sometimes surprisingly cold. Caroline Brandon's French nightgown of flimsy black silk was inadequate to protect her from the cold, but the truth of the matter was that she had no other nightwear and had to make do with what she had brought with her.

Perhaps it was the cold that kept her awake as she huddled beneath the blankets on her bed in her covered wagon, but it was even more likely that boredom was responsible. The days all seemed alike, as the endless journey eastward went on and on and on; the evenings were unbearably dull, and there was absolutely nothing to do. Caroline discovered soon after the wagon train left Virginia City that she had few, if any, suitors in the company. The military officers were too disciplined, and most of the civilians were married men traveling with their wives and children. Ted Eannes, who appeared to have fallen in love with her, was, in her opinion, a hopeless fool. She had been pleased by the presence of Bernhard von Hummel on the wagon train, but to her extreme disappointment he had been avoiding her. Not that he was going out of his way to snub her; he was pleasant enough, but to her private disgust he seemed to be developing an interest in Beth Blake, who was in Caroline's opinion a totally inadequate female.

Whip Holt was a fascinating man, but Caroline soon learned that he was totally impervious to her charms and that no matter how hard she flirted with him she had no effect on him. She couldn't help wishing he were as malleable as his son, Toby, who had the advantage of being exceptionally handsome and who, although naive, was better than nothing.

She counseled herself to exercise patience. She had sold her property in Virginia City for a handsome profit, prices there being wildly inflated, and she had accumulated a substantial nest egg. Now she intended to start life anew as Mrs. Douglas de Forest. She would relish having dozens of house slaves to wait on her, and she looked forward eagerly to assuming her new role. The thought flicked through her mind that the current war between the states was a distracting influence, but she saw no way that it could interfere with her life. It didn't matter to her in the least whether the North or the South won the war; Caroline was interested in herself, not in politics.

She stared up at the canvas roof of her covered wagon with unseeing eyes, and only the chill prevented her from climbing out of bed. She desperately wanted a drink of brandywine, but it was far too cold to cross the wagon for it.

Reviewing her own life in recent years, she had every cause to be satisfied. She had been a nobody, a nonentity married to a New England professor, but her existence had changed drastically when he had gone to Denver to analyze the gold in the Colorado mines and had taken her with him. His death had more than set her free; it had signaled the beginning of a new existence for her. Granted she had suffered torment and humiliation when she had been forced to work in a Denver brothel, but her own ingenuity had come to the fore, and as usual, her luck had been marvelous. Caroline believed in luck, and with good cause. She had attracted a large following in Denver before she had gone to Nevada, and she had become the highest priced courtesan in Virginia City. Now she would be leaving the life of a prostitute for all time, thanks to the willingness of

Doug de Forest. She smiled softly to herself and decided she had no need for any brandywine.

Suddenly the canvas covering at the rear of her wagon parted, and a man whom she could not make out in the dark entered.

Caroline was curious about his identity and felt no fear. It had been a long time since she had had cause to be afraid of any man. "Hello," she called softly, seductively. "Who are you?"

The man moved closer but made no reply.

She found his silence disconcerting, so she struck a phosphorus match and lighted the small oil lamp that sat on the clothing box that served as a bedside table. By its light she made out the uniform of a Union officer, which surprised her. Toby Holt wasn't the sort to come to her unbidden, and to the best of her knowledge she had made no other conquest in the battalion.

Her surprise turned to sheer astonishment when she recognized the swarthy man who loomed over her. "Doug!" she exclaimed.

Douglas de Forest gestured vehemently for silence. "Quiet," he muttered. "For God's sake don't mention my name again."

Caroline was silent as she reached for a filmy black negligee, which she donned over her nightgown. Then she sat up in bed. "I had no idea," she said, taking care to speak quietly, "that you'd accepted a commission in the Northern Army. When did you do that?"

De Forest had no intention of explaining that he had come to the camp disguised as a Union officer in order to avoid calling attention to himself. If Caroline thought that he truly had obtained a commission from his enemies, so much the better. He trusted her no more than was absolutely essential, and he had no respect whatsoever for her intelligence. He grinned at her but made no reply.

"If you'd like a swallow or two of brandywine to ward off the chill," she said, "you'll find a bottle and glasses on the wall shelf behind you. As a matter of fact, you could pour a sip or two for me."

De Forest complied, and after handing her a drink, he adjusted the wick of the oil lamp so that it burned as low as possible, casting a faint glow on the interior of the wagon.

Caroline, mindful of the fact that this was the man that she was going to marry, played her role of his future wife to the hilt. "You have no idea what a wonderful surprise this is, darling," she said. "I was just thinking about you."

De Forest smiled broadly and addressed her with an insincerity that matched her own. "I always think about you," he replied.

She beamed at him.

"I've come here privately," he told her. "Very privately. No one must know of my visit."

"I see." Actually she saw and understood nothing but hated to admit her ignorance.

He had no intention of enlightening her. What she didn't know couldn't hurt him. The entire battalion would be in an uproar, as he well realized, if they discovered that a Confederate spy had penetrated so close to the wagons that contained the precious silver bullion.

"I've come to see you," he said, "at considerable risk to myself—never mind why I'm taking chances. In time of war it's often safer not to explain."

"Of course," Caroline replied promptly, having no interest whatever in the war.

He raised his glass in a silent toast to her, then sipped the excellent brandywine. "I have a desperate need to know something that only you can tell me," he declared. "Soon the wagon train will be leaving the Nevada Territory and can follow any one of many routes. I've got to know which route this wagon train is going to be taking for the next two weeks."

Caroline had no idea of the train's location at any given time, and she neither knew nor cared where they went. Her only concern was that Whip Holt was leading the company toward the East.

"I'm afraid I have no idea, darling," she murmured.

De Forest concealed his impatience. "I'm well aware

of that," he said, "but you can find out for me. In fact, it's imperative that you find out." He tempered his words by taking her in his arms and embracing her. "I can hardly wait until we're married," he murmured. "I see you in my mind's eye now as mistress of my widower father's estate. When you stand at the base of the marble staircase, you're going to look as though you've always belonged there."

She nestled close to him, envisioning the scene that he depicted.

"I'll be back in a couple of nights," De Forest told her. "See to it that you have the wagon train's itinerary for me by then." She stirred in his arms, faintly disturbed.

"Wherever am I going to get information like that?"

He shrugged, and his voice became harsh. "I don't know, Caroline, and I don't care. That's strictly up to you. All I know is that it's vital that I obtain this information, and I am depending on you—only you—to get it for me." He kissed her savagely, then released her. "I'll be back in two nights," he said. "You'd best turn off your lamp now."

She obediently extinguished the lamp, and no sooner was it dark in the wagon than Douglas de Forest silently took his leave, vanishing as suddenly as he had arrived.

He thought that he was totally escaping detection, but he was mistaken. Ted Eannes, unable to sleep, was sitting on the back stoop of his covered wagon, and he caught a glimpse of a Union officer departing from Caroline's wagon. A wild stab of jealousy aroused the former rancher and left him trembling. It was too much for him to even contemplate that this young woman, for whom he had conceived such a grand passion, could have been entertaining another man in private.

Thanks to a halt made the previous day at an army fort in the Humboldt River valley, in the eastern section of the Nevada Territory, the wagon train had acquired sides of bacon and considerable quantities of flour, among other supplies. So the battalion cooks prepared bacon and hot biscuits for breakfast, a fare that they would serve so frequently that the troops would grow heartily sick of the meal.

For the present, however, the biscuits and bacon were still something of a novelty, and Toby Holt, who had grown up on such fare, stood by himself a short distance from the cooking fire, where he used the ledge of a large rock as a table. He ate with relish, taking occasional sips of the hot black coffee that the battalion cooks had prepared. He saw a civilian coming toward him, and he braced himself for questions and requests.

Ted Eannes looked gaunt and hollow eyed after a sleepless night. He clenched his fists as he stood in front of Toby. "Damn your soul, Holt!" he exclaimed.

Toby blinked at him in surprise. The former rancher was mild mannered and had caused no problems for anyone on the journey so far, and his sudden outburst was not typical of him.

"You needn't stand there smirking and being so damned satisfied with yourself," Eannes stormed. "I'm going to take care of you, all right. I'm going to challenge you to a duel, right now, with pistols."

Toby concealed his astonishment. He knew of no earthly reason why he should fight Ted Eannes, and looked at the man curiously. "What have I done to get you so riled up, Mr. Eannes?" he inquired politely.

The man clenched his fists and rocked back and forth on his heels, color burning in his face. "You can pretend all you want," he said, "but I saw you with my own eyes, coming out of Caroline Brandon's wagon last night."

Toby looked at him and smiled politely. "I had no such luck, my friend," he said. "I was nowhere near Miss Brandon's wagon. I suspect you mistook someone else for me."

Eannes shook his head fiercely. "I know damn well I saw you," he said between gritted teeth, "and I demand satisfaction."

The conversation was nonsensical, and a day's march loomed ahead. "Look here," Toby said flatly, "I've already told you that you were mistaken. I was nowhere near Miss Brandon's wagon at any time last night. So I have no intention of fighting a duel with you. If I did, I'd put a bullet through your heart, and that's that, sir." He picked up his coffee mug, turned on his heel, and stalked off. Ted Eannes glared at him, muttering under his breath.

Toby paid no further heed to the man and tried to dismiss the matter from his mind. It niggled at him, however, and he found himself speculating on the identity of the unknown officer who had apparently visited Caroline.

The day's march started when Whip gave the order for the wagon train to move out, and the wagons headed in a drawn-out line toward the passes that would take them safely through the next of the interminable Nevada chains of mountains.

Whip rode ahead, having been informed by one of the military scouts that he had seen some Paiute Indians in the mountains they were approaching, and Toby rode at a sedate pace beside Andy Brentwood. "I guess Caroline Brandon has made a conquest in the battalion," he said, making conversation.

Andy was not interested in Caroline's romantic conquests, and he shrugged. "She manages to keep busy," he replied vaguely.

"I wonder who the lucky officer could be, that's all," Toby explained. "She's as attractive a woman as ever I've seen."

Andy could not conceal his scornful smile. Young Holt was even more naive than he had assumed. "Caroline Brandon," he said succinctly, "is nothing more and nothing less than a damned whore."

Toby was shocked, and he was about to respond angrily but stopped himself just in time to avoid a nasty confrontation with the battalion commander. Regardless of what he thought of Caroline, regardless of Andy's opinion of her, he could not afford to lose sight of the fact that he was a first lieutenant and that he was dealing with a major who was his immediate superior. Had any other officer insulted Caroline, Toby would have been inclined to challenge him to a fight. If he went too far—and it was possible that he might if he gave free rein to his temper—he would be risking court-martial for insubordination and conduct unbecoming to an officer. He was no longer a civilian and could no longer enjoy the privileges of civilian life that he had always taken for granted.

He swallowed his anger and told himself that he would not forget Andy's slur against Caroline Brandon. He could, in fact, almost understand the jealous anger that Ted Eannes had displayed.

At the same time he wondered anew about the officer who had been fortunate enough to visit her in her wagon the previous night. He couldn't help envying the lucky devil.

From now on, he thought, he would keep his opinions to himself in Andy Brentwood's presence. His dislike for the major was becoming strong and active, and it was a damned shame that Andy was the son of the man that his father considered his oldest and closest friend.

Toby rode in silence for the better part of the morning and was relieved when Whip rejoined the column shortly before noon. "There are a half-dozen Paiute warriors hunting for game up yonder," he said, nodding toward the mountains into which they were heading. "But they're harmless, and I can't see them causing us any damage."

"How do you tell whether Indians are going to be friendly or hostile?" Andy asked. "It seems to be a fine art."

Whip grinned at him. "Blamed if I can tell you," he said. "You just plain feel in your bones that they're going to get unpleasant. Ask your pa sometime."

Andy chuckled. "I've discussed the subject with him often," he said, "and he gives me virtually the same answer—word for word—that you have, Colonel."

Whip became thoughtful. "It's a matter of experience, I reckon," he said. "You see just so many Indians under all kinds of circumstances for just so many years, and your instinct tells you whether they're going to offer you wampum or the sharp edge of a tomahawk blade."

"I see." Andy nodded. "It's like everything else, then."

"Exactly," Whip exclaimed. "It's like looking at a woman and knowing at a glance whether she's a lady or a trollop. If you were an inexperienced youngster, you wouldn't know, but any man of experience can tell at a glance."

Color flamed in Toby's cheeks. His father had inadvertently touched a very sore spot. Andy had called Caroline Brandon a whore, but he refused to believe it. He had seen prostitutes in Oregon and in Virginia City, and Caroline did not fit their image. She was far too attractive, and her manners were far too ladylike. There was no question, of course, that Caroline was a woman of the world and had known men of wealth and means, but that only made her more attractive. It was strange, he mused, but Andy's insulting remark about her had impelled him to become more her champion than ever, and he was determined to offer her whatever protection he could.

That evening the civilians and military alike were served a steaming beef stew with meat, onions, and carrots. Only Toby and a few others knew that the dish was not really made up of beef but of venison, the scouts having isolated several deer when they had encountered a herd several days earlier.

Feeling restless, Toby ate quickly, then started to wander through the camp. He stopped short when he saw Caroline sitting on the rear stoop of her wagon. She looked particularly attractive in a gown of yellow silk with a low, square-cut neckline and a slit skirt. On a sudden impulse he headed for her wagon.

"Evening, ma'am," he called. "Do you mind if I join you?"

Caroline bestowed one of her ravishing smiles on him. She was bored to distraction, and here, at least, was a good-looking young officer who could amuse her for a time. "I'd be delighted if you would, Lieutenant," she replied.

He seated himself below her on the steps. "If you don't mind my saying so, ma'am, you sure do look pretty tonight," he declared.

Again Caroline beamed at him. She could never accept enough compliments about her appearance.

They chatted about inconsequentials for a time, and suddenly Toby felt bold. He could satisfy his curiosity about her visitor the previous night, perhaps, without arousing her ire. He was thoroughly confused because the officer, whoever he was, kept his distance from her at all other times.

"Tell me to mind my own business if you like, ma'am," he said, "but I can't help wondering who the officer was who paid you a visit last night."

Caroline smiled steadily, mindful of the fact that Douglas de Forest had stressed the secrecy of his visit. "Last night?" she asked as she frowned prettily, as though trying to remember.

"Ted Eannes," he said casually, "happened to mention that an officer visited you, that's all, and I was curious."

She laughed heartily, and the tinkling soprano sounded like a small waterfall breaking over rocks. "Poor Ted Eannes," Caroline said. "He's enamored of me, or thinks he is. Anyway, his imagination keeps playing tricks on him, and he's sure that I'm carrying on a secret romance with someone. He doesn't know who, and frankly, neither do I." She laughed again.

Toby felt greatly relieved. It hadn't occurred to him that Eannes had made up the entire incident out of whole cloth, but now that he thought about it, he wasn't surprised. In any event, that was that, and it was evident that he had no real rival for her interest, at least on the wagon train.

Caroline studied the chiseled face of this earnest young man, and a sudden thought struck her. Doug had asked her to use any means at her disposal to learn the wagon train's itinerary, and Toby Holt was an officer who obviously knew it.

"Now it's your turn to tell me something," she said. "I find that I get terribly depressed by the Nevada scenery.

We seem to be crossing one chain of mountains after another, and they're about as endless as the desert. Are we going to be in Nevada much longer?"

Toby shook his head. "No, ma'am," he said. "We'll soon be leaving Nevada and heading into the Utah Territory. You'll find the terrain is very different there."

"That's good," she murmured, listening to him with rapt interest.

"We'll be heading north toward Great Salt Lake," he said, "and then we're going to follow the basic trail that leads by way of Fort Bridger. Thousands and thousands of travelers have used it, most of them heading in the opposite direction of the way that we're going, and you'll find that there are plenty of trees and lots of rivers that make the scenery a great deal prettier. Then—and I guess there's nothing wrong in my telling you this—we're going to go to Denver."

She nodded and thanked him, surprised at the ease with which she had acquired the information.

They chatted at length, and Caroline was pleased to have the company of this personable young man, whose politeness and eagerness made it obvious that he admired her. As for Toby, he couldn't remember when he had enjoyed himself more. Ordinarily he was shy and retiring in the presence of females, but he found it no strain to be in Caroline's presence, and he was able to speak freely and with self-confidence. He was vaguely aware of the fact that her attitude was somehow responsible. She had a knack for encouraging a man, for causing him to forget his inhibitions and to speak freely. She devoted her total attention to him, and even when he was talking about inconsequentials, he felt that he had captured and was holding her undivided attention.

Twice he started to rise, intending to cut the visit short. But each time Caroline pouted prettily, shook her head, and waved him back to his seat, so he hastened to accede to her wishes.

Eventually others in the company finished their suppers and retired for the night; the wagon train began to settle down. Toby became self-conscious and decided that he would definitely take his leave. Caroline extended a hand to him and held his own hand in a firm, warm grasp for some moments before she released him.

His hand felt as though it glowed, and as he made his way toward the battalion's bivouac area, he thought that Caroline Brandon was unique, that she was the most interesting and most beautiful woman he had ever known. It was strange, he reflected, that Andy Brentwood had gone out of his way to insult her by calling her a whore. He supposed that Andy had been letting off steam because of some slight, real or fancied, in his own relationship with Caroline. Whatever the cause, Toby thought firmly, the charge was malicious and uncalled for.

As for Caroline, she surprised herself by watching Toby with regret as he left her wagon. Certainly she felt sorry and slightly ashamed of herself for having used him to obtain the information that Douglas de Forest had demanded of her. Not that Toby had suffered any harm, but she had the feeling that she had been taking unfair advantage of him.

Examining her reactions to him, Caroline realized that here was a man who truly liked her for herself. He sought her company and went out of his way to be pleasant to her, asking nothing. More men than she could count had made a fuss over her, to be sure, but that was part of the game that males played when they wanted to bed a popular prostitute. Toby Holt seemed to have no idea of her profession, and she was sure that he would be shocked and more than a little stunned if he were to learn it. His admiration for her was genuine, and it was patent that he truly liked her for herself. Consequently, she was flattered far more so than she had been by the attentions anyone else had paid her in a very long time. Just as she was someone special to Toby, she began to regard him as someone special, too.

It was still daylight when Susanna Fulton and Alison White finished eating their supper, so they adjourned to the back stoop of their wagon and sat there, gazing out at the peaks of the last chain of mountains they had crossed. Alison had already inquired as to the name of the mountains, but she couldn't remember what she had been told, and she was reluctant to inquire again. There were so many chains, so many mountains that her head spun, and she couldn't keep them straight in her mind any longer. It was no matter, she supposed, and she sighed gently.

Susanna looked at her, then broke the silence. "Is something the matter?"

Alison shook her head. "You have no idea how educational it is traveling by wagon train. I'm beginning to gain a very good idea of the size of the United States now. It's truly enormous—much larger than I'd imagined. It's a remarkable country, really."

Susanna nodded soberly. "I don't wear my patriotism on my sleeve as a rule, but I have enormous feeling for my country. That's why I'm so worried now by this dreadful war. It could destroy so much that so many of us believe is precious."

"If you'll forgive the judgment of an outsider," Alison said, "I believe that the war between the states is going to strengthen rather than dilute or harm America's principles. You're the only nation on earth, I think, that believes in a form of government based on freedom and has actually developed a government that fits those beliefs. You're unique."

"Hear, hear!" a man declared in a deep voice.

The two women were startled to see that Major Andy Brentwood had approached the wagon.

"We're devoted to an ideal," Andy said, "and a great many men are going to die for that ideal before this war ends—more's the pity."

Susanna nodded, and Alison, based on her limited knowledge, had to agree, too.

Andy changed the subject. "This is far too lovely an evening for gloomy observations," he said. "I hope I'm not interrupting."

"Certainly not," Susanna replied, and her emphatic manner spoke volumes.

Andy grinned at her in obvious appreciation. "Do you

suppose I could persuade you to take a stroll with me as far as our sentry lines? I don't know if you feel as I do, but on a night like this I just can't sit still."

"I know exactly what you mean." Susanna smiled at him warmly as she rose eagerly to her feet. "You don't mind, Alison?"

"Certainly not," Alison replied.

She watched them as they strolled away together with Andy offering Susanna his arm, which she grasped firmly. They made an exceptionally attractive couple, Alison reflected. Both were good-looking, and both were devoted to the principles in which they believed. Susanna might not yet be aware of it, but Alison was sure, by the way that Susanna looked at Andy, that she was on the verge of choosing him.

Alison was glad for her, certain that her friend would lead a happy existence. Of course, marriage to an officer in the standing army would mean her life would be somewhat nomadic and she might know any number of homes in the years to come. But Susanna's own past as a newspaperwoman had prepared her for just such a life. Unlike most women, she wasn't particularly attracted by the prospect of having a permanent home and establishing roots.

It was strange, Alison thought, but she herself would give a great deal for such a home, which she had never known. There was no point, however, in dwelling on the impossible. She had no serious suitor, and as a singer-actress she was condemning herself to years of life as a transient. Moreover, her present activities as an espionage agent made the thought of marriage and home even more remote. So be it. There was nothing to be gained by yearning for the unattainable.

A male voice sounded close at hand, and Alison jumped.

"I'm so sorry," Captain Scott Foster said. "I didn't mean to startle you."

"That's perfectly all right. My thoughts were very far from the mountains and deserts of Nevada."

"I see." He loomed above her, looking large and solid

in his uniform. "I gather that Susanna isn't about at the moment."

"I'm afraid not," Alison replied politely, protecting her friend by not revealing her whereabouts.

Scott sighed, stared off into space for a moment or two, and then asked suddenly, "Mind if I sit down for a spell?"

"I'd be delighted," Alison told him. For some reason that she couldn't quite fathom, she felt very much drawn to Scott Foster. Perhaps it was because his air of self-assurance so epitomized the American spirit that she had come to admire. It might have been her imagination, to be sure, but he was a younger, more robust, and more vibrant version of the late Sir Charles, and the thought had flitted through her mind that if Charles had possessed some of Scott's obvious qualities, it would have been far easier for her to love him.

She realized, of course, that he was seeking her company simply because Susanna wasn't available at the moment, but she felt no shame at being second best. She was sufficiently experienced in the ways of the world to realize that a man and a woman could always establish new relationships, even if they cared for someone else.

Scott lowered himself to the step beneath the one on which Alison sat and asked her politely, "Could I fetch you a cup of coffee from the cook fires? No, come to think of it," he added hastily, "you always prefer tea."

Alison was flattered that he had paid enough heed to her to have learned which beverage she preferred. In any event, she shook her head. "I'm quite comfortable, thanks, but if you want some coffee or tea, by all means help yourself."

He shook his head. "I hate to admit this, but I'm careful about the amount of coffee I drink at night. More than one cup keeps me awake."

"It does precisely the same thing to me," Alison said.

Scott grinned at her. "You know, I'm ashamed to admit to any limitation, even one as trivial as being kept awake by drinking coffee. My father always taught us to be strong, and so naturally I hate any sign of weakness.

To be weak means not to be free to do the things you want."

She smiled at him. "You take freedom very seriously, then?"

"I reckon I do."

"But we're all subject to limitations of one kind and another," Alison said. "I don't think anyone is completely free to do what he or she wants in all things at all times."

"Maybe not," he admitted reluctantly.

"Take the most obvious of restrictions," she said. "You wear your country's uniform, so you're obligated to obey the commands of your superior officers."

"Sure," Scott admitted, "but this war isn't going to last forever. I'll be a civilian again one of these years, and then it will be up to me to make of my life whatever I can."

She clasped her hand over one knee, and looked at him thoughtfully. "That's an interesting way to look at life, I suppose. As a singer I've always been aware of my talents—and of my limitations. I would never apply for a role that I knew I could not fulfill."

"I guess that's true enough of the way that I feel," Scott admitted, "but I'm always tempted to push a little beyond my capacity in the hope that somehow I can force myself to succeed."

Alison began to understand how men with attitudes similar to his had conquered a wilderness that had stretched across the entire North American continent. "Aren't you sometimes afraid you'll fail?" she asked, very interested now.

Scott shook his head. "Failure," he said, "is strictly a state of mind. I've lived by the creed of never refusing a challenge."

She nodded, deeply impressed.

Suddenly he grinned, then chuckled. "Of course, by accepting any and every fool dare that's come along," he said, "I've stumbled and fallen flat on my face more often than I care to admit."

Alison was fascinated. "But you've always picked

yourself up, dusted yourself off, and come back for more, I gather."

"Sure," Scott admitted. "Nobody keeps track of the times that I've fallen. All that counts is succeeding in something that you've set your mind to."

"I think that's rather wonderful," Alison said, and meant every word.

Her admiration made him uncomfortable. "I don't see anything extraordinary in my attitude," he said. "On the contrary, I think it's a fairly common approach, but you're a fine one to talk. You're really achieving something."

She looked at him in astonishment. "I am?"

"You bet!" Scott declared. "Most women are happy as clams sitting home and doing nothing. They're satisfied with their lives if they find a husband, bring his kids into the world, and make a home for their families. But not you! You had talent, and you were darn well determined to do something about it. You must have studied for years before you went on the stage."

She was embarrassed by the sudden turn of conversation that had placed her in the spotlight. "Oh, well, yes, that's true," she admitted. "I did study voice for five years—five years of hard labor!"

Scott interrupted. "And after seeing you perform in Virginia City, I know how hard you work. At the end of a performance you're nearly wiped out, and I sure can't blame you."

She sought something appropriate to say, but her mind was suddenly blank.

"Anyway, you're the one who deserves admiration," he declared.

"Not necessarily." She spoke quietly, gently. "I saw an opportunity when I was quite young of assisting my family. My parents had a difficult struggle financially, and when I began to achieve success as a singer, I was able to give them considerable material assistance." She refrained from adding that those same motives had impelled her to marry Sir Charles White.

Scott said, "I doubt if many people would have done what you did."

She smiled in return, basking in the rapport that they had created. Suddenly he spoke again, and his voice became confidential. "If you don't mind," he said, "I want to tell you something in confidence. I think I've lost out in the race for Susanna Fulton's hand."

Alison privately agreed with him, although she hesitated to tell him as much. So she said nothing.

"Not that I ever got my hopes up too high," he continued. "She's like quicksilver, that one. I suppose what drew me to her in the first place is that she's so different. I never knew another woman like her."

She felt very sorry for him, and she gazed at him intently.

"It isn't at all like meeting you, for example," Scott continued. "You're a star—a person of consequence in the theater—so I suppose I should have been in awe of you, but I found I could hit it off with you right away. It was like—no offense intended—pulling on an old shoe."

She knew that he intended the remark as a compliment, so she tried to accept it as such and tried to smile, although the effort was painful.

"I've never felt that way with Susanna," he said. "I guess I've got this feeling that she's a lot smarter than I am and that no matter what I say, she's already thought of it." He stood and sighed almost inaudibly. "I'm sorry," he said. "I sure don't mean to burden you with my problems."

"They're no burden," Alison assured him.

"You're sweet and generous to say so, ma'am, but that's exactly what I've come to expect from you." He grinned at her, shifting his weight from one foot to another.

Alison was emboldened and took the initiative. "Anytime you're at loose ends and feel like chatting, I'm available," she told him.

Scott looked uncomfortable. "I don't want to take advantage of your good nature—"

"You'll be doing no such thing," she cut in. "In fact, I

shall be very annoyed if you don't come to chat with me from time to time."

He squared his shoulders. "Then I reckon that's something I'll just have to do," he said. Bowing to her, he went off slowly to the bivouac area.

Alison sat unmoving and watched him as he departed. Susanna Fulton was far more fortunate than she knew, and it was remarkable that she could afford to turn down a man of such sterling qualities.

Given her own choice, Alison would instantly opt for Scott Foster ahead of every other man she had encountered. He was ruggedly good-looking, extremely personable, and self-reliant almost to a fault. Above all, he had so many of the qualities that made her admire America and look up to Americans; come to think of it, he personified America in her mind.

Alison warned herself, however, to watch her step and not become too deeply involved with Scott. He was so much in love with Susanna that he did not know that any other woman existed in the world, and if she lost her heart to him, she would be certain to regret it. What was more, there was the little matter of her espionage assignment. She smiled ruefully and shook her head. It was one thing to give herself sound advice, it was something else again to accept that advice.

Beth Blake unexpectedly slept late the next morning and was one of the last members of the company to appear for breakfast. For reasons she made no attempt to analyze, she was starved and therefore accepted two slabs of bread, onto each of which she placed several slices of bacon. Then, moving away from the cooking fires, she began to eat ravenously.

She was still consuming her meal when Toby Holt appeared. He had been acting as officer of the day, an assignment that each of the officers took in turn, and his duties had kept him so busy that he had not had an opportunity to eat breakfast until now. When he went to the cooking fires, however, the sergeant in charge of the military mess was apologetic.

"I'm sorry, Lieutenant," he said, "but we've plumb run out of bacon, and there's no time to fix another batch. The colonel will have us on the march at any time now."

Toby contained his disappointment. "Just give me some bread," he said, "and I'll be fine." He walked away, munching on the dry bread, then stopped short when he caught sight of Beth with a bacon sandwich in each hand. A wave of annoyance engulfed him, and he went to her, seething inwardly.

"I reckon," he said unpleasantly, "that you've never heard of sharing food on the trail."

Taken aback by his unexpectedly harsh tone, she blinked at him. "I beg your pardon?" she inquired icily.

"On the trail," Toby said, "folks take their fair share of rations, no more or less. They don't eat like hogs and deprive others of a meal." Giving her no opportunity to reply, he stalked away.

Beth was furious and would have followed him, not caring if she created a scene as long as she had a showdown with him. But at that moment, Bernhard von Hummel, who had overheard the entire exchange, materialized suddenly beside her. "I urge you," he said quietly, "to forget what the lieutenant just said to you. His anger was justified, from his point of view, just as you have every right, from where you stand, to be angry in return."

Beth was surprised and amused by the interference of the good-looking, earnest foreigner. "May I ask what you know about it?" she inquired.

Bernhard chuckled. "To be sure," he said. "You were hungry this morning, so you took a double order of bacon. That is not a capital offense, even in a wagon train company. Lieutenant Holt was busy with his military duties, and when he appeared for his breakfast, there was no bacon left. He saw you with a double order and took out his resentment on you. It is all very simple and very foolish."

Beth couldn't help giggling. "I'm much obliged to you for clarifying the matter, Baron," she said.

He held up his hand. "Please," he said, "the name is Bernhard."

"Very well, Bernhard," she replied. "I suppose the least I can do after all your trouble is to offer you part or all of my second bacon sandwich." The twinkle in her eyes told him that she was joking.

Bernhard howled with laughter. "If I were hungry enough to eat more bacon and bread," he said, "I would run the risk of being called to fight a duel with Lieutenant Holt. Thank you, miss, but I think I will leave well enough alone." His whole manner indicated his fondness for Toby as well as his obvious interest in Beth.

Giggling quietly, she examined him surreptitiously. He was even more handsome than she had thought, and he was obviously self-assured. The trip promised to be even more exciting than she had anticipated.

Precisely forty-eight hours after Douglas de Forest first visited Caroline Brandon in the wagon train, he reappeared. She had spent another evening with Toby Holt, and his obvious admiration and interest had buoyed her, putting her in an exceptionally cheerful frame of mind.

When de Forest silently eased his way into her wagon, her mood changed abruptly, and her euphoria vanished. She suddenly realized how much she resented Douglas de Forest, and she not only knew it, but she recognized the reason for her reaction. He was using her for his own purposes, taking it for granted that she would assist him because she was engaged to marry him.

Knowing men as well as she did, she suspected that he was the type who would always take from the women in his life, giving grudgingly while expecting them to support him unstintingly.

De Forest smiled at her, signaled for silence, and then dutifully embraced and kissed her. "What have you learned?" he asked without preamble.

"Tomorrow," Caroline told him in a low tone, "we leave Nevada and enter the Utah Territory. We're going to travel by way of Great Salt Lake and Fort Bridger, and then we're going to Denver."

She had provided him with precisely the information that he had sought. When the wagons were just outside Denver, he would use the funds his superiors had sent him to pay Southern partisans in the area to sabotage the train. Pleased with himself, de Forest embraced Caroline again more fervently, and his kiss was passionate.

Caroline coolly placed her hands on his shoulders and managed to disengage herself. De Forest stared at her in astonishment. This was the first time that she had failed to respond with wholehearted enthusiasm to his love-making.

"Too many people are still awake in camp," she said. The excuse was a flimsy half-truth, but Douglas de Forest reluctantly accepted it.

Later she wondered why she had rejected the advances of this man to whom she was betrothed. Perhaps, she decided, it was her way of punishing him for using her and then assuming that he could pay his debt to her by making love to her. She hated that attitude and hoped that if he stopped to think about it, he would learn a lesson from the experience.

De Forest was more upset than Caroline knew. His hold on her was strictly physical, or so he thought, and he assumed that he had to continue to make advances to her in order to assure her cooperation in the future.

Ordinarily he would have persisted in forcing his attentions on her, but if she objected in any way, the ensuing commotion could attract the attention of others. So he desisted, privately promising himself that he would more than compensate for his failure to make love to her. He was not forgetting that Caroline was a prostitute, and under no circumstances did he want her to get too high an opinion of herself.

De Forest went to the cabinet and, not bothering to ask for Caroline's permission, poured himself a stiff drink of brandywine. He neglected, however, to offer her a glass, which increased her irritation with him. He raised his own glass in silent salute, then drained the contents.

Caroline had to remind herself that her marriage to this man, boor though he might be, would make her mistress of a large plantation in Mississippi. It was worth being annoyed a bit in order to make a lifelong dream come true.

Not indicating when he intended to see her again and not bothering to thank her for the information that she had obtained for him, de Forest walked to the flap, peered out into the night, and vanished with a wave of his hand.

He did not know it, but he was observed. Ted Eannes had been overcome with jealousy for two nights and two days and had refused to accept the word of Toby Holt that he had not visited Caroline in her wagon. All that Eannes saw now was a Union officer's uniform of about the same cut as Toby's, and he immediately jumped to the conclusion that he indeed was seeing Lieutenant Holt. He was so convinced that he would have been willing to take an oath that the young officer was Toby.

Again he spent a sleepless night, and in the morning he was fatigued, and his brain was muddled. Seething in impotent rage, he stumbled to the cooking fires for breakfast and, as luck would have it, caught a glimspe of Toby off to his left. Through happenstance, Caroline had just emerged from her wagon and had paused on her own way to breakfast as Toby engaged her in conversation.

Seeing the woman he thought he loved chatting intimately with the man he regarded as his rival was more than Ted Eannes could bear. He completely lost control of himself and raced toward the couple, cursing loudly.

A half-dozen other people saw him, stepped out of his path, and stared at him in wonder.

He halted in front of Toby, shouting and gesticulating wildly. Toby was startled, and a swift glance at Caroline told him that she, too, was upset.

Eannes became even more abusive, his curses becoming vicious. Toby might have been able to shrug off the incident had Eannes come to him in private, but the fact that Caroline heard him using language that was not intended for any lady's ears put a far different light on the matter. "See here," Toby said, "I don't know what this is all about, but I'm telling you plain, clean up your language in a hurry, mister, when you're talking in the presence of ladies."

Eannes responded by cursing at him again and swinging at him.

Toby had no choice. The man had hit him, and Toby had to defend himself. Measuring the man carefully, he cocked his right fist and threw a short, sharp punch from the shoulder.

The blow landed on Ted Eannes's cheekbone directly below his eye. Eannes staggered backward, then stumbled and fell to the ground. He was immediately surrounded by military men and civilians alike, and Whip Holt swiftly pushed his way through the crowd.

Toby told his father what had happened. The witnesses nodded emphatically, corroborating his story.

Whip gestured to a pair of troopers, who hauled Eannes to his feet. They continued to support him by the arms as he swayed groggily.

"I made the rules of conduct very plain to everybody in this company at the beginning of our journey," Whip said coldly. "You've chosen to break the peace, Mr. Eannes, and in so doing you've disobeyed my rules. By rights, I'd heave you out of the wagon train right here and now, but we're in too deep a wilderness, and you'd never survive in country like this by yourself. So I'm going to let you come with us as far as Denver. The minute we reach Denver, however, you are no longer a member of this wagon train company, and I'll be very much obliged to you if you get yourself gone and stay gone!"

No one ever disputed the word of Whip Holt when he spoke authoritatively. Ted merely nodded dumbly. Toby felt almost sorry for the poor devil.

The two troopers escorted Eannes to his wagon, and there one of them went to the water supply, found an extra bucket of water, and emptied it over the head of the luckless former rancher. The dousing in cold water, combined with Whip Holt's strong words, was enough to sober Ted Eannes. He knew, now that it was too late, that he had indeed gone too far. He realized that Caroline Brandon had never encouraged him and that any romance that he had enjoyed with her had existed in his mind. She had the right to entertain anyone she saw fit in her wagon, and he knew it. The one thing that continued to irritate him was Lieutenant Holt's flat denial that he had visited her in the wagon. Eannes knew better, and nothing would ever convince him otherwise.

The incident had taken just a few moments, and Toby and Caroline walked to breakfast together. He ate his hot biscuits with sizzling bacon, and she contented herself with a mug of steaming tea.

"I'm sorry that you've been annoyed by that fellow Eannes," Toby said. "I reckon he's loco."

"He certainly isn't sane," Caroline declared, "and why he has chosen to keep watch on me and my alleged visitors is beyond me. I scarcely know the man, and I've never discussed anything personal with him."

Toby nodded sympathetically. It occurred to him that a woman of her outstanding beauty must be subjected to all kinds of annoyances from men.

"What gets me," he said, "is the fellow's insistence that he's seen me leaving your wagon. You and I know that I've never set foot in your wagon—in the daytime, after dark, or any other time!"

"I know," Caroline said, and looked perturbed. "I do hope that others don't take Ted Eannes's claims seriously, because no man has visited my wagon any night that we've been on the trail."

Toby never understood, either then or later, how he detected a false note in Caroline Brandon's voice. She spoke with great, seeming sincerity and appeared to be truthful as well as forceful, yet Toby nevertheless knew, beyond all doubt, that she was telling him a deliberate falsehood.

He was so startled that he could only nod, and later that day, as he sat in his saddle riding behind his father on the trail, he had an opportunity to sort out the facts of the incident. Why had Caroline told him a deliberate untruth? He had no idea. Why had she been so insistent that *no* officer had visited her wagon? Her denial made no sense.

All that Toby could figure out was that she was trying to make as good as impression on him as she could and therefore was denying the existence of a competitor for her affection, but something in her attitude made that possibility appear unlikely.

As he reviewed the whole incident again slowly, reliving every detail, the thought struck Toby forcefully that Caroline had spoken with a sense of bravado—a surface certainty that had concealed uneasiness, perhaps something more.

Ah, that was it! Fear! She had lied to him because she had been afraid.

But what was there for her to fear? The young officer had no idea. The more he brooded on the matter, the more confused he became, and finally he realized that he was getting nowhere. Based on the information that he possessed, he could not possibly solve the mystery. But he made up his mind to get to the bottom of the matter. He would keep an eye on Caroline—which he intended to do in any event—and this would constitute no hardship for him. Sooner or later, perhaps, he would learn something more.

It didn't occur to him that there might be a serious problem involved, and Toby kept the whole matter to himself, just as he kept his interest in Caroline to himself. He found her to be a lovely, charming, and alluring young woman, and he believed she was growing more and more interested in him, too.

VII

The growth of Denver was phenomenal, and those who were familiar with the city, especially Susanna Fulton and Scott Foster, were astonished by the solidity of the new buildings that were springing up everywhere. The city had been transformed almost overnight from a gold-mining boom town into a metropolis of stature.

As the procession went through the city and approached the local garrison, Ted Eannes rode to the head of the column and spoke diffidently to Whip Holt. "May I have a word with you, Colonel?" he asked.

Whip nodded. "I reckon so," he replied abruptly.

The man fell in beside him and was silent for a time. "I deserve the punishment you handed to me, Colonel," he said at last. "I had it coming to me, and I'm not asking you to change your mind in any way. I just wanted to let you know that I bear you no grudge."

Whip was aware of the effort that it cost the man to make that simple statement, and he felt admiration for him.

"I'm not the first to make a damn fool of myself over a woman, and I guess I'm not the last, either. I'm well rid of the wench, and I wish the lieutenant well with her."

Whip privately hoped that his son had more sense than to become involved with Caroline Brandon.

"I've decided," Eannes said, "to stay in Denver. I hear tell that there are all kinds of business opportunities in the town, so I guess I won't be too bad off."

Whip looked the man squarely in the eyes and said sincerely, "I hope everything works out for you."

Eannes smiled for the first time in a long while. "Thanks, Colonel." Then he turned back abruptly and vanished from sight.

Whip couldn't help feeling sorry for the man, but the rules of the road were strict and had to be obeyed by everyone. Those who failed were required to pay the consequences.

Colonel Whip Holt and Major Andy Brentwood made the silver bullion wagons secure in the garrison and made arrangements with the chief of the quartermaster corps for the replenishment of supplies. Then, telling Andy he had private business that required his attention, Whip went alone to the far side of the military compound and soon was sequestered with the regimental physican, Dr. Logan.

The doctor, hiding the awe he felt for the legendary mountain man, listened carefully as Whip described his arthritis. "I'm not much for complaining," he said, "but spending hours every day in the saddle is blame near killing me. I've come to you, Doctor, for some kind of medicine that will give me relief."

Dr. Logan shook his head. "I must be honest with you, Colonel," he replied. "The only permanent relief you're going to get will.come in the form of absolute rest. Which means you'll have to give up your present assignment."

Whip shook his head grimly. "Sorry," he said crisply, "but that's impossible."

The physician saw the set of Whip's jaw and knew that it would be useless to argue with him. Surely the command of a wagon train was not all that important, but Dr. Logan was too sensible to enter into a dispute with Whip Holt. He went to a supply cabinet where he rummaged for a time, and finally he handed his visitor some packets of powders.

"These may give you some temporary relief, Colonel," he said, "but on the other hand, to be honest with you, they may accomplish nothing. All I can suggest is that you try them, and if you're one of the fortunate ones, you'll find that your hip will become less bothersome."

Whip stuffed the packets into the pouch suspended from his belt. "I'm obliged to you, Doctor," he said, "and I'll be grateful to you if you'll keep this visit of mine private."

"I never discuss my patients and their ailments," Dr. Logan assured him.

"Ordinarily," Whip said, "I wouldn't give a hang, but there's more than meets the eye in my present assignment, and I'd just as soon that gossip about me be held to a minimum."

The physician nodded, his mind racing. This was no ordinary wagon train, he felt certain. A man of Whip Holt's caliber would not be wasted on conducting a group of nondescript civilians and carrying ordinary freight across the country. As a regimental physician, however, he knew better than to ask any questions. "Try the powders," he said, "and if they don't help, come to see me again, and we'll dig around for another prescription. Unfortunately there's no known cure for what ails you."

Whip managed to smile. "I reckon that my sins are all coming to roost," he said. "Anyway, I've learned to live with this condition."

Wade Fulton, the energetic publisher who had established such a success with his Denver newspaper, was delighted to see his daughter. Ever since his wife had died during childbirth, Susanna had been the most important person in his life, and when she arrived in Denver after being in Nevada for so many months, father and daughter made up for lost time. They spent hours together in the parlor of the apartment Wade kept above the newspaper plant, and Susanna talked incessantly, her father listening carefully, interrupting quietly from time to time in order to clarify a point.

At last, when she paused for breath and stirred the cup of hot chocolate that she had made for herself, Wade leaned back in his chair. "I'm not at all surprised that you couldn't make a profit with the paper in Virginia City," he said. "Conditions aren't what they were here, and they didn't resemble what we faced when we first arrived in Sacramento, either. Denver and Sacramento are basically family towns, and both of them are establishing solid roots. Virginia City will last only as long as there's silver in the mountain. When it runs out, I'm afraid the community will be a ghost town."

Susanna's violet eyes shone brightly. "That's just how Scott and I feel, and I'm glad you think that way, too."

Her father shrugged. "We've enjoyed two great successes," he said, "and I'm satisfied with our lot."

Susanna sucked in her breath. "Do I have your approval for traveling with this wagon train? That's been worrying me ever since we set out from Nevada."

The publisher grinned at her. "You've had an uncanny nose for news as far back as I can remember, Sue," he said. "I don't quite know how you learn where all the big stories are, but you appear to have the instinct of a true reporter, and that's a quality that you can't be taught. I reckon you're born with it. Naturally, I'll go along with whatever you wish. I'll grant you that it seems odd that there are so many troops attached to this wagon train and that both Colonel Holt and Andy Brentwood are assigned to it, so you do whatever you think is necessary and right, and whenever you put your story together, telegraph me and I'll throw the paper wide for you."

The young woman smiled at him. "Thank you, Wade," she said, using his first name as she had done since she was a little girl. "You won't regret this. I'm convinced that there's a major news story in this train."

A tap sounded at the door, and Wade Fulton rose to his feet, then admitted Scott Foster to the apartment.

"I hope I'm not intruding," Scott said, glancing from father to daughter.

"Not at all," Wade replied. "Come in and take a load off your feet."

"What I have to say won't take very long," Scott said earnestly. "I had to come to you, Mr. Fulton. My conscience would have given me no peace if I hadn't. I feel that I owe you an apology for our failure in Virginia City."

Wade raised an eyebrow and shook his head. "Failure?" he asked. "I'd say that you and Sue performed miracles. Your Virginia City paper broke even, so your experiment hasn't cost me a nickel, and that's really extraordinary. Usually a new newspaper runs in the red for at least a year, but you earned as much as you spent. You have every right to be proud—damned proud—of what you've achieved, Scott."

Scott thought that the publisher was merely trying to put him at ease. "I'm not a quitter," he said, "but the call to duty was too strong for me."

"Of course it was," Wade said emphatically. "If I were younger I'd have accepted a commission and gone on active duty, just as you've done."

Scott's spirits rose, and he grinned.

"Furthermore," the publisher told him, "I'll prove to you that I'm not making an idle speech. When the war ends, your job here as business manager is waiting for you."

Scott expressed his thanks with great sincerity.

Fulton was curious as to whether or not Susanna had shown a preference for either of her admirers. He glanced at Susanna and the former Californian, sitting side by side but not touching, and he had no idea how Scott's suit was progressing. He knew better than to ask, however. He approved of both young men and hoped that one of them would become his son-in-law, but he knew that only time would determine the answers to the questions that crowded his mind.

Alison White had nothing better to occupy her, so she went sightseeing in Denver, wandering through the streets of the city's shopping district and marveling at the quantities and quality, as well as the variety, of merchandise that was being offered for sale. She couldn't resist buying a length of silk cloth, and as she emerged from the shop, she suddenly remembered the letter she had in her pocket, which told of the wagon train's present whereabouts. She had addressed it, according to her instructions, to a Mr. Graves in Chicago, and she was debating with herself whether she would actually go to the post office to mail it, when she beheld a familiar figure waiting patiently for her on the other side of the street. Alison was so startled she nearly dropped the bolt of cloth she was carrying.

Poole raised his hat as he joined her, then took her arm as he fell in beside her. "We'll go to a quiet place I know for some tea and a private chat," he said, and led her to a small, surprisingly clean establishment with marble-topped tables. There he ordered tea and cakes, and did not speak again until their waitress had deposited their order and had retreated to the kitchen. "I suppose you are wondering how I found you, since we obviously have received no word from you regarding your whereabouts," he said. "Well, let me tell you that it was not easy, but in light of the fact that I have received no further instructions from Lord Palmerston, I made it my business to track you down, going first to Fort Bridger, then to Fort Laramie, trying to pinpoint the location of the train."

Alison made no attempt to conceal the relief that she felt. Perhaps the British prime minister had forgotten all about her existence, and Poole had come to tell her to give up this foolish espionage mission.

"In the absence of any directions from His Lordship," Poole said, "I have other—urgent—orders for you."

Alison's heart fell. "Oh?" was all she could say as she began stirring her tea.

His expression remained unchanged. "It is imperative," he said in a quiet, guarded voice, "that the wagon train be crippled by an act of sabotage."

The young woman stared at him, scarcely able to believe what she was hearing.

"You will perform such an act," Poole said forcefully. "You've spent a considerable period of time on the train now, so you're far more familiar with it than I am.

Therefore, I leave the details up to you. All that I care is that the act be performed successfully."

Alison stared at him, indignation rising within her. "Performing acts of sabotage," she said coldly, "was not a part of our original agreement."

Poole shrugged. "I'm well aware of it, my dear Lady White, but circumstances alter cases, and I regret to say that your active participation has become essential."

Alison now felt a deep surge of anger. It was bad enough that she had to act as a spy for Great Britain, a position for which she had no training and which she strongly disliked. It was an outrage to ask her to do something to harm the progress of the train on which she had developed so many lasting relationships. She shook her head vigorously. "I'm sorry," she said. "If I'm forced to give information to the Crown regarding the wagon train I shall do so—with great reluctance—but nothing will persuade me to do anything that will harm or slow the train or cause injury to anyone traveling with it!"

Poole's face stiffened. "You seem to forget, Lady White," he said icily, "that you are in no position to give orders or to determine what you will or won't do. If you do not comply, you will never be able to return to England."

Taking care not to raise her voice, she replied with spirit. "You appear to forget, Mr. Poole," she said, "that I did not volunteer for the assignment that I've been given. I was more or less forced into it, and there's a vast difference between supplying information and committing harmful acts of sabotage. I am in no way disloyal to the queen or her government when I flatly refuse to take advantage of friends who have come to trust me, but if you and His Lordship still want to take away my citizenship, so be it. I'll make a life for myself right here in America."

The spymaster stared at her incredulously. "We've gone to a great deal of trouble to establish your credentials and the validity of your position," he said. "Our agents do what they're told."

"In me you see a reluctant agent who will not budge beyond the bounds established by her conscience," Alison said firmly. "You've told me that my late husband was in your employ, and I must take your word for it, but I am not Charles, and I am obliged to do only what I myself deem essential. I have earned enough money in Virginia City to support myself and live wherever I choose, so I am not beholden to you or the prime minister in any way. I have no idea why it should be so vital that an act of sabotage be perpetrated on the wagon train, but that is none of my concern. I only know I refuse to participate in any such shady venture, and that, sir, is final."

Poole well knew when he was defeated. He could not counter her arguments, and since she had gained a measure of financial independence, he had lost control over her. What was more, her willingness to remain in America removed the only threat he had over her: taking away her British citizenship. So he had to bow out gracefully and return to England with a feeling that he had failed.

But Alison felt no sense of achievement when she saw Poole sullenly leave the room. In fact, as far as she was concerned, she now faced a real dilemma. She had no way of knowing if Poole had other agents who were willing to work for him; all she knew was that an act of sabotage by the British might very well take place. She wanted to warn Colonel Holt and Major Brentwood to be on their guard, but she could not go to them without betraying Poole's confidence, and that, she realized, would be an act of disloyalty to the British Crown. For the moment she could do nothing. Perhaps she could figure out some way to help her new friends without committing an act of disloyalty to her own native land.

Residents of Denver had been amazed to see the unusual wagon train rumbling through the town's streets. None had been more surprised than Ezekiel and Patricia, who quickly learned that many of their old friends were among the wagon train party. They hurried to the military compound, where Ezekiel shook hands warmly with Andy and Scott, and Patricia promptly went to see Beth Blake, whose mother had been her employer.

Ezekiel had not yet enlisted in the army as he had planned, due to his preoccupation with selling the store, so he asked to see Major Andy Brentwood in private. At Ezekiel's request, the commander of the expedition was also present.

Whip Holt was unacquainted with Ezekiel, but he liked what he saw and heard. The man was sincere beyond question, devoted to the Union, and his offer of help was heartening. A man of his size and physical strength would be a valuable addition to the protectors of the train's precious cargo.

Andy listened without comment as Ezekiel explained that they had inherited the general store, which he had now sold because of his determination to join the Union Army. His only remaining concern was to see his wife safely to Massachusetts, where she would join her family.

Andy did not speak until Ezekiel finished his recital. Then the officer said, "There's no question about your enlistment. I'll tell you right off that the army is going to be fortunate to have you, but I urge you to wait to enlist until we reach Fort Kearny, Nebraska. Colonel Holt and I would be obliged to give you a private's rating, but the adjutant general's office has a representative at Fort Kearny, and if you'll wait, we can get a sergeant's stripes for you there."

Ezekiel's face fell. "How do I get myself and my wife to Fort Kearny?" he demanded.

Andy laughed. "I guess I didn't make myself clear. You join the wagon train right now, and we're happy to have you with us."

Whip added, "I reckon you and your wife can make arrangements to travel in Beth Blake's wagon. She has plenty of room for you, I'm sure."

A smile creased Ezekiel's face. "You make it seem easy," he said. "The way I been worrying I imagined all kinds of blocks to my joining."

173

Whip shook his head. "We have a special place for you in this train, Ezekiel," he said. "Never fear, you'll get all the workouts and all the responsibility that you can handle."

"What's more," Andy added, "your wife can travel with us as far as New York. Then I can grant you a brief leave while you escort her up to Massachusetts."

"Major," Ezekiel said fervently, "this is too good to be true."

"To be honest with you," Andy replied, "we'd be foolish not to go out of our way to latch onto a man of your caliber. It isn't every day that the Union Army gains volunteers like you."

The only member of the wagon train company who did not venture into Denver was Caroline Brandon, who was tempted by neither the eating places nor the many shops of the city. Denver was the place where she had started her career as a courtesan, and she was well known here—far too well known for comfort. Not wanting to see any of her former clients, she decided to remain in her wagon on the grounds of the military compound.

The Denver sojourn was dull, but she preferred a touch of boredom to complications that could prove embarrassing. So she slept late every morning, then spent hours primping before a mirror, and somehow the time passed.

To the best of her knowledge, no one in Denver even knew that she was in town, so Caroline was surprised when a corporal brought her a tightly sealed note with her name printed on the envelope. She broke the seal, wondering who could have learned that she was in town. She removed a single folded sheet of paper from the envelope and opened it. The message was carefully printed in black ink, and it was succinct: *Urgent! Absent yourself from the wagon train the second night out of Denver! Do not fail to do this!*

It was unsigned, but Caroline decided immediately that Douglas de Forest must be the author of the communication. No one else had any idea that she was in Denver traveling on the wagon train, and only Douglas would have some reason to plan an act of sabotage that might place her in danger.

From the outset she took the warning seriously. It was no hoax, she felt certain. She showed the note to no one and kept the information it contained to herself for more than twenty-four hours, but it was not a simple matter, and she could not dismiss it from her mind. The advice given by her supposed benefactor was simple but almost impossible to follow. Caroline had no objection to absenting herself from the wagon train the second night after leaving Denver, but she knew that, for all practical purposes, there was nowhere else she could go. It was all well and good to warn her to put a distance between herself and the train, but she felt certain that the wagons would be stopping in unpopulated country, and she had no intention of wandering off alone into the wilderness.

Having decided that, for better or worse, her future was tied up with that of the wagon train, Caroline realized she had to act accordingly. She was afraid to go to Whip Holt with her information because his steely glance made her extremely uncomfortable. For the same reason, she chose to avoid Major Brentwood, who had amply demonstrated his lack of regard for her. Lieutenant Toby Holt would give her a sympathetic hearing, she knew, but she was afraid to go to him with the letter she had received, for it might somehow implicate her and might lower his esteem of her. She would do nothing that would change the adoring expression she saw in his eyes when he looked at her.

Therefore, she decided to leave the note in a place where Toby Holt would be sure to find it. She supposed she could have just as easily left it for Whip Holt or Andy Brentwood to find, but somehow she felt better knowing it would be found by her handsome young admirer. Then he could be the one to do something heroic.

On the day before the train was scheduled to depart, Caroline saw Toby supervising the loading of food and medical supplies for the coming journey. Showing a rare degree of patience, she waited a long time until he and his men finally disappeared behind one of the wagons. Then she quickly went to the stack of crates, left the note on top, and withdrew behind the wall of the garrison's supply depot, just as Toby and his men returned and resumed their work.

She watched from a distance as Toby spotted the note, picked it up, and read it, and she saw from the intent expression on his face that he was absorbing the full impact of the message. Now she knew that something would be done to ensure that there were no acts of sabotage on the wagon train. She felt no guilt over the possible betrayal of Douglas de Forest. If her own safety were being threatened, she was entitled to do whatever she felt was necessary to protect herself.

As Caroline sneaked back to her wagon, Toby studied the message for a time in silence. Then he carefully refolded the single sheet and replaced it in its envelope. Slipping the communication into the inner pocket of his tunic, he left his men to continue with the loading of the supplies and hurried off to join his father and Andy at dinner at one of the city's leading hotels. Toby explained the circumstances by which he had come into possession of the letter and handed them the communication.

Whip read the note in silence, then stared out the window at the crowded Denver street. "Ordinarily," he said, "I wouldn't pay much heed to a warning like this, but somehow this has an authentic ring to it."

Andy raised an eyebrow and waited for his superior to continue.

"A rattlesnake always sounds a warning before it strikes," Whip said. "Even when it could attack far more effectively in silence, it always sounds a rattle before it lunges. I got me a hunch that this note was written by a human rattlesnake."

"But why would such a warning be left like that for me to see?" Toby asked. "That's what confuses me."

His father exchanged a puzzled glance with Andy.

The major was the one who replied. "The way I see it," he said, "the writer of this thing wanted to protect you. He—or she—has information that you don't and has chosen a rather crude but effective way of warning you."

"But surely whoever wrote this would know I'd pass it along to the two of you," Toby said.

Whip shrugged. "Maybe, maybe not," he said, drumming lightly on the tablecloth with the fingers of one hand. "The big question in my mind is how much credence do we give to this warning? It sounds real enough, but maybe the person who wrote it is just trying to scare us. Stranger things have happened."

"Well," Andy replied, "I guess all we can do is to keep our powder dry."

"Exactly," Whip said. "This note may mean we have a saboteur on the train, or it may have come from someone on the outside, but whatever the case, we'll notify our sentries to be on their guard for anything unusual, and I'll feel more at ease in my own mind if we take one additional step. Toby, you have a special duty to perform the second night on the road. Keep your eyes and ears open and look for trouble."

"Yes, sir." Toby was becoming more deeply involved in the affair than he had imagined.

"If you see or hear anything that arouses your suspicions," Whip said emphatically, "let Major Brentwood know right off. This is about as far as we can go to prepare for trouble."

"I just hope that nothing unpleasant develops," Andy said.

"So do I." Whip's voice became grim. "But I can't help thinking that so far our trip has been easy—too confounded easy—and we're ready for an explosion of some kind."

Beth Blake gladly shared her wagon with Ezekiel and Patricia. The man who had been looking after Beth's wagon while she served as monitor returned to his own wagon, which his wife had driven in the meantime, and now Patricia sat on the box of Beth's vehicle, taking the reins as the wagon train left Denver shortly after daybreak one morning. Ezekiel, mounted on a horse he had purchased for the purpose, rode with Andy Brentwood, who promised to teach him as much as he could absorb about the operations of the train.

The time of the company's departure was a surprise to both soldiers and civilians. They had been told to assemble the previous night and had awakened an hour and a half before daybreak to make ready for the early morning departure.

The heavy special wagons, surrounded by armed troops, rumbled through the streets of Denver, and the open countryside east of the city was reached before most residents of the community were awake. That, of course, had been Whip's intention. Rarely had any wagon train begun a journey so early in the day.

The wagons began their long, slow descent from the mountains toward the flat country of the Great Plains that lay ahead. Eastern Colorado was being populated rapidly, and the wagons passed numerous farms where the soil was surprisingly productive. It had been discovered that sugar beets grew in this soil and climate better than any other crop, and members of the company gazed out at acre upon acre of beets, already a major staple that in time would prove as valuable to the state as the mineral wealth found in the mountains west of Denver.

That evening a halt was called in an unpopulated region, and the cooking detail went to work while the sentries took up their positions for the night.

The preparations being made for the following evening were vague, as it was impossible to prepare for the unknown. It might have been wise to alert the whole company to the possibility of impending danger, but Whip had ruled out such a course on the grounds that civilians in the company would become unnecessarily tense and, in the event that a crisis developed, might give in to hysteria.

The second day of the journey east of Denver began routinely. The company enjoyed the luxury of eating scrambled eggs with their breakfast bacon, and spirits were high as the wagons slowly moved into position for

the day's journey. On impulse Andy Brentwood told
Ezekiel about the threat Toby had received for that
night, and Ezekiel nodded but made no comment. Andy
noted, however, that a short time later Ezekiel drew the
long butcher knife that he carried in his belt and
thoughtfully tested the edge of the blade with his
thumb. He was as prepared for possible danger as was
anyone.

The road that led to the valleys was broad and
straight, and the train covered a distance of almost fifteen miles before plunging into a forest of fragrant
pines. Whip, who was thoroughly familiar with the territory, called a halt beside a swift-running stream.

At supper Toby Holt presented a calm façade for the
others' sake, but he felt far less tranquil than he appeared. He made it his business to speak to every man
who had been assigned to the sentry watch for the
night, and he urged the soldiers to maintain a sharp
vigil. He gave special instructions to the corporal in
command of the detail and the two corporals who were
his assistants: they were to notify him instantly of anything untoward that they noted.

The evening passed uneventfully, and families drifted
off to their wagons to sleep. Of all the civilians, only
Bernhard von Hummel—perhaps because of his Prussian
military background—sensed that something unusual was
going on. He maintained his own private vigil, sitting
wrapped in his blankets, looking out into the darkness
and shadows beyond the wagons to detect any strange
movements or sounds.

The cooking fire burned low, and at Toby's request it
was fed with just enough firewood to keep it alive. The
wagons were arranged, as always, in a circle, with the
horses and pack animals grazing inside the enclosure.
The guard detail was somewhat stronger than usual, and
a total of thirty men were on watch. Toby decided he
could function more quietly on foot than mounted, and
he began to circle the enclosure slowly, pausing briefly
beside each sentry and listening intently. As the hours
passed, nothing of consequence developed.

In spite of himself, Toby felt a letdown. Perhaps the note he had found had been a hoax of some sort; it did not appear that anything adverse was going to happen. The sentries, who had also been keyed up, began to relax somewhat.

It was well after midnight when the crisis suddenly erupted, and it was Whip Holt rather than one of the younger men who first became aware that something was amiss. The old mountain man lay sleeping on the ground, curled up in his blanket, but his sixth sense, developed over many years of wilderness living, warned him of impending danger and he awoke instantly, alert and ready for action.

There was no time for him to voice a warning. It was enough that he sensed the presence of intruders in the forest beyond the circle of wagons. They had crept close to one of the silver wagons, and he knew immediately that they intended to isolate it, to hitch up the team of mules and make off with it. Whip's reaction was instinctive and spontaneous. He snatched up his rifle, took careful aim at a dark, blurred shape in the forest beyond the wagons, and pulled the trigger.

A shriek of pain told him his bullet had found its target.

By the time he fired again, the entire military unit had been alerted. The sentries in that sector responded at once as Toby instructed them to open fire on the unseen foe in the forest, and the entire camp was aware of the crackle of rifle fire.

Andy Brentwood soon appeared and rallied his men, placing Scott Foster's volunteer Nevada militia on his left flank and his regulars in the center and on the right.

A spirited return fire from the forest told the defenders that they were indeed under attack. As nearly as Toby could judge, there were about forty men in the force of intruders. He passed this information along to Andy and to his father, who were sprawled together on the ground directly behind the troops who were facing the forest.

"Your count isn't off by too much, Toby," Whip told

him. "I'd say the total enemy out yonder is closer to fifty men than to forty."

Civilians who were awakened by the sound of fire and who emerged from their wagons were urged to return at once to their beds and leave the matter in the hands of professionals. Bernhard von Hummel, roused from his vigil into action, assisted in the task, shepherding frightened men, women, and children back into their wagons. He saw that Beth Blake was also instructing the civilians to return to their wagons, and he was impressed anew by the spirit of General Blake's pretty daughter.

At Whip's direction, Andy's troops kept up a steady rain of fire. "Station a whole company the length of that first silver wagon," Whip said. "They plan to cut it away, and they've concentrated practically their whole force opposite it."

Andy obeyed the order, and Scott's company of Nevada volunteers poured a steady stream of lead into the forest just beyond the exposed silver wagon.

It was almost impossible to determine the progress of the battle, even though a half-moon was shining and the sky was filled with stars. The enemy had chosen its attack site with great cunning; it was so dark in the forest that it was virtually impossible to see how many enemy troops were deployed there.

The commanders weighed the situation carefully. "It seems to me," Whip said quietly, "that we'll have to send some men out yonder to clean out the attackers once and for all."

Andy nodded. "I'm afraid you're right, sir," he replied. "Whoever is conducting this assault has a disciplined force of veterans. Amateurs would have dispersed long before now under fire as heavy as ours."

"The only reason I hesitate," Whip told him, "is because I hate to cause needless casualties."

Scott Foster was close enough to the two commanders to hear their conversation. "Colonel," he said, "let my men have the honor of counterattacking, if you will. They're volunteers who are at home in the mountains, and they've had experience in Indian fighting. I think you'll find that they can look after themselves."

Whip chuckled aloud. "Go to it, Captain," he said. "Your lads are on their own now."

Scott gave quiet orders, and his volunteers began to crawl forward, some of them leaving the circle in the openings between wagons, while others wriggled toward the forest by going under the wagons. What none of them realized at first was that they were accompanied by Ezekiel, his butcher knife in one hand. He was not yet a member of the Union Army, but he was not to be denied his part in the battle. He wriggled into the clear, under the silver wagon, and then entered into the forest. His eyesight was almost equal to Whip's and certainly was far better than that of Scott and his militiamen. He saw a number of men concealing themselves behind clumps of trees and boulders, and he hurled himself at them, his knife flashing wickedly, moving with lightning speed, not pausing long enough to make himself a target for the foe. He lunged and slashed at his victims, and the combination of the darkness and his great agility prevented the enemy from taking a bead on him.

The militiamen were inspired by his example and fought in the manner to which they were so well accustomed, moving within a short distance of a foe and then discharging either a rifle or a pistol before moving on to the next enemy.

The intruders were unaccustomed to this unorthodox type of frontier warfare and were forced to give way. Their casualties heavy, they had the unhappy choice of holding firm and facing almost certain death or of withdrawing from the scene in order to save their lives.

They proved, however, that they were well trained; even now they did not panic and conducted their withdrawal in good order. Heeding the shouted commands of a slender officer brandishing a sword, they pulled back little by little, increasing their pace slowly, and eventually they broke off contact with the Nevada militiamen.

Even Ezekiel gave up the chase when the enemy

mounted horses secreted in the depths of the forest and rode away rapidly. Scott Foster had the good sense to order his men to bring several bodies of the slain foe into the circle.

The corpses were examined, and neither Whip Holt nor Andy Brentwood was surprised when they found that their slain foes carried documents that, in spite of their civilian appearance, identified them as members of the Confederate Army.

It was clear that this had been an attack planned and executed by Rebels and its target had been the capture of a silver wagon. So there was no longer any shred of doubt left in Whip's mind: the Confederates were aware of the exceptionally valuable cargo that had been entrusted to his care.

The excitement subsided gradually, and one by one the civilians returned to their own wagons to sleep for what little remained of the night. Bernhard von Hummel, however, was unable to sleep. His mind was filled with the night's events. The silver that Colonel Holt was transporting was worth a fortune, as he well knew. But the Confederates had now shown their hand, and the outcome of the journey was very much in doubt. Ordinarily three hundred men would have been more than sufficient to protect the precious cargo, but the Rebels were resorting to desperate measures to stop delivery of the silver to New York and to gain possession of the cargo. Bernhard couldn't help hoping that Whip Holt and his subordinates succeeded in their efforts; after all, his own interests coincided with theirs, and if they succeeded, there was no question that the munitions makers of Prussia would be paid the vast sum due them.

Susanna Fulton was ecstatic. The story behind the wagon train journey was turning out to be much more important than even she had imagined. She lighted a candle in her wagon and immediately went to work with pen and paper, writing down notes about the abortive attack and the reason it had been conducted. The dispatch of the story itself would have to wait until the leaders of the wagon train gave their authorization, but Susanna was content. It was enough for her to know that she had obtained a major scoop and would be the first in America to report the story to the public. The gamble she had taken was well worth her while.

Alison White went back to bed, but lay wide eyed, hearing no sound but the steady scratching of Susanna's pen as she wrote her notes for the sensational news story.

Alison was deeply troubled. Tonight's raid might have very well been the work of men Poole had hired after her refusal to partake in an act of sabotage. If so, she was partly reponsible for not informing the wagon train leaders of her association with Poole. It was true that Alison's patriotism for Great Britain had prevented her from speaking out, but now the knowledge that Britain was not only sympathetic to the Confederacy but was perhaps actively working with the Rebels put the entire matter in a new, somber light. Her own sympathies lay completely with the North, and her friendships with the members of the wagon train company solidified her stand. Under no circumstances could she allow herself to be disloyal to them.

At the same time, however, she was still mindful of her obligations to her native land. Never mind that Poole had threatened her with loss of citizenship: she was still British, a loyal subject of Queen Victoria, and she did not presume to stand in judgment on the government of Great Britain. The decision to back the Confederacy was wrong, in her opinion, but she was willing to grant that government officials be privy to information that might make a difference.

All she knew for certain was that she could and would do nothing that would place her friends in jeopardy. Perhaps, she thought, she should go to Scott Foster and tell him about her relationship with Poole and the request made of her by the spymaster, but still she hesitated. Just as she could do nothing to allow her friends to be harmed, so she could take no action disloyal to Great Britain.

She was trapped, and she faced the future gloomily, not knowing what might develop next. But her common sense told her to move one step at a time and to let the future take care of itself.

Of all those on the wagon train, the least sleepy was Caroline Brandon, who sat in her wagon, staring at her flawless features in a mirror by the light of a large, flickering candle. Caroline knew little about the issues that had divided the United States and had set brother against brother in a catastrophic civil war. Her ignorance did not trouble her, and she gave it no further thought. Her one concern was herself. Caroline had come to know and understand what she wanted, ever since she had been widowed in Denver and had been cast adrift to fend for herself, and she well realized that she was a survivor. Questions of morality and ethics did not bother her in the least, and she gave them no heed. Her one aim in life was survival—and something more. She wanted to live in comfort and ease, and she devoted herself single-mindedly to the pursuit of that goal. Never vicious and rarely vindictive, she nevertheless could be utterly ruthless when her own interests were jeopardized.

Still, the attack on the wagon train had shaken her severely, especially when she realized that a stray bullet fired by either side could have snuffed out her life. The only consolation was that by leaving the warning note for Toby to find, she had at least done what she could to foil Douglas de Forest's plans.

Forcing herself to study her relationship with De Forest, she began to see him in a new light. If she knew anything in this world, she understood men and their motives, and she realized now without a doubt that de Forest had been using her for his own purposes. It was obvious that he had no intention of marrying her and making her mistress of his family's plantation in Mississippi. He was using her to obtain information on behalf of the Confederates. Equally obvious was that de Forest had put the attack on the wagon train ahead of her safety, that he had been willing to place her in jeopardy in order to win a victory for the Rebel cause. The warning note, which she was now certain he had sent her, was impractical at best. Surely if de Forest had bothered to think about her welfare, he would have realized there was no way Caroline could absent herself from the wagon train in the middle of the wilderness.

Caroline's perspective changed, and her resolve hardened. She knew now what had to be done: to the devil with Douglas de Forest and all that he represented! Her own welfare took precedence, and she had to act accordingly.

Her mind made up, Caroline acted swiftly. She freshened her makeup, brushed her long blond hair, and donned a provocative peignoir of yellow silk. With it she chose a pair of very attractive, silver-colored high-heeled pumps. Then she crept out of her wagon.

The military were still active. Soldiers were continuing to search the bodies of the Confederate dead for information, and patrols were roaming through the forest searching for stragglers. Caroline waited unobtrusively in the shadows until she saw Lieutenant Toby Holt returning to the wagon train compound from the forest, and then she stepped boldly into the open. Toby saw her, was astonished, and hurried to her side.

She contrived to look very meek and somewhat perplexed. "I must speak with you, Toby!" she exclaimed. "It's urgent."

Assuming that she was still overwrought because of the battle, he tried to soothe her. "There won't be any more fighting tonight," he said. "You can depend on it. The enemy has been routed."

She shook her head. "That isn't what concerns me," she said. "You remember that warning note you received? I was the one who left it for you to see, and I want to tell you the whole story now." Somewhat to her own surprise, she spoke breathlessly as the words tumbled out. There were times when it paid to be completely honest, and this was one of them. She explained Douglas de Forest's promise to marry her and his subsequent appearances on the wagon train seeking information.

Toby listened in silence, realizing now who the mysterious visitor to the young woman's wagon had been and why Caroline had appeared so fearful. He wondered if this exceptionally attractive woman knew that she had been used by a very clever Confederate spy. He heard her story, then touched her arm. "Would you mind repeating what you've just told me to my father and Major Brentwood?" he asked.

Caroline looked worried.

"I give you my word that no harm will come to you," Toby said, "but it's imperative that they be told the whole situation."

She knew she could control Toby without any difficulty, but she doubted that she would have any ability to influence Whip Holt and Andy Brentwood.

Toby, conscious of her hesitation, said, "Take my word for it, I'll stand behind you all the way."

She smiled at him, feigning a timidity that she did not feel, and then slipped her arm through his as he escorted her across the wagon train circle to the spot where Whip and Andy had established their temporary command post.

Both were surprised by the appearance of the scantily clad young woman, but they forgot all else as she repeated her story. Whip was surprisingly gentle as he asked a number of questions, which Caroline answered, and then he nodded solemnly.

"We're much obliged to you, Mrs. Brandon," he said. "You have no idea how valuable this information is."

"My conscience wouldn't allow me to rest until I told you the whole story, Colonel," Caroline replied, putting the best possible light on her situation.

Even Andy was impressed. "I don't suppose you happen to know whether this de Forest holds a commission in the Confederate Army?" he asked.

Caroline shrugged. "I have no idea, Major," she replied. "We haven't discussed such matters, and so I don't know. I assume he is a Confederate officer, though, because he comes from an influential and wealthy family in Mississippi. Although politics mean very little to me, I know he's dedicated to the Rebel cause."

Whip thanked her for her cooperation and asked Toby to escort her back to her wagon, which the young officer was delighted to do.

"I wonder what impelled her to speak so freely?" Andy asked, looking after the retreating figure in the peignoir.

Whip shrugged. "Maybe she had a falling out with de Forest, or it could be that she's just trying to protect herself now that the war has come so much closer to home for her. There's no telling, but I'll say this much, Andy: I'm convinced her story is genuine."

"So am I, sir. And she has revealed to us far more than she realizes."

"I know," Whip replied nodding slowly. "It's obvious now that the Rebels have known all along about the plan to transport silver by wagon train. We've got to act accordingly."

"First off," Andy said, "I'm going to double the watch on sentry duty."

"Fair enough," Whip said. "I can't help wondering whether there's something else we might do, though."

Andy was lost in thought for a time. "I'm blamed if I can think of anything."

"Neither can I," Whip said. "We have ample manpower. I think it's just a matter of being vigilant enough, and since we've been warned of the Confederate knowledge of the situation, we should be able to deal with it."

"I sure hope so," Andy replied.

"You and I," Whip told him, "will take turns standing guard duty ourselves from now on. One or the other of us will be in personal command of the sentries at all times."

"Yes, sir," Andy replied, agreeing heartily with the order.

Toby was beaming when he rejoined his father and Andy, and it was obvious that he was filled with wonder at what Caroline had done. "It took real courage for her to come out in the open with her story," he said. "She could have kept quiet about it, but she made a real gesture of patriotism."

Whip and Andy exchanged a swift glance, and neither replied. It was apparent to both of them that whatever her reasons may have been, Caroline was motivated by pure selfishness; the making of a patriotic gesture was far from her thoughts.

Whip studied his son and was troubled. The expression in Toby's eyes, the timbre of his voice told Whip that his son was more than impressed at what Caroline Brandon was doing; he actually appeared to have fallen in love with her.

This presented Whip with a dilemma. He had no doubts in his own mind regarding Caroline's profession and lack of virtue, but apparently Toby was blind to the obvious. As a father, he knew better than to warn his son to deal carefully with the woman and to avoid becoming involved with her. Such an attitude on his part would force Toby to rebel and to become all that much more interested in her.

Whip was grateful to her, to be sure. Thanks to her timely warning, he was far better prepared to meet any Confederate threat. He could only hope, however, that Toby's proximity to Caroline Brandon would result in his son's regaining his balance and a measure of wisdom. Whip guessed that the right way to handle the problem was to give his son his head and hope for the best. Eulalia would know, of course, what to do and what was right, but she was far away at the ranch in Oregon, and he had to depend on his own instincts.

Unfortunately, he could discuss the problem with no one—not even Andy Brentwood, in whose face he read flat contempt for Caroline Brandon and all that she represented. He wanted to go on record, however, as being fair to her. "The United States," he said, "is in that young woman's debt. I just hope that she gets her just deserts."

VIII

Brigadier General Henry Hayward sat at his desk in the Richmond headquarters of the Confederate Army and read with great care Captain Douglas de Forest's detailed account of the assault on the wagon train. Then, frowning faintly, he stared for a long time out the window.

Unfortunately, young de Forest was a hothead who was totally lacking in insight, despite his personal courage. He seemed well pleased with the attack he had conducted, but Henry Hayward could not agree with his estimates. It was apparent to the general that the failure of the Confederate attackers to isolate and steal a silver wagon was far more serious a matter than de Forest realized. Primarily it was significant because it alerted the Union forces guarding the wagon train to the fact that they were under observation and subject to attack. That meant that in the future they would be more on their guard than ever, and it would be that much more difficult to succeed in preventing the silver bullion from reaching New York.

General Hayward took his time, and ultimately he summoned his aide. "Go down the hall," he said, "and tell Lieutenant Colonel Roger Stannard that I'd like to see him at his earliest convenience."

Perhaps Stannard, an officer who combined the passionate idealism of a Confederate supporter with the levelheaded, realistic approach of a veteran intelligence officer, was needed to transform the defeat into victory.

Roger Stannard, wiry and with shaggy, sandy-colored hair, hurried down the corridor to his superior's office. He had been an intelligence specialist in the United States Army for some time, working directly under Henry Hayward in the department headed by Lee Blake. Now the Georgia-born officer was one of the most valuable intelligence assets of the South. Equally at home in a headquarters job or in the field, he was competent almost beyond measure.

He tapped at the door of the general's office, entered, and saluted smartly. Hayward waved him to a chair and said, "Roger, how familiar are you with the situation of the Nevada silver that the Union is currently transporting to New York?"

Carefully adjusting his gray uniform trousers in order to preserve their crease, Roger Stannard smiled slightly. "I've been following the progress of the wagon train, sir, because I happen to be a lifelong admirer of Whip Holt. I think he's unique, and his abilities are second to none."

The general raised an eyebrow. "Do I gather that you disapprove of our efforts to interrupt the train?"

Stannard was as subtle as he was clever. "It isn't my place to approve or disapprove, General," he said. "I wouldn't have assigned an officer of Douglas de Forest's qualifications in charge of our efforts to disrupt the delivery of the silver bullion, but my criticism is unfair, perhaps. I realize that we had to make do with the officers that we had in the field and that de Forest was handy. I'm not in the least surprised, however, that he bungled his attack. That assault was doomed from the outset."

"How so?" his superior demanded.

"The Union has three hundred men assigned to defend that silver bullion. We know that for a fact. So an attack by fewer than a hundred men who tried to detach one silver wagon from the train was inadequate."

The general shifted his weight and stared hard at his subordinate. "Just what would you have done instead?" he demanded. "How would you have handled the problem had you been in charge?"

Roger Stannard sighed gently. "Frankly, I don't really know what I would have done, General," he said, "and I think it's a waste of time and effort to speculate on what might have been."

"I advise you to start thinking about it in detail," General Hayward told him, "because I'm assigning you to the project, and I'm giving you the personal responsibility of halting the delivery of that silver bullion to New York."

If Roger Stannard was surprised, he did not show it. In fact, his colleagues said that it was impossible to surprise him, that he had a genius for anticipating problems before they occurred. "How much time will you give me to carry out this mission, General?" he asked matter-of-factly.

Hayward shrugged. "All that matters to President Davis and the Cabinet," he said, "is that the silver be diverted from its destination. If we can get our hands on it, so much the better, naturally, because we're dealing with a treasury that's half empty. But if there's a choice between destroying the bullion or allowing the Union to keep it, we'd prefer that no one benefit by it. Lincoln is counting on this money to pay for very large supplies of artillery his War Department has purchased in Prussia, and we've got to neutralize that purchase before it's completed."

"What restrictions are you placing on me, sir?" Colonel Stannard demanded.

The general shook his head. "None."

"What assistance will I be given?"

"What are your needs?" Henry Hayward countered.

"Obviously I'm in no position to make specific plans now," Roger Stannard said slowly, "although I want to be well prepared when I go north and would like to take with me certain supplies. But my first task will be paying a visit to Captain de Forest and finding out what he and his subordinates know. If possible, I'd like to see the wagon train for myself, which will help me to make a definitive judgment."

The general had known Stannard would react in this way. Promising the officer full support and all the supplies he wanted, he wished him well and urged him to complete his initial survey as rapidly as he could.

Colonel Stannard set out immediately for the route that de Forest had said he would be following. The war between the states was raging in the East, but no action had commenced in the West, and it was a relatively easy matter to travel there. Accompanied by several subordinates, who guarded the crates containing firearms and ammunition, Colonel Stannard traveled by rail as far as Missouri, then—changing into civilian clothes for good measure—he and his men rode three nondescript wagons into the Nebraska Territory. Leaving the wagons under guard, Stannard traveled another hundred miles alone on horseback, and the next evening, he found de Forest and his partisans in the thick woods of the hill country that marked the line of demarcation between Colorado and Nebraska. Stannard and de Forest sat in front of a campfire, where both men sipped mugs of steaming coffee, and they conferred.

Douglas de Forest had an invisible chip on his shoulder. "Do I gather that you're relieving me of my command, Colonel?" he asked stiffly.

Roger Stannard smiled and shook his head emphatically. "You've done well, extremly well with the men under your command, and the Confederacy is grateful for your efforts. I have specifically requested that you be kept as my field commander for this enterprise."

De Forest was somewhat confused. He was being replaced as chief of the mission, there was no question about that, but Colonel Stannard was allowing him to save face by leaving him as head of the troops assigned to the difficult task, and he took comfort in that thought.

"Where is the wagon train at present?" Colonel Stannard asked.

"They're only about ten miles from here," de Forest told him. "I'll show you in the morning when they're pulling out of their camp."

"Good," Roger said. "I'm anxious to see those silver wagons and their defenders for myself." He paused, then asked, "How many men do you have in your command at present?"

"Twenty-seven effectives, Colonel," Douglas replied. "We started with almost double that number, but our casualties were very high in that attack we made east of Denver."

"I daresay," Stannard said dryly.

Sensing his disapproval, Douglas looked at him intently.

Roger Stannard never indulged in outright criticism of another's mistakes; that was not his way. "I gather, Captain de Forest," he said, "that you feel you can actually defeat the defenders of the wagon train in open combat and can detach at least one wagon carrying silver bullion from the main body of the train."

"I'm convinced of it, Colonel." Douglas came to life and spoke eagerly. "The civilians who are traveling with the train were intended as a cover-up and serve their purpose, but now they get in the way, and I'm sure that with enough men, we can bring the Union column to its knees."

"You're aware that their forces are commanded by Whip Holt, I presume?" Stannard asked softly.

"Yes, sir." De Forest was unperturbed.

His superior smiled faintly. "I heard one of our leading generals remark recently that Whip Holt is equal to at least a whole division of infantry with a couple of regiments of cavalry thrown in for support. Don't ever underestimate him. He knows more about the protection of wagon trains in the wilderness than you and I and just about everybody else in the Confederacy put together." Roger Stannard shook his head. "I'm afraid a direct assault on the wagon train isn't the answer to the problem. We'd need at least a thousand men, and the very logistics of sneaking them through Union lines, finding some way for them to travel unobtrusively, and keeping them supplied with food gives me the shudders."

De Forest could not conceal his surprise. "You really think you'd need a thousand men, Colonel?"

"I've already told you we're facing Whip Holt," Stannard said emphatically. "The biggest mistake we could make is to underestimate him as an adversary. I'd say that even with one thousand men at our disposal, I'd be dubious of the success we might achieve. We cannot allow ourselves to forget that our primary goal is to prevent that silver from being delivered to the Union Treasury Department in New York. If we're able to get hold of the bullion for ourselves, so much the better, but to prevent the North from using it to buy weapons is our first consideration."

"How do you propose to accomplish those goals, Colonel?" De Forest could not conceal a note of disdain in his voice.

Roger Stannard smiled steadily, and his reply was cheerful. "I have no idea, Captain," he said. "I prefer to move one step at a time when taking over a mission. I'll study the situation as best I'm able, and you'll be the first to learn my plan."

He spoke so firmly that Douglas de Forest felt as though he'd been doused with a pail of cold water. If the stories about Stannard were true, he was a calculating, cold-blooded devil, who was totally unorthodox in the achievement of his ends. Certainly there was no telling what he had in mind, and de Forest, aware that his own position depended on the friendship of Colonel Stannard, decided that discretion was necessary. So he held his tongue.

The following morning they sat side by side on their horses at the crest of a hill, looking at the wagon train in the valley below as the escort began to fan out and the civilians' wagons moved slowly into line.

Stannard concentrated his attention on the four oversized silver wagons pulled by the mule teams. The silver they contained was considerable, judging from the size of the wagons and the struggles of the mule teams in starting to move.

Douglas de Forest began to speak, but his superior silenced him with an abrupt gesture. His mind was be-

ginning to function now, and he wanted no interruption.
An idea was germinating.

"Where will the wagon train and the silver be transferred to railway freight?"

"In Missouri, sir," de Forest replied.

Stannard's shrug was noncommittal. It would be a
simple enough matter to obtain the assistance of some of
the many Confederate sympathizers in Missouri, and a
plan of action was developing rapidly in his mind. Suddenly he chuckled softly to himself.

De Forest looked at him, waiting for him to speak, but
Colonel Stannard remained silent. The idea that occurred to him was so bizarre, so outrageous that he
could tell it to no one.

Watching the wagon train as it began to creep eastward on its long journey, he weighed his audacious
scheme in his mind. It needed refinement, to be sure,
but he was on the right track at last, and he felt certain
that, after he refined his idea, the days of the Union
wagon train would be numbered.

Following the South Platte River, which provided the
travelers and their animals with ample supplies of water,
the wagon train crawled eastward through the hills of
eastern Colorado and western Nebraska into the heart of
the Great Plains in Central Nebraska. Whip Holt was astonished by what he saw. The last time he had been in
this land was when he had led the first wagon train to
Oregon, and the limitless prairie had been uninhabited.
Now, however, farms were springing up in the region,
varieties of crops were being grown in the fertile soil,
and telegraph lines had been strung up across the plains.
Nebraska had become a formally recognized federal territory seven years earlier, and the population was increasing so steadily that there was talk of it being
admitted to statehood.

All the same, there were signs of the great prairie that
had existed for so long. Huge herds of buffalo subsisted
on the tall prairie grass. Bulls, cows, and calves—often as
many as one thousand and more—still roamed freely and

ventured relatively close to the farmhouses of the pioneer settlers. The buffalo was still an important source of food and clothing for the inhabitants of the Nebraska Territory.

Also, ferocious Indian tribes still hunted in the Great Plains. Every settler kept firearms close at hand and banded together with his neighbors to prevent raids by hostile Indians.

Whip ordered his military scouts to travel in pairs and directed them not to venture too far from the main column. They were unaccustomed to Indian warfare, and he wanted them to take no unnecessary risks. The wagon train moved far more rapidly through the Great Plains than it had through the mountains of the West, and Whip finally gave in to temptation. "We're staying put for the next twenty-four hours," he announced at breakfast one day. "We can stand some supplies of fresh meat, and we're going to take time off for a buffalo hunt." The younger members of the party, who had heard of buffalo hunting from their elders but had never participated in the sport, grew excited.

The majority of the troops were ordered to stay behind and guard the wagon train. Only a few were selected to take part in the hunt. Among the fortunate were Andy Brentwood and Scott Foster. Toby Holt was selected as a hunter, too, and enjoyed a natural advantage over his companions, for, as a small boy, he had been taught the principles of hunting buffalo by his father.

Accompanying the expedition strictly in the role of an observer was Bernhard von Hummel. Whip had noticed him watching the preparations being made for the hunt and felt compelled to beckon to him.

"I think we can show you something today that you've never seen in Europe, Baron," he said. "Come with us if you like, and we'll show you how we hunt buffalo."

"I would like nothing better, Colonel," the delighted von Hummel replied.

"Just remember this much," Whip said. "Don't interfere and do exactly what you're told. Once the buffalo start thundering, I can't be responsible for the safety of any man."

As Whip headed toward the northeast with his dozen companions, he instructed them in the do's and don'ts of buffalo hunting. "It's customary to hunt the buffalo on horseback," he said, "but since we're dealing with inexperienced men, we're going to ambush them on foot. Now, when we see a herd, make sure your rifles are loaded, then dismount and leave your horses behind. One skittish horse can cause a whole herd of buffalo to stampede."

"Why is a stampede to be avoided?" Andy asked.

Whip grinned at him. "If you had ever seen buffalo by the hundreds—weighing thousands of pounds—thundering across the plains toward you, you wouldn't have to ask that question, Andy," he replied. "The trick of our hunt today will be to sneak up close to a grazing buffalo and to dispose of it as quickly as you can, using as few shots as you can. You'll see that certain animals are natural leaders; avoid them at all costs. Resist the temptation to shoot them, and stay as far away from them as you possibly can."

The younger members of the party listened carefully and nodded.

"Eventually," Whip said, "there's going to be a stampede, you can bet your boots on it. When this happens, don't waste any time. Mount your horses and consolidate your positions. Get together and stay together. Any man who is caught by himself stands a good chance of being trampled to death. Use your ammunition sparingly during a stampede. You never know when some stupid bull is going to charge you, and you've got to be prepared to halt him before you're killed."

Toby half listened to his father as, taking the lead, he followed a trail of trampled prairie grass. "From the looks of it," he called, "we're on the trail of a substantial herd, and I guess they're no more than five miles away."

Whip studied the signs and nodded agreement. "If anybody doesn't understand what needs to be done and what needs to be avoided," he said, "speak up now. Once we sight the herd, we'll have no talking."

The younger men exchanged glances, but no one spoke. Ezekiel, who was learning to use a rifle for the first time in his life, cleared his throat. "Where's a buffalo the most vulnerable, Colonel?" he asked.

"Between the eyes," Whip replied. "But you've got to be in perfect position for a shot in order to put a bullet there. Behind the ears is good, and any head shot is effective. Don't bother, though, to put one or more bullets into the body of a buffalo. You won't be able to halt a bull that way, or a lively cow, either. I've seen adult buffalo come on strong and keep heading straight for you with a half-dozen bullets in their carcass." He called out to his son, who had taken the lead of the caravan. "Can you think of anything I've left out, Toby?"

"Just this," Toby Holt replied. "You've probably heard that the buffalo is a stupid animal. Well, he is, and he isn't. He lacks the intelligence of a horse or of other domesticated animals, but when his survival is at stake, he is shrewd and resourceful, so don't underestimate him. I think we're getting close now," he added.

The herd was still nowhere to be seen, but Whip took his son's word and imposed silence on the group. The riders spread out, with Andy Brentwood moving the farthest to the left flank while Ezekiel stayed relatively close to Whip.

Suddenly Toby gestured for a halt, half stood in his saddle, and pointed.

Directly ahead in the distance was the grazing herd, and Scott, who had never seen, much less hunted, buffalo, was impressed. Several mature bulls roamed the outskirts of the herds and prevented straggling; they nudged cows and their calves who lingered behind the main body to graze. Here and there, too, were young cows that were not bothering to eat the prairie grass. Instead they stood quietly, their heads raised, sniffing the breeze that blew steadily across the flat countryside.

Now the hunters understood why Whip had constantly tested the wind, and they saw that it was blowing from the direction of the herd toward them. Had it been blowing in the opposite direction, the animals would have smelled the men and would have taken themselves elsewhere immediately.

Toby awaited no signal and dismounted on his own initiative, looping his reins over his horse's head and leaving his mount as he crept through the tall grass toward the grazing buffalo. Whip watched him for a moment, grinned approvingly, and then gave a signal for the entire company to follow his son's example.

Ezekiel, who was a less accomplished rider than the others, more than compensated for his lack of skill with his natural grace. When forced to rely on his own two feet, he moved lightly, making no sound as he followed Toby.

Whip headed toward a young bull, advancing several feet, halting and freezing, and then going forward again.

The others watched his technique and followed his example. Andy and Scott could understand the intense excitement of a buffalo hunt now. The trick, it appeared, was to move as close to one's quarry as was possible without alarming the entire herd, and the challenge was considerable.

Bernhard, following the example of the others, moved forward cautiously, remaining just behind Scott and Andy. He had never beheld a spectacle such as this, and his heart was pounding.

Ezekiel had a hunter's natural instinct and inched closer and then still closer to a cow and a calf, which the cow shielded as it grazed beside her.

Toby was the first to strike, neatly putting a bullet behind the right ear of a grazing bull. The beast was caught completely by surprise and made no sound as it collapsed slowly onto the ground.

What amazed the neophytes was that the death of the bull did not alert or alarm any of the other animals in the herd. They continued to graze peacefully, unmindful of what had just happened to the bull.

Ezekiel displayed dexterity as well as courage by moving almost within arm's length of the cow, putting a bullet into her head and then whirling on the calf and disposing of it with a single shot, too. It was difficult to believe that he was still learning to handle a rifle.

Andy brought down a large cow, as did Scott, but when Toby felled a second bull, something awakened the herd to danger, and a cow raised her head and emitted a curiously high-pitched, prolonged sound.

All at once the entire herd seemed to become aware of its danger. The young bulls, acting as monitors, moved closer together to prevent strays from wandering away, and the mature bulls seemed to take command.

Whip did not hesitate. "Mount your horses and rally to me!" he shouted. "Be mighty quick about it!"

Toby set an example for his comrades by abandoning all dignity as he sprinted as fast as he could to his waiting mount and hurled himself into the saddle, simultaneously digging his heels into his horse's flanks and sending the animal hurtling toward Whip's stallion.

The others did not hesitate, either, and soon virtually the entire company was mounted and on the move. By the time the dozen horsemen had managed to cluster behind Whip, the entire herd of buffalo was in motion. The sight was awesome.

The bulls who led the wild charge seemed indifferent to the presence of the men and their mounts and raced right by Whip and his companions. Soon the ground trembled as hundreds of the ungainly beasts thundered at full tilt, charging heedlessly across the plains.

It was impossible for Whip to give any orders now, as the steady drumbeat of the buffalos' hooves reverberated so loudly that his voice could not be heard, but the men needed no instruction. They instinctively formed into a wedge behind him and moved as close together as they dared. Quieting their frightened horses as best they could, they sat in wonder as the bulls, cows, and calves roared past them, some almost close enough to touch.

It was no longer possible to distinguish one buffalo from another, and the members of the party realized that it might prove to be extremely dangerous if they shot any of the herd now. A falling beast might cause others to stumble or to lose their sense of direction, trampling horses and riders.

The tall grass vanished beneath the heavy hooves of the buffalo, and clots of dirt flew high in the air. It was astonishing how fast such a vast number of large beasts could move across the prairie. Then suddenly the ordeal came to an end. The last of the herd thundered past them, with the young bulls who were acting as monitors bringing up the rear, and the entire procession moved off.

Andy Brentwood was surprised to discover that his hand was slightly unsteady. Scott Foster, too, was trembling, and Bernhard von Hummel sat in a daze, knowing that he had enjoyed a unique experience.

As the roar of the buffalo hooves subsided, Whip raised his voice. "A good day's hunting, lads," he said.

Toby was obviously pleased. "We brought down more than twenty of the critters," he announced. "We'll be eating fresh meat for days to come."

Whip supervised the next step, which was the skinning of the buffalo and the butchering of the carcasses. The task was not easy, but he explained patiently. "Buffalo hide," he said, "is valuable. I don't know anything that offers better protection from the cold in winter. As for the meat, all of it is useful, so don't throw anything away."

Two of the men rode off to the wagon train for reinforcements, returning with several empty wagons to carry the meat. Meanwhile, the majority of the men paused in their labors to watch Toby as he skinned the hide of the first bull he had shot.

The preparation of the meat required far more time and effort than had the hunt itself, and it was mid-afternoon by the time the hunters returned to the wagon train. There, a cooking fire glowed in welcome to them, and Toby gave the cooks special instructions. "Buffalo meat," he said, "is tougher than beef or any other meat that we eat, so it needs to be cooked much longer in order to make it edible. When it's undercooked, you can chew it forever, but you can't swallow it."

Chunks of buffalo meat were combined with wild onions gathered by the women and children of the company, and that night everyone feasted on buffalo stew, a delicacy that had sustained countless pioneers who had crossed the country. Those who tasted it for the first time never forgot the unique flavor. Here was the essence of America, and most of the members of the wagon train knew it.

After supper Toby busied himself with the tanning of a buffalo hide, performing the messy job with skill. The following morning, just before the journey was resumed, he asked Caroline Brandon's permission to stretch the hide in the sunlight on the roof of her wagon, and she readily agreed. He continued to work the leather during the nooning and again when the wagon train halted for the evening, and some of his colleagues were amused when he used a bone needle and thread of sinews. He was not satisfied with his work until he had fashioned a creditable cape, which impressed his colleagues.

Beth saw Toby at work on the animal skin late one afternoon after the train had halted for the day, and she lingered beside him for a moment. "I know what you have in mind," she said, "and I urge you as best I'm able not to do it."

He looked up from his labors, perplexed by the intensity of her tone. "What do you mean?"

She drew a deep breath, realizing she was treading on delicate ground. "I know you're sweet on Caroline Brandon," she said. "You ought to have better sense, but I'm not going to lecture you on that. Just don't, for the sake of your parents, if nothing else, get too involved with her."

Toby looked her up and down slowly. It occurred to him that despite his earlier resolve to keep his interest in Caroline a secret, everyone in the wagon train could see how he felt. Well, that couldn't be helped, but he certainly wasn't going to let anybody—least of all the nosy Beth Blake—interfere. "Did anybody ever tell you to mind your own business?" he snapped at her.

She sighed and walked away rapidly. She should have

known better than to interfere, and she deserved his rebuke.

Toby returned to work on the cape, and when it was finished that evening, he presented it to Caroline.

Caroline was pleased and modeled the cloak for him. "I've never received a gift quite like this," she said. Men had showered her with many presents, but no one had ever presented her with a cape of buffalo leather that he had made himself from the hide of an animal he had shot.

The gift, to be sure, was anything but useful. Having realized her relationship with Douglas de Forest was terminated, she knew she would have to start life anew on her own. She had been given permission to accompany the others to the East Coast, and she had a vague plan of buying a home for herself in New York or Philadelphia or Boston. In none of those cities would she wear an ungainly and heavy buffalo cloak.

But she knew that Toby had expended considerable time and energy in the making of the cape for her—far more time than most of her admirers had ever spent on the gifts they had given her. Thus, she began to treat him seriously.

She could do far worse than attach herself to Toby Holt, she knew. Certainly he was exceptionally good-looking, even though he was a few years younger than she and was almost painfully naive. On the other hand, his father was one of the most renowned of living Americans and was a man of considerable means. She had no idea what his ranch in Oregon might be worth, but she knew it comprised a large property and that he had invested a fortune in the horses he raised and sold.

Life with Toby might be dull, but it would be a safe, secure existence. Therefore, it was worth her serious consideration.

Alison White sat on the stoop of her wagon, savoring the warm, dry night air. Her wagon partner, Susanna, had gone for an evening stroll with Andy Brentwood, as was becoming more and more her custom, and Alison was glad to be alone. Indeed, she had kept almost entirely to herself since the Confederate attack on the wagon train, unable to deal with what she regarded as her conflicting responsibilities to her friends and her native country.

"Hello."

Alison was startled to see Scott Foster standing almost in front of her, grinning broadly.

"I'm sorry if I frightened you," he said. "You were so lost in thought you didn't even hear me approach."

"Yes, I guess I was," Alison said, shifting uneasily on the stoop.

"I sure haven't seen much of you the last few days," Scott said, taking a step forward. "Is anything wrong?"

"Nothing, nothing at all," Alison replied quickly, wishing with all her heart she could confide in Scott.

The young man took a seat on the step below her. "You know, I think I can guess what's bothering you," he said.

"You can?" Alison was startled anew. Had Scott found out about Poole?

"Sure," he said. "Everyone's been a little on edge since that attack on the train, and I imagine you're more upset than most, being a stranger to this country. Well, if it's any consolation let me just tell you that we know who was responsible."

"You *know*!" Alison was so alarmed now that she was trembling.

"Yes. I can't tell you everything we know, but I'm sure my superior officers wouldn't mind if I told you that Douglas de Forest from Virginia City was responsible for the attack and that he's working for the Confederate government."

Alison was vastly relieved. Poole's men had had nothing to do with the sabotage attempt, and she was in no way responsible for not telling the others about her interview with Poole in Denver. What had become of the English spymaster she had no idea, but clearly he was not committing any acts of sabotage, with or without Alison's help.

Impulsively Alison reached down and hugged Scott around the neck, and the young man was so surprised he could not move. When she released him, all he could say was, "I didn't think it would mean that much to you."

"Oh, oh, it's not that," Alison stammered, eager to glide over the issue and forget the whole matter once and for all. "I guess it's just nice to know that you think enough of me to try and make me feel better."

"I think a lot more of you than just that," Scott said, and his face reddened as he looked down at the ground. It occurred to him forcibly now that there was someone else in his life besides Susanna Fulton.

It was essential to the purpose of his grand scheme, Colonel Roger Stannard knew, to throw the wagon train defenders off the track, so he planned his initial move with great care. It was a simple matter to gain the cooperation of one of the most ferocious Indian tribes that inhabited the Great Plains, the Sioux. Long disgruntled because of the loss of their hunting grounds to the settlers who poured through their territory en route to California and Oregon, the leaders of the tribe were amenable to the deal that Roger offered them. He supplied five hundred Sioux warriors with modern rifles and large quantities of ammunition, sending fifty of the Indians to retrieve them from the wagons located in the southern part of the territory. All he asked in return was that the Sioux make life miserable for Union supporters, and particularly for the wagon train that was now moving across the Great Plains. The sachems, war chiefs, and medicine men of the Sioux needed no urging, and their scouts watched the train from a distance for a number of days.

One evening a halt was called in the open near the bank of the South Platte. The wagons were drawn up in the customary circle, and the usual sentries were established, paying particular attention to the silver bullion wagons. The cooking detail began to prepare the evening meal, and the water-gathering detail formed a bucket brigade from the river.

The Sioux attacked suddenly about an hour before sundown. Unlike most Plains Indians, they were at home on horses, and the entire attacking force was mounted. The sentries had no sooner given the alarm than the braves, riding in single file, surrounded the wagon train and pumped bullets into it.

It was astonishing, but the only members of the wagon train band who were experienced in fighting Indians were Whip Holt and a number of men from Scott Foster's company of Nevada volunteers. But the others learned very quickly.

The civilians were ordered into the center of the circle, where they were promptly requested to wait quietly and not interfere with the military operation.

Alison White, seated near Susanna—who was busily jotting down notes in a little pad—waited expectantly for the battle to begin. Perhaps, because she didn't know what was in store, she was far calmer than she otherwise would have been. Susanna Fulton did not enlighten her, however. Susanna exulted inwardly, telling herself she was once again in luck. Here was a genuine Indian attack that she could describe at length in the article she was writing about the train trip across the country.

Beth Blake could scarcely contain her own excitement. She was eager to take part in the battle herself but knew that if she even dared to suggest that she participate, Whip Holt would tell her to behave herself. Rather than risk an open rebuke, she decided to bide her time and hope that she would have an opportunity to join in the fray.

One person who did not hesitate to approach Whip was Bernhard von Hummel. "Colonel," he said, "I have a request to make, and I will be brief. I spent three years as an officer in the Prussian Army, so I can handle firearms. May I join your forces?"

"By all means," Whip replied, "and we're mighty glad to have you. Report to Captain Foster, if you will, and just remember this: don't waste ammunition."

Major Andy Brentwood and the troops of his battalion quickly learned to take cover behind the wagons and not to expose themselves unnecessarily. They also picked up one of the primary principles of Indian fighting: they learned to hold their fire until they had a clearly defined target and then to waste no time shooting at their foes.

The Union regulars were disciplined and held their fire while they concealed themselves behind the bulk of the wagons in the circle. Andy instructed them to fire at will, and they seemed to enjoy waiting until they could aim at clearly defined targets. Certainly they gave as good as they received.

Scott Foster's Nevada militiamen, with the enthusiastic Bernhard von Hummel among their number, did even better than that. Presenting no targets of consequence themselves, they exercised great patience and held their fire until the Sioux attackers edged closer and closer to the wagons. Then the militiamen rained a steady hail of fire at them, and the marksmen took a heavy toll.

Whip was satisfied with the way the battle was progressing. In spite of the inexperience of most members of his command in dealing with Indians, the troops were quick to learn, and the results they achieved held the Sioux at bay.

"It doesn't appear to me," Andy said, "as though they're concentrating on the silver wagons."

"I reckon they aren't," Whip agreed. "They're using the old Indian technique of going round and round and round while they look for a break in our lines. If they find it they'll pour into the circle."

"Not today they won't, Colonel," Andy replied grimly. "Our boys are holding firm up and down the entire line."

The battle eased off about a quarter of an hour after it started, and the Sioux withdrew, pulling back beyond range of their foes' rifles. "Do you suppose they've had enough?" Andy asked.

Whip shook his head. "Not by a damnsight," he said. "Unless I'm very much mistaken, this is just a temporary respite. You notice they're holding their positions even though they're beyond range now."

"So I see," Andy said. "What's the idea?"

Whip shrugged. "It's a good thing when fighting Indians," he said, "never to anticipate what they'll do next. Our way of thinking isn't at all like their way, and we cause ourselves more trouble than good when we try to anticipate them. I think our best bet is to wait and see what develops and then react accordingly."

Andy began to understand why his superior had achieved such renown as an Indian fighter. The key to Whip Holt's success was his monumental patience.

The defenders held their battle positions and remained alert while the Indians withdrew still farther. Andy continued to observe them closely.

"Here they come again!" he said at last.

It was true that the Sioux were returning to the fray, but they had adopted new tactics. They were armed with bows and arrows rather than the modern rifles that they had used. They began igniting their arrows from a torch one of the braves carried, then fired flaming arrows into the compound. One moment the air was clear; the next instant fires were raining on the defenders and the civilians.

Horses and mules, unnerved by the flaming arrows, whinnied and pawed the ground. Some of the women and children and a number of the civilian men, as well, became panicky when burning arrows lodged in the canvas of their wagons and the fires began to spread.

Before Whip could react and issue instructions on the most effective method of countering this attack, Alison White's common sense told her what needed to be done. She saw an arrow lodge in the canvas roof of her wagon, and she knew that within moments the roof would catch fire and place the contents of the wagon in jeopardy. Indifferent to her own safety, Alison scrambled onto the wagon box, where she made a tempting target, and snatched the burning arrow from the roof, hurling it to the ground. Then she jumped down. Several civilians began to cheer.

In fact, the women were so impressed by Alison's efforts that one of them almost lost her life. A flaming arrow landed on the ground directly behind her, and she was so absorbed watching Alison that her dress caught fire before she realized what was happening.

Beth Blake proved equal to the emergency, and at last had her opportunity to make her contribution to the cause. She shouted a warning to the woman who, in her panic, began to run in circles. That was the very worst thing she could have done, as Beth well knew. Ignoring her own safety, Beth threw herself at the taller, huskier woman, bearing her to the ground. Then, clutching her hard, Beth rolled over and over with her until the flames were extinguished.

Once the woman realized she was out of danger, her gratitude was so great that she broke into tears.

Embarrassed, Beth retreated. She hadn't anticipated being treated as a heroine, and she suddenly craved anonymity again.

The troops continued to hold their lines and to fire at the braves whenever the opportunity afforded, and the civilians, taking their cue from Alison, extinguished the fires that the flaming arrows started. They proved equal to the task, and surprisingly, no one showed more courage or worked with greater zeal than did Caroline Brandon. The spirit of adventure that had led her to become a courtesan took another form now, and she reacted recklessly to the threat. Again and again she pulled flaming arrows from the roof of a wagon, indifferent to the risk that she was taking and unmindful of the incongruity of the sight that she created. She seemed to have forgotten that she was wearing a figure-hugging gown of green velvet, and she leaped up repeatedly to snatch an arrow and hurl it to the ground.

Not until later, after the battle had ended, did she realize that she had suffered burns on her hands. Toby, who discovered that she had injured herself, obtained quantities of salve from the first-aid supplies and personally bound her wounded hands.

The failure of the Sioux to start a major fire or to cause the defenders to panic brought the battle to an abrupt halt. The attackers were suffering heavily from their temerity, the sharpshooters among the defenders taking a steady toll, and the sachem abruptly withdrew his entire force. The Indians retreated as rapidly as they had advanced, streaking across the plains in loose formation.

Whip shrugged. "That's the last we'll see of them tonight," he said flatly.

Andy Brentwood didn't feel as confident. "Isn't it possible that they've just withdrawn to regroup?" he asked. "They could come back and attack again in force."

Whip shook his head. "Not the Sioux," he said. "They tried two different methods of assault, and we held firm under both. They've had enough for one day, and they won't fight again."

The alert remained in force, however, and Whip congratulated all those who had distinguished themselves in combat.

He thanked Bernhard von Hummel for his appreciable help, and the Prussian, true to form, merely clicked his heels and bowed in return. Whip was especially lavish in his praise of Alison White and of Caroline Brandon. Certainly he was forced to revise his estimates of Caroline. He couldn't help admiring her courage, and although he regretted his son's interest in her, he could well understand Toby's reasons for being fascinated by her.

The defenders' casualties were exceptionally light, three soldiers having suffered slight wounds, and Andy was obviously relieved as he sat down to eat a bowl of buffalo stew. "I don't know what that attack was all about," he said, "but I believe the Sioux will think twice before they attack us again."

"Maybe so," Whip answered quietly.

Andy studied his superior in the light of the cooking fire. "There was more to this attack than meets the eye. Is that what you're trying to tell me, Colonel?"

Whip shrugged. "Could be," he said. "It's too early to tell." Whip sighed, then continued. "The Sioux are a brave nation, and by and large they're pretty sensible. They never attack without knowing something about their enemies, so they're bound to have learned our strength before they conducted their assault."

"I see," Andy said. "You're telling me that it was odd for them to send a force of only five hundred men into combat against three hundred experienced defenders."

"Right," Whip replied emphatically. "Don't forget that our three hundred men know firearms and how to use them. But these Sioux were such bad shots with their rifles that it was quite plain they were using completely unfamiliar weapons."

"That, sir," Andy replied softly, "puts a different light on the entire matter."

"So it does," Whip said.

His subordinate was silent for a few moments and then said, "The obvious question has an obvious answer. Where would the Sioux nation, living in the remote Great Plains of the Nebraska Territory, get their hands on five hundred modern rifles? The only possible source of supply for them has got to be Douglas de Forest and his Confederates."

"That's the way I see it," Whip said.

Andy chuckled. "Well, at least we won this encounter easily."

"I'm not so sure we've won it," Whip replied as he stared into the fire. "It could be that the Confederates were simply trying to agitate us and didn't expect the Sioux to beat us. That makes a lot of sense to me."

"I'm afraid you're right," Andy said heavily. "They couldn't have expected the warriors to accomplish more than they did. But what's their ultimate plan?"

Whip reached for a blade of grass, plucked it from the ground, and concentrated on nibbling the tender white end of the green shaft. "If we knew the answer to that," he said, "we'd be in a far better position to counter the major threat that the Rebels are mounting. All I know for sure is that they have something in mind—something far more serious than an obvious attack by Sioux braves. I'm damned if I know what it is, or how they plan to attack us, but I'm afraid that this incident today was no more and no less than a preliminary for what's to come next. What's more, I don't believe this is the work of Douglas de Forest alone. I think the Confederates have got someone else directing the activities in the field, someone with capabilities beyond those of de Forest. We're not facing an amateur now, and our greatest challenge still lies ahead of us."

Averaging almost twenty miles per day, the wagon train at last drew near to Fort Kearny, a major army post on the bank of the Platte in eastern Nebraska. Scouts from the fort had been keeping track of the train's progress, and on the last day of the journey, one hundred cavalrymen rode out into the plains and acted as an escort.

Colonel Jacob Watson, the commander of Fort Kearny, was on hand to welcome Whip and Andy. "I've been keeping watch for you, gentlemen," he said, "and I've already telegraphed the War Department that you were arriving today. I'm sure that the President will be very much relieved to receive the good news."

The civilians, including the women and children, were the guests of the garrison at supper, and Whip and Andy dined with the commander in his private quarters. He listened with great interest to the stories they told of the difficulties encountered on the journey. "It strikes me," Watson said, frowning, "that the Rebels have somebody who is both clever and resourceful nagging away at you. I think we'll take no unnecessary risks, and I'll give you a cavalry escort for the rest of your journey to Independence."

"I appreciate that, Colonel," Whip replied. "I don't know what the Rebels have in mind, but I've got to admit that they've made me a mite jittery."

"I'd like to ask a favor of you, Colonel Watson," Andy said. "I hope your adjutant will be good enough to swear a man into service and grant him an official promotion to the rank of sergeant."

Colonel Watson raised an eyebrow. "We'll be glad to oblige naturally but isn't this rather unusual?"

Whip grinned. "I reckon it is," he said, "but Ezekiel

has already demonstrated on the wagon train that he's a very unusual fellow."

Immediately after they finished the meal, they went to the adjutant, and then they found Ezekiel.

Patricia was present, naturally, to watch her husband being sworn in and so were Scott Foster, Susanna Fulton, and Beth Blake.

Ezekiel treated the occasion with the solemnity it deserved, and did not smile as the oath was administered to him. The garrison quartermaster quickly found that the newest member of the Union Army was so big that ordinary uniforms would not fit him, and considerable effort was expended to find a tunic and hat, trousers, and boots large enough for the man. At last Ezekiel's uniform was complete, and Andy presented him with the three stripes that were the insignia of his rank. "Maybe you could persuade your wife to sew this on your sleeve, Sergeant," he said. "Effective immediately you are assigned to my headquarters."

Ezekiel beamed. "Yes, sir!" he said heartily.

When Whip had first seen Independence, Missouri, a quarter of a century earlier, the community had been a tiny frontier town perched on the edge of the Great Plains and had been isolated and remote. Then it had become a thriving metropolis, one of the most renowned cities in America. It had been the jumping-off place for thousands of immigrants bound for California, Oregon, and in latter years, other destinations in the far West. Now, however, another city had developed and was flourishing, Saint Joseph, which was served by railroads that connected it with the great population centers that lay to the East.

The success of Independence and Saint Joseph was mirrored in the growth and prosperity enjoyed by Sam Brentwood, the one-time wagon train guide and close friend of Whip Holt. He and his wife, Claudia, had grown and prospered, first with Independence, then with the other burgeoning Missouri cities. Now Brentwood warehouses covered many acres on a number of sites and were filled with the provisions and supplies that the westward-bound travelers required for their long journeys. The tiny ranch house in which Andy Brentwood had been born had given way to a great mansion, one of the showplaces of Independence. But wealth and stature had not changed Sam and Claudia Brentwood. They were still unassuming people who put on no airs. They extended a hearty welcome to Whip, Toby, and Beth Blake, their niece. They were delighted at the unexpected reunion with their son, and that evening they gave a grand dinner to celebrate. At Andy's request, Susanna Fulton and Alison White also were present, and the atmosphere was festive.

The chinaware, silver, and glasses that Claudia used were imported from England and France, and the menu was a far cry from the stews that she had prepared when she and Sam had first been married. The soup was made according to a continental recipe, the beef was roasted to perfection, and the vegetable dishes seemed endless.

Conversation was lively, but the most significant talk took place at one end of the table where Sam, Whip, and Andy spoke quietly.

"I've been expecting your arrival for several days," Sam said, "and I sent wires to the White House and the War Department the minute I saw your caravan heading up the hill toward town. The President is going to be mighty relieved to hear that you've made it this far."

"I estimate that the worst of our journey is over," Whip said. "Are the special railroad cars that were ordered for us on hand?"

Sam Brentwood nodded. "They arrived in Saint Jo about three weeks ago from Chicago. They were built for the carrying of very heavy loads—specifically for silver bullion. I've examined them thoroughly myself, and they're strong enough to hold a great many bullion bricks."

Whip was pleased. "I want to have a look at them myself, before we make up the railroad train that's going to take us the rest of the way to New York. Are we going to encounter any difficulty in getting hold of passenger cars for our military escort?"

Sam smiled and shook his head. "Apparently you don't realize, any of you, the importance that President Lincoln has given your mission. You get first priority up and down the line. The railroad people tell me that you'll have all the passenger cars and other rolling stock that you'll need. I know that a special engine and coal car are being held for your use."

Whip sighed gently. "It's going to seem mighty strange to be traveling all the way to New York by train," he said. "It seems like just yesterday when we crossed the states either on horseback or on our own feet."

Sam nodded. "The whole country is shrinking," he said. "The marvels of transportation are greater than anything you or I ever dreamed of when we were young." Sam paused, then said, "We gather from Cathy and Lee that Beth here will stay on board the train until you reach Ohio."

Andy nodded. "That's right, Pa. We're going to drop her off at school at Antioch."

"Are there any other civilians traveling with you?"

"Originally," Whip replied, "we weren't planning to carry any, since the civilians who came with us from Nevada are going to remain in Missouri, but one way and another our party has grown."

Andy smiled somewhat sheepishly. "Sue Fulton asked for permission to ride with us, and Colonel Holt was kind enough to give his approval," he said. "And that meant that we had to allow Alison White to come, also. Then, after I was lucky enough to get Ezekiel as a sergeant, the problem of transporting his wife to the East Coast was presented, and we solved it by offering Patricia quarters, too."

Whip glanced down the table and in the direction of his son, who was engaged in animated conversation with Claudia. "Unfortunately," he said, "Toby has obligated us to give some space to Caroline Brandon, too."

Andy Brentwood frowned. "I don't see Caroline as a

beneficial addition to the company," he said. "In fact, I regard her as a potential troublemaker. However, I couldn't reject Toby's request after the way she conducted herself during the Sioux attack. I figure that we owe her the courtesy of transporting her to the East."

Whip shrugged. "It appears that we're going to have all the railroad cars we'll need," he said, "so I don't think it matters if we carry a few more civilians with us. The presence of some young females in our company sure won't do any harm. I'll grant you that the Confederates have kept abreast of our plans and undoubtedly know that we're making the rest of the journey by rail, but a stranger—an outsider—seeing the young ladies might get confused and not realize that we're going to be transporting bullion."

Early the following morning Whip and Andy rode up to Saint Joseph and presented themselves at the main office of the railroad company, and there they found that Sam had not exaggerated when he had said that they were being given whatever they required for the journey.

Whip had already determined that he could cut the size of his escort by one hundred men for the rail portion of the journey, so he had arranged for a company of regulars to return to Fort Kearny with the cavalry escort that Colonel Watson had provided. Consequently, he needed fewer coaches for the two hundred troops who would provide the escort for the final phase of the trip, and he decided that two dining cars, each of them equipped with a woodburning stove, would be ample for his purposes. He also requisitioned only one sleeping car, which would accommodate his headquarters personnel and the five young women whom he was allowing to travel to New York on the train. The sleeping car, which was divided into individual compartments, was unique for this time and was very luxurious.

He and Andy inspected the special cars being provided for the silver bullion. The cars were sturdy, with floors and walls of steel, capable of carrying very heavy loads. A corridor ran the length of each car, which meant that twenty-five to fifty soldiers could be assigned to guard duty in each of the two cars at any given time, with the remaining soldiers staying in the coaches. Whip could find no fault with any of the equipment.

The transfer of the silver bullion took place early the following morning, and all available troops, including the cavalry escort from Fort Kearny, were pressed into service to stand sentry duty. The special wagons that had served their purpose so well were hauled by the mule teams to the railroad yards, which were cleared of all nonessential personnel. Then teams of baggage handlers began the laborious, back-breaking task of transferring the silver bullion bricks to the two railroad cars that would carry the fortune the rest of the journey. The soldiers, each carrying a loaded rifle, surrounded the area. Whip stayed in one spot and watched the bullion being moved into the railroad cars, while Andy and Toby rode from one end of the area to the other, ready to alert the troops in the event that trouble of some kind threatened. But nothing untoward took place, and the operation was completed without incident. The troops were immediately assigned to sentry duty and were ordered to keep watch on the silver until further notice. Plans were made for departure the following morning, and Whip ordered the train's engineer and firemen to report then for duty. All passengers were notified by Toby to have their personal effects on board the train in ample time.

Sam Brentwood gave the young women a good price for their wagons, which were no longer needed, and Beth, Susanna, and Alison went off to pack their belongings, then to say good-bye to the wagon train members who had accompanied them to Independence. Meanwhile, Caroline Brandon impatiently waited in her hotel room for their departure the following morning.

A last-minute addition to the company was Baron Bernhard von Hummel.

"I think," Bernhard said after taking Whip aside, "that I should stay near the silver, wherever it may be, until it reaches its final destination. Only in that way can I report on its safety to my superiors in Berlin. Naturally, I will compensate you, Colonel, for my passage on the train."

Whip smilingly refused. "We have the space, Baron," he said, "so you're more than welcome. It's important that you see for yourself that our cargo is delivered to New York safely."

That evening Sam and Claudia entertained the departing travelers at supper again, and later Claudia had an opportunity to speak privately with her son. "I approve of your taste, Andy," she said. "Susanna Fulton is a lovely young woman."

Andy grinned at his mother. "There's no question about that," he said. "The only problem is whether she's going to pick me instead of my competitor for her hand."

Claudia's smile broadened. "What I like best about her," she said, "is that she has a mind of her own. She reminds me of myself when I was her age, and all I can say to you, son, is that you can consider yourself very lucky indeed if she accepts you. Have you proposed to her?"

"I propose regularly," Andy replied, "and I'm astonished by the infinite variety of ways in which she puts me off."

Claudia laughed. "Good for her," she said. "Anyone who marries you won't be leading an easy life. Marriage to a regular army officer means moving from one post to another, as Cathy has done for so many years. But it is also true that you're going to inherit a rather substantial sum of money when your father and I die."

"She's no gold digger," Andy assured her. "I don't think money means very much to her."

"So much the better," his mother said. "I trust your judgment, and I hope for your sake that she chooses you."

Since the young women were sharing guest rooms in the Brentwood house prior to the train's departure, Claudia made it her business to seek Susanna early the following morning.

"I hope we meet again, Miss Fulton," Claudia said pointedly.

Susanna reddened but held her ground. "I'm sure we shall, Mrs. Brentwood," she said.

Claudia studied the younger woman. If she knew anything at all about human nature, she was sure that Susanna Fulton was no flirt. She sounded as though she had made up her mind about Andy, and it was curious that she had not yet told him, so his mother decided to speak bluntly. "Andy doesn't give his affections lightly," she said, "and I know what he thinks of you."

Susanna looked even more flustered. "I—I've been putting him off for a reason," she said. "I know now that I've made up my mind about him, but there's someone else in the picture. Someone whom I'm very reluctant to hurt."

"I see." Claudia smiled. "When I was young," she said, "we had a surefire way of handling a predicament like that. We used a little subtlety and persuaded a friend to keep an unwanted swain occupied." Still smiling, she went on to the dining room to attend to the needs of her guests.

Susanna stood still, and a smile appeared on her lips. Of course! The solution to her problem had been present the entire time, but she hadn't seen it. Alison had shown her in a dozen ways that she was interested in Scott Foster, and, indeed, they had been spending more and more time together. With a little encouragement she and Scott well might become absorbed in each other, and that would leave Susanna free to do as her heart dictated, without hurting anyone.

There was no time like the present, and she deliberately seated herself at the breakfast table in such a way that Alison, who was following her, would be placed adjacent to Scott.

Immediately after breakfast, Andy sought out Susanna and was surprised when she greeted him even more warmly than usual. "I wonder if you'd do me a favor?" he asked.

"Of course," she said.

221

"My mother has provided us with some meats and baked goods for the journey. I'm sure you ladies will find them more palatable than the government fare that's being provided for the troops," he said. "I've got to see to it that the men and their gear go aboard the train now, so I'll appreciate it if you'll go with me to Saint Jo and take charge of packing away the food in the kitchen car."

"I'll be delighted," Susanna said, smiling. She had no idea that her smile was ravishing and that it had an immediate, deep effect on Andy.

He stared at her for a moment, bewildered by her attitude.

"When will we see each other aboard the train?" she asked.

"I'll be pretty busy," he said, "but I should be able to steal a little time to see you."

She could not resist saying, "Perhaps you'll be inclined to ask me a question that you've repeated on a number of occasions. I think you'll get a definite response now."

Before he could say a word, she picked up her skirts and fled.

Claudia, who overheard the exchange, had no doubts about Susanna's meaning, however. She looked in triumph at her husband, who was finishing his breakfast at the opposite end of the table. It appeared that Andy's bachelor days were numbered, and she approved heartily of her prospective daughter-in-law.

Scott Foster was also aware of Susanna's growing interest in Andy, but strangely he wasn't bothered by it. He couldn't sort out his own thoughts, but he suspected that Alison White was responsible for his declining interest in Susanna. He hadn't deliberately turned to Alison, but he found himself thinking about her more and more frequently, and he found her proximity comforting. The rail journey to New York promised to be an exceptionally pleasant interlude.

Whip Holt rode off to Saint Joseph immediately after breakfast and arrived in the railroad yard that afternoon. He found the train's engineer, Tim Zachary, waiting for him. A veteran of more than twenty years of railroading, Zachary viewed the coming mission calmly. "Colonel," he said, "I've arranged for double coal cars behind the engine so we won't need to make any special stops for fuel. We can load up with coal whenever we come to a major city and are going to stop anyway."

Whip, who was unfamiliar with railroads as a means of transportation, nodded. "I'll go along with whatever you say, Tim. You're the expert."

Zachary chewed on his wad of tobacco in silence and finally spat, sending a stream of tobacco juice flying across the yard. "All I ask of you, Colonel, is that you assign a couple of husky soldiers to keep the engine supplied with fuel, and I suggest that you change the detail regularly. It isn't easy to get competent firemen these days. Most of the men who work for the railroad are a mite lazy, and I like to work up a good head of steam and to keep it up."

"Consider it done," Whip said.

Soon therafter the troops marched onto the train, depositing their luggage in the coaches, and then, under Andy's direction, sentries lined the corridors of the two bullion cars. The passengers boarded the train, occupying some of the private rooms in the sleeping car, and they were followed by members of the staff. The most conspicuous was Ezekiel, who towered above the other soldiers in his flat-crowned hat and who saw to it that he was always within hailing distance of Major Andy Brentwood. A pistol was strapped to Ezekiel's thigh, a rifle was slung over his shoulder, and his razor-sharp kitchen knife protruded from his belt. The knife was a nonregulation weapon, but Andy conveniently failed to see it, knowing that the black man felt far more at ease when armed with his knife. Ezekiel grinned broadly when Patricia followed Beth Blake onto the train and disappeared into the compartment that they would share. He was ready for anything that might develop.

The troops that were returning to Fort Kearny lined the siding in the railroad yard and raised their rifles in silent salute as the engine worked up its head of steam and slowly began to haul the ten-car train forward on its journey. Sam Brentwood, who had ridden up to Saint Joseph with his wife to see them off, raised a hand and waved. Claudia, standing beside him, gestured broadly with a handkerchief. Whip and Andy saluted the couple, and Claudia was heartened when, as the passenger car began to gain momentum, she caught a glimpse of a handkerchief returning her farewell gesture and recognized Susanna. She felt certain that the next time she saw Andy, he would be accompanied by his bride.

The train gradually gained speed, and Whip was satisfied. He preferred to travel by wagon train, but railroading was far simpler and more luxurious.

"This way of travel is so easy," he said, "that I can't quite believe it. But with luck we're on the last stage of our assignment."

IX

Soldiers were stationed in Tim Zachary's engine and coal cars, and others rode on the rooftops of every car in the train. All were armed with rifles, and all were ready for any emergency. Whip sat in the stateroom that was his private headquarters and reviewed the overall situation with Andy Brentwood and Toby. "The worst dangers," he said, "will present themselves in the first twenty-four hours. Keep in mind, gentlemen, that Missouri is a divided state, and it elected by a very narrow vote to stay in the Union."

Andy nodded gravely. "There are a great many Confederate sympathizers in Missouri, as well as in Illinois, especially in the southern part of the state."

Unfolding a map of Missouri, Whip said, "Precisely so. Independence and Saint Joseph are firmly in the Union camp, and Saint Louis is a Union stronghold. Unfortunately, the rail route from Saint Jo to Saint Louis goes through territory that's pro-Confederate." He traced a line on the map with a sturdy forefinger. "And when we leave Saint Louis and enter southern Illinois, just above Kentucky, we'll be in a no-man's land until we get close to Louisville. I'm a mite apprehensive about what may happen."

"Do you think serious sabotage will take place?" Toby asked.

Whip shrugged. "The Confederates haven't told me their plans," he said, "but it wouldn't surprise me if they do pull some shenanigans in the region. Remember, that Sioux attack was just a warning of what's to come."

"We're doing everything possible to protect ourselves," Andy said. "We have details assigned to Tim Zachary and his assistants night and day. We have enough coal to take us as far as Saint Louis, and there we'll load up again."

There were two sets of tracks that ran parallel to each other, and rail traffic on both was heavy with troops and freight. But Colonel Holt's train had been given the unquestioned right of way, and other trains were shunted to side tracks to make way for it. The special train traveled at a rapid clip, its pace seldom varying as Tim Zachary, who was familiar with every inch that the train would cover, let out the throttle.

Whip had taken all possible precautions, so there was little else that he could do. But he remained vigilant, all the same, and was ready in the event that an unexpected crisis developed. He had to admit that the mode of travel was helpful to his physical condition. His arthritis bothered him far less than it had when he spent hours in the saddle every day.

Andy and Toby remained vigilant, too, and the younger officer toured the train incessantly, going from the engine to the dining car at the rear and back in a never-ending round. His father and Andy were being overly cautious, but they felt it was better to take as few risks as possible.

Andy also made several trips to the special cars in which the bullion was stored and was reassured by the sight of the blue-clad sentries whom he saw in the corridors. There was literally nothing else he could do, he realized; if the Confederates were planning a move, they were free to take the initiative.

On his way back to his own quarters in the command car, he saw that the door to the compartment shared by Susanna and Alison was open. Alison, who had decided to relax and enjoy her journey, now that Poole was no longer an issue, was reading a book. Susanna, meanwhile, was scribbling furiously on sheets of foolscap. She looked up and gave Andy a broad smile. "It's quite an art to write while the train is jolting and jostling," she said, "but I think I've mastered it."

"Do I assume that you're starting the first of your articles about the train?" Andy asked.

She nodded. "I'm putting together all my notes about the earlier part of the journey, and with your permission I'll dispatch the article to Denver from Louisville when we arrive there."

"I've already talked with Colonel Holt about it, and it's fine with us, provided you make no mention of our itinerary or of any stops that we plan to make. But since the existence of the train is well known to the Confederates, we see no reason why the people of the Union shouldn't also be informed."

Susanna thanked him and resumed her writing. It occurred to Andy that the pieces she was working on about the transfer of the silver bullion would give her a national reputation. Not only would her father's Denver newspaper print her articles, but key papers in New York, Chicago, and other metropolitan centers would also buy them.

She had invited him in so many words to propose to her again, but this was not the appropriate moment. He hoped that soon he would find an opportunity to see her alone, if only for a few minutes. He had no idea what she was going to say to him, and he was, in fact, a little nervous. Perhaps she was asking him to propose again in order to tell him that she was not going to marry him.

Feeling the need to keep himself occupied, Andy relieved Toby and undertook the chore of patrolling the train himself.

Toby had nothing else to keep him busy, so he wandered back to the command car, and as he started toward his own compartment, he hesitated at the quarters occupied by Caroline Brandon. The door was ajar, and giving in to temptation, he tapped lightly. She called to him to come in, and he stepped into the compartment,

then stopped short. Caroline was reclining on the sofa
bed that occupied the greater part of the cabin and was
clad in a flimsy peignoir of flesh-colored silk that she
had exchanged for the dress she had been wearing when
she left Saint Joseph.

She smiled at him. "Well, hello," she said. "You've
been so busy that I've scarcely seen you."

"I've just been relieved and had nothing to do," he
told her.

Her smile broadened, and she made room on the sofa
for him. "Do join me, then," she said. "We're making a
very long journey, and I don't know of a better way to
pass the time than to spend it with you."

Flattered, Toby quickly sat down.

The truth was that Caroline was already thoroughly
bored. There had been a measure of excitement in the
wagon train journey, but the monotony of travel by rail
was suffocating, so she began to flirt with Toby, mildly
at first and then with far greater intensity. Toby could
not help responding to Caroline's gestures. She was rav-
ishingly beautiful, the most attractive young woman he
had ever seen. By now he had certainly admitted to himself the nature of her profession and was under no false
illusions about her, but that knowledge made her no less
attractive. She concentrated her complete attention on
him, and he enjoyed himself thoroughly.

Caroline's boredom vanished. Here was a young man
who was sensitive to any move she made. When she
reached out and touched his arm, she was aware of the
inner excitement that took hold of him. When she
shifted her position slightly to make more room for him,
she noted how quickly he took advantage of the opportunity, and his eager, slightly bedazzled smile told her
that she had made a total conquest.

A hedonist who lived for the pleasures of the moment,
Caroline gave no thought to the future or to the possibility that she might be creating complications in her relationship with Toby. It was enough for her that she was
passing the time pleasantly with an exceptionally good-

looking, virile admirer, who was so attracted to her that he responded to her slightest gesture.

It amused her to lean forward slightly, her lips parted, and look up at him guilelessly.

Toby seemed to lose himself in the depths of her huge green eyes, and suddenly he took her in his arms. Caroline gave a gentle sigh and yielded to him. Scores of men had made love to her, but Toby was different; his adoration of her was as intense as it was genuine, and she loved being the object of his open worship.

Skillfully guided by Caroline, who resorted to subtleties of movement and suggestion, Toby's lovemaking became more intense. Before he knew it, this most desirable of women had gone to the compartment door and locked it, then slowly returned to where he sat, gazing down at him, a smile on her lovely lips. Then she shed her peignoir and was offering herself to him in the nude. He swept aside all caution, all sense of restraint, and soon he had removed all his clothes, too. He took her in his strong arms, and they kissed passionately. Then Caroline led him onto the sofa bed, where they quickly became one. Toby's experience with women was limited, and the intensity of Caroline's passion left him breathless.

At last his world righted itself, and he dressed slowly, watching Caroline. She took her time donning her peignoir, allowing him to feast his eyes on her superb figure.

More than an hour had passed, Toby discovered with a glance at his watch, and he realized he should offer to relieve Major Brentwood of his chore.

Caroline opened her arms for his farewell kiss. She had killed an hour in the most enjoyable of all ways and was content.

As Toby left her compartment, he realized that the door of the adjacent chamber was open, and glancing inside, he saw Beth Blake, who was looking out the window at the Missouri countryside.

To his surprise she seemed to be expecting him, and she beckoned to him.

He hesitated for a moment, then stepped into her compartment. "Close the door, please," she commanded.

He did, and she said, "This is none of my business, Toby, but I think you're getting involved in something you can't handle."

When he merely looked at her blankly, Beth had to force herself to continue. "This isn't easy for me to say," she said in embarrassment, "but I—well, I—have a pretty fair idea of what's been going on there in the last hour or so. You and I have never been particularly close, but our parents are such good friends that I felt it was my duty to warn you before. Now I'm warning you again."

"Warning me of what?" he demanded irritably.

She took a deep breath. "I can understand that any man would be fascinated by Caroline Brandon," she said. "She's gorgeous, and the way she dresses and uses makeup—well, she's hard to resist. So I'm not blaming you or pointing any finger at you, but she's a woman of great experience, Toby, and you're, well—you're over your head."

He glared at her and stiffened, but she plunged on. "I don't pretend to know what she has in mind or what she sees in you, but a woman like that is certain to cause serious trouble for you."

He drew himself to attention, and his spurs clanged. "Thank you for your warning," he said. "I'll be sure to keep it in mind."

Beth heard the contempt in his tone, and her own anger flared. "It doesn't matter in the least to me," she said. "You're free to do as you please and to make a total jackass out of yourself if that's what you wish."

Toby glowered at her. She matched his hostility and stared at him without blinking.

He raised his hand to the visor of his flat-topped uniform hat, and in a curious gesture that was half salute and half farewell, he turned on his heel and stamped out of the compartment.

Perhaps he was too deeply involved with Caroline, but that did not concern him. He was so enamored of her that he could pay no heed whatsoever to Beth's warning.

Time passed slowly on the train, especially for those who had no responsibilities. The man who was the least occupied was Bernhard von Hummel, who enjoyed watching the passing scenery by day but had literally nothing to occupy him after night came. He surprised the other occupants of the sleeping car by offering his services as a cook, and Beth, who had volunteered to prepare the group's meal that evening, promptly accepted his offer. She regarded it as a challenge and was pleasantly surprised when he proved to be adept at cooking several vegetables quickly and neatly and making a sauce to go with the beef dish that she prepared.

"You astonish me," she told him, laughing.

Bernhard grinned and shook his head. "You Americans," he said, "make the mistake of thinking in stereotypes. Men enjoy food as much as women, so who is to say that they are not qualified to cook it? The preparation of food has long been a hobby of mine."

"That's obvious," Beth said, and it was plain that she was impressed by his skill.

The ice was broken, and they chatted amiably all through dinner, then retired to Beth's compartment, where Bernhard sipped a small glass of cognac as he talked about his family and the life he had led in Prussia.

Speaking completely without self-consciousness, Bernhard said, "I do not look forward to returning to my own country."

"Why ever in the world not?" she asked, surprised.

He grinned at her. "Because I will be pestered every day of my life by the mothers of daughters who are eligible for marriage," he said.

"Oh," Beth replied, unable to think of anything else to say.

"Unfortunately," he said, "I have been left a rather considerable fortune by my grandfather and father who, by no efforts of their own, acquired large sums of money. I have a title as well, and titles still are very important in Europe. Add all these factors together, and you see why the mothers of young ladies will chase after me." He sighed deeply. "Forgive me," he said, "I don't mean to burden you with my problems." Clicking his heels, he bent over her hand and kissed it, then took his departure.

Andy Brentwood had passed the open door of the compartment several times, and soon after Bernhard went off to his own quarters, the young major reappeared. He closed the door firmly behind him and sat down opposite Beth.

"I believe in adults leading their own lives as they see fit," he said, "but circumstances alter cases. You're not only my cousin, but you're young and naive and lack experience."

Beth was reminded of her own previous conversation with Toby Holt and was secretly amused. She nodded but made no reply.

"Bernhard von Hummel," Andy said, "is a nice fellow, and he's an honorable man. But he's a European, and he doesn't think the way Americans think. What I'm trying to tell you is—"

"What you're trying to tell me," Beth interrupted sweetly, "is his attitude toward women isn't like that of American men."

Andy was relieved that he didn't have to spell out his meaning. "Exactly," he said.

"What you fail to take into consideration, Andrew Jackson Brentwood," Beth said primly, "is my reaction, my feelings. I'm not only an American, but I've been raised to accept certain ideals in which I believe wholeheartedly, so you may rest assured that I have no intention whatsoever of being seduced by Baron von Hummel."

A scarlet-faced Andy retreated hastily. At least he knew that his young cousin was not as naive and as lacking in experience as he had thought.

The following morning they arrived in Saint Louis, having encountered no difficulties on the trip across Missouri. The train was immediately surrounded by a cordon of Union infantry, the coal cars were refilled, and supplies of food and water were taken on board. Meanwhile, Whip Holt and Andy Brentwood entertained a visitor in the commander's private quarters. Major Ed Thomas, the commandant of the local garrison, had been a classmate of Andy's at the U.S. Military Academy at West Point and was on the friendliest of terms with him.

"Three days ago," the visitor said, "I received a message from Washington that I'm duty-bound to pass on to you. I don't want to alarm you, but the Confederates have assigned some powerful personnel to keep watch on this bullion train, and I don't like it."

"Be specific, will you, Ed?" Andy asked.

"Sure," Major Thomas said. "For one thing, an agent we had planted in the Confederate War Department has informed us that no less an officer than Brigadier General Henry Hayward of Rebel intelligence is following the moves that your train is making."

Andy whistled under his breath. "There's none better than H.H.," he said, then turned to Whip to explain. "Hayward was a full colonel in the Union Army and served as Lee Blake's deputy in intelligence. I don't know of a more competent officer anywhere."

"With the possible exception of Lieutenant Colonel Roger Stannard," Ed Thomas said.

Andy nodded and smiled wryly. "Stannard was about two years ahead of us at the military academy," he said, "and we saw him in action even before he created his reputation. He has a rare ability to put himself in the minds of other people and to divine what they're going to do even before they do it. He's a formidable opponent, and I just wish that he were spending the war on our side."

"Unfortunately," Major Thomas said, "Colonel Stannard is not only active in Confederate intelligence, but he's been assigned to this silver train as a special project by General Hayward."

Andy exchanged a look with Whip. "So now we know

233

who the mastermind was behind the Sioux attack," he said. "This is very bad news."

"I'm afraid I can't offer you any consolation," Major Thomas declared. "In fact, you're going to feel even more frustrated when I tell you that you know all that the War Department has been able to glean. If Stannard has any plans that involve the silver train, Washington is ignorant of them."

Whip slapped the arm of his chair. "We'll have to be more vigilant than ever," he said. "All we can do in a situation like this is to hope for the best."

All two hundred of the soldiers on board the bullion train were placed on an alert when the train left Saint Louis. The guards stationed in the engine and on the roofs were doubled, and additional sentries were assigned to stand duty in the two bullion cars as well. In spite of the natural apprehensions of Whip Holt and Andy Brentwood, however, there were no incidents. Then, at mid-morning, as the train was passing through a heavily wooded section about twenty miles outside Saint Louis, Tim Zachary was forced to slow down. Something appeared to be blocking the track ahead.

He reduced his speed to a crawl and finally was forced to grind to a halt; he sent a corporal ahead to investigate. The noncommisioned officer returned after a few moments. "There's a dead cow lying plumb on the tracks, Mr. Zachary," the noncommissioned officer reported. "It's a big cow and very dead."

Zachary grimaced. It was a frequent but annoying occurrence for livestock to wander too close to the railroad tracks and get hit by passing trains. "Take your detail and move it, corporal," he said. "We can't allow this train to be stopped by a dead cow."

The corporal and the men of his squad left the engine and started to move up the track in the direction of the dead animal. Meanwhile, Whip Holt, sensing something was amiss, headed immediately for the front of the train.

Suddenly all hell broke loose. Heavy rifle fire broke out from the direction of the woods on both sides of the stalled train, decimating the ranks of the sentries stationed on the roofs of cars.

The Union forces rallied quickly, none more rapidly than the militiamen from Nevada. Captain Scott Foster dashed into the open and stood in the space where two cars were joined. "Hold steady, men!" he shouted. "We've run into a Rebel ambush!"

The Union troops returned the enemy fire with gusto, but their efforts were unsuccessful. The trap had been prepared with infinite care, and the Confederates had assigned more than four hundred well-concealed sharpshooters to the task of neutralizing the train's protectors. Volley after volley was fired, and Union casualties were heavy.

While the Confederate infantry kept the bulk of the defenders occupied, a special Rebel force dashed into the open and raced to the train. Another one hundred men hurled themselves at the defenders, concentrating on the troops that guarded the two bullion cars and on the command sleeper.

Before Whip and the other staff members could organize for the defense of the train, they were overwhelmed. Pistols were jammed into their backs, and they were forced to abandon the fight before they could get truly started.

Whip suffered the ultimate humiliation when two young Confederate officers converged on him, cocked pistols in hand, and a wiry officer wearing a Confederate lieutenant colonel's uniform materialized out of nowhere and said, "I'm sorry to inconvenience you, Colonel Holt, but you are my prisoner, sir. I'm afraid that under the circumstances I'll be obliged to have you bound for a time in order to immobilize you."

Whip gritted his teeth as one of the young officers produced a length of rope and began to tie his ankles and to make his wrists secure behind his back.

In spite of his humiliation, however, his mind continued to function sharply, and he deliberately tensed the muscles of his wrists and legs as much as he possibly could. He was taking a long chance, but it was the only opportunity available to him.

Another pair of officers conducted Andy Brentwood into the compartment. "I'm sorry we have to meet under these unpleasant circumstances, Andy," Colonel Roger Stannard said. "I'd have much preferred to meet you for a friendly supper and a drink."

"Roger," Andy replied ruefully, "I'm afraid this round is yours. All I ask of you is that you deal respectfully with the ladies who are traveling as our guests."

"Of course," Stannard assured him. "The Confederacy doesn't make war on ladies."

Even as he spoke, however, there was a complication. Stannard's immediate subordinates were rounding up the civilians in the sleeping car, and two of the officers discovered Patricia. "Well," one of them said, "here's a slave."

"She is no slave," Beth Blake replied tartly. "She's as free a woman as I am."

"Maybe so by your standards, ma'am, but not by ours. People of color are slaves, and that's the way we see them."

A bellow of rage sounded behind them, and Ezekiel, maddened by the sight of his wife being held by two Rebel officers, lunged toward them, wielding his sharp butcher knife.

An immediate scuffle ensued, and although Ezekiel fought furiously, he was badly outnumbered and was at last overwhelmed. He was bound hand and foot, and a disheveled Confederate captain looked at him in awe. "I've got to hand it to you, black man," he said, "you sure can fight. You're going to bring a top price at the Montgomery auction."

"No!" Beth screamed. "Can't you see that he's a sergeant in the Union Army and not a slave!"

The Rebel struggled for breath. "I can see that he's wearing a sergeant's uniform," he said, "but that doesn't make him a sergeant or a free man, either. Take him down to the end of the car, boys," he told the enlisted men who were standing guard over the trussed Ezekiel.

"He's a bull, this one, and we don't want to take any chances that he might escape."

Ezekiel was hauled away, and Patricia was in despair, tears filling her eyes.

"Have patience," Beth whispered to her, "and trust Colonel Holt. He'll think of something."

Colonel Stannard had planned the operation with infinite care, the earlier Sioux attack merely a diversion from his ultimate plan. He had cleverly realized that the Union forces traveling in railroad cars would not have the freedom of movement and the ability to defend themselves that they had had on the trail, and so he had led a company of Confederate soldiers into the forests outside Saint Louis to overtake the train. Then, when the rails divided slightly farther east, Stannard and his men would take the train south, through Confederate western Kentucky and into Tennessee.

His men knew precisely what was expected of them, and the Confederate takeover of the train was accomplished smoothly and efficiently. Two hundred of the men boarded the train, and the soldiers assigned to the engine and coal cars descended swiftly and dealt with their Union counterparts. They took possession of the engine at once, and Tim Zachary and his two helpers were held at gunpoint, forced to do the captors' bidding.

The occupation of the special freight cars containing the silver bullion was also achieved quickly and completely. The Rebels concentrated their largest individual force on this effort, and before the defenders quite realized what had happened, they had been made prisoners, their uniforms taken from them and donned by their captors.

By now, all the Union officers, including Toby Holt and Scott Foster, were bound and left under guard in their individual compartments in the sleeping car. Colonel Stannard sympathized with their plight, but in no way did he weaken. "I realize this is a heavy blow to your dignity," he said to Andy Brentwood after the takeover had been completed, "and I'm sorry about that, but it can't be helped. The important thing, as you well real-ize, is for me to make the entire train secure."

Andy strained at the bonds that tied his wrists and ankles and smiled ruefully. "I'm afraid I've got to hand it to you, Roger. You've outsmarted me."

Stannard nodded but did not reply.

"May I ask what disposition you're making of the ladies?"

Colonel Stannard replied loftily. "As I told you, the Confederacy doesn't make war on women. We're requir-ing a pledge of neutrality from the ladies, and once they give it, they'll be treated as our guests rather than as our prisoners."

Andy was inclined to doubt that a firebrand like Susanna Fulton or a true patriot like Beth Blake would give any such pledge, but not wanting to anticipate trouble for any of the women, he kept his own counsel. What really bothered him was what disposition would be made of Patricia. She and Ezekiel were in real jeop-ardy, but he decided to remain silent on the subject, at least for the time being. It would be time enough to lodge a protest if and when they were mistreated in some way.

The young women reacted sensibly to the shock of the attack. Captain Douglas de Forest had been charged with their security and supposedly would require them to pledge their neutrality, but his vanity interfered with his sense of duty. Showing off for Caroline Brandon's sake, he assured the young women that no harm would come to them, and he asked nothing in return, other than to say softly to Caroline, "I shall visit you in pri-vate when the occasion permits."

In spite of his seeming carelessness, however, he was taking no unnecessary risks, either. Four armed Rebel sentries were stationed in the corridor, two of them at either end of the rooms occupied by the women.

The situation that Ezekiel and Patricia faced was even more hazardous than Andy Brentwood had guessed. Ezekiel fought so furiously before he was subdued that as a further deterrent to escape, his shoes and stockings were removed when his feet were bound. After this had been done, one of the Rebel guards noted an old brand mark on the sole of his left foot.

"This man is an escaped slave," he said.

The lieutenant in charge of the detail examined the brand and promptly agreed.

This sealed Ezekiel and Patricia's fate. His status as a sergeant in the Union was ignored, as was his marriage. He would be treated as a runaway slave and undoubtedly would be sold to a new master. Similarly, Patricia was certain to be sold into slavery, too; it was irrelevant that she had been born and reared in freedom in the North.

Confederate troops wearing the uniforms of Union soldiers occupied the roofs of the railroad cars, and the train started up again and continued on its journey.

Andy Brentwood was anxious to learn all he could from the Confederate commander, and when he glanced out the window as the train gathered speed again, he guessed what was in store. "I gather," he said, "that we're headed for some point south of the Mason-Dixon line."

Roger Stannard nodded. "That's a fair enough guess," he said.

Andy glanced at Whip Holt, who was also bound hand and foot and occupied the seat opposite him, but Whip appeared to be paying no attention. "I must admit you make the operation seem simple, Roger," he said. "You disguise an appropriate number of soldiers as you pass through Union lines and then replace them with others in gray uniforms before you enter the Confederate lines."

Stannard smiled but made no comment.

Andy made a supreme effort to speak calmly. "We were always taught that simplicity was the essential key to any espionage or sabotage operation," he said, "and you've carried that principle to its logical conclusion."

"You're quick to see the whole scheme," Stannard told him.

"I wasn't quite quick enough," Andy said, "and I

reckon I'll be spending the rest of the war in a compound for prisoners, where I can mull over my shortcomings." He sighed and shook his head. "As much as I hate to do this, I'm forced to offer you my congratulations, Roger. You've delivered a tremendous blow to the Union."

Not until Colonel Stannard left the compartment, closing the door behind him, did Colonel Whip Holt come to life. "I wouldn't congratulate the Rebels just yet," he said. "The train isn't securely in their hands until it reaches its destination."

The engine's whistle sounded, its plaintive, high-pitched call echoing through the forests of southern Illinois, and Andy Brentwood winced. "We'll be past Confederate lines any minute now," he said. "From there on we'll be moving deeper and deeper into Rebel territory. I'm afraid we've lost the silver that President Lincoln so badly needs."

"Lost," Whip replied gently, "is pretty strong language. I'd say that we've misplaced the silver temporarily."

Andy stared at the older man. "You have something in mind," he said.

Whip shrugged as best as he was able with his hands securely fastened behind his back. "I've never been one to give up too soon," he said, "and I have a congenital hatred for surrendering prematurely."

Andy stared at him in wonder. This was the Whip Holt of legend. The facts were discouraging, to say the least. A strong Confederate force had taken control of the train, which was rolling unhampered into Rebel-held territory. The Union forces had been captured, their weapons had been removed, and there was literally nothing that they could do to regain command of the train. But Whip Holt refused to give up hope.

Andy was reminded of the stories his father had told about Whip fighting seemingly insurmountable odds against Indian warriors and other foes during his younger days in the mountains. Apparently he was incapable of admitting defeat.

Being more practical, Andy could not possibly agree with him, and he shook his head slowly. "I wish I could share your view," he said, "but I see no grounds for optimism."

"Optimism?" Whip raised an eyebrow. "I'm far from optimistic. I'd say our chances of regaining control of the train and returning to the North with it are very small. Maybe one in a hundred. But the way I grew up, we've got to take that chance. Are you with me?"

"You know I am, sir," Andy replied firmly. "No matter what may happen, I'm with you all the way."

Whip grinned for an instant and then looked complacent. "Glad to hear it," he said. "You might as well rest for a spell. There's nothing we can do until tonight, and I just hope that the Confederates save lamp oil by leaving us in the dark after night comes."

He offered no explanation and seemed to drift off to sleep.

Andy Brentwood lapsed into silence and glanced gloomily out the window at the thick foliage of the forest. Perhaps, he decided, Whip was trying to make him feel better by telling him that they had one chance in a hundred of salvaging the train and resuming their mission. In his opinion, the odds made their situation totally hopeless. Every passing moment brought them closer to defeat; he and Whip had been outsmarted by Roger Stannard.

Perhaps, if he could call attention to their plight when they reached the border, the train might be stopped by Union forces, but that faint hope faded when two Confederate officers, both of them armed with pistols, entered the compartment. "Colonel Holt, Major Brentwood," the senior of the pair said, "I trust you'll forgive me for speaking what is sure to sound like a threat. We're approaching the border now, and we'll be passing the last Union lines in a few minutes. I've been requested, gentlemen, to warn you to make no attempt to get in touch with any Union sentries we may pass. If you do, I'm under orders from Colonel Stannard to shoot both of you dead. Colonel Stannard says you know him well enough, Major, to realize that he means the order and expects it to be obeyed."

Andy stared at the pair's drawn pistols. "I take Roger Stannard's words literally, and I'm sure Colonel Holt does, too."

Whip said nothing but looked out the window at the passing scene.

The woods thinned, and the unhappy captives saw the heavy guns of Union artillery protecting what obviously was a major railroad yard. Then they saw breastworks raised for infantry, and as a final mortification they were forced to watch soldiers in blue waving cheerfully as the silver train sped past them.

The disguised Confederate troops returned the greetings of their supposed comrades.

If any officers in the Union camp wondered why the special train was rolling on and heading into Confederate territory, they did not think about it until it was too late to do something about it. One moment the train loomed up in the yards, and the next it disappeared. The senior Union officers on the site discussed the phenomenon but were unable to find a satisfactory answer and were forced to drop the matter. All they knew was that they were under orders to give freedom of passage to the special train, and they did.

The commander took the precaution of sending a telegram to the district commander in Saint Louis, and by the time the Union officers figured out that they had been fooled and that the train had been occupied by Confederates, it was too late to act. The train with its valuable cargo had moved safely into Confederate-held territory.

Somewhat to their surprise, the women passengers on the train were treated with great courtesy. They were asked to remain in their own compartments and not to wander anywhere on the train, and two sets of sentries saw to it that the order was obeyed. Otherwise, however, the young women were left to their own devices. Later in the afternoon a pair of lieutenants, now wearing their Confederate uniforms, went from room to room, lighting oil lamps, and Susanna Fulton, who had shown good sense by keeping very quiet, decided to find out what she could about their present situation. "What plans are being made for our supper?" she inquired innocently.

"Our cooks are at work," one of the lieutenants replied, "and your meal will be ready at about the time that ours is ready."

"But don't complain to us if you don't like the food," his companion added, grinning. "We're using up the Union supplies that we found on board the train." He spoke as much for Alison White's benefit as he did for Susanna's.

Alison smiled dutifully at the little joke. She already discovered that the Confederate officers treated her with great respect after learning that she was a British subject, and she had decided to take full advantage of their friendship.

"Where are we now?" she asked.

The elder of the Confederate lieutenants lowered his voice. "We're not supposed to answer questions like that, ma'am, but I don't mind telling you that we've crossed the border state of Kentucky, and we're now well into the Confederacy. We'll be going first to Memphis and then to Alabama."

Susanna's heart sank, and she was so afraid that she would reveal her feelings that she averted her face. The crossing of the train into the Confederacy meant the total failure of the Union's plans for the train. She was not concerned for her own safety, regarding it as likely that she—and any other woman who wished it—would be sent north after the train reached its destination. But she grieved because the Union had suffered a severe blow, and she was afraid that Andy Brentwood's military reputation was ruined. He would be known for the rest of his career as an officer who had been bested in a duel of wits by the Rebels.

The two young officers nodded and went on to the next compartment.

Caroline Brandon brightened when they came in and automatically began to flirt with them. She had been irritated by the upset in the train's arrangements, and the sudden reappearance of Douglas de Forest did not please her. He had used her in the past and undoubtedly planned to use her again in the future.

She had no idea what had become of Toby Holt, but she knew better than to ask outright about his whereabouts. It was far better to proceed cautiously and to learn what she could.

The young Confederate officers, influenced by her beauty and dazzled by the warmth of her reception, lingered for a time in her compartment but knew they had a duty to complete. So, vying with each other to leave the more lasting impression on Caroline, they took their leave and went on to Beth Blake's compartment.

There the atmosphere was far different. Beth sat erect in stone-faced silence and regarded the Rebel lieutenants with open contempt.

They had already learned that her father was a major general in the Union Army, so they were uncomfortable in her presence.

"Where is the young lady with whom I was sharing this compartment?" she demanded.

The elder of the officers had no idea what she meant and looked at her blankly.

The junior lieutenant believed that he grasped her meaning, however. "If you mean the black woman—"

"That's precisely who I mean!" Beth said emphatically.

The Confederate lieutenant shrugged. "Begging your pardon, ma'am, but she's no lady. Her husband is an escaped slave, so she's tarred with the same brush. If you want to see her again, you'll have a chance to buy her when they put her up for sale at the slave auction in Mobile."

Beth was so outraged that she was afraid she would only lose her temper and create serious problems for herself if she replied. So she clenched her teeth, digging her nails into the palms of her hands, and said nothing.

It was outrageous, inhuman, that Patricia and Ezekiel should be held as escaped slaves and treated accordingly, but she knew that there was nothing she could do to help her friends to overcome their predicament.

The Rebel lieutenants were aware of her intense displeasure, but they had no idea what caused it. They did not linger in the compartment to find out. A general's daughter—even the offspring of an enemy general—was best avoided.

At the opposite end of the car, Whip Holt appeared to be growing rigid, then relaxing, then straining once again against his bonds.

Andy Brentwood regarded him curiously. "If I didn't know better," he said softly, "I'd be inclined to believe that you're trying to break or slip out of your bonds, Colonel."

Whip grunted. "There's an old trick that your father and I used more than once when we were captured by Indians," he said. "I'll show you how it's done when we have a little time to spare. Meanwhile, just keep your ears open for possible visitors and hope that the Rebels don't bring us any supper soon."

Andy nodded and continued to watch him.

Whip worked steadily, first relaxing then straining, and ultimately, to the young officer's surprise, he freed his wrists.

Then, his lethargy vanishing, he acted with great, deliberate speed. Producing a short, sharp knife that he had somehow concealed in his shoe, he slashed the bonds that held his ankles and quickly set Andy Brentwood free, too.

He was wasting no gestures and was in dead earnest. This was the Whip Holt whose name had become a national byword and who was regarded throughout the United States as a legend in his own time. Certainly he was living up to his name. How he had managed to conceal the knife in his shoe from the Confederates was beyond Andy's knowledge, and as the younger officer watched him now, he realized that Whip Holt was far from helpless. He began to unwind his belt from his waist, and the realization dawned on Andy that instead of a belt, he was wearing the rawhide whip that had given him his nickname. When he grasped it firmly by the handle, he looked ready for anything.

It was almost dark in the compartment now, but Andy could make out the older officer as he gestured for silence and quietly opened the compartment door. A faint light showed in the corridor, and there, about fifteen feet from the compartment entrance, were two Rebel sentries deep in conversation. They were standing with their backs to the compartment door, and Whip instantly took advantage of that tactical error. His whip hissed as it snaked through the air, and before one of the sentries even knew what was happening to him, the leather had wrapped itself securely around him, pinning his arms to his sides.

Whip tugged at the leather, pulling it taut, and the sentry was rendered helpless. Andy Brentwood needed no instruction now; he rushed forward and snatched the rifle from the Rebel soldier's hand. Then, wielding it like a club, he brought the stock down with all of his strength on the head of the second guard.

The man staggered against the side of the car, then slumped to the floor, unconscious.

Whip took his rifle and hastened to jam a gag into the mouth of the sentry he had immobilized. Only then did he loosen the whip and tie the man's hands and feet.

Andy dragged both of the guards into the compartment that he and Whip were vacating and closed the door. The liberated pair hurried into the adjoining compartment, where a trussed Scott Foster and Toby Holt stared in surprise at them.

Whip made short work of their bonds with his knife, and now there were four officers who had attained at least temporary freedom.

Conversation was kept to a minimum. The need for weapons was self-evident, and Whip and Andy repeated their tactics with two more sentries, which gave the group more rifles and ammunition.

Toby and Scott were ecstatic, but Andy, evaluating the situation more cautiously, knew that the odds against them were still overwhelming. They were traveling deeper into Confederate territory, and the Rebels remained firmly in control of the train. A great deal remained to be done before the tide could be reversed.

Going from compartment to compartment, the quartet set a number of other officers free, and it soon appeared that the sleeping car, at least, could be reverted to their control. The key to that goal, although they didn't know it, developed almost by accident. Scott and Toby cautiously opened the door of a compartment that had previously been unoccupied and found two young Confederate officers standing guard over Ezekiel, who was tightly bound hand and foot. The Rebels were startled to see the two Union officers, and Scott struck the first blow before they could recover. Hurling himself at a Confederate lieutenant, both fists flailing, Toby attacked the other officer and subdued him after a brief but vicious fight. Now the freed Union officers acquired pistols and swords, as well as rifles.

Ezekiel's bonds were cut, and so great was his rage that he seemed on the verge of rampaging through the train. Andy Brentwood was required to exercise control over him immediately. "Sergeant," he said, "we have a long way to go. Follow orders and do nothing to alert the enemy."

The humiliated and deeply angered Ezekiel curbed his rage. "All right, Major," he muttered, "but I've got to find my wife."

"We'll find her," Andy said, and turned to his subordinates. "We'll try the women's compartments." With Scott close behind him, he went to the compartment occupied by Susanna and Alison. As he thrust the door open, expecting the worst, he was surprised to find the two young women sitting quietly, sipping mugs of coffee.

Before the astonished Susanna could recover, Andy embraced and kissed her. She was so elated over seeing him that she returned the gesture in full measure. There was no question in her mind about her feelings for Andy Brentwood.

Scott and Alison smiled at each other, but both were self-conscious and restrained.

Andy took in the situation quickly and spoke accordingly. "Thank God you women are all right," he said. "Now I want to see to it that you stay that way. We have some nasty business ahead, and I don't want you getting mixed up in it. Stay right here and don't leave this compartment, no matter what may happen."

Toby Holt went straight to Caroline Brandon's compartment and was astonished when she greeted him with wild enthusiasm, silently throwing her arms around his neck and pressing close to him. He had no way of knowing that Douglas de Forest had just succeeded in forcing his attentions on her and Caroline was still smarting, insulted beyond measure by his cavalier treatment, by his assumption that she was available whenever he felt like making love to her.

Toby whispered instructions to the young woman, telling her to stay out of harm's way.

Caroline shook her head. "I didn't give a damn one way or the other about this war," she declared, "but all that is changed now. I'll do anything to help you win! Anything!"

She was so obviously sincere that Toby stared at her for a long moment. "I'll keep that in mind," he said, "but in the meantime, stay out of trouble. Don't leave this compartment, no matter how much hell may be raised elsewhere in the car."

Ezekiel found his razor-sharp knife resting near his boots in a compartment at the end of the corridor. He put on his stockings and boots again, and now, having regained possession of his knife, his whole personality seemed to change. His wild, seething anger subsided and was replaced with a mood far more deadly, a calm, cold, determined air that boded ill for any man who stood in his way. Whip saw the expression in his eyes and knew that the black man was determined to have his own way.

"Now," Ezekiel announced, "I've got to find my wife."

Whip had no intention of denying him that privilege and decided to accompany him.

The door of the compartment adjoining Caroline's was closed, so it was possible that Patricia was being held there. Whip nodded toward the door, and the black man bounded to it, opening it cautiously inch by inch as he peered inside.

A single oil lamp was lighted, and in its soft glare they could see Patricia bound hand and foot and gagged, doubled on a seat. Nearby a pair of Confederate officers assigned to guard her were eating their supper, laughing and chatting, ignoring the frightened, miserable woman.

Ezekiel took in the scene and launched a furious, cold-blooded assault.

He made short work of the two unfortunate Rebel officers. One moment they were relaxing, enjoying their supper, and no doubt congratulating themselves on the ease of the assignment they had drawn. The next instant they were dead. One toppled to the floor with his throat cut from one ear to the other, while the other, attacked so swiftly that he had no chance to defend himself, succumbed as the knife plunged deep within him.

Ezekiel quickly set his wife free, and the grateful Patricia clung to him, tears dampening her lashes.

This was no time for long reunions, and Whip tapped Ezekiel on the shoulder. "There's work still to be done, Sergeant," he said brusquely.

Ezekiel promptly freed himself, murmured soothingly to his wife, and then asked, "Where can I leave Patricia, sir? I want to make good and sure she's safe."

A young woman's voice sounded behind them. "Leave her with me," Caroline Brandon said. "I'll see to it that no harm comes to her."

Ordinarily Caroline would have been the last member of the company whom Whip would have selected for the responsibility, but his judgment of character stood him in good stead. He heard the conviction in Caroline's voice and saw the sincerity in her face. Beth Blake would bristle at his giving Caroline such an assignment, but Caroline was a woman of far greater experience than Beth, and he knew that Patricia would be far better protected in her hands. He nodded and said to Patricia, "Stay with Caroline." There was no time to explain, and he hastily left the young women.

The freed officers worked out a rough plan of action. Scott and Toby volunteered to recapture the engine and coal cars from the Confederates, and when Ezekiel reappeared, Scott clapped the giant on the shoulder. "You're just the lad we need, Sergeant," he said. "Come with us if you want to see some real action."

The trio left the sleeping car and cautiously began to make their way forward through the train.

In all, seventeen officers had been freed, and Andy Brentwood assigned them the task of finding their troops, setting them free, and obtaining weapons for them. It was obvious that at least some of the prisoners were being held in the special cars that held the silver bullion, so a number of officers made their way toward the rear, intent on carrying out their mission promptly.

The element of surprise continued to benefit them. Whip had set the officers free to handle the problem as they saw fit, admonishing them only to abstain from using firearms whenever possible. Most of the Confederates on the train had no idea that their captives were regaining their liberty, and Whip wanted no shooting to break out prematurely and distract the enemy. The odds would favor the Union men now, provided they could maintain the element of surprise.

Whip was concerned about the whereabouts of Lieutenant Colonel Roger Stannard. He realized that the Confederate officer had provided the spark that had enabled the Rebels to succeed in capturing the train, and he wanted to neutralize the brilliant intelligence officer as rapidly as possible. There was no way of determining where he might be found on the train, but Whip had a hunch and acted accordingly.

So far, in freeing the prisoners in the sleeping car, one person had been noticeably absent. He had yet to see

Baron Bernhard von Hummel, and he had an idea that wherever the Prussian munitions maker might be, there Colonel Stannard would be, as well. He beckoned to Andy Brentwood, then led the way to the last remaining private quarters in the sleeping car, a double compartment that stood at the end of the car. They could hear voices inside, and Whip gestured for a halt, then eavesdropped.

"There's no reason for your company or any of the other Prussian manufacturers to lose business because of our capture of the train, Baron," Colonel Stannard was saying. "The silver is as good in our hands as it is in Union hands, and we're willing to pay you precisely what the North would have paid for the heavy guns that you're about to ship over. In fact, our need is even greater than the Union's."

Bernhard interrupted, sounding both incredulous and amused. "One moment, Colonel," he said. "Let me understand you correctly. First you and your men steal the silver in this train from the Union forces, then you propose to replace the Union in the business arrangements that they have made with the munitions makers of Prussia. You propose to replace them and to use the silver you have stolen to pay for the cannon that you wish delivered."

Roger Stannard laughed lightly. "That's exactly correct, Baron," he said. "You gain, and we gain. Only the North loses."

Andrew Brentwood did not wait for a signal from Whip Holt before acting. He pushed the door open and entered the compartment, a cocked pistol in each hand. "Sorry to interrupt you, Roger," he said, "and my apologies to you, Bernhard, but I think this is one deal in which the Union is not going to be disappointed and is not going to lose out."

The trio worked their way forward slowly through the coal cars. The Confederate soldiers who were feeding the engine were stripped to the waist, concentrating on moving considerable quantities of coal forward into the maw of the engine. So it was no great trick to take them by surprise.

Ezekiel was in the lead. His knife in his hand, he loomed over the Rebel soldiers one by one, and gesturing in pantomime, he gave them a clear, immediate choice. Either they would surrender or they would die. Without exception, they chose to live.

They were herded by Scott Foster and Toby Holt to one side of the rear coal car, and their weapons were confiscated, rendering them helpless. It was an easy matter to replace them with the Union soldiers whom the Confederates previously had captured, and soon the coal again flowed uninterruptedly.

Meanwhile, Scott and Toby made their way forward to the engine. There they made short work of dispatching the sentries who guarded Tim Zachary, and then they conferred with the engineer.

"It seems like my helpers and I were struck and had to cooperate with the Confederates," Zachary declared. "I'm the only professional engineer around, and nobody else on this train knows how to operate a steam engine. It may seem simple enough, but it ain't. Especially when you've got to switch tracks and you're carrying a mighty heavy cargo."

Scott peered out through the gloom of night at the dimly seen shapes beyond the railroad tracks. "Do you have any idea where we are, Tim?" he wanted to know.

Tim Zachary grimaced. "I'm familiar with every inch of these here tracks," he said. "I know the whole line blame near as well as I know my own hand. We're deep in Tennessee now, and we're heading straight for Memphis."

"Memphis," Toby said, concerned, "is a major Rebel military headquarters. We sure don't want to wind up there."

The engineer shrugged. "We ain't got too much choice, Lieutenant," he said. "There's nowheres on the tracks that we can make a loop and head back in the opposite direction. Besides, we'd be askin' for a heap of trouble if we did. The Rebels would be sure to halt us because they'd figure there was somethin' fishy about our travelin' back toward the North."

The problem was one that had to be presented to Whip. Whether he could find a solution for the dilemma was questionable, but no one else in the Union command was in a position to do so.

Leaving Ezekiel in charge of the detail assigned to assist the engineers, Scott and Toby made their way back to the sleeping car. They instructed the sergeant to take no risks in the event that trouble erupted with the Confederates again; he was under orders to shoot to kill.

By now, the recapture of the train was complete. The Union officers had freed their own men and were now holding the Confederates prisoners. Douglas de Forest, who was in the dining car drinking a glass of brandy, was furious when he was overcome and captured. Behaving with typical recklessness, he put up a fight, and it required three men to subdue him and take him captive.

Scott and Toby found Whip and Major Andy Brentwood closeted with Baron von Hummel and the deposed Confederate commander of the train.

"I admire your spirit, gentlemen," Lieutenant Colonel Roger Stannard was saying genially, a steely undercurrent in his voice, "but you'll have to come to some sort of an accommodation with me. You're deep in the Confederacy now, and your troops are badly outnumbered. Perhaps we can come to an arrangement of some sort whereby you and your men will be returned to the Union lines, and in return for setting you free, the Confederacy will take possession of this train and its contents."

Whip smiled faintly and shook his head. "I don't rightly regard that as much of a bargain, Colonel," he said. "Besides, I believe in living up to my obligations. President Lincoln is expecting me to deliver the bullion this train is carrying to the Treasury Department in New York City. As you well know. The President has a great many problems that are plaguing him these days, and I'd be the last to want to disappoint him."

Baron von Hummel looked at the mountain man with undisguised admiration. Granted that Whip Holt had regained control of the train, but the odds against him were still overwhelming. He did not appear discouraged, however, and his atitude was quietly defiant without being boastful.

Andy Brentwood had to admire his superior, too, Had he himself been in overall command of the train, he might have been inclined to listen to Roger Stannard's offer and, perhaps, to bargain with him in order to avoid unnecessary bloodshed. Certainly he could see no way that the train with its clumsy cargo of silver could be safely returned to Union hands. But Whip apparently thrived on challenges.

Just then, Toby and Scott appeared. They asked to speak with Whip privately, and when he joined them in the corridor outside the compartment, they brought him up to date on the situation.

He frowned thoughtfully as he listened. Then placing two guards in charge of Roger Stannard, he retired to his own compartment with Andy, Scott, and Toby.

"Tell me about Tennessee's loyalties in the war," he said. "I'm a mite confused about just where the state stands."

"I don't blame you for being confused, sir," Scott replied. "The people of Tennessee share your confusion. The eastern part of the state is one hundred percent pro-Union, but Memphis is strictly in the Confederate camp, as are the other towns of the western and southern part of the state. As to Nashville, I'm blamed if I know."

"From the intelligence dispatches I've read," Andy said, "I'd be inclined to believe that Nashville is split wide open. There are as many people in town who are Union supporters as there are Rebels."

Accompanied by the two young men, Whip made his way forward to the engine to speak with Tim Zachary. The engineer turned over control of the train to one of his assistants and retired to the rear of the cab.

"Tell me what you know about the tracks in Tennessee," Whip commanded.

The engineer pushed his cap onto the back of his head and shrugged. "There ain't much to tell, Colonel," he replied. "There's one double set of tracks that goes from Memphis to Nashville, and at Nashville you have a choice. Either you take the tracks that carry you down deeper into the Confederacy, or you follow another set that will take you north, to Louisville, Kentucky."

Whip was silent for a moment. "Are you familiar with the switches in Nashville that would put us on one or the other of these tracks?" he demanded.

Zachary nodded. "Sure," he said, "but that ain't sayin' much, Colonel. First we gotta get there." The engineer scratched his head. "Now, it sounds easy enough: the tracks comin' into Memphis follow the river, and from there they head due east, so all I gotta do is open up the throttle, and we'll head straight for Nashville. The same is true once we get there. The tracks to Louisville are so easy to find that I could locate 'em blindfolded, but that ain't our problem."

"I know," Whip replied. "We're trapped in the midst of tens of thousands of Rebel troops, and one false move can mean the end of us and the destruction of our mission. It seems to me we'll have to proceed with caution so we don't make any false moves." He returned to the sleeper car and, summoning Andy Brentwood, sat down with him, Scott, and Toby to plan the audacious scheme he had in mind. The odds against his success were overwhelming, but he pointed out emphatically, "We have everything to gain and blame little to lose. We're obliged to take some terrible chances because we have no choice."

The four officers sat up for the better part of the night as they went over every detail of the complex plan, leaving nothing to chance. In the morning, after snatching a brief rest for a couple of hours, Whip summoned his entire officer corps and outlined the scheme.

"What we've got to do, lads, is to convince the Rebels in Memphis that we're Confederates, too," he said. "Major Brentwood will act as our spokesman because he speaks with a Missouri accent that's close enough to

Southern to pass without arousing suspicions. Every Rebel on board this train—and I include every officer, every enlisted man—will be incarcerated under lock and key during the time we're actually in Memphis. If need be we'll gag every last one of them to make certain that they don't give us away. We've had a taste of Rebels disguising themselves in our uniforms, and now the shoe is on the other foot. We're going to help ourselves to their uniforms. Any questions?"

A company commander raised his hand. "How do we prevent Rebels from boarding the train in Memphis, sir?" he asked.

"That," Whip replied flatly, "is very simple. We make it clear that no one boards the train. We'll invent some phony orders from the Confederate War Department to that effect, and the rule will apply to everyone, including generals and colonels. Your men will threaten prospective boarders with rifle fire, and if necessary they'll actually use their rifles to prevent boarders. That's basic. If we can convince the authorities in Memphis that we're genuine Rebels, we'll be well on our way to achieving an impossible victory. In that case I don't anticipate another crisis until we reach Nashville, and with Memphis behind us, the obstacles in Nashville should be relatively easy to overcome."

His confidence was contagious, although the more sober of the Union officers had to admit that the risks were breathtaking.

Roger Stannard was bound, gagged, and kept under heavy guard in a locked compartment. The officers of his staff were similarly treated and locked in an adjoining compartment, although the bound Douglas de Forest struggled and swore so violently that he was put into a compartment by himself.

"I'll show you, damn Yankees," he muttered between gritted teeth. "I'll get out of here if it's the last thing in the world I do!" His captors paid him no heed as they left him and locked the door. Under no circumstances, Whip ordered, was anyone to be admitted to that compartment.

Now the Confederate enlisted men were herded into one of the silver bullion cars where they were stripped to their underwear and held under lock and key. Since it was not feasible to gag that many men, the Northerners made the position of their prisoners very plain to them. "Some of you," Major Brentwood told the captives, "may get the bright idea of calling for help or notifying your comrades in Memphis that you're being held prisoner and that the men who are presumably Confederate troops are nothing but impersonators. If any man has conceived the idea of becoming an instant hero, I urgently advise him to change his mind. My troops are under orders to open fire on any man who dares to make a sound, and I assure you that they'll shoot to kill at short range, so if you want to survive, you'll keep your mouths shut and will remain very, very quiet."

Andy Brentwood encountered some difficulty in putting together a Confederate uniform that was large enough to fit him but managed at last. On his shoulders were Roger Stannard's insignia as a lieutenant colonel.

Whip, whose fame was as great in the South as it was in other parts of what had been the United States, agreed to remain undercover during the halt in Memphis.

Every Union soldier was taking part in the deception, and Tim Zachary and the assistant engineers had been drilled in the roles they would play, as well. The train gradually slowed its pace as it drew nearer to Memphis, and when it reached the town on the Mississippi River that had become an important port for cotton and agricultural products, it slowed to a crawl.

Obviously its arrival was expected. Confederate troops bearing rifles were in evidence on both sides of the tracks, and grinning broadly, they waved the train on. Eventually a signal to halt was given by an officer who stood on a tower platform near the tracks, and the train ground to a stop. What happened next would be critical.

Andy Brentwood, disguised as a Rebel lieutenant colonel, dismounted from the train and was followed by Toby Holt, who was disguised as his aide and wore a captain's insignia. They walked only a few paces and halted when they were confronted by a full colonel of Rebel infantry, whose staff was clustered behind him. "I'm Auguste Leland, Colonel Stannard," he said, returning Andy's crisp salute. "I offer you my felicitations. I didn't think you'd be able to carry off such an elaborate hoax, but damned if you didn't do it. Is the cargo what you anticipated?"

Andy exaggerated his Missouri accent somewhat. "The cargo didn't disappoint us, sir," he said. "In fact, we're considerably richer because of it."

Colonel Leland chuckled approvingly. "Glad to hear it," he said. "I assume you'll be heading south to Alabama now."

The Union men faced their first real crisis. "No, sir," Andy replied. "My orders have been changed, and I've been directed to proceed to Nashville."

Colonel Leland was surprised. "The War Department didn't tell me," he said. "That's strange."

Andy knew that the less explanation he offered, the better it would be for him. "I have no idea why the plans were changed, Colonel," he said.

Leland shrugged. "No matter," he said. "We've taken possession of this train, and that's what matters. What can I do for you, Colonel?" he asked.

"Well, sir," Andy said carefully, "we'll appreciate whatever you can spare in the way of rations."

"Certainly," the Confederate officer replied. "Just tell my supply officer where you want his men to put the food cases, and they'll be brought right on board."

Again Andy had to maneuver delicately. "If it's all the same to you, Colonel," he said, "the crates and boxes can be left next to the tracks, and my own men will attend to taking the supplies onto the train."

Colonel Leland was surprised and raised an eyebrow.

"I'm just following my orders to the letter, sir," Andy explained. "I'm under strict instructions to allow no one but my own personnel on board the train."

The Confederate colonel was disappointed. "I had my

heart set on getting a glimpse of all that lovely silver," he said.

Under no circumstanses could Andy permit him to enter one of the cars where the bullion was stored, as he would see scores of Rebel prisoners being held at rifle point.

"I suppose," Colonel Leland continued, "you could get around your orders?"

Andy thought rapidly. He was being invited to disobey the supposed instructions he had received from the Confederate War Department, and inasmuch as the Rebel officer outranked him, it would be extremely awkward to refuse the request. By giving in to it, however, he knew he would be obliged to take Colonel Leland prisoner and to hold him as a captive. So be it. He had no real choice in the matter. "When we're ready to pull out, Colonel," he said, "perhaps you can join me on board for a bon voyage drink."

Leland grinned and winked.

Andy Brentwood's mind raced, and he looked meaningfully at Toby, trying hard to convey a message to him. Whatever lack of rapport they had experienced earlier throughout the journey was now completely forgotten. Toby knew precisely what his superior had in mind. He nodded, then slipped away and reboarded the train. It would be necessary to prepare a special reception for Colonel Leland.

The food that the Confederates were supplying for the rest of the voyage was piled adjacent to the train, and the soldiers disguised in Confederate uniforms appeared and proceeded to load the cartons and crates on board. They worked swiftly but without displaying undue haste, and within a short time they completed the task.

Hoping that Toby had prepared an appropriate reception for the high-ranking Confederate officer, Andy knew the time had come to act. "Colonel," he said, "perhaps you'd like to ride with us a short distance. I suggest that your staff meet you at the point where we pass the Wolf River."

"A splendid idea," Colonel Leland replied, realizing he could not be accused of delaying the train's departure. He smiled jovially.

Andy indicated with a gesture that he wanted the Rebel officer to precede him onto the train. Colonel Leland climbed on board, and as Andy followed, he gave a prearranged wave that would tell Tim Zachary to begin the next phase of the escape. The train was beginning to move as the two officers reached the corridor of the sleeping car where Toby Holt awaited them. "This way, sir," he said, leading the Confederate to the open door of a compartment. There Caroline Brandon, smiling provocatively, awaited him. She had had almost no time to prepare for the role that Toby had quickly outlined for her, but she was fully made up as usual, and her off-the-shoulder gown of yellow velvet was just right for the part she was expected to play.

Colonel Leland was astonished. The last sight he had expected to see on board the train was an exceptionally attractive young woman. He blinked at Caroline, whose smile broadened.

"This is a great honor, Colonel," she said, and Andy was startled to hear her speak in a thick Southern drawl.

If her accent was less than perfect, the bemused Colonel Leland did not know it. He returned the smile of the green-eyed beauty and chuckled as he addressed Andy over his shoulder. "Your cargo, Colonel Stannard," he said, "is even more impressive than I imagined it would be."

"Let me offer you a drink, Colonel," Caroline said, handing him a stiff whiskey and water that had already been prepared in great haste.

Andy and Toby withdrew discreetly but left the compartment door ajar. This was not the moment for Andy to express his surprise. He had anticipated that Toby would enlist the support of Susanna Fulton, perhaps, but it hadn't crossed his mind that he would enlist the services of Caroline. Come to think of it, however, Caroline was far better suited to the part that she was playing so perfectly.

He waited impatiently in the corridor. Toby stood beside him, listening intently, and when Caroline's high-pitched laugh floated out of the compartment, it appeared to be a signal that the time had come to act. Toby promptly drew his pistol and stepped into the compartment, again with Andy at his heels. Colonel Leland was taking his ease. His tunic was unbuttoned, and somehow Caroline had managed to persuade him to rest his pistol on the seat beside him.

Toby Holt moved swiftly. "Colonel," he said pointing his own pistol directly at the Confederate officer, "I regret to inform you, sir, that you are our prisoner."

The astonished Leland began to sputter. Andy Brentwood cut him short. "I'm afraid you won't be rejoining your staff today, Colonel," he said. "And it won't be possible to show you the silver, either. You'll be made as comfortable as the circumstances warrant."

He and Toby proceeded to bind Colonel Leland's ankles and wrists securely, then helped themselves to his handkerchief, which they intended to use as a gag. Before they stuffed it into his mouth, however, he stared at the two officers, then at the lovely young woman who appeared unperturbed by his capture. "I refuse to believe," he said, "that this beautiful lady is a bandit!"

"You're quite right, Colonel," Andy agreed. "She's no more a bandit than we are. She happens to be a patriotic citizen of the United States, who is doing her duty in a wartime mission."

He jammed the handkerchief into the officer's mouth, then led him away to join the real Lieutenant Colonel Roger Stannard in closely guarded captivity.

Toby lingered behind for a moment. "That was perfect!" he told Caroline. "You did everything I asked of you and then some. The Union Army is very much in your debt."

Caroline was pleased with his praise. She was also happy that she had helped to settle a score of her own. She would not forget the lies and deceits to which Douglas de Forest had subjected her, and the more she was able to help the Union men, the more she could get back at the Southerner.

The train gathered speed slowly, and it sped past the spot where Colonel Leland had arranged to meet the members of his staff. They had not yet arrived at the rendezvous, which was all to the good. By the time they realized that he was not going to appear, the train would be well on its way to Nashville. The first step had been successful in surmounting the crisis that faced the little Union force.

X

"We're doing well," Patricia commented as the bullion train rocketed eastward through Tennessee. "In fact, we're doing so well I'm afraid that this whole scheme will blow up in our faces."

Beth Blake thought she was being unduly pessimistic, and the other women were inclined to agree.

"I grew up listening to my father, who has fought in more than his share of battles," Beth said. "And I learned something from him. When your cause is right and just, you never give in to despair or fear. Those are the worst enemies of anyone who takes part in a battle. You persevere, you know your cause is right, and somehow you win. I have no idea how we're going to make out on this journey, but I'm truly not worried about it. The men in charge of our forces know what they're doing, and I'm positive we'll triumph."

Despite Beth's courageous words, tensions soared when they passed a Confederate troop train traveling in the opposite direction. But to the intense relief of all the Union adherents on board, nothing untoward developed. The engineers exchanged whistles, and Confederate troops exchanged waves with their supposed colleagues on the silver train. No one suspected the real identity of the operators of the bullion train.

When they reached the outskirts of Nashville, they encountered the first signs of trouble. In a railroad yard just outside the town, where unused freight cars sat unattended, the train unexpectedly ground to a halt.

Almost immediately, Whip and Andy Brentwood rushed forward to the engine. They noted as they approached it that members of the crew they had assigned under Ezekiel's command were hastily refilling the coal cars with coal that they shoveled from a large pile that stood beside the tracks.

"What's wrong?" Whip demanded. "Why have we stopped?"

Tim Zachary looked deeply troubled as he said, "We've hit a real snag, Colonel, and that's for certain. The main line between here and Louisville is closed."

Whip stared at him in dismay, and Andy swallowed hard. Catastrophe had struck swiftly and unexpectedly.

"According to a signal man," Zachary went on, "there was fighting between partisans somewhere in the hills north of here, and they tore up the tracks for a mile or two. They destroyed enough to make the line useless, and it won't be repaired for days."

Whip Holt was at his best in moments of supreme emergency, never giving in to a sense of panic and calmly considering all alternatives to the plan on which so much depended. "What's our choice, Tim?" he demanded.

The engineer sighed heavily. "We ain't got no real choice, Colonel," he said. "We can either head back to Memphis, which I don't like, or we can follow the southeastern line that'll take us down toward Georgia and Alabama by way of Chattanooga."

Andy's heart sank. "Chattanooga," he said, "is the most important Confederate military base in all of Tennessee."

Whip made no comment as he looked out of the engine. Ahead were assembled at least two companies of Rebel infantry, and there were enough mounted troops in the vicinity to indicate that there were cavalry units in the local garrison, too. Clearly, the Confederates in Nashville were still in control of the city, and there was no way the train could linger here without many questions being asked. His train had become a potential land mine that could explode at any minute.

He made up his mind at once. "We can't just sit here

taking on coal indefinitely," he said. "The Rebel garrison of Nashville is nearby, and the senior officers are sure to be curious. We were lucky—incredibly lucky—that we got out of Memphis without any trouble, but we can't count on that sort of thing happening again. Take the line to Chattanooga, and we'll see what we can develop that will get us out of an even worse predicament."

Zachary sighed, recalled the troops loading coal, and once the men climbed aboard, he started forward again, taking the switching to the line that bore to his right and would carry the train toward the southeast.

Andy was silent as he followed Whip back to their compartment, where Toby was elected to bring every railroad map of the area that he could find. A portable table was erected, and the maps were spread out on it.

Andy studied them in silence. "Well," he said, "with the Louisville line out of use, it looks like we don't have much choice."

The symbols and signs on a railroad map meant very little to Whip, and he deferred to his son, whose fledgling career in railroading made him a valuable asset at this critical time.

"Do you agree that our situation is hopeless, Toby?" he asked.

His son bent low over the map, examining it with infinite care. "Maybe so, maybe not," he said. He was silent for a long time, then said, "The way I see it, we have two problems. We've got to have clear access to the North in order to get clear of the Confederacy, and unfortunately we're going to be badly in need of fuel. We didn't stop long enough in the Nashville yard to fill the coal cars, and they'll be just about empty by the time we reach Chattanooga."

Andy hated to admit that the cause appeared hopeless.

Toby took a knife from its sheath and used the point to illustrate his words. "Look here," he said, and the others bent low over the map. "You see this thin line near Chattanooga? That indicates a spur line that loops

265

around the city in order to direct trains from the busy main tracks. It also reroutes trains north."

Andy began to take heart.

"I have a suggestion," Toby said, "and even before I make it, I'll grant you it isn't perfect, but it's the best I can come up with under the circumstances. I suggest we get ourselves onto the loop, which will make it possible for us to avoid going into Chattanooga itself and encountering the local Confederate garrison there. We follow the loop until we find ourselves well outside the town, heading north." He made a sweeping circle with the knife.

"Then," he continued, "comes the tricky, dangerous part of my scheme. We'll have run out of coal, more or less, by that time, so I propose we halt and wait for another train to come up behind us. You'll note that the track is single line, so that means that sooner or later another train is bound to appear. What kind of a train it'll be, I have no idea, and it's a waste of time to speculate. All I want to point out to you is that there's obviously no way we can be moved off the track by the train that comes up behind us." He took a deep breath. "I suggest we steal their coal and make a dash for the Union border, by which time the tracks to Louisville should be repaired."

Andy shook his head slowly. "I hate to think of all the things that could go wrong with that scheme," he said. "The possibilities are endless."

"I know," Toby said, "but we're in a desperate situation, and I don't think we have much choice."

"We have none," Whip said flatly. "I'm open to any other idea that you want to present to me, Andy, but I'm afraid that whether we like it or not, we'll have to adopt this scheme of Toby's."

Whip ordered food and water rationed as the train started toward Chattanooga. There were twice as many mouths to feed as there were supplies, thanks to the Confederate captives, and there was no telling when additional food and water might be available. "We'll have to make do with what's on hand," Whip said grimly, "and we'll have to tighten our belts."

To the credit of the Union Army regulars and the Nevada militiamen alike, not one man objected or grumbled. All recognized the extreme difficulties under which their officers were laboring, and they accepted the short rations cheerfully. A few suggested that the Confederate captives be denied food and water, but the majority agreed that, regardless of the outcome of the strange adventure, their adversaries should be treated with decency and respect.

Late in the night, shortly after the train left Nashville, the sounds of sustained rifle fire could be heard in the distance. It appeared that a battle was in progress. Those on the train never learned any details of the engagement, but they were heartened to know there were others who believed in the cause of the Union who were fighting nearby.

The journey to Chattanooga was interminable, and tempers began to grow short. The train had been meandering through the South for some time now, and the Union men were eager to end their wandering and to bring their journey to a successful conclusion.

In spite of the ever-present danger of traveling through Confederate territory, the motion of the train was monotonous, conducive to sleep, so the young ladies—who had no real responsibilities and no reason for staying alert—became drowsy, and one by one they went off to bed.

As she lay in her berth, Susanna Fulton stayed awake, composing in her mind the startling news story she intended to write when the train finally reached Union territory. Lying in the other berth, Alison White was preoccupied with thoughts far more personal. She couldn't help worrying about Scott Foster, hoping that he was all right and was not subjecting himself to undue risks.

In the adjoining compartment, Beth Blake felt strangely powerless, unable to do anything, unable to contribute to the cause that meant so much to her. It was strange, she reflected, but this was one time when she could do nothing to help. Meanwhile, Patricia was too frightened to think clearly. She and her husband had narrowly escaped being enslaved, and the threat of the fate that awaited her if the train again fell into the hands of Confederates haunted her. She prayed constantly that the Union forces would prevail.

Bernhard von Hummel sat alone in his private compartment, sipping brandy from a snifter and ruminating on the strange fate that had led him into this weird adventure. He spent little time thinking of himself, however, and found his thoughts centering more and more on Beth Blake. He had to admit to himself that he was growing increasingly interested in her. She was far livelier, far more independent, infinitely more forthright than any European woman he had ever known. He found it difficult to imagine her in Prussia as his wife, but he told himself he didn't yet know her well enough to project her into that role. He was moving too fast, and he warned himself to act more slowly and think more slowly, progressing one step at a time.

A bored Caroline Brandon was the last to extinguish her oil lamp, and after a time she dropped off into a light sleep.

Suddenly she was jolted wide awake. A hand was clamped over her mouth, making it impossible for her to speak, and her shoulders were pinned to her berth. She recoiled in terror and opened her eyes. As she became accustomed to the gloom, she made out the familiar features of Captain Douglas de Forest.

"Don't make a sound, or I'll be obliged to kill you," he said. "I'm not joking."

She knew by his tone that he meant every word, and she nodded as vigorously as she could to indicate her agreement.

De Forest stared at her for a time and finally decided to take a chance on her. He released his tight grip over her mouth.

"You needn't be so rough," Caroline complained. "I'm

sure I'm going to be bruised after the way you handled me."

He shrugged, and his indifference was also apparent in his tone. "Sorry," he muttered, "but there are some things that are necessary, very necessary."

"Is it needful to press my shoulders down as though I were in a vise?" Caroline demanded bitterly. "You ought to know by now that you're bigger and stronger than I am, Douglas. I'm hardly in a position to hurt you."

She sat up in her bunk, conscious of her negligee. De Forest immediately caught hold of her wrist. "Oh, no, you don't!" he exclaimed.

"Really," she said indignantly. "This is too much. I don't see what harm it does you if I put on my robe."

De Forest laughed a trifle sheepishly. "I reckon my nerves are on edge," he said. "Don't mind me."

Caroline pulled on her peignoir. "Whatever in the world happened to you, Doug?" she demanded. "The last I knew, you were a prisoner of the Union forces— you and all the other Rebels on this train."

His laugh was harsh, and there was a quality in it— something Caroline could not quite define—that sent shivers up her spine. "You're right," he said, "I was a prisoner, but I'm not anymore. Because of this!" He pulled out a knife that had been cleverly concealed in his boot. "And I don't mind telling you that a Yankee lieutenant and three of his enlisted men have gone to meet their Maker."

Caroline gasped.

He could not resist posturing for her benefit. "That'll teach the Yanks to treat Doug de Forest with the respect he deserves," he said. "They should have known that I would not submit all that easily."

Caroline stared at him and felt certain that he was not exaggerating. Somehow he had succeeded in killing a Union officer and three of his men. What stunned her was not so much that he had committed the deed—after all, she had seen and had become accustomed to a great deal of violence on this journey—but it was his attitude that upset her. He was calm, and in no way did the violence in which he had participated disturb him. Apparently he could commit murder with a totally clear conscience.

"Now," he said, "I need your help. I've got to have your help."

So he had remembered her existence and had turned to her! Making no attempt to hide her resentment, she said, "Why me?"

Never had Douglas de Forest's smile been more charming, never had his voice been more ingratiating. "Why, honey," he said, "you're the natural person for me to come to. After all, you're going to be my wife." He reached out and deliberately fondled her breasts beneath the thin fabric of her silk nightgown.

Caroline's instinct was to shrink from him. His very touch made her flesh crawl, and she wanted no part of him. How dare he! He had taken her for granted and then had forgotten her entirely. Now he needed her, apparently, so he was remembering her existence, thinking she would do his bidding.

"What is it you want of me?" she demanded, her voice hoarse.

He thought he heard a sound in the corridor outside her room and, gesturing for silence, drew a pistol from a holster at his side and cocked it. She knew from his expression that he would indeed shoot to kill. He was desperate.

Having satisfied himself that no one was abroad in the corridor outside the compartment, he went to the door and locked it. Then he relaxed again somewhat and lowered his arm.

"Put that firearm away," Caroline said. "It makes me nervous."

He looked at her and laughed savagely but complied with her request.

She was able to breathe a bit easier. "I repeat: what is it you want me to do?"

He chuckled, but his grin was mirthless. "I've tried to think of some way to regain control of this train, but I'm afraid that it's beyond me. So I have another plan. In about two hours from now, at dawn, we'll be passing a major Confederate military installation. I'm going to ask you to create a disturbance of some kind that will cause the train to be slowed down temporarily. I'll make my way to a platform at the end of a car, and I'll drop off at the Confederate camp. Then I'm going to tell the commandant about this train, and you can bet your last dollar that every soldier in the Confederate Army will be gunning for it."

Caroline was too unfamiliar with military tactics to know whether his scheme was sound. All she realized was that she had to discourage him, and she hit on what seemed to her to be a likely reason. "There are sentries stationed on the platforms at the end of each car," she said. "They'll kill you."

He laughed again. "I think you got that a mite mixed up, honey," he said. "I'll be looking for them, but they don't even know that I've escaped and that I'm on the loose. I'll just add a few more Northern scalps to my belt, that's all."

She was afraid he would succeed in doing precisely what he said. She had not realized that he could be so determined. This man whom she had contemplated marrying was actually a cold-blooded fanatic, who would do anything for the cause in which he believed.

"You can use any excuse you please for convincing the Union people of your sincerity," he said. "Tell them you had a bad dream or something of the sort, anything just so they've slowed or stopped the train. They might not like it, but there's not much they can do about it." He chuckled dryly.

"Then what will happen to me?" Caroline asked sharply.

"Why that's simple," he said glibly. "Our troops—thousands of them, if need be—will stop this train. You and the other young women on board will be safe, naturally. I'll have told the Confederates of the key role that you've played, and you'll be treated as you deserve—like a heroine."

She nodded but made no comment. It was obvious to her, as he improvised, that he hadn't really concerned himself with her future.

Unaware of her lack of enthusiasm, he enlarged on his theme. "As a matter of fact, we'll both be celebrated," he said. "I'm certain to get a promotion—maybe even a double promotion—after the silver rests safely in Confederate hands. So when we go off together to my father's plantation in Mississippi, everybody will look up to both of us."

Once again Caroline was overwhelmed with disgust and loathing for this man. That he could think she was so gullible that she would still swallow his story! But she decided that the best way to gain control of the situation was to remain calm and pretend to go along with him, so she said pleasantly, "You paint a very attractive picture."

Convinced that he had impressed her, he caressed her again, failing to notice that she shrank from his touch. He eyed her with greater interest, and suddenly he chuckled. "Since we have an hour or two to kill before dawn breaks," he said, "I suggest we pass the time in the most pleasant of all possible ways."

Caroline's blood ran cold. Under no circumstances could she accept this man's lovemaking now. The mere thought of it turned her stomach. But she was not for a moment forgetting that de Forest was armed with a pistol and a sharp knife, both of which he was capable of using. So she smiled broadly, and before he could stop her, she climbed swiftly out of her bunk.

"Where are you going?" he demanded.

Never had her voice been so innocent nor her expression so guileless. "Why, I'm—going to get us some brandywine, naturally. I know how much you enjoy it."

He considered the offer, then nodded. "Well now, that's right nice of you," he said. "You're going to be just the right wife for me."

His words filled her with bitterness and sealed her resolve. She knew now what needed to be done.

She made her way to a metal cupboard in the bulkhead, and while Doug divested himself of his boots and the belt on which he carried his pistol, she opened the cupboard and then tapped lightly at the door that separated her chamber from Beth Blake's.

"What was that?" de Forest demanded sharply.

"What was what?" she replied blandly.

"I heard a knocking of some sort," he said.

She shook her head. "The train was probably jolting over some stretch of roadbed," she said calmly. "I didn't hear anything." With one hand she poured brandywine into two glasses, and with the other, she silently unlocked the door. She could only pray that Beth would awaken and would have the good sense and the courage to come to her assistance. She needed help, she knew, and she could not possibly handle a desperate Douglas de Forest alone.

He seized his glass, downed it in a single gulp, and then reached for her, pulling her to him roughly. Caroline yielded to him because she had no choice. As he kissed her, she heard the door creak open a few inches and remain ajar. Opening her eyes, she saw the bewildered Beth standing in the frame, clutching her bathrobe around her. Caroline knew that she needed to reveal more of the situation to her as soon as possible.

Breaking away from de Forest, although he still cradled her in his arms, Caroline said, "I'm afraid for you, Doug. You're proposing that you take on the whole Union Army, and I don't care how many more of them you may kill, you're still outnumbered on this train by hundreds to one." There! That should be sufficient to inform Beth.

De Forest chuckled but made no reply, and his grip tightened.

Caroline continued to stall for time. "How will I know," she asked, "when to make the fuss that will cause the train to slow down? It's far too dark outside this window for me to see a Confederate military camp."

"Never fear," he said, pressing closer to her. "You just do what you're told, and everything will be fine. Right now, all you've got to do is relax and enjoy yourself." He lowered her to the bunk, his weight pressing on top of her.

Beth Blake had heard all she needed to hear. She advanced silently into the compartment, braced herself, and looked around wildly. Her glance fell on de Forest's double-edged knife, which was lying now on a chair beside his boots, and she seized it, taking a firm grip on the handle.

De Forest's lovemaking became more intense, and Caroline wriggled in pretended ecstasy, praying that Beth would hurry. She did not have long to wait.

Suddenly Beth's cold, crisp voice filled the compartment, and although she did not realize it, she sounded remarkably like her father. Any of Major General Leland Blake's subordinates would have known instantly that she was his daughter. "Rebel," she said, "raise your hands high above your head and stand up slowly. Very slowly. Don't try any tricks or stunts because this knife of yours is sharp, and I guess you know it can do a lot of damage." She pressed the point into the small of his back.

De Forest stiffened, his mind working rapidly. He realized that he'd been bested, at least for the moment, so he did as Beth directed. His eyes smoldering, he looked at Caroline, whose bland, broad smile told him all too clearly where she stood.

"You damn little bitch," he said. "You tipped her off! I don't know how you did it, but you told her I was here!"

Caroline made no reply; none was necessary.

Suddenly de Forest lunged for his pistol in his holster on the chair.

Caroline knew him well—almost too well—as she later confessed to Toby. She had been anticipating just such a move, and she leaped into action. Her responses were quicker than de Forest's, and her hand closed before his did on the butt of the gun. She drew it, although she was unable to control the shaking of her hand.

Douglas de Forest looked at the two young women, glancing first at one and then at the other. Caroline had beaten him to his pistol, but he very much doubted that she had the courage to fire it at him. As to the other woman, he was convinced that she was capable of using his knife and probably would relish carving him with it. He was in a serious spot and had to do something quickly.

"We'll call for attention," Beth said, "and wake up some of the officers. They'll take charge of this prisoner."

De Forest was about to comment but changed his mind. The young woman with the Northern accent seemed to have ice water running in her veins. He shifted his position in an attempt to become more comfortable.

"None of that," Caroline warned. "You keep your hands over your head and don't try any of your stunts. I'm as sick of them as I am of you."

He knew his only chance lay in his ability to distract her. "Do you mean to say that you're not going to marry me?" he demanded.

"Not if you were the last man on earth." Caroline replied contemptuously.

All at once Douglas de Forest was in motion. Reaching out with his right hand, he shoved Caroline violently, pushing her backward with such force that she crashed into Beth Blake. Both women lost their balance, and before they could recover, de Forest had darted into the corridor.

He had left his boots behind him, as well as his pistol and his knife, but in his need to escape as soon as possible, he could not take even a few seconds to retrieve his belongings. He ran wildly down the corridor.

"Stop him!" Beth called. "Stop him!"

Caroline had the presence of mind to scream at the top of her lungs. As the sound echoed through the car, de Forest reached the metal door at the end of the sleeper and opened it.

The sentries on the platform at the end of the car had been alerted by Caroline's loud scream, but they were unprepared for the wild man, suddenly endowed with superhuman strength, who appeared in their midst. Before they could stop him, Douglas de Forest had wrenched open the outer door of the platform and thrown himself into space off the rapidly moving train.

The sentries recovered, and the noise of their rifle shots awakened everyone in the car. Andy Brentwood ordered the train halted; then he listened intently, as did Whip and Toby Holt, while Caroline related the story of what had transpired and Beth picked up the tale from the point where she had intervened.

The train was still halted, and when the young women had finished their recital, Toby rose and, offering no explanation, quietly vanished. He left the train and started walking down the side of the track.

After he had proceeded a short distance, he found what he was seeking. There, in a gully surrounded on three sides by a copse of pine trees, lay the crumpled, lifeless body of the fiery Confederate officer who had been Douglas de Forest.

The blood of Union soldiers was still fresh on his hands, and he had paid for their deaths with the loss of his own life.

Toby ordered a military detail to disembark, and graves were dug for de Forest, as well as for the men he had killed. De Forest was an enemy, but he had served his country to the best of his ability, and he deserved to rest in peace.

That, at least, was a soldier's point of view. Caroline Brandon reacted far differently. She felt only infinite relief that de Forest was gone and that he would never menace her again.

The greatest trial of all still awaited the passengers of the silver train. Tim Zachary guided the train on the spur line and made a loop around Chattanooga that enabled them to avoid any contact with the large garrison stationed in the Confederate stronghold. Supplies of coal were dwindling so rapidly that when a halt was called on the line heading north out of the city, Tim Zachary breathed a sigh of relief.

"In another two or three hours," he said, "we'll be out of fuel completely, and the only way we'll be able to move this here train is to get out and push!" The tired Union troops were alerted, and with a minimum number guarding the Confederate prisoners, the rest settled down to await the arrival of another train on the line behind them.

Later, in retrospect, the officers agreed that the wait for the arrival of an unknown train was by far the most difficult part of the journey. They were dealing with the unknown, and the uncertainty made them increasingly apprehensive. They halted late in the afternoon, and by dawn the following morning nerves were ragged.

"It's possible, isn't it," Captain Scott Foster demanded, "that no other train will show up on this spur behind us?"

"Anything is possible," Toby replied hotly. "All I know is I can find no indication on the maps that the line is unused. What trains do utilize it is anybody's guess."

The hours continued to drag, and by mid-morning an air of crisis hung over the stalled train.

Then, in the distance, they heard the steady chugging of an engine. At last another train was using this section of track and was moving up behind the bullion train. The troops were alerted and were told to prepare for any contingency.

Whip went to the dining car at the rear of his train, and from that vantage point, he watched the approach of the other train.

"What is it, Toby?" he asked impatiently. "A passenger train or a freight?"

Toby's reply was somber. "I'm afraid," he said, "it's a Confederate troop train."

Andy Brentwood's deep sigh spoke volumes. They had avoided the garrison, only to be directly confronted with another Rebel force.

The other train pulled to a halt only a short distance from the back end of the dining car, and while the officers concealed there watched, they saw an irate Confederate general alight from the troop train, followed by a captain, who obviously was his aide-de-camp.

With Whip continuing to remain undercover, Andy was fully in charge, and he said to Toby, "It looks like we're in for it now, but come along, and we'll try to stall as best we can." He descended to the ground slowly, straightening the tunic of his borrowed Confederate uniform. Toby joined him and saluted smartly as they approached the Rebel leader.

It was clear before he spoke a word that the general was annoyed. His face was flushed, his eyes blazed, and he stalked rapidly up to the pair who were coming toward him. "What in tarnation is the meaning of this, Colonel?" he thundered. "I'm moving eight hundred men to another sector at the front on the direct orders of the War Department in Richmond, and I tell you that this delay is intolerable. I won't stand for it."

Andy knew that he was in deep trouble. "The delay is unavoidable, General," he replied earnestly but vaguely. "We're traveling under direct orders of Richmond, too."

"I don't give a damn what your orders may be," the general roared. "I tell you plain that my train has got to get through, so the only question is how do you get these confounded cars off the tracks for me?"

Andy began to sense that there was only one way to deal with the irate Rebel commander, who obviously was not amenable to reason. "If you'll come with me, sir," he said, casting a meaningful glance at Toby, "I'll be pleased to show you my orders, and perhaps we can work out some solution." Toby hurried ahead to the sleeping car. The tactics that had been used to neutralize Colonel Leland could be utilized again.

Caroline Brandon stood in the open door of a compartment, with Susanna Fulton and Alison White directly behind her. None of the young women had been prepared for the emergency that had arisen, but all three had instantly volunteered their services in response to Toby Holt's urgent request.

Caroline, self-possessed as always, smiled broadly as she came forward. "Why, General," she said in her imitation Southern accent, "You don't know what a real pleasure this is."

The general halted and gaped in astonishment at the three young women. It was inexplicable that they were present on a train he believed to be some sort of a Confederate military transport, and his rage was so great that he sputtered.

Caroline was sufficiently familiar with the moods of men to know that this middle-aged Confederate officer was beyond her reach, impervious to her charms. Nevertheless, she had volunteered to neutralize him as best she could, and she was trying to keep her word. Her smile unwavering, she continued to move toward him.

Putting his hand on his pistol, the general angrily turned toward the officer in a Rebel lieutenant colonel's uniform, about to demand an explanation.

His aide-de-camp was thoroughly bewildered by the developments, but he loyally followed his superior's example and reached for his pistol.

Alison White ended her neutrality in the American Civil War at that instant. Paying scant regard to her own safety, she stepped forward and grasped the Rebel captain's arm, making it impossible for him to draw his weapon. The general, however, succeeded in removing his pistol from its holster.

Either because she was ignorant of the danger to which she was exposing herself or because she was determined to keep her word, Caroline did not falter and reached for the general's arm. In his blazing anger he squeezed the trigger. There was a loud, sharp report, and Caroline Brandon collapsed in a heap on the floor of the compartment.

Major Andrew Brentwood, who prided himself on his ability to maintain his calm under any circumstances, promptly saw red. A man who shot a defenseless woman deserved no protection, no sympathy. Hastily drawing his own pistol, Andy fired two shots.

The first struck the Confederate general in the heart, and he staggered back against the bulkhead of the train and slowly slid to the floor, an expression of utter astonishment on his face as he died. The second shot was equally effective, landing between the eyes of the unfortunate aide, who expired on the spot, too.

The uproar of the next few moments was indescribable. The junior soldiers hurried forward, and Andy crisply ordered them to remove the bodies of the general and his aide but cautioned them not to throw them from the train. In the meantime, Susanna Fulton dropped to one knee beside the stricken Caroline Brandon and was joined by Alison and by Beth Blake, who hurried into the compartment from her own adjoining chamber.

"Thank God she's still alive," Susanna declared.

"We need hot water—a lot of it," Beth said, "and somehow we've got to stop her bleeding."

Andy was anything but heartless, yet he knew that a crisis had arisen that demanded his immediate attention. He would have to leave Caroline to the ministrations of the women while he tended to a more urgent matter, that of getting the silver bullion train in motion again.

Andy started forward to the engine and was quickly joined by Scott and Toby, who had been in the rear, watching to see if anyone else emerged from the Confederate train. "Somebody else is heading this way," Toby said breathlessly.

Andy looked out from between the cars and saw a major in his mid-thirties making his way forward along the tracks. Andy braced himself and then dismounted from the train, followed by his two subordinates.

The major looked concerned as he hurried forward and saluted. "Sorry to bother you, Colonel," he said, "but I'll be obliged if you can tell me the whereabouts of the general. The last I saw of him he was heading forward to speak to the commander of this train."

Andy realized he had to stall for time. "I'm commanding the train," he declared, "but I'm afraid I can't give you any information on the general's whereabouts."

The Rebel major blinked and looked confused. "I saw him with my own eyes walking this way," he said flatly.

Andy braced himself and then shrugged. He had no idea whether he could carry off this deception and knew he would be forced to resort to violence again if his efforts failed.

The Confederate major said, "If you don't mind,

Colonel, I'd like to send somebody through your train to search for him."

Andy swiftly debated with himself whether or not to act high-handedly and decided that a friendly, seemingly cooperative approach was preferable. "Instead of sending some junior officer," Andy suggested, "why don't you look yourself? You're welcome to make yourself at home." He waved at his train.

The major beamed. "I thank you right kindly, sir," he said, standing aside to let Andy climb aboard first.

Andy Brentwood hoisted himself up the steps, and Scott and Toby fell in close behind the major. It was unnecessary to give them any instructions; they already knew precisely what had to be done.

Scott Foster drew his revolver from his holster, held it by the barrel, and using the butt end, hit the unsuspecting Rebel officer hard on the head.

The major slumped and would have fallen backward onto the ground but Toby caught him and eased him into the railroad car. He was unconscious as he was trussed and locked in a compartment.

There was no time to waste, but Andy reacted with the calm that was the hallmark of a first-class officer.

"The Rebels on that train behind us are going to get mighty suspicious when their major, as well as their general, doesn't reappear," he said. "We've got to load up with coal, then get moving as fast as we can." He quickly went to the front of the train and ordered Ezekiel and his detail to take as much coal as they could from the troop train.

Ezekiel knew that time was pressing, and he needed no urging. He formed his men into a bucket brigade and seeing several other soldiers at the rear of the train, pressed them into service, too. He remained out of sight, however, knowing the appearance of a black man would be sure to arouse the suspicions of any onlookers.

Several Confederate officers traveling on the troop train had disembarked and were looking curiously at the supposed Confederate enlisted men, who were transferring coal from one train to the other, apparently on the orders of the trains' commanders. The maneuver was as strange as it was inexplicable, but being soldiers, the Rebels asked no questions. They apparently assumed that the men had received authorization for what they were doing, so they did not interfere.

Working at top speed, Ezekiel's men completed the operation in a remarkably short time.

If the troop train's officers began to suspect the true situation, if they gleaned any notion of the fate that had befallen their general, his aide-de-camp, and his second-in-command, they would be certain to launch an attack on the occupants of the smaller train. If that happened, as Andy well knew, there was no way he and his men could win. They were badly outnumbered by the Rebels, and even if they distinguished themselves in battle, they still couldn't win, for they were in the middle of Confederate territory.

Scott and Toby were also aware of the precariousness of their situation, but they behaved with equal aplomb, and their expressions revealed nothing of what they were feeling. Scott concentrated on the coal that Ezekiel's men were moving, and when he saw that approximately three-quarters of the troop train's load had been transferred, he knew the time had come to call a halt and to proceed to the next stage of the operation.

"That's good enough, Sergeant," he said. "Get your men back on board the train."

Ezekiel obeyed with alacrity, and within moments an apprehensive, stewing Tim Zachary sent his engine forward again. The bullion train began to roll.

As Andy and his subordinates well knew, their secret would be revealed when the train started forward and the Confederate officers did not reappear. From that moment there would be no turning back, and their problems would be complicated accordingly.

A few soldiers emerged from the troop train, their suspicions aroused, their rifles ready. Others, also armed, appeared on the roofs of the cars and leaning out the windows. Andy took a deep breath. "As soon as the enemy sees we're under way," he said, "the fat will really be in the fire."

The words were scarcely out of his mouth when a volley of rifle shots broke the silence. The train in front was gathering speed, the general, his aide, and the major had not reappeared, and the surviving Confederate officers had no doubt that there were enemies on board the shorter train that blocked their use of the track.

"Should we return the fire, Major?" Toby asked as the troop train also began moving, the Confederate soldiers continuing to fire.

Andy shook his head. "I see nothing to be gained," he said. "We'll save our ammunition. There's no telling what lies in store for us, and we've got to be prepared for anything that may turn up."

Zachary achieved a comfortable speed that enabled him to draw away from the Confederate train. Everyone breathed a sigh of relief, and before long, the train passed again through Nashville and was given the green flag, indicating the tracks to the north had been reopened. But Zachary became ill at ease as he peered ahead down the track. "I was afraid of this," he said at last.

The officers stared ahead, and they, too, quickly realized the gravity of the situation. Directly ahead now lay the border that separated the Confederacy from the United States, and an undetermined number of Rebel troops were stationed behind substantial breastworks. Equally important, in order to prevent a railroad train from being sent into the Union across the border, a barrier consisting of a series of wooden planks blocked the tracks ahead.

Toby Holt did some rapid calculations in his head. The silver train was running at approximately twenty miles an hour now, and he tried to judge the size of the planks, particularly the thickness of the wood. "If we increase our speed by about ten miles an hour," he said, "I believe we're capable of smashing through the barriers. Whoever erected them obviously was none too familiar with what a railroad train can and cannot do."

Andy Brentwood weighed the situation and knew he had to take the risk and order the train to make the attempt to crash through the barriers. If he slowed to a halt and had his men remove the planks, the Confederate troops stationed behind the breastworks would become suspicious, and a battle would become inevitable. His only chance of carrying the precious silver across the border into Union territory depended on the element of surprise.

He took Toby's word that the train was capable of smashing through the barriers because he had no real choice. The ultimate decision, he supposed, was Whip Holt's, but Whip was in the sleeping car, and Andy was in the engine. So that placed the full responsibility on the shoulders of the younger man.

Andy spoke decisively. "Mr. Zachary," he said crisply, "be good enough to increase your speed by at least ten miles an hour."

A crooked smile of delight lighted Tim Zachary's homely face. Tugging at his cap, he pulled the acceleration throttle all the way back.

The train seemed to leap forward, and those on board felt a series of sharp jolts as the metal cowcatcher came in contact with the stout wood of the barriers. The sounds of crunching, splintering wood seemed to fill the air.

It was clear to the Confederate troops stationed at the border that the train, for whatever its reason, was trying to escape from the Confederacy. The officers in command of the units gave the command to open fire.

The sounds of wood splintering were drowned by the steady, loud explosions of rifle fire.

Whip Holt had been content to allow his younger officers to remain in charge of the attempted escape, but now he felt compelled to intervene. He promptly gave orders for all personnel to return the Rebel fire.

The Union regular and the Nevada militiamen needed no urging. They had been masquerading for what they felt was a very long time as Rebels, and now, at last, they were being allowed to enter open combat.

Concealing themselves as best they could as bullets whined overhead, they returned the Confederate fire with vigor as the train continued to hurtle forward. Scott crouched behind the open window of the cab and fired his pistol repeatedly at the troops who were defending the border. Toby did the same, and in his exuberance he actually laughed aloud. Only Andy Brentwood refrained from joining in combat. He was tempted, but he had to pay the penalty exacted of a senior commander. He alone was in a position to decide what tactics to employ, and he had to keep his mind free so he could concentrate on the larger issue.

It was impossible to determine whether there were any casualties in the strange battle between the Confederates at the breastworks and the men on board the rapidly moving train. Only one thing was clear: the Rebel defenders were not able to halt the forward thrust of the train, which gathered still more speed after the wooden obstacles had been swept aside.

The area directly north of the Confederate position was a no-man's-land that belonged to neither side. It was impossible to determine whether the railroad tracks had been mined by either Union or Rebel forces, and the only way to find out was to press forward. Tim Zachary was concerned, and Andy hesitated but gave the order to continue because he had no real choice. True victory was within reach at last.

The three officers at the rear of the cab saw someone struggling forward to join them, and suddenly Toby Holt broke ranks, hurried forward, and assisted his father, who was finding it exceptionally difficult to make his way through the open coal cars to the engine. Whip's arthritis was causing him severe pain, and he made no secret of that fact now.

He was carrying something voluminous in his arms, and Toby looked bewildered when he opened it and saw it was an American flag.

"Raise that banner in a hurry!" Whip ordered. "We should be reaching the Union line soon, and they'll shoot at us with every weapon in their arsenal unless we identify ourselves properly. And while we're about it, have our troops change out of Rebel uniforms into their own, without delay. We haven't come all this distance to be killed by our own men."

Knowing Whip was right, Andy and Toby struggled with the flag and managed to hoist it on a pole. In the meantime, Scott hurried back from the engine to the train proper to give the order for the troops to don their own uniforms at last.

Soon they were approaching breastworks remarkably similar to those erected by the Confederates, and again Whip intervened. "Tim," he said to the engineer, "you'd be right smart to slow down to a trot. If you send this iron horse galloping through Union lines, you're inviting a lot of shots from troops in Louisville who are suspicious of just about anything that comes from the Confederate side."

Zachary nodded and immediately slowed the train to a crawl.

Union troops by the thousands were stationed behind the breastworks, and they stared in wonder, but at the direction of their officers they held their fire as the train flying the flag of the United States penetrated deeper into Union territory. Then blue-clad men appeared at the windows of every car and at the openings between cars, all of them waving their hats and cheering. The troops guarding the border cheered in return, although they had no idea what they were celebrating.

At last the engine approached a group of officers standing on a siding; most prominent in the group was a man whose gold braid identified him as someone of consequence, and Whip ordered the train to halt. He was the first to alight, and his immediate subordinates followed him. A major general watched his approach curiously, and said something in an undertone to one of the half-dozen staff officers who had accompanied him.

Whip limped forward and raised his hand to the brim of his hat in salute. "Colonel Michael Holt, at report, sir," he said. "I'm carrying a load of silver at the request of the President, and I'm as surprised as you are to find myself in your territory."

The general laughed and shook his head. "I'm Jim Jones," he replied, "and I really will be damned. So you're Whip Holt, and this is the bullion train."

Whip nodded and grinned.

General Jones shook his head in amazement. "The entire Union Army has been looking for you for days, Colonel Holt," he replied. "We'll go straight to my headquarters and telegraph the War Department in Washington that you've been found. How in the name of all that's holy did you get on the wrong side of the Confederate border north of Chattanooga?"

"It's a long story, General," Whip replied, "and I scarcely believe it myself."

XI

The train came to a halt on a siding a short distance from General Jones's headquarters, and no sooner did it grind to a stop than the senior physician of the command and two of his associates boarded the sleeping car and examined the unconscious Caroline Brandon. When they were finished, they spoke to Alison, Beth, and Susanna, who was busy finishing the news story of the astonishing adventures that had befallen the company.

"The young lady has lost a great deal of blood," the senior physician said, "and I'm sorry to report that a bullet is lodged in her body, near her heart, and needs to be removed. She requires immediate surgery."

The young women were concerned, and Alison quickly asked, "Will she survive, Doctor?"

The military surgeon shrugged. "She's young, and she's healthy, both of which are in her favor. Beyond that, I hesitate to say. Unfortunately, we're afraid to move her for fear the jarring and jolting she'd undergo would start her bleeding again. That means we'll have to operate on her right where she is now."

"Do whatever you think is necessary, Doctor," Susanna said.

The doctor nodded and said, "Does she have any relatives in the vicinity?"

"No," Susanna replied carefully. "There's no one on board the train who's related to her."

The use of anesthetics was relatively new. Caroline was kept asleep by the application of ether during the long, complicated operation that followed. The physicians finally succeeded in removing the bullet that had caused her so much damage, and the surgery came to an end. At General Jones's order, his orderlies stood guard over the patient and were instructed to attend to her needs.

But Caroline, even after she awakened, was too weak and too miserable to make any demands. She sipped a little water into which sugar had been dissolved, and most of the time she slept. The physicians visited her repeatedly, and after they had called again for the fourth or fifth time, Susanna halted them in the corridor outside the compartment that had been transformed into a sick room.

The long, detailed article that Susanna had written was ready for dispatch and lacked only definitive information about Caroline to complete it.

"How is your patient?" she asked.

The principal physician shook his head and shrugged. "That's almost impossible to say," he replied. "I've seen many in her state, especially in the months since the war started. Whether she'll survive or not is anybody's guess."

Susanna felt a wave of sympathy for Caroline. She had never admired the other woman but had to admit that Caroline had proved herself to be a heroine of the first order. "Is there anything I can do for her?" she inquired.

The doctor shook his head. "Only if you know her sufficiently well to supply her with some strong motivation for wanting to live," the doctor replied.

Susanna was blank, and so was Alison. Neither of them knew Caroline that well, and they had no idea of her likes and dislikes.

Toby Holt had learned of Caroline's condition just after their arrival in Louisville, but he had been obliged to spend several hours in General Jones's office, giving his account of the events on the silver train. Thus, it wasn't until late in the day that he was able to come to the sleeping car to see her. He was wearing his dress uniform for the ceremonies that were to take place shortly, ceremonies to which all the civilians on board had been invited, but he was gravely concerned about Caroline and wanted to see her before he became involved in any more military matters. He listened wide-eyed as Susanna repeated what the doctor had told her, and then he said, "I had no idea it was that bad. I wish I knew of something that would motivate her."

"All I know," Susanna replied, "is that the doctor seems to feel that she'd be helped if she had some strong reason to want to live."

Toby hastened into the sickroom. He was alarmed by Caroline's appearance. She was deathly pale, and wearing no makeup, she looked very young and vulnerable. He smiled down at her, feeling very sorry that someone as beautiful as she had suffered so much. "You're quite a heroine, you know," he said. "The Union commander in Tennessee intends to pay you a visit as soon as you're well enough, and it wouldn't surprise me if he gives you an official commendation for bravery."

"That's nice," Caroline whispered, and her green eyes were enormous as she looked up at him. "I'm going to die, Toby," she murmured.

"Oh, no, you're not," he replied firmly but without conviction, "You're going to be just fine."

She shook her head. "No, I'm not going to live, but there's something I want. Very badly. Will you help me?"

"I'll do everything for you that I possibly can," he said.

Caroline swallowed painfully. "I have no reason to be proud of the life I've led," she murmured. "In fact, I'm ashamed of a great many things that I've done."

Toby stirred uncomfortably. "Don't think about that now," he said. "Don't dwell on the past."

"I can't help it," she replied, and all at once her voice seemed to grow stronger. "I want—so very much—to wipe out what's been bad and to dwell on what's good."

He didn't know what to reply, so he nodded.

She indicated with a gesture that she wanted a drink

of water, and he propped her up in his arms and held the glass for her so that she could drink. She had lost so much weight that he was shocked. "I want to be a—a respectable woman in my last days," Caroline said sincerely, "I want it more than anything in the world." She hesitated. "If I marry a decent man, I'll bear his name," she said, "and that will save me." Her hand inched across the covers and suddenly reached out and grasped Toby's hand. "Would you do that for me? Would you marry me so that I could die without shame?"

Her request stunned him, and he didn't know what to respond. He could not in all conscience reject the tragic appeal of those huge green eyes that were fixed on his. He was fascinated by her; he continued to yearn for her; and he was helpless. "Sure," he muttered. "Sure, Caroline, I'll marry you. Don't you worry."

A tremulous cry shook her entire being, and she smiled as she leaned back against her pillows and closed her eyes. "Thank you, Toby, and God bless you," she whispered. "You just don't know how much this means to me."

She appeared to be asleep when Toby crept out of her sick room. Deeply troubled by their exchange, he went at once to the quarters that had been provided for his father at General Jones's garrison.

Whip was dressed in his gold-trimmed blue uniform and was buckling on his dress sword when his son entered his quarters. He took one look at Toby's face and instantly demanded, "What's wrong?"

Toby repeated his entire conversation with Caroline. "I have no idea what got into her to make the request of me, Pa," he said, "but I didn't have the heart to turn her down. I kept remembering what Susanna Fulton had told me about Caroline needing motivation in order to get better."

Whip stared out the window at the rolling green hills of Kentucky. "I don't see where you had any choice, boy," he said. "You've been caught in a trap, there's no two ways about it. She performed a courageous act, which is how she got wounded in the first place, and you wouldn't be much of a man if you turned her down."

Toby nodded but was unable to speak. He was struck with the enormity of what he had done. As much as he had been attracted to Caroline before, he was now aware that he had made a commitment he might regret.

"I'll grant you," Whip said dryly, "that Caroline isn't the wife that your mother and I have had in mind for you."

"I've found her very attractive, and I'm the first to admit it," Toby said. "As to wanting her for a wife—well, I know she's been a—woman of the world, and the thought of marriage had never occurred to me."

"Your mother will be upset at first, but I'll straighten her out," Whip said. "I reckon you'll have to go through with this marriage."

"I reckon so," Toby replied.

Whip looked at Toby with admiration. "You're doing a fine thing, son, making a noble gesture, and you won't regret it."

"I have written to my employers," Bernhard von Hummel said. "I have not only assured them that the Union is solvent and can pay for the field artillery units ordered from the Prussian plants, but I have also made it clear that in my opinion the North is certain to win the war."

Whip was pleased at the news, but at the same time he was curious. "What makes you so sure that we're going to win?" he asked.

"I have been through an incredible experience," the young Prussian nobleman replied. "I was filled with admiration for the Confederacy when they stole the silver train, and I still cannot overcome my total astonishment at what you and your subordinates did in recovering the train and returning it to the North. The feat is extraordinary."

Whip smiled modestly. "My boys don't know when they're beat," he said, "and that's the real key to victory."

Watching Whip depart, Bernhard felt great admiration for him, as he did now for all Americans. They were unique, he decided, a breed apart.

He saw Beth Blake approaching and smiled to himself. She, too, was unique.

"I was supposed to go directly from here to my college in Ohio, but I persuaded Colonel Holt to let me go the rest of the way east before returning to school," she said. "Have you ever heard of Antioch?"

He smiled broadly. "I spent time this very day doing research on Antioch," he said, "and I would not be surprised if I know more about it now than you do. In any event, I shall be there in the near future."

She was surprised. "Really? You have business there?"

He looked at her hard and long. "Personal business," he said slowly.

Later in the day, a full-dress, public ceremony was held at the army post outside Louisville. There the Confederates who had stormed and captured the bullion train formally surrendered, and Whip accepted on behalf of the Union.

Lieutenant Colonel Roger Stannard made a point of presenting his own sword to Major Andrew Brentwood. "If it weren't for the extraordinary efforts of you and your lads," Stannard declared, "the bullion would be safely deposited in the Confederate Treasury right now. Much as I hate to admit it, you deserve the victory you've won."

Andy accepted the sword graciously, then deferred to Whip for a formal reply.

Unaccustomed to public speaking, Whip Holt was uncomfortable, but as always, he did what had to be done and spoke briefly of the terrible events that were tearing the nation asunder. The war was a nightmare, he said, but when foes treated each other with compassion, there was hope for the future. "I have thus recommended to the War Department—and my suggestion has been accepted—" he concluded, "that the Confederate officers and men that participated in the abortive assault on the silver train should not be treated as ordinary prisoners of war. We're sending you back through the lines to Chattanooga, Colonel Stannard, and you'll take your entire command with you."

Those who were watching the ceremonies were treated to the rare spectacle of seeing the Union men applauded by the Confederates whom they had defeated. The double theft of the silver bullion and the astonishing conclusion of the event would be remembered for many years after the war ended; it would have a permanent place in history.

General Jones received special instructions of his own from the War Department; several cars were to be added to the train, and an additional three hundred infantrymen, fully armed, were to be added to Whip's command for the rest of the journey. The army had learned a lesson, and no risks were being taken with the precious bullion.

Immediately after the ceremony, Andy Brentwood sought out Susanna Fulton, who had watched the display from the grandstand erected for General Jones's guests.

"I'm glad," she said, "that Colonel Stannard is being returned to the Confederacy. A man that clever shouldn't be forced to languish in a prisoner of war camp, and I have another story to write as a result." She smiled happily. "I received a telegram from my father after I wired him my long story, and he was just ecstatic. I gather that scores of newspapers all over the United States are going to buy my article on the bullion train."

Andy fell in beside her, and they strolled across the military compound. "I guess," he said, "you're well on your way to a new career as a war correspondent."

She nodded. "I've thought of the possibility," she admitted, "although the opportunities for a woman are rather limited."

"You'll have no problems getting what you want," Andy assured her.

"I hope so," she said, and a mischievous expression appeared in her eyes.

It was obvious that she intended the statement as a leading remark, and Andy became uncomfortable.

She waited for him to speak and was disappointed when he remained silent. "Major Brentwood," she said, "I sometimes think you're far too disciplined for your own good."

He reddened. "How so?" he demanded.

She took his arm, led him off the path to a spot hidden from the road by a large supply shed, and there she halted. "As you've no doubt gleaned from my reports of your exploits," she said, "I find you an officer of great courage and ingenuity. What I neglected to put into my analysis of you was my private opinion of you."

Andy braced himself. The train journey had been so hectic that he had never managed to make a formal marriage proposal to Susanna, and now he expected the worst. "I'd be much obliged to learn your private opinion, Sue."

She moved a step closer to him. "You exasperate me beyond measure," she declared.

He was astonished. "I do?"

"You proposed marriage to me regularly," she said, "at a time when I was torn between you and someone else. What I completely fail to understand is why you stopped asking me to marry you from the moment I made up my mind that it was you I wanted."

Amazement registered on his face. "I had no idea," was all he could say.

"Well, I gave you enough hints!" Something perverse in her nature caused her to refuse to make things easier for him.

Andy continued to stare at her for a time, and suddenly he knew the time had come for him to take direct action. He reached for her and pulled her toward him.

Susanna sighed in gratitude and relief as she yielded to his embrace.

Unmindful of the fact that others using the path might chance to see them, he kissed her soundly and at length. "When did you make up your mind and choose me?" he demanded as he released her.

The starry-eyed Susanna shook her head. "I'm not really certain," she said. "I've asked myself the same question, and I can only tell you that my thinking didn't crystallize until your mother asked how I felt about you."

He blinked in surprise. "You knew that long ago?"

"Oh, yes," Susanna said casually.

"I—I had no idea," he muttered.

"I know," she replied, taking his arm as they resumed their walk. "You've had other matters on your mind."

"I have some leave coming once we deliver the bullion to New York," he said. "Will you marry me then?"

"With all my heart," Susanna replied. "Ordinarily I'd insist that my father be present for my wedding, but the war has changed many things, and we'll need to take advantage of any time you can get away from your duties." They walked in silence for a few moments.

"I hope that Scott Foster isn't too upset by your decision," Andy said at last. "He's a fine fellow and a first-rate officer."

Susanna smiled and shook her head. "Don't waste any sympathy on Scott," she said. "It's the last thing in the world that he wants or needs."

Susanna did not know it, but Scott Foster was not enjoying clear sailing in the development of his romance with Alison White. Alison's conscience was responsible, and as she found herself becoming more and more deeply involved with Scott, she felt compelled to tell him her whole story.

"I want to speak to you about something terribly important," she said as they walked together across the military post toward the tent that had been erected for her use until the train journey was resumed. Scott went into the tent with her and lighted the oil lamp that stood on a small table; then he seated himself on one of a pair of camp chairs and looked at her expectantly.

Alison needed all of her inner strength to ask, "How would you react if I told you I was a British spy?"

Scott stared at her incredulously and burst into laughter.

She shook her head sadly. "I wish it were funny," she said, "but it isn't." Speaking haltingly, she told him about her late husband's profession, about the visits that the British agent named Poole had made to her, and about her unwilling entanglement in the affairs of nations. "I managed to avoid making a report of any kind to Mr. Poole," she said, "but he was terribly angry."

Scott's incredulity gave way to slow-burning anger. "I'd like to be present the next time he threatens you," he said.

She shook her head. "I doubt if he'll threaten again. He made it very clear that unless I did his bidding, I'd be refused permission to return to London, and I expect that's the next step on his agenda."

He digested the information in silence and then asked, "Why are you telling me all this?"

"Because I don't want to be accepted by you under false pretenses. I want you to know me for what I am."

"I know you for exactly what you are," he said. "You're a loyal and honorable woman, as well as a very lovely one. I hope that you aren't too worried about the doors of the British Empire being closed to you. I'd be honored if you'd accept whatever protection my name can offer you."

She realized that he was proposing marriage to her somewhat clumsily, and there was amusement as well as tenderness in her eyes.

"I find it hard to explain how I feel," Scott went on. "I was in love for a long time with Susanna. In fact, my love for her became a habit, an unthinking process that became farther and farther removed from reality, especially after you came into my life. It took me a long time to wake up, but it finally dawned on me that it was you I loved, not Susanna. I hope that's all right with you."

She nodded silently.

Scott grinned at her. "Then everything is going to work out for the best," he said.

"It doesn't bother you that I'm a widow?" she asked.

"Not in the least," he replied quickly.

"I'm very glad," she said. "It was an arranged marriage, and I never loved Sir Charles." She took a deep breath. "It doesn't bother you that I was an espionage agent?"

"You weren't," Scott said. "You were recruited as an agent, but you never served as one. For your own protection and for the information of our government, I wish you'd put the whole experience with this man Poole on paper. I'm sure that Secretary Seward and his people in the State Department will be interested in learning what you have to tell them."

It occurred to Alison that she was burning her bridges behind her, but she nevertheless nodded. "I'll do whatever you think best," she said.

"I think it best," Scott replied, "that you marry me as soon as we reach New York. I've been told I'm being granted a brief leave before I'm reassigned to new duty. We'll not only be married, but I'll make certain that your future is well taken care of when I return to the army."

The thought occurred to Alison that her worries about her future were ended. Scott had calmly assumed responsibility for her future and was planning for her in his own way.

He rose to his feet and embraced her.

As Alison returned his kiss, she felt secure for the first time since she had come to the New World. Scott Foster's love enveloped her, and she knew she was safe.

Whip quietly made the arrangements for his son's unorthodox wedding. He enlisted the aid of the chief chaplain of the Kentucky command, to whom he confided the whole story, and then he went to Beth Blake and asked her to be present for the ceremony as a witness. Beth was startled by the totally unexpected development, and she was of two minds regarding it. She had to admire Toby's willingness to make the sacrifice for the sake of the young woman who was not expected to live, and she could understand, too, why Caroline Brandon sought refuge in a respectable marriage, hoping to salvage what she could of her shattered reputation before she died.

On the other hand, however, Beth was very conscious of the fact that her own mother and Eulalia Holt had been hoping for years that she and Toby would find each other and would marry, although she was the first to admit that they irritated each other and they had virtually nothing in common. But nevertheless, she had accepted him as a passive suitor. Now that he was about to be married to someone else—and a notorious courtesan at that—she saw him differently and viewed the situation through new eyes.

Toby had far more strength, far more integrity, and infinitely more courage than she had given him credit for having. She had been in the habit of thinking of him as a boy whom her parents had tried to foist on her. Now she knew that Toby Holt was no boy. He was a man, a worthy successor to his father.

But it was too late for regrets. Caroline might have only hours to live at best, and Beth could not begrudge her the faint shreds of happiness that marriage to Toby might give her. It was the role that fate had determined that she herself would play, but she accepted the part with all the good grace that she could muster.

The physician had advised them to proceed as rapidly as they could, so the chaplain came forward and began to read the marriage ceremony in a low voice.

Caroline recognized the familiar words, and a faint smile appeared on her pale lips. The others understood her amusement at the prospect of becoming a married woman after the way she had lived.

A crisis arose when the time came to slip a wedding ring onto Caroline's finger. No one, it appeared, had remembered to provide a ring.

Whip met the emergency by removing his own gold wedding ring, which Eulalia had given him on the first anniversary of their wedding. He had worn it ever since, and his hand felt strange without it. Caroline stared down at the worn band shining on the fourth finger of her left hand, and her eyes filled with tears. She had truly achieved respectability at last.

When the chaplain pronounced the couple man and wife, Toby leaned down and brushed his bride's forehead with his lips.

Caroline blinked away her tears and clutched his hand. "I'll remember this forever," she murmured.

Her gratitude continued to embarrass him. "I'll get you a ring that fits you properly the first chance I get," he said.

She shook her head feebly. "No," she murmured. "I just want this ring."

Toby had to agree that he would not take it from her, and he promised that when they reached New York, he would have it made smaller for her.

Caroline was satisfied and smiled as she drifted off to sleep. Whip hoped that Eulalia would understand Toby's reason for making his sacrifice, and he hoped, too, that she would forgive her husband the loss of his own wedding band.

Toby and Beth followed Whip and the chaplain as they made their way back to the headquarters of the camp. "You and I have never been friends," Beth said, "but I want you to know that I think you're doing a grand thing by going through with this ceremony tonight."

Toby shrugged. "I didn't have much choice," he said. "Caroline requested it, and I'd have been selfish if I'd refused."

Beth shook her head. "A lot of men would have found an excuse not to go through with it," she said, "but you didn't, and that takes a special kind of courage. I'm afraid I have an idea that your mother and mine may not approve, but I just want you to know that I do."

She held out her hand. She was offering a truce in their private war, and he shook her hand and then smiled. Beth had made a friendly gesture, and the least he could do was to accept it in the spirit she had shown when offering it. Perhaps, he reflected, she wasn't as badly spoiled a brat as he had always assumed. He grinned at her as their hands met.

Whip was aware of the byplay between them and thought it odd that it had been necessary for Toby to marry someone else in order to end his long-standing feud with Beth Blake.

Prime Minister Palmerston was busy, so his visitor was obliged to wait interminably in his reception room. Hours passed, and it occurred to Poole that perhaps His Lordship was punishing him for his failure in the United States. Well, he couldn't help what had happened—he was in no way to blame. He straightened his shoulders, gritted his teeth, and continued to wait.

Dusk was falling when he was finally admitted to the prime minister's office. Palmerston wasted no words. "What have you to say for yourself?" he demanded.

Poole sighed. "I did my very best, Milord, but for once my best wasn't quite enough. The Yankees have a chap named Holt who is a conjurer and who performs miracles."

"That he does," the prime minister replied coldly. "The greatest of all miracles is that he's forced Her Majesty's government to change its policies. We still hope privately for a Confederate victory, but we're going to be obliged hereafter to be far more even-handed in our treatment of the combatants in the American Civil War. In fact, we'll be obliged to lean toward the Union from time to time." He hooked his thumbs in his waistcoat pocket, glowered at the secret agent, and added, "Thanks completely to your inefficiency."

Poole thought his superior was being eminently unfair but knew it was useless to complain.

"When you return to your own headquarters," the prime minister said, "you'll find a new assignment awaiting you. There's new turmoil in the Balkans. You'll be briefed on the particulars. You're being sent to Sofia, and I hope you enjoy better luck dealing with the Bulgarians than you did with the Yankees." He nodded curtly, terminating the interview.

Bulgaria was the end of the earth, but Poole could not protest, and he crept out quietly, utterly defeated.

Plans for the resumption of the silver bullion train's journey were completed the morning after Toby Holt and Caroline Brandon were married. The additional cars were added to the train for the augmented troops who would stand guard, and ample supplies were taken on board.

At Tim Zachary's request, he would remain as chief engineer for the rest of the journey. "When I start somethin'," he said, "I like to finish it!"

The train was granted a priority on the line that led toward the northeast, and when it rolled into the District of Columbia, a large military guard was on hand. An aide to Abraham Lincoln was sent to tell Whip that the President wanted to see him. A short time later, he was escorted into the President's private office.

"The saga of your experience is extraordinary, Colonel Holt," Lincoln said. "Maybe you can help me to reward you as you deserve by telling me what you want. And if it's in my power to grant, you shall certainly have it."

Whip shook his head. "That's kind of you, Mr. President," he said, "but I can't think of a thing that I want. I'm reverting to a civilian status as soon as we deliver the bullion to your Treasury people in New York, and it'll be none too soon. I promised my wife that I wouldn't stay on duty a day longer than was needed, and I aim to keep my word to her."

"By all means," the President murmured, and thought it refreshing to be meeting with a patriot who wanted nothing for himself.

"Come to think of it, sir," Whip said, "there may be something you can do for me, after all. I succeeded against overwhelming odds because I was assisted by first-rate men, especially my troop commander. If you saw fit to grant a temporary promotion to Major Andrew Brentwood and transferred him to the combat command I know he wants, I'd be very much grateful and more than satisfied."

"That's the very least I can do," the President said. "What about others who served with you through the ordeal you suffered?"

Whip grinned. "If you look after Andy Brentwood, Mr. President, he'll take care of the others. One reason the lads worked so well together is that they're a team, and everyone looks out for everybody else's welfare."

President Lincoln's personal physician examined Caroline Brandon while the bullion train was in Washington and reported that she was holding her own. "The young lady is very weak," he said, "and she has a terrible struggle for life on her hands. But she's managed to survive from one day to the next—from one hour to the next—and that's saying a great deal."

Toby took advantage of the brief stay in Washington to visit a jeweler, who cut down his father's wedding ring to fit Caroline's slender finger.

During the halt, Andy Brentwood reported to his superiors in the War Department and was filled with wonder. President Lincoln had acted with dispatch in keeping his word to Whip Holt.

"I've had a brevet promotion to lieutenant colonel," Andy told Susanna. "And I'm being given a combat battalion of my own, with the right to name my own staff. Not in my wildest dreams did I think I would be this lucky!"

"I don't think luck has played any part in what's happening to you," Susanna said. "You've earned your way."

Andy acted swiftly now that he knew what lay ahead for him, and the first person he summoned was Captain Scott Foster. "I hear," Andy said, "that you're planning on being married, too, once we reach New York."

"I sure am, sir," Scott said, grinning broadly.

"Well, now," Andy said, "since the women we're marrying are such good friends, it strikes me they might take up wartime residence together, especially if you and I share assignments. I'm being given a combat battalion of my own, and I'm pleased to give you a staff position as my operations officer. Naturally, there will be a promotion to major that goes with the job."

"I accept, sir, and I'm flattered," Scott said.

They shook hands, and Andy grinned at him. "I'm not doing you any favors, you know," he said. "I just don't believe in breaking up a winning team."

Scott nodded. Together they were formidable.

Toby Holt was the next to be summoned to Andy's compartment and was asked to sit. "You and I," Andy said, "have never had any love for each other, Lieutenant. We've had the natural antipathies of regular army and reserve officers toward each other, and there have been a lot of personal elements that have influenced our relationship as well."

Toby wondered why his superior was speaking to him so bluntly, and he could only nod in agreement.

"If you want to get as far from me as you can for the rest of the war, I won't blame you," Andy went on. "But on the other hand, if you think you can stand the sight of me, I have an offer that may interest you."

"You bet I'm interested," Toby replied instantly.

Andy was heartened by his positive response. "I've been given a combat battalion of my own, and I have a need for a liaison officer to make contact with other headquarters. I think you'd fill the bill nicely."

Toby straightened his shoulders, stood, and held out his hand. "Colonel Brentwood," he said, "you're my idea of a real man. I am with you all the way—for the duration of the war."

Their eyes met as they shook hands, and Andy was satisfied. He had acquired the services of a reliable, highly competent officer on whom he knew he could depend. Come to think of it, he should have realized long before that Toby Holt was exceptional. After all, he was the son of Whip Holt, and thus his talents were necessarily formidable.

The last meeting that Andy held was with Ezekiel, who saluted smartly as he entered his superior's compartment.

Andy invited him to sit and then asked, "How do you like the army? Does it live up to your expectations?"

"I didn't know what to expect," Ezekiel said, grinning, "but I like it just fine."

"You couldn't have been any more active," Andy replied. "I had to devote more than a full page to your exploits in my report to the War Department."

The big black man sighed gently. "I got kind of riled up when the Rebels said they were going to sell my wife into slavery," he declared. "I guess I kind of lost my temper."

Andy smiled. "You were awe-inspiring," he said, "and I want to give you the chance to equal your performance. How would you like to be my battalion sergeant major?"

"That's fine with me," Ezekiel said, "but I don't know the first thing about what's expected of a sergeant major."

"You'll learn fast enough," Andy assured him. "I'm certain of that."

The final stage of the long journey from Virginia City, Nevada, to New York was uneventful. The Union authorities were taking no chances, and at every community through which the train passed—beginning with Baltimore, Maryland, and Wilmington, Delaware—the stations were crowded with armed troops who kept the curious at a safe distance. When the train finally pulled into New York City, a surprise awaited Whip and Andy. High-ranking government officials, including senators and congressmen, were on hand to greet them, and in ceremonies held outside the station, they heard themselves being hailed as heroes.

"Whip Holt has added another chapter to his illustrious saga," the general who commanded the New York military district declared. "He is unique among Americans."

Susanna Fulton hurried off to the nearest telegraph office to file what would be her second story to her father's newspaper in Denver and to all the other newspapers that were buying her articles. "The Treasury

Department," she wrote, "had representatives on hand to take charge of the precious silver bullion, which was being escorted to vaults below the surface of the earth at the corner of Broad and Wall Streets. The long journey had indeed ended in success."

What Susanna had not anticipated was that she herself would be greeted as a heroine. To her astonishment a half-dozen or more of her fellow reporters clamored for interviews with her, and she became so flustered that Andy Brentwood had to intervene. The representatives of the press questioned him regarding his identity, and not until later did the significance of the event dawn on Susanna.

"Oh, dear," she said laughing ruefully. "I've been scooped on the story of my own romance and forthcoming marriage. My father will blister my hide for this."

Andy smiled and shook his head. "If I know Wade Fulton," he said, "he's bursting with pride over what you've accomplished already."

Whip had an errand that kept him busy from the moment the ceremonies were completed. He purchased a railroad ticket for Antioch, Ohio, and put Beth Blake on the train that would take her back to college for her final year there.

He escorted her to the train, supervised the boarding of her luggage, and saw her to her compartment. Then he turned to her, put his hands on her shoulders, and kissed her lightly. "It's odd how things turned out," he said. "Eulalia and I always hoped that you'd be our daughter-in-law some day, but I guess that wasn't meant to be."

"Apparently not," Beth replied, and before she could say anything more, they were interrupted when someone else arrived at her compartment.

Bernhard von Hummel was breathless as he thrust a large bouquet at Beth. "I hurried as fast as I could," he said. "I was afraid I would miss you and that your train would leave before I could bid you good-bye. But I hope to see you soon."

Beth hid her face in the flowers to hide the tears that

threatened to fall. She was unaccustomed to the emotions she now felt, but she hoped with all her heart that Bernhard would keep his word and visit her in Antioch.

Whip looked at the young woman, then at the young Prussian, and decided to withdraw. He had had no idea that they were interested in each other, but that interest was obvious now. He said good-bye to Beth, telling her to be sure to telegraph her parents at Fort Vancouver when her train arrived safely in Antioch. Then he withdrew to the platform and waited for Bernhard to emerge from the train.

After a time Bernhard joined him, and they stood together, waving to Beth, who waved back from the window of her compartment.

"I understand," Bernhard said, "that you and your family have been close to Beth all her life."

"Indeed we have," Whip said. "We've been close friends of her parents since before she was born. I may be prejudiced," Whip added guardedly, "but in my opinion, she is a splendid young woman."

"That she is, Colonel Holt!" Bernhard said enthusiastically. "I came to know her well only on our railroad journey, but to me she is typical of American womanhood at its best."

As Whip nodded, meanwhile waving again to Beth, he wondered about the extent of the baron's commitment to Beth. Lee and Cathy, he knew, would be deeply disturbed if she married a foreigner and made her home elsewhere than in the United States.

"She has given me permission to call on her at her college," Bernhard said. "I have completed my assignment, now that the silver is safely in the hands of the federal Treasury officials, so I have decided I owe myself a holiday—in Antioch, Ohio."

It appeared that the romance had progressed much farther and faster than the surprised Whip realized, and he knew he would have to report in full detail to Lee and Cathy, who would demand to know all that he could tell them.

It was not his place to interfere in what was none of

his business, but he decided to make it his business. His long association with Beth's mother and father throughout the years gave him special privileges and, even more important, special responsibilities.

"She is a typical American girl, Baron," he said quietly. "She thinks she knows her own mind, and she's headstrong and stubborn, but she's far more naive than she looks, and far less sophisticated than she acts. I think she'd gasp and flounder like a fish out of water in any environment but her own." The train began to move, and there was a fixed smile on Bernhard von Hummel's face as he removed his hat and waved it at Beth.

"I am not insensitive to the problems of paying court to Miss Blake, Colonel Holt," he said quietly. "I am aware of the problems, and I realize they are formidable."

His sensitivity surprised Whip. "I don't claim I know what's right or wrong for Beth, any more than I will for my own daughter when she's Beth's age," he replied. "But I'm pretty darn sure of one thing. It would be a mistake to rush somebody that young and impressionable off her feet."

"Quite so," Bernhard said. "It might be a simple enough matter to win Beth's hand at this stage in her development, but to assure her lasting happiness is another matter entirely. No doubt you will be in touch with General Blake?"

Whip nodded and eyed the young Prussian warily.

"I will be grateful if you would give him a message for me, Colonel Holt," Bernhard said. "I am sure that you intend to inform him of my interest in his daughter and of her response to me."

"Quite so," Whip admitted.

"Then, sir, be good enough, if you will, to tell him also that her welfare is my primary concern. I think—but I am not certain—that she would be the right woman for me to marry. I do not know, however, if I am the right man for her. I hope to find out when I visit Antioch."

Whip was deeply impressed by the young Prussian's

attitude, and he knew that Lee and Cathy would share his view.

Bernhard appeared to read his mind. "Be good enough to assure General Blake," he said, "that I seek for his daughter what he seeks, her contentment and the opportunity to fulfill herself in life. Rest assured, sir, that I shall do nothing that will interfere with her achievement of that goal."

Whip had to admit that the young nobleman was being forthright, honorable, and considerate. He revised his opinion somewhat, and even wondered whether it was possible for Beth to find happiness if she lived in far distant Berlin as this man's wife. Anything was possible, and he told himself not to make premature judgments.

No sooner had the bullion train pulled to a halt in New York City than Caroline Brandon Holt had been transferred to Midtown Hospital on East Fourteenth Street, a special ambulance taking her there. It was the first time she had left her compartment on the train since she had been shot. Lieutenant Toby Holt was fully occupied with guard duties pending the transfer of the fortune in silver to the Treasury's underground vault in the financial district. He was on full duty, as were all of his colleagues, until the bullion had been safely moved and was no longer Whip Holt's responsibility.

Only then did the young officer have time to pay a visit to the hospital. He had the foresight to buy a bunch of flowers on his way to visit Caroline, and when he arrived at the hospital, he was admitted without delay to her room. To his astonishment Caroline was sitting up in bed and, thanks to her lavish use of cosmetics, looked like her old self. Her flaxen hair was neatly brushed, the eye shadow that ringed her eyes made them look larger than usual, her mouth was rouged, and artificial color on her cheeks further enhanced her appearance.

Toby, who had braced himself for a farewell meeting with a woman whom he expected to die at any time, stared at her in astonishment.

Caroline smiled at him slowly. "Thanks to you," she said huskily, "I'm going to be all right. I'm going to live."

"That—that's truly wonderful," he stammered.

She held out a hand. "I'm in your debt for all time," she said. "I'll never be able to repay your wonderful gesture."

Completely nonplussed, Toby didn't know what to do, so he thrust the flowers at her.

She buried her face in the blossoms, inhaling deeply. "Thank you, Toby, dear," she murmured. "You have no idea how much pleasure I get from simple joys. I've truly come back to life."

Toby struggled to regain his composure. "What happened to you?" he demanded. "When they brought you here only seventy-two hours ago, you were barely conscious, and the doctor in charge of the ambulance indicated that there wasn't much hope for your life."

Her green eyes glowed. "I developed the will to live," she said. "You gave me the incentive."

He stammered incoherently.

"I don't pretend I was an angel," Caroline said softly. "Far from it. But the knowledge that an honorable man was willing to give me his good name strengthened me beyond measure. You have no idea how you inspired me to live."

He was burdened now with a wife whose past was highly unsavory, and he fought a sense of panic that arose within him. His mother would never understand how he had come to marry Caroline, and he was not too sure that he understood himself just what had happened. But he was married to her for better or worse—that much he knew.

He took his leave as soon as he reasonably could, promising to return to the hospital the following day. He had no chance to speak to his father in private until that evening, when Whip signed the last of the papers that transferred the possession of the silver to the Treasury Department.

"Come along, Toby," he said cheerfully. "The War

Department has provided us with splendid quarters in a hotel on Madison Square. We've seen the last of the train." They hailed a hansom cab and soon were clattering over cobbled streets en route to the hotel.

Toby took a deep breath and told his father that Caroline was now well on the road to recovery.

Whip stared at him. "Well, now," he said, "well, now."

Toby knew precisely how he felt.

"I'll write to your mother immediately," Whip said, "and I'll explain the circumstances as best I'm able."

"Thanks, Pa," Toby muttered.

Whip stared out the window of the cab, shaking his head slowly; then he turned to his son and addressed him in a solemn tone of voice. "There are things in our lives that we can control and other things that we can't," he said. "What determines the measure of a man is the way he handles himself when he's in a situation that he can't control. It's a matter of showing grace under pressure, that's what Lee Blake calls it."

"I've been thinking of little else," Toby said. "Caroline's a beautiful, desirable woman, but she sure isn't the type I would have married, or that any man in his right mind would have married. I admit that I deserve what's happening to me."

"How so?" Whip demanded.

"I lost my head over Caroline," Toby said frankly. "I was so fascinated by her that I completely lost my perspective. I knew deep inside myself that she was a courtesan, but I couldn't for the life of me admit it. I had to pretend that she was misunderstood and maligned. Well, all that is past history now. She had a narrow brush with death, and she's become my wife, and those are the things that matter."

"Your future together is what matters," Whip told him.

"My future," Toby replied, "belongs to the Union for as far ahead as I can see. I can't worry about anything except winning this war. After that I'll tackle my personal problems."

*   *   *

Not only were both of the brides uncommonly attractive, but one of them had achieved a measure of fame as the author of a series of articles on the silver train. Both of the grooms had been prominent in the daring exploits that had preserved the silver for the Union, so the wedding attracted a great deal of public attention. The mere fact that the renowned Whip Holt was giving away the brides guaranteed that Trinity Church would be filled to overflowing, and crowds of curious people lined the street outside.

Susanna Fulton had never looked lovelier, and Alison White was breathtaking. Andy Brentwood and Scott Foster, both wearing full-dress uniforms, were dashing. They satisfied even the most romantic of the onlookers.

But it was the recuperating Caroline Brandon Holt who attracted the most attention. Crowds craned for a glimpse of her, jostling and shoving, and excited murmurs followed her in and out of the church. Caroline was well aware of the stir she was creating, but she remained demure as she clung to Toby's arm.

Even at the reception that followed the ceremony, she continued to draw attention, and the press, which was in full attendance, concentrated on her.

Andy and Susanna, Scott and Alison were planning a short honeymoon, since the new combat battalion that Andy Brentwood would command was being mustered on Governor's Island, a military fort off Manhattan Island, and the assembly of the subsidiary units would take time to accomplish. So the newlyweds were able to stay together, renting a small house on rural Staten Island, where the women would live while their husbands went off to war. They invited Patricia to join them, and she was tempted to accept the invitation but finally turned it down, electing instead to go off to Boston and join her family for the duration of the hostilities. She also decided not to have Ezekiel escort her to Massachusetts. She would stay in New York City with him so that she could see him off to war, and then she would take the train north by herself—to which Ezekiel reluctantly agreed.

Nothing was said to Caroline about joining the other young women. They were polite to her, and without exception they took care to treat her as an equal, but an invisible barrier still separated her from the truly respectable. Caroline had expected no other treatment and was not surprised. She had lived for a long time beyond the pale of honorable people, and she knew that her marriage to Whip Holt's son would not automatically open doors for her.

She faced her situation with courage and candor as she expressed herself to Toby. "It's going to take time before I'm accepted," she said. "The decent people want to make sure that I've reformed before they'll hold out a hand to me."

Toby was impressed by her honesty and sincerity. The bullet that had almost taken her life appeared to have changed her whole attitude, and he was encouraged.

Caroline gauged his reaction carefully. She was conscious of the fact that her new husband had not taken advantage of his marital prerogatives. On the contrary, he carefully remained at arm's length from her. Perhaps this was due to his consideration of her while she recuperated, but Caroline knew there was more, that his attitude was more complex than that.

She sensed that he had not expected her to live when he had married her and that her recovery left him somewhat confused. There was only one way that she could deal with the situation: Toby was young, virile, and impressionable, and she was expert at making herself irresistible to the opposite sex. She had to exert very little effort in order to nudge Toby into consummating their relationship. Now they were truly married, and she felt infinitely more secure.

"I think," she told him one evening when they returned to the quarters on Governor's Island that they shared, "that I want to go out to Oregon with your father when you march off to war next week with the battalion."

"I would have thought you'd prefer to stay in New York," Toby said.

She shook her head. "For one thing, we'd be spending far too much money, which we can't afford. Living at the ranch, as I understand it, will cost us nothing. For another thing, I know no one in this city except the other women who traveled with us on the wagon train, and they're far more comfortable in my absence than in my presence. I really think it will be best for everyone if I go with your father."

Toby had to admit that he would enjoy a far greater peace of mind if his parents were looking after Caroline, but some lingering doubts remained in his mind. "You're accustomed to glamour and excitement in your life," he said, "and you could find both here in New York. You'll lead a quiet life on the ranch, far quieter than you could imagine."

"That's what I want," Caroline replied promptly. "I plan to get my excitement marking off the days and weeks and months on a calendar until you and I are reunited."

Toby was reassured by her answer and believed that her reformation was sincere.

Other people were not quite so certain. "I've known Caroline for a long time," Susanna Fulton Brentwood told her bridegroom. "I knew her, as you did, when she came to Denver initially with her late first husband. She was flighty then and couldn't help flirting with every man she saw, but it's possible that she's changed. Her near-fatal shooting may have reformed her."

"Reformation is always possible," Andy replied carefully.

"I've talked to Alison about this, and we've come to the same conclusion. We'd invite Caroline to move in with us, but neither of us wants to take the chance. Suppose she really hasn't reformed, the complications in all our lives would really be horrendous."

"Toby hasn't asked that you take her in," Andy said, "and I gather that Whip is intending to escort her back to Oregon, so I suggest that we leave well enough alone."

The following week the new battalion held a full-dress parade in honor of Colonel Whip Holt, who was being retired from active duty in the Union Army that same day. Whip accepted the salute, and then Andy Brentwood read a commendation written by President Lincoln, which took note of the major contributions Whip had made to the Union cause.

Immediately following the ceremony, the troops and the members of their families adjourned to the Battery by boat, and there the women said their farewells to their husbands.

Susanna remained dry-eyed, as befitted the wife of a battalion commander. Alison struggled hard to match her friend's dignity, and almost succeeded. Patricia wept without shame, and Ezekiel tried in vain to comfort her. His tremendous physical strength made him equal to most occasions, but in this instance he was powerless.

Whip shook his son's hand and then stepped aside to permit Toby and Caroline to have a final, private word. Caroline reached up and toyed absently with the row of brass buttons on her husband's tunic. "I just want you to promise me one thing," she murmured. "I want you to swear that you aren't going to worry about me."

Toby started to reply.

She reached out and gently placed a hand over his mouth. "Hear me out," she said. "You're not going to have an easy time of it. This battalion is going to see action and more action. You're going to have to keep your wits about you and stay alive and healthy. I want you to know that nothing is going to happen to me while you're gone. I'll be safe and sound—and very content with my lot at your parents' ranch."

Toby searched her face, and the expression in her green eyes told him that she meant what she said.

He took her into his arms and kissed her. Caroline clung to him for a very long time.

Then whistles blew, a bugle sounded, and an entire battalion fell in, formed ranks, and marched off to war, its initial destination known only to Colonel Andrew Brentwood and the members of his staff.

Caroline's eyes were moist as she joined Whip and took his arm.

In that instant, his doubts about the future vanished. He felt a deep wave of sympathy for the young woman and for the difficult situation in which she found herself. Toby had meant well when he had married her, and now, as his wife, she deserved the unswerving support of his family. Whip was prepared to give her that support.

He still felt that same way late in the day when a carriage took him and Caroline to the docks on the Hudson River. There, an armed passenger ship, manned by civilians but protected by U.S. Navy warships, was waiting to carry Whip and his daughter-in-law on the first stage of their journey to Oregon. They would go by way of the Isthmus of Panama, and President Lincoln had obtained their reservations on the vessel; they would be afforded the fullest protection available in wartime. They boarded the ship and went to their separate cabins in a suite that had been provided them, and there they supervised the unpacking of their belongings. As the ship cast off and started toward the mouth of the Hudson River, its engine causing the entire vessel to vibrate, Whip went to the main deck, where he joined the other passengers to watch the sailing.

There Caroline joined him, and her appearance created an immediate sensation. She had freshened her cosmetics and had changed into one of her more spectacular costumes, a gown with a provocatively low neckline and a slit skirt. The cloak that she had thrown over her shoulders in no way detracted from her appearance.

The other passengers gaped at her, and several of them glanced at Whip as well.

The old mountain man knew what they were thinking. He had made it clear that he was escorting his daughter-in-law to his home in Oregon, but Caroline did not look like any man's daughter-in-law. Whip felt certain that at least some of their fellow passengers were convinced that he was traveling with his mistress.

That was one of the burdens that he would be required to bear in his association with Caroline. Although her intentions were honorable, she was incapable of living down her past completely and changing her whole nature. She dressed and made up as she did out of habit. Perhaps it didn't occur to her that any man who saw her would regard her appearance as enticing and that every woman would think her a trollop. On the other hand, Whip reflected, maybe she was well aware of the effect she created. She was one of those women whose appetite for male admiration was insatiable and who was indifferent to what other women thought of her.

As she stood beside him on the deck, her hand resting lightly on his arm, he knew that the months ahead would be stormy for all the Holt family. How Eulalia would react to such a flamboyant daughter-in-law with such a lurid past was anybody's guess. What their friends would think was another matter entirely—there was no way that he could predict the future. How he himself would get along with Caroline was an open question, and he was worried, too, about the young woman's stability. He prayed that she would be able to achieve and maintain an inner balance.

Whip Holt had faced countless dangers without flinching, but he guessed that no problems he had yet encountered were as complex as those connected with the contradictory young woman whom his son had married in a humanitarian gesture.

By the year 2000, 2 out of 3 Americans could be illiterate.

It's true.

Today, 75 million adults... about one American in three, can't read adequately. And by the year 2000, U.S. News & World Report envisions an America with a literacy rate of only 30%.

Before that America comes to be, you can stop it... by joining the fight against illiteracy today.

Call the Coalition for Literacy at toll-free **1-800-228-8813** and volunteer.

Volunteer Against Illiteracy. The only degree you need is a degree of caring.

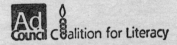

Ad Council Coalition for Literacy

LWA

★ WAGONS WEST ★

A series of unforgettable books that trace the lives of a dauntless band of pioneering men, women, and children as they brave the hazards of an untamed land in their trek across America. This legendary caravan of people forge a new link in the wilderness. They are Americans from the North and the South, alongside immigrants, Blacks, and Indians, who wage fierce daily battles for survival on this uncompromising journey—each to their private destinies as they fulfill their greatest dreams.

☐	26822	INDEPENDENCE! #1	$4.50
☐	26162	NEBRASKA! #2	$4.50
☐	26242	WYOMING! #3	$4.50
☐	26072	OREGON! #4	$4.50
☐	26070	TEXAS! #5	$4.50
☐	26377	CALIFORNIA! #6	$4.50
☐	26546	COLORADO! #7	$4.50
☐	26069	NEVADA! #8	$4.50
☐	26163	WASHINGTON! #9	$4.50
☐	26073	MONTANA! #10	$4.50
☐	26184	DAKOTA! #11	$4.50
☐	26521	UTAH! #12	$4.50
☐	26071	IDAHO! #13	$4.50
☐	26367	MISSOURI! #14	$4.50
☐	27141	MISSISSIPPI! #15	$4.50
☐	25247	LOUISIANA! #16	$4.50
☐	25622	TENNESSEE! #17	$4.50
☐	26022	ILLINOIS! #18	$4.50
☐	26533	WISCONSIN! #19	$4.50
☐	26849	KENTUCKY! #20	$4.50

Prices and availability subject to change without notice.

THE EXCITING NEW FRONTIER SERIES
BY THE CREATORS OF

WAGONS WEST
STAGECOACH
by Hank Mitchum

"The STAGECOACH series is great frontier entertainment.
Hank Mitchum really makes the West come alive in each story."
—Dana Fuller Ross, author of *Wagons West*

- [ ] STATION 1: DODGE CITY (26383 *$2.75)
- [ ] STATION 14: CIMARRON (26303 *$2.75)
- [ ] STATION 23: EL PASO (25549 *$2.75)
- [ ] STATION 24: MESA VERDE (25808 *$2.75)
- [ ] STATION 25: SAN ANTONIO (26180 *$2.75)
- [ ] STATION 26: TULSA (26229 *$2.75)
- [ ] STATION 27: PECOS (26193 *$2.75)
- [ ] STATION 28: EL DORADO (26332 *$2.75)
- [ ] STATION 29: PANHANDLE (26467 *$2.75)
- [ ] STATION 30: RAWHIDE (26571 *$2.75)
- [ ] STATION 31: ROYAL COACH (26712 *$3.50)
- [ ] STATION 32: TAOS (26856 *$3.50)

Prices and availability subject to change without notice.

**FROM THE PRODUCER OF WAGONS WEST
A SWEEPING SAGA OF WAR AND HEROISM
AT THE BIRTH OF A NATION.**

THE WHITE INDIAN SERIES

Filled with the glory and adventure of the colonization of America, here is the thrilling saga of the new frontier's boldest hero and his family. THE WHITE INDIAN SERIES chronicles the adventures of Renno, his son Ja-gonh, and his grandson Ghonkaba, from the colonies to Canada, from the South to the turbulent West. Through their struggles to tame a savage continent and their encounters with the powerful men and passionate women in the early battles for America, we witness the events that shaped our future and forged our great heritage.

Special Offer
Buy a Bantam Book
for only 50¢.

Now you can have Bantam's catalog filled with hundreds of titles plus take advantage of our unique and exciting bonus book offer. A special offer which gives you the opportunity to purchase a Bantam book for only 50¢. Here's how!

By ordering any five books at the regular price per order, you can also choose any other single book listed (up to a $5.95 value) for just 50¢. Some restrictions do apply, but for further details why not send for Bantam's catalog of titles today!

Just send us your name and address and we will send you a catalog!

BANTAM BOOKS, INC.
P.O. Box 1006, South Holland, Ill. 60473

Mr./Mrs./Ms. _____
                    (please print)

Address _____

City _____ State _____ Zip _____
                                          FC(A)—10/87
Please allow four to six weeks for delivery.